CAST IN BLOOD

Also by *New York Times* bestselling author Michelle Sagara

The Chronicles of Elantra

CAST IN SHADOW
CAST IN COURTLIGHT
CAST IN SECRET
CAST IN FURY
CAST IN SILENCE
CAST IN CHAOS
CAST IN RUIN
CAST IN PERIL
CAST IN SORROW
CAST IN FLAME
CAST IN HONOR
CAST IN FLIGHT
CAST IN DECEPTION
CAST IN OBLIVION
CAST IN WISDOM
CAST IN CONFLICT
CAST IN ETERNITY
CAST IN ATONEMENT

And "Cast in Moonlight" found in HARVEST MOON

The Wolves of Elantra

THE EMPEROR'S WOLVES
SWORD AND SHADOW

The Academia Chronicles

SHARDS OF GLASS
HEIR OF LIGHT

Praise for Michelle Sagara

"*Shards of Glass* is a spellbinding fantasy with a powerful tale of friendship at its beating heart. With vivid world building and compelling characters, this is a treasure of a book."

—Kylie Lee Baker, author of *The Scarlet Alchemist*

"[An] elaborate, magic-filled tale . . . A treat."

—*Publishers Weekly* on *Shards of Glass*

"A puzzling, absorbing mystery . . . Recommended for readers who have been caught up in the fantasy mystery trend, anyone looking for a way into Elantra without wading through its vast lore, and those who fell away from the series and are looking for a route back." **—*Library Journal* on *Shards of Glass***

"First-rate fantasy. Sagara's complex characterizations and rich world-building lift her above the crowd."

—Kelley Armstrong, *New York Times* bestselling author

"Sagara swirls mystery and magical adventure together with unforgettable characters." **—*Publishers Weekly* on *Cast in Silence***

"Sagara's remarkable Cast novels are a voyage of discovery into one young woman's fearsome destiny. Filled with time-release plot threads and intricate details, these books are both mesmerizing and unforgettable. If you're a fan of rich fantasy, this is the series for you!" **—*RT Book Reviews* on *Cast in Secret***

"This world feels so complex and so complete."

—*ReadingReality.net* on *The Emperor's Wolves*

"This magical thrill-ride is a treat."

—*Publishers Weekly* on *Cast in Wisdom*

A Chronicles of Elantra Novel

MICHELLE SAGARA

CAST IN BLOOD

HANOVER SQUARE PRESS

ISBN-13: 978-1-335-00148-1

Cast in Blood

Hanover Square Press
22 Adelaide St. West, 41st Floor
Toronto, Ontario M5H 4E3, Canada
HanoverSqPress.com

HarperCollins Publishers
Macken House, 39/40 Mayor Street Upper,
Dublin 1, D01 C9W8, Ireland
www.HarperCollins.com

Printed in U.S.A.

26 27 28 29 30 LBC 5 4 3 2 1

This is for Terry, a West reader who followed me to the Cast books and has read every word, in raw first draft, from the beginning.

01

Kaylin was late to work for the first time in weeks. Months, maybe. The intense betting pools about her time of arrival had died down to a tiny trickle. Tanner raised a brow as she made her way up the stairs. Clearly they hadn't completely gone away. That was the expression of a man who was going to lose money.

"Lord Sanabalis is in the West Room," he said.

Kaylin grimaced. "What day is it today?"

"Magic lesson day. Severn's queued for your Elani beat after the lesson." He paused, and then asked, "Midwives' guild?"

She shook her head. There was no reason she'd slept in; no reason that she'd made her way past the breakfast table—against Helen's admonitions—and out the door half an hour late. It wasn't Mrs. Erickson, who was awake, and in whose hands breakfast prep now resided; it wasn't the visiting gold Dragon.

Something felt *off* in her house, and Helen hadn't seen fit to complain about whatever it was. Kaylin had even asked, once. Helen's lack of answer made clear that her instincts were right: something was wrong.

Terrano and Mandoran, often at the breakfast table, were notably absent, not that she'd intended to join them. She half suspected they were avoiding her. Neither of them was much good at keeping their thoughts to themselves.

If she had another day like this—or two, maybe—she'd have to ask more than once. She knew that if she demanded answers, Helen would have to give them. But if she forced Helen to answer—if she pushed through the barrier of preference and choice—she'd be damaging something important, and she might never be able to repair it.

She paused in the aerie—the towering atrium in which Aerian Hawks practiced their maneuvers. She had, in her earliest years with the Hawks, loved it here. Here, where she could watch and daydream and even yearn at a great enough distance that nothing she could do could break or destroy anything of beauty. She'd once believed that if she'd been born with wings, she'd have freedom.

She knew better now, but some hint of those old dreams lingered.

Hope squawked loudly in her ear. She covered it reflexively.

Back then, she'd had no familiar. She'd had few friends. She'd had very little in the way of responsibility. But she'd had the Marks of the Chosen, even then, and she could feel them almost vibrate.

That's what was wrong. It was subtle; they weren't glowing. But it almost felt as if they were jostling for position against her skin, butting into each other, moving in a flat, unseen frenzy.

Ugh.

Hope bit her hand.

"Sorry. I just didn't get enough sleep last night."

Squawk.

"Or the night before. Or the night before that. Okay?"

He huffed and deflated, returning to his shawl position across her shoulders.

"We *all* have days like this." She wasn't sure if she was arguing with a winged lizard or talking to herself. Probably both.

But: she was late for the first time in a couple of months, and this time she didn't have an excuse.

The general mood in the office made it clear that people had persisted in betting; not as many as before, when Kaylin's time of arrival had been far more flexible. But some were annoyed and some were cheerful.

"Are you coming down with something, dear?" Caitlin asked, as Kaylin drifted past her desk.

"I don't get sick. You know that."

"There's a first time for everything."

"I'm not coming down with anything that I'm aware of. No fever, no coughing, no chills, no anything."

"And you haven't been out drinking with the Barrani Hawks?"

"No." Strictly speaking, this was *mostly* true. But she hadn't gone out in the past week.

Caitlin had that mother hen expression Kaylin found so difficult. She liked what it meant. Caitlin was worried for her. Her worry implied affection, even love of a kind. But she hated to be seen as a child that was in need of mothering. It hurt her pride.

You are a child, the condescending voice of Ynpharion said, which didn't help. It had been weeks since she'd last heard Ynpharion. They'd been busy weeks, but still. The voice of this particular namebound didn't make her day any brighter.

She managed not to snap at Caitlin, so gratitude won out—but it was awfully close.

Why are you even talking to me? Kaylin demanded, as she stomped toward the duty roster.

A loud growl diverted her. Right. Sanabalis was waiting in the West Room.

I have been asked to inform you that there might be some trouble in the near future.

What kind of trouble?

I am uncertain. The Lady asked that I reach out; she did not command it. Had she, Ynpharion would have had no choice. If Kaylin reluctantly knew his name—and she did—he had offered it—willingly—to the Consort. It was the Consort he served; he was grateful to serve her. Whatever Kaylin had done to save his life paled in comparison; he accepted it because it had allowed him to find the lord he truly wished to serve.

Ynpharion didn't correct her; it was true. But it was also true that he avoided all contact with Kaylin where possible these days. If the Consort thought there might be difficulty in the future, it was serious.

But her job was serious as well, and she was late to meet Sanabalis. The Arkon. The new Arkon. She had taken a distinct dislike to the changing of names. People had had perfectly *good* names before, and now it was all up in the air, and Kaylin made mistakes constantly.

She'd gotten a bit better about it, but she imagined it'd take months until the new names became the normal ones.

The Arkon was sitting in a large chair at the otherwise empty conference table. His eyes, when he looked toward his tardy student, were orange. To her surprise, there was no candle in front of him. Candles had been the implement of teaching torture that he had previously employed.

"You're late."

"Sorry. I didn't realize you were coming today."

"I believe you were informed."

"I've been a bit busy, and your lessons aren't an emergency."

The Arkon exhaled a small stream of smoke. "We have heard from Lannagaros; he believes you aided Lord Bellusdeo, with the help of Mrs. Erickson."

Kaylin nodded.

"Lord Bellusdeo's situation is now *extremely* unusual, but she does seem to be far less prone to tantrums."

"She isn't prone to tantrums at all." Kaylin pulled out a seat and took it, with very little grace.

"She wouldn't throw them in your presence—you might not survive. If you disbelieve me, you must speak with Lord Emmerian. *After* we have finished this class."

"There's no candle."

"No. Unfortunately, this is not that kind of class. I have surrendered some of my authority as your teacher—as Arkon, I have other duties that occupy too much of my time. It is a wonder to me that Lannagaros did not torch most of the collection in the Imperial Library centuries ago. And before you defend him, I understand that to Lannagaros, they were the remnants of his desire for the scholarship offered by the lost Academia."

"I thought he took most of that with him?"

"You are incorrect. He felt that it would teach me needed patience to be forced to look after what remains of the collection. From time to time, information from his various relics and artifacts has proven essential—but not in a reliable or dependable way."

Sanabalis—ugh, the Arkon—had never struck Kaylin as particularly impatient. Had the Dragon who replaced Lannagaros as Arkon been Tiamaris, she might have agreed or at least found it less implausible.

"Your interference—your *welcome* interference—in Lord Bellusdeo's difficulties made clear to us that your magic, as Chosen, is not strictly the talent-based magic of Imperial mages."

"Or Arcanists."

"You're a Hawk. That goes without saying."

"Teela was an Arcanist."

The Arkon's eyes reddened.

Kaylin murmured apologies. Hope snickered.

"Your magic seems very tied to context and circumstance. It seems—from observation—to respond to your will and your need. It does not respond in predictable ways. But the few documents the palace has retained that concern the Chosen imply that this has always been the case. My attempts to teach you how to channel your magic have resulted in very little conscious, deliberate control."

"Meaning?"

"I have been attempting to teach you mathematics. I should instead have been attempting to teach you art."

Kaylin blinked. She didn't hate math. At least there were right and wrong answers. She knew when she'd made a mistake. She knew when she hadn't.

Art wasn't something taught in the Halls of Law.

"I have therefore arranged supplementary lessons. Before you ask, no. I am not an art teacher. Creativity is about expression."

"Then . . . why are you here?"

Sanabalis smiled. With teeth in it. "Rumors have reached the ears of the Emperor." He fell silent.

"Does this have something to do with the dead?" Kaylin finally asked, when Sanabalis failed to speak.

"Possibly the future dead," he replied. "Although it is not clear, given my brief interactions with Mrs. Erickson, that the Barrani leave ghosts in their wake."

Kaylin winced. "This is about the High Court?"

"There has been movement there that might become cause for concern. Our informants are not highly placed at the moment, for obvious reasons. In normal circumstances, we would ignore any difficulties from that quarter, unless the High Lord intended to foment open rebellion and war."

Kaylin nodded.

"You are aware—of course you are—of the changes in the High Halls the most powerful of the Barrani call home."

She nodded again.

"The changes have caused some social unrest. Those who might once have perished when they underwent the Test of Name do not perish now. The Lords of the High Court were once designated as such by the simple expedient of their survival. Now that is not the case. While some fail to pass that test—or so we have been informed—many have not. The number of Lords of the High Court has grown."

Kaylin shrugged. "They can't have as many as the human caste court."

"Ah, no. But they consider the human caste court almost irrelevant. There are a handful of lords with significant economic power, but the rest are unremarkable. Adding to their number gives the lords of actual power people to rule, in a fashion that does not imply treachery.

"Prior to the recent changes in the Halls of Law, the hallowed Barrani ceremony weeded out those of insignificant will or power. It apparently does not do so now."

"You want me to talk to people." By *people* she meant either Teela or Sedarias. She preferred Teela.

"I leave that decision in your capable hands. But you are aware that much of the Barrani economic power resides in the streets of Elantra. If divisions are brewing, if a Barrani war begins, it is from those streets that economic power will be withdrawn or leveraged."

Kaylin nodded. "You think it's that big?"

"We are uncertain, but we are concerned. That is not, however, the entirety of the reason I chose this block of time. I have, as you have noted, dispensed with the candle. Any attempt to force you to channel the power of your Marks through acceptable traditional means has failed to take. While you have managed, once or twice, to light the candle, you have scorched the table, melted the candle, and missed the wick."

"So . . . what did you want me to do?"

"I want you to consider who, and what, you are. I want you to access the emotions that seem to be the largest driver of the power you use. Do not look at me like that; it is considered disrespectful—at best."

"Like what?"

"As if I have taken leave of my senses."

"You realize that almost *all* of my training has been about *suppressing* random emotion, right?"

"Acceptable. Do not punch people in momentary rage."

"I mean it, Sanabalis." Ugh. "Arkon. You have my Records. You know what happened before I became an official Hawk."

"If you are referring to the slaver, yes, I am aware. He was skinned alive—and the shock did not allow him to pass out before he had experienced all of it." He spoke without horror. Teela spoke of the same incident with a complete lack of horror as well.

Kaylin couldn't quite manage it, and she'd been the person who'd killed the man.

Kaylin believed the slaver had deserved to die. But she could have killed him by breaking his neck. Or stabbing him in the heart—if she could find it. The death itself had been horrific. Teela felt death was death, regardless of how it arrived. She'd said that. She'd said that a hundred times while Kaylin had hyperventilated as she crashed.

"I believe that is the source of your problem. You did not control, did not even consider controlling, your emotions. Your power flowed naturally into your rage, and you used it. We do not intend for you to run around Elantra in a rage, but you are not the child you were on that day. You have used the power of the Marks in the years since then—but desperation seems to be your driver. It is a better driver than rage, but it is, as you are well aware, unreliable.

"I can set fire to this city without any deep emotion. I can transform into my draconic self without rage. Rage does not help our kind. It is control that we measure and value.

"That control does not entirely work for you. You must find a way to access the emotions that drive your connection to your own power if you wish to avoid situations in which desperation is your only option.

"Awareness of your emotional state does not depend on rage. If it did, we would not be having this discussion; the risk to the rest of us would be too great. The only way you use your Marks in deliberate fashion is to heal. It is proof that something other than rage can drive the conscious use of real power. The healing is impressive," he added, voice softening. "But healing is often something done after the fight, not before."

"What kind of fight are you even expecting?" She didn't bother to keep her tone neutral.

"At the moment, not a fight we cannot win."

That wasn't exactly comforting.

"We are content to leave this in the hands of Hawks. I have an appointment with Lord Grammayre after our lesson is concluded. I will request flexibility in your schedule in the near future."

The lesson ended up being much shorter than the usual candle torture. Sanabalis asked questions that were personal in nature. Kaylin punted. If it was true that she needed to somehow invoke emotion on command, she sure as hells wasn't going to do it in front of the new Arkon.

For once, Ynpharion—whose presence lingered—agreed. Agreement meant silence; he couldn't possibly be agreeable in actual words that might sound like approval.

This is what the Lady wanted you to warn me about, isn't it?

Perhaps. She does not allow me to spy on you; she feels it is beneath her.

But not you, clearly.

I serve her. Information that might become relevant is just that: information. How it is gathered is a minor concern.

And you're going to tell her that the Imperial Court has spies in the High Halls.

This time, his obvious contempt was clear. *Do you expect us* all *to be as naive and foolish as you? Of course they have spies in the High Halls. We have spies in the Imperial Palace.*

The funny thing was: she was far more comfortable with this version of Ynpharion. When he was actually polite and respectful, it made her suspicious.

Because you fail to understand the bond itself. Again. I must assume it's deliberate.

It wasn't. *I don't spend my free time thinking about you.*

Or any of those whose names you hold.

She might be more comfortable, but that didn't mean she enjoyed speaking with Ynpharion. *What exactly is the Lady afraid of?*

Ynpharion did not reply. No, of course not.

Kaylin exhaled. *Ask her if it would be acceptable if I visited.*

The silence was quantitatively different, but it was there. *She does not think it particularly wise at this time. If, however, you feel it urgent, she will grant that permission; she will not take the risk of extending an invitation. She asks, however, that you visit in the company of a guard you trust. She does* not *consider An'Teela to be a suitable guard.*

Does she think any *of the cohort would be suitable?*

Silence again. It lasted longer. *No. They are too linked with Mellarionne. Understand that she is not particularly concerned for your cohort. It is your safety that concerns her.*

Can I come with Severn?

I fail to see how that would be any protection at all. No pauses there; he hadn't bothered to ask.

Well, it's Severn or Bellusdeo. I suppose I could ask Nightshade, but I was under the impression that outcastes would be far worse.

She suggests perhaps Lord Andellen.

Kaylin frowned. Barrani names were so similar she sometimes had to sort through them before she could come up with a person to attach them to.

Lord Andellen was Nightshade's second-in-command. The most loyal of his Barrani lieges. Kaylin's work in the High Halls had allowed her to ask that Lord Andellen, exiled but not outcaste, be allowed to return to the Halls until she passed away. She certainly hadn't asked for that boon for her own sake—the High Halls gave her hives.

Everything about this felt wrong, off-kilter.

If you visit, she will instruct the guards to allow you to enter; they will take you directly to her. Give me some warning should you think it necessary to meet with her. Pause. *She feels Severn would also be acceptable because she suggests, if you visit, you visit as a Hawk.*

Kaylin froze on the spot. It took her a moment to find her own feet. *She wants me to come as a* Hawk*?*

She feels it will emphasize your caste. You are human. Those who wish to harm their rivals on opposing factions will think several times about adding human bodies to the brewing conflict, especially if they are Hawks.

Is she in danger? Kaylin began to walk, her steps slow. She wasn't always the best at reading undercurrents and subtext, because she had so little of either to offer. But Ynpharion wouldn't have made the attempt to contact her if the circumstances didn't involve the Consort, at least peripherally. *Ynpharion, tell me.*

Silence.

Severn looked up as she approached. He nodded, falling into step beside her as they left the Halls for their Elani beat. They'd be a bit early, but Kaylin was now too restless to pause or make small talk. She needed to be moving. She needed to do something.

Maybe that was why her Marks seemed almost jittery: she was. Something was happening, or about to happen.

Severn glanced at her; she felt his muted concern. Of course he was concerned. Even her thoughts were loud. She'd never quite figured out how to mask or obscure them, how to slide into a superficial layer of thought while avoiding the thoughts that were actually important.

"Try not to kick Margot's sign over."

"I didn't do it last week."

As beats went, Elani was harmless. Most of the regulars were so accustomed to Kaylin's familiar they no longer made the attempt to purchase him. People less familiar with the Hawks still asked. She almost hoped someone would try to swipe Hope. It would give her something to respond to, some way to relieve some of her building steam.

No one did.

You look like thunder, Severn observed. *If you want to start an incident—or have an incident start—try looking friendly.*

Kaylin shook her head. She had paused in front of Evanton's. She almost entered. But Evanton's wasn't where she was meant to be. Had Evanton wanted to see her, Grethan would have opened the door as she approached the faded lettering of the store window.

The only silver lining on the cloud she'd become—Severn being right, no doubt—was the fact that there were no incidents, and reports would be minuscule enough even Kaylin could get them in on time.

But she'd been ill at ease for a couple of days now, and she expected bad news.

In the end, she didn't worry about reports. She didn't worry about Elani.

When news came, it arrived in a way no one else could hear.

She felt it first, on her tattooed cheek; she lifted a hand to touch the mark Nightshade had left on her face. It felt like years ago. It had been maybe two—at most.

Severn stopped as Kaylin did, his steps so naturally in time with hers the pause was instinctive, automatic.

She lowered her hand.

"Your cheek is bleeding."

A single streak of blood reddened the palm of her hand. She nodded, turning toward the streets that led to the bridge to Tiamaris. It was the only way anyone with legitimate business entered the fiefs anymore. *Nightshade?*

There was no answer.

Kaylin began to run.

02

She hadn't heard from Nightshade in almost a month. Helen kept the namebond contact out of the house, because she didn't completely trust the fieflord. But Helen let him into the house, in person, whenever he wanted to visit Annarion. If she didn't entirely trust him, she didn't entirely distrust him, either. Kaylin, sprinting all out, didn't disagree.

Ynpharion's warning, Sanabalis's information, and her own sense of restless anxiety had come together in a visceral near certainty. That and her bleeding cheek. Severn kept pace with her; they could run without break through a quarter of the city, but not at an all-out sprint. Gaining the bridge across the Ablayne required slowing to a quick jog.

They were wearing the Hawks' tabard. The guards situated on the fief side of the bridge frowned but made no attempt to stop them. They jogged across the bridge, into Tiamaris proper. The Dragon had made significant changes to the fief he ruled in the short time he'd captained the Tower; it now felt like a poorer district within Elantra. Not the warrens, but a place that was slowly struggling its way out of that almost lawless state.

She hit the fief side of the bridge and shouted. "*Tara!*" She then continued to jog.

She wasn't surprised to see the shadow of a Dragon's descent before she'd reached the streets that formed part of the Tiamaris-Nightshade border.

"This had better be an emergency," the Dragon fieflord said, his orange-red eyes the size of Kaylin's face.

"I need to get to Nightshade."

"That fief is not under my jurisdiction."

"No—it's Nightshade's. At least for now."

"Your cheek is bleeding." He exhaled a stream of smoke; that was his only pause. "Very well. Get on. If this causes diplomatic issues, the Halls of Law will hear about it. Tara is concerned," he added, which explained the speed of his appearance. Kaylin had expected that. He lowered himself to ground so Kaylin could scrabble up his side.

Severn leaped up onto Tiamaris's back, behind Kaylin; they both braced themselves as the Dragon launched his bulk into the sky. The city shrunk beneath Tiamaris, but not too much; he flew as close to the ground as the aerial demands of flight permitted.

"Where?" he asked.

"I don't know—I just know something's wrong!"

"Do you know where he was?"

"I just said—" She stopped. "He didn't answer. When I reached out, he didn't answer at all. It's namebond stuff. I don't always understand it."

"Clearly." The word was more felt than heard; Tiamaris vibrated with the sound of his own voice. "You can, however, find him if he still lives."

She felt the hair on her arms rise in a ripple of goose bumps and sensitivity. Tiamaris, in draconic form, was casting a spell—a traditional one, in Sanabalis's terms. Severn snaked an arm around her waist as she closed her eyes; she wasn't certain which came first.

Nightshade.

Silence.

Tell us where you are. We're coming on dragonback.

Silence.

She'd been told she would know if he was dead. No one whose name she held had died—not yet.

Ynpharion said, *So, it starts. And it ends.*

If you can find it in yourself, be helpful or shut up.

The Consort believes he was traveling to see his brother.

Why? She cursed. *Never mind. Not important.* It wasn't. How the Consort knew could wait. Nightshade himself couldn't. She inhaled, exhaling slowly as wind whipped strands of hair from her face.

If it was true that she'd know if Nightshade was dead, he wasn't. Not yet. But Ynpharion believed she could find him. Somehow. It had been a long time since she'd been the one to initiate contact with the fieflord. He, like Ynpharion, was aware of where she was or what she was doing—or he could be.

But he hadn't reached out either, and if she were honest, she was comfortable with that. She wasn't comfortable with his death. Didn't examine the why of that. Instead, she listened as she tried to find Nightshade through a namebond she didn't really understand.

But Ynpharion, curse him, was right. She could sense *something*, a flicker of light she could almost see, although her eyes were closed.

"We need to cross the border," she told Tiamaris. The familiar painful tingle of magic made her arms highly sensitive to the cloth that was rubbing against them. "Can you stop that?" she asked, trying—and failing—to sound less annoyed.

"Stop what?"

"The spell. Whatever you're casting, stop."

Silence.

Kaylin frowned. "It wasn't you who cast the spell, was it?"

"No. I will have to have a word with the Arkon if you can even ask that question."

Kaylin was at a loss for words. This level of magic, at a distance she couldn't even see, was the equivalent of an Arcane bomb. A very big one.

But the buildings beneath Tiamaris's massive wingspan hadn't been destroyed, and a bomb that felt this large at this distance could level part of a city block. Maybe the border buildings were different. Or maybe there was no Arcane bomb.

Nightshade couldn't have been in Castle Nightshade; the Tower's defenses were ferocious. Even if an invited guest had tried to harm or kill him, the Tower would have prevented it. She didn't think he could be in the streets of his fief, although there, assassination stood a better chance.

If what had threatened him had come from *Ravellon*, the Tower's defenses would aid him within the boundaries of the fief itself. But what if the threat wasn't Shadow? How useful could the Tower be?

She felt *certain* that he was in the border zone. She didn't bother to put that into words. Tiamaris was already flying there.

"Have Shadows been more active recently?" Kaylin shouted in what she hoped was the direction of draconic ears.

"Not notably. Some of the Norranir remain at our borders; most have migrated to the fief of Bellusdeo. They are very, very sensitive to incursion; no alarm has been raised. Do you fear Shadow has managed to infiltrate Nightshade?"

Did she? Or was she just hoping? And if she *was* hoping it was Shadow, what in the hells was wrong with her?

The border zone emerged beneath Tiamaris's wings. She wanted to tell the Dragon to fly lower, to fly more slowly. The latter he could do, but not without circling, and that felt like almost no movement at all. But as he wheeled, as he came closer to the ground, as his shadow darkened buildings, she felt the painful slap of magic grow stronger.

She shouted directions.

"She means the other left," Severn said, raising his voice.

"There—the building on the very edge of the border zone from the Nightshade side. You can see the smoke rising from it."

"I do not have permission to land within the fief itself."

Kaylin almost shrieked in frustration—and pain.

"Set us down at the edge of the border!"

"Where the bodies are," Severn added. He didn't seem to be shouting—Kaylin certainly was—but his voice carried.

Tiamaris offered no further argument; he landed.

Severn had been right. There were bodies. Some were missing limbs, some missing heads—although the heads, detached at the neck, weren't far away. Not all of them were dead, but most were dying. They were armed and armored in a style consistent with the High Halls, the High Court—and its many members.

They are, Ynpharion said. His focus was so intent, she could almost feel it and pushed him back. *They are not Nightshade's people.*

They aren't anyone's people anymore, she snapped. She didn't understand how she hadn't seen this from Tiamaris's back.

Magic, Severn said.

But you could see it?

I cheated. Be careful.

She nodded, waiting beside the Dragon until Severn had fully dismounted. She waited until he was armed. He'd pulled the twin blades of his most significant weapon but hadn't unwound the chain.

Kaylin had long knives, and she drew one. She then glanced at Tiamaris.

The Dragon glinted red as he nodded. He didn't return to the air or his own fief, but he didn't cross the almost invisible line that marked the edge of the border zone, either. Then again, his breath had range. Kaylin's daggers—or Severn's weapon—lacked that.

Together, the two Hawks walked toward the building Severn had indicated from the air. One wall was a blackened mess; stones—for it was a stone building—had cracked and fallen, both outward and inward. She passed over headless bodies, choosing a path that wasn't littered with the dying. Dying Barrani could still take out two human Hawks if that was their intent.

She counted twelve bodies. She wanted to sprint ahead, but training overtook impulse. *Ynpharion, what's the smallest unit of a Barrani war band? What are the numbers?*

Between twelve and fifteen, historically.

Twelve to fifteen. She counted twelve and glanced at Severn.

"It's a war band," he said, hearing the question she hadn't put into words. Maybe hearing the question that followed—*how do you know this?*—but ignoring it for now.

Barrani played games of politics—their polite word for assassination—but this was different. There was no subtlety in it. Someone had sent a *war band* into Nightshade.

They could not afford subtlety if they intended to remove Nightshade, Ynpharion said. His interior tone had sharpened, not in his usual condescension, but almost in earnest.

Do you recognize any of the dead?

No.

Does the Consort?

She is our Lady. This meant yes. Ynpharion's next question made clear that the Consort was far less concerned with the war band. *Can you sense Nightshade?*

Kaylin frowned. *I'm not certain. I think—I think he's in the ruins of that building. It would be a better place to deal with greater numbers of assailants, but a worse place to use his sword—it's too large, and buildings this size weren't meant for all-out combat. Not that way.*

The sword, Ynpharion said in the same urgent tone, *was not the only reason he was feared.*

Severn tapped her shoulder, as if aware of her ongoing conversation with Ynpharion. He probably was. *I want to enter the building first—I have some protection against magic.*

I have Hope. She poked the familiar. Hope sat up. His eyes were wide open, his head scanning the streets.

"Wing," she told him.

Hope lifted a wing and placed it across only one of her eyes. He didn't even smack her with it, which meant he knew it was serious. She had seen the bodies of the Barrani only when she landed. If a spell of concealment had been cast, it was large enough to cover the whole of the building and the streets surrounding it. The magic that had been invoked seemed to be a barrier of some kind—a way of keeping the immediate battle from being noticed by anyone not involved in it.

The rest of the smoking building looked normal from the wing-eye view. *Has my cheek stopped bleeding?*

Severn nodded. *The mark is still there.*

Would it vanish if he were dead?

I don't know. If I had to guess, I'd say yes.

There had been whole years when she wished Nightshade dead. Years in the streets of his poorly ruled, neglected fief. Years. Sometimes, though, she didn't think about him at all. She was an orphan, protected by another orphan; there was no reason she'd ever cross even his shadow.

There are worse fieflords.

There are way better fieflords, Kaylin shot back. Severn had never resented Nightshade—person or fief—as much as she had.

Although she had Hope, she let Severn move a yard or two in front; Hope was scanning the streets, as was she. The windows of buildings across from this one seemed closed; she caught no glimpse of assassins there.

The door that Severn approached had been blown off one of

its hinges and listed in the blackened frame. Given the state of the walls, the door should have been destroyed.

Severn stationed himself on the hinge side of the doorframe.

Have you found him? Ynpharion's voice was sharper. Too sharp.

Kind of busy right now. Kaylin matched his tone.

Silence. Anger. Something else in the mix. Worry? Fear?

She cursed him in Leontine, which had less of an effect when the words weren't verbalized, although he did hear them through the namebond.

Ready? Severn asked. At Kaylin's nod, he lashed out with his left foot and kicked the door. Whatever had preserved the hinge was gone; the door flew in.

Lightning flew out.

Kaylin took a risk. "Nightshade?"

The lightning wasn't followed by any other attack. "Lord Kaylin?" Not Nightshade's voice.

"Andellen? Is that you?"

"I have my lord with me; he is injured. He is unconscious."

"The rest of the attackers?"

"Very dead. There were only two who made it through the door."

Kaylin immediately swung round and rolled through the doorframe, coming up on her feet prepared to throw herself forward if necessary. Severn was less than a step behind.

Hope, however, leaped off her shoulder before he could become part of her somersault. He squawked very, very loudly, in august displeasure.

Nothing attacked. Kaylin saw another door—this one was open. Through it, she could see Andellen. He was bleeding but appeared to have all of his limbs; he'd taken a quarrel wound on his right shoulder.

His thigh was slashed, his hands slick with blood; she

couldn't tell how much of it was his own. She moved toward him quickly, while Hope flapped around her head, squawking.

Andellen stepped aside before she could touch him. As he did, she could see Nightshade. His hand had a white-knuckled death grip on *Meliannos*, but that hand was still attached to the rest of him. She could see no visible wound, but he was unconscious.

Unconscious. He couldn't do what Andellen had just done. He couldn't avoid her touch. She hesitated.

Do not do it, Ynpharion snapped.

Why not? I already hold his name.

Ynpharion knew this but was outraged at her casual statement. *You know very well why not. Are you a fool? The secrets of the powerful are not yours to know unless they are offered. Lord Nightshade is among the very powerful.*

He might die if we don't move him.

Silence. It was a longer silence, and there was heat in it, fear, even disagreement. Ynpharion was arguing with someone. Kaylin could guess who.

She wants me to save him.

She has not yet decided!

No—you haven't decided. She wants me to save him.

She acknowledges the danger to you; it is the only reason she feels conflicted. She points out that you bear the mark of the Erenne. She says you understand the danger.

She did. Immortals didn't want to be healed. Ynpharion hadn't wanted to be healed. She'd forced herself into his life because she'd wanted to heal him. She'd taken his name. If she'd had any way of scrubbing that knowledge from her brain, she'd've done it in an instant.

She looked at Nightshade, kneeling by his side to gauge his level of injury. His limbs had not fallen in a way that implied they were broken—but back injuries weren't always obvious either. If she wasn't careful—if they weren't careful—moving him could finish him off.

There was no wound that implied loss of blood would kill him. He was pale, but Barrani were often pale. They didn't tan or burn the way normal people did, unless they *wanted* to.

She looked up at Andellen. "Do you know what caused this?"

Andellen was silent for a long beat.

"It's not Shadow?" This was asked with more force.

"It is not Shadow as I understand it. I would guess poison, if I were pressed; I would not like my lord's life to depend on that ill-formed guess."

"What did you see?"

"Nothing. I heard him grunt. I heard him fall. At that point, the attackers who managed to follow us into the house were still alive. They did not remain so for long."

Long enough.

She frowned, sheathing the one long knife she carried. She closed the eye that wasn't behind Hope's translucent wing, and focused. Through Hope's wing, Nightshade's pallor was subtly different. She looked for exposed skin, for any sign of a needle, a dart, but could find nothing.

Andellen's injuries were far more obvious.

"Is it safe to take his hand from the sword?"

"I would not, were I you. *Meliannos* is a weapon meant for fighting many things; not all are, or can be, easily seen. It is possible that his grip on the sword has preserved him."

They were as far away from Castle Nightshade as they could be while remaining within the fief's boundaries. Taking him to his Tower when he was in this shape would be deadly if any of the attacking Barrani remained. Andellen could—and would—fight, as would Severn, but the Barrani wouldn't need a small war band to finish them all off. Andellen's skills could be trusted, but he'd be saddled with two humans as comrades.

"How many of Nightshade's Barrani servants can be trusted?"

She could feel Ynpharion's deep annoyance at the question. Fine. "Did any of the Barrani take a blood oath of service?"

Andellen failed to reply. She looked up at him and revised her opinion about his ability to fight. Neither he nor the lord to whom he'd devoted his life were going to be much help should they be required to fight their way to the Tower where Nightshade would be safest.

"Is there such a thing as magical poison?" she asked instead. *Ynpharion?*

It would not be called poison, Ynpharion replied. *Wait a moment, if that's possible for you.*

If it was magic, Kaylin's healing might be hampered. If the magic had done damage, she might be able to alleviate that—but she was no longer certain.

She called his name. *Calarnenne.*

He didn't answer.

She called it again, with more force, with true intent. When she did, she almost felt his familiar, lurking presence—but there were no words, no deliberate response.

Hesitating, she continued to study his pallor. "Hope, do you see what I see?"

Hope squawked; it was the affirmative squawk, but it felt slightly hesitant.

Severn?

"No."

But you could see the attackers from the air.

I could see past the barrier. I'm almost certain that barrier wasn't erected by Nightshade. Would you recognize his magic?

Kaylin shook her head. *I never saw him cast a magic powerful enough to leave a sigil. Either that or the magic he used didn't require one. I'm not sure how the Towers function in that regard.* She'd never considered it before.

She hesitated and then reached out to touch Nightshade's pale cheek with her left hand.

His skin was hot.

The cheek that carried the Erenne mark burned at the contact; she hadn't expected that. She didn't even need Severn to tell her that her cheek was bleeding again. Closing both eyes, she started to examine his physical body the only way she knew how. She built the bridge of power she had always crossed to heal.

She touched nothing.

She felt nothing. Only the fevered heat beneath her palm made clear she hadn't lost the necessary physical contact. That made things simpler.

"He's feverish. I don't know enough about Barrani physiology to know how much of a fever Barrani can safely maintain, or for how long." She couldn't read him at all. She couldn't tell if there were internal injuries she couldn't see.

"We won't make it back to the Tower. We have a Dragon waiting in the street at the edge of the border. If he had permission to fly—and land—we could ask him to take us to the Tower. But the Tower will be a problem. I can't wake Nightshade. I can't *get* his permission, if Tiamaris would even ask it."

"I highly doubt a Dragon is capable of the subtlety required to pass beneath the Tower's notice." Andellen's voice was stiff. Tiamaris was standing at the very edge of Nightshade, and Nightshade had a death-grip on *Meliannos*, one of The Three, weapons considered dragonkillers by the Barrani.

Kaylin grimaced. "Fine. We need Nightshade not to be here. I don't know how much time we'll have. I don't know if there are spies who are waiting until they feel enough time has passed that they can approach. Help me carry him."

"What do you intend?"

"I don't have a Tower. I could ask Tiamaris to shelter him while we try to figure out what's wrong. Tara might have some idea." Before Andellen could reply, she said, "Or I could take him to my home. Helen used to be the home of a sorcerer. She might be able to give us information."

The Consort would prefer that, Ynpharion said.

Andellen carried Nightshade across the border. Tiamaris was, as Kaylin had said, waiting—and he hadn't bothered to transform again. He was a large red Dragon whose scales reflected the day's light. His eyes were orange, but red flecks—far more visible in eyes of this size—were moving in.

"I need you to carry us to Helen," Kaylin told him, without preamble.

"I cannot legally do so in this form."

"I don't think the city streets will be safe," she said, ignoring the question of legality, although technically she was on duty. "Can you pick him up in your claws?"

"By unsafe, what do you mean? Corpses seldom pose a problem, except in that they must be removed."

"Fourteen Barrani are dead by my count. Does that mean much to you?"

"War band, perhaps." Tiamaris's voice was a rumble. He knew flying in draconic form was illegal but knew as well that exceptions were often made in emergencies. In what the Emperor deemed an emergency.

Severn nodded. "There may be Barrani in the houses or streets who are waiting to confirm Nightshade's death. If another gathering of Barrani soldiers is waiting, they'll be waiting within the city itself."

"You believe they would be foolish enough to attack in the Emperor's streets?"

"They were foolish enough to attack Nightshade in his own fief."

Tiamaris rumbled. "Your request does not appear to be entirely foolish, given Lord Nightshade's condition. Fine," he said, dropping High Barrani for Elantran for the single word.

"Andellen is coming with us." Kaylin let the statement tail into a question by tone alone.

"He will not be an encumbrance. But Kaylin, I do suggest we move."

Severn hadn't sheathed his weapon. He turned. In the distance, Barrani, armed and armored, could be seen. None were carrying bows.

Ynpharion cursed. To Kaylin's surprise, he chose Leontine. In any other circumstance, she might have been amused.

"Two war bands' worth of Barrani," Kaylin murmured. She leaped onto Tiamaris's back. Severn sheathed his weapons in a single gesture. He joined her. Andellen did the same. If he had reservations about riding a Dragon's back, the obvious danger overwhelmed them. He trusted Tiamaris more than he trusted the Barrani.

Fool. It's you he trusts.

It didn't matter. Tiamaris pushed himself off the ground. Any thoughts Kaylin might have shared with Ynpharion were lost; she needed to hold on tightly, his ascent was so steeply angled.

Nightshade, he dangled in his forepaws.

Kaylin had no easy way of communicating with Helen at a distance. None of her namebound lived in her house. Severn was directly behind her. Nightshade was unconscious. Lirienne was in the West March. Distance didn't destroy the bond—it couldn't.

That left only Ynpharion, and in this particular case, he couldn't be of much use either.

"You're going to have to land on the lawn!" she shouted. Tiamaris was flying quickly; he kicked up enough wind to make shouting necessary.

He roared a *yes*.

It didn't take long to reach Helen from the fiefs; the Dragon's speed and the lack of any aerial traffic made the distance seem trivial.

He did land on the lawn, as Kaylin had suggested. Helen *had* a tower large enough to contain a landing Dragon—it was what she opened when Bellusdeo came to visit, because Bellusdeo didn't particularly care about petty Imperial laws that made being an actual Dragon illegal without the Emperor's permission.

Kaylin suspected that blanket permission had been granted. The Emperor was pragmatic at heart. Bellusdeo would continue to be Bellusdeo. She was not his liege, and she was necessary, absolutely necessary, for the future of the race.

Tiamaris was necessary as a fieflord. But Tiamaris retained his position on the Dragon Court, and some of the funding—she'd heard this through Tara—for the reconstruction of the fief had come from Imperial coffers and taxes. Tiamaris was going to be called up on the figurative carpet to justify his draconic form—and his flight across the city proper.

Kaylin wasn't too worried. The fiefs were important to the continued existence of the city, and Nightshade was a fieflord. Towers that lost their captains declined over time; the denizens of *Ravellon* could find larger and larger cracks through which to pass. None of that was good for the Emperor's citizens.

Andellen dismounted first and moved immediately toward his lord; Tiamaris had taken care to set him down as gently as he could, given his form. Severn followed, although he turned to offer Kaylin a hand, should she need it.

She accepted it. Tiamaris's flight to Helen had been far faster—and far less careful—than his flight toward Nightshade. She found her footing and took two steps toward her house.

The door flew open long before she could reach it. Helen was standing in its frame, eyes obsidian. Kaylin shouted, "We need a room!"

Before Helen could answer—not that it was necessary—the Avatar of Kaylin's home was pushed to one side. Annarion, Mandoran following close behind, ran out to the lawn. He didn't appear to notice Tiamaris at all.

Tiamaris turned his enormous head to Helen. He nodded, the nod deep with genuine respect. Her eyes remained obsidian, but she returned the Dragon's nod with a nod of her own before her gaze fell to Annarion's back.

Tiamaris then pushed up, gaining height without the encumbrance of passengers, and headed straight toward the Imperial Palace.

The moment Annarion appeared in the open door, Andellen rose and stepped back from Nightshade. He stood at a distance as his lord's younger—and only—brother ran to his side. Annarion knelt there, as if months of argument and bitterness had been a lie. He checked for a pulse, for breath, and for the sword that Andellen had carefully resheathed. He then lifted his brother's limp body. Mandoran would have helped, but Annarion had turned to Helen.

He didn't speak—or didn't speak out loud. The cohort, like Kaylin, mostly avoided masking their thoughts. It was so natural for them to speak through their namebonds that they often didn't speak aloud at all.

Helen stared at Nightshade as Annarion carried him through the open door. Andellen, after a long pause, turned to Helen. "My apologies for our abrupt arrival. The situation was grave. We did not have time to offer advance notice."

Annarion was often so thrown by his brother's presence, Helen had asked that Nightshade make an appointment to visit, to better prepare herself for the possibility of conflict.

Nightshade had clearly respected what was only barely a request.

"Emergencies have their own imperatives," Helen replied,

voice gentle. "Lord Nightshade arrived with Kaylin; it is clear she meant to carry him here. She is the master of the house; what she desires is paramount. Do you wish to share the rooms your lord will convalesce in?"

"If it will not trouble you, yes. I do not believe he will find my presence encumbering."

"Not in his current state, no." Helen frowned. "You might consider convalescing yourself. I will have food prepared. You will eat."

Andellen stared at the Avatar of Kaylin's home as if she were losing her mind.

"Don't argue with her," Kaylin told him. "I do it all the time and it doesn't do any good."

Andellen's gaze clearly said *then what does she mean by master?* But he didn't say the words aloud. Then again, Helen didn't give him much time.

"An'Teela will be joining us shortly. I should warn you that the cohort is very loud at the moment. Would you like me to examine Lord Nightshade?"

"If possible. I tried to do it—but my healing magic has been thoroughly blocked. Andellen thought Nightshade's state might be due to poison." Poison, Kaylin was certain, she could deal with. But something had prevented any attempt at healing.

"Lord Andellen?" Helen asked, adding the requisite title she felt the guest deserved—and that Kaylin in particular should be using.

"There was no obvious wound that would have caused the collapse. Kaylin has suggested, however, that she found no dart wound, no way poison could be delivered. She believes that the poison, such as it is, is entirely magical in nature."

Helen smiled. "Kaylin does not feel she has to mask or obscure her thoughts when she is in her own home. Or on its property. Come, enter. I can provide clothing, but it will not last when you step beyond my gates. The cohort, however, has physical clothing, and I am certain that they would be willing to gift it for your use in the current emergency."

Severn didn't accompany them into the house.

"You're not coming in?"

"I have some research to do," he replied. "The Halls of Law will almost certainly demand information about what occurred."

"The Halls don't interfere in the fiefs."

"The *Hawks* don't interfere in the fiefs. The fiefs don't fall under legal jurisdiction—but the fiefs are an Imperial concern. News of Nightshade's possible assassination would be of great interest."

"You want to talk to the Wolflord."

"No. But I want access to information about the High Court. It might be a waste of time." His tone implied the opposite.

Kaylin nodded. "Let me know if you find anything relevant."

Severn turned and walked—quickly—away.

Helen had created rooms for Nightshade's use. She'd probably had them ready to go before Annarion had crossed the threshold, carrying the brother he both loved and hated. She didn't insist that Andellen eat the moment he entered the house; he was, given blood and damaged clothing, not yet fit for the dinner table.

She did ask him questions as they walked toward the new guest quarters, which were down the hall from the regular guest rooms. Andellen answered her.

Kaylin, however, frowned. Or frowned differently; not much had happened today that didn't deserve a frown. "You said you notify Helen before you visit."

Andellen nodded.

"Which means Nightshade wasn't coming here."

Andellen fell silent.

"Who were you meant to meet? Clearly whoever that person is—or was—information about that meeting was leaked to someone who didn't have your best interests at heart. You were the only person to attend Nightshade."

Andellen nodded again, but the nod was stiffer.

One guard. One meeting, not held in the fiefs. Whoever Nightshade intended to meet couldn't enter the fiefs openly. But the intended meeting must have involved Barrani; there was no other way the Barrani war bands would be so ready for action. Only one guard. Someone Nightshade had trusted, inasmuch as he ever trusted Barrani.

He didn't usually bring Andellen on his visits to Helen.

Ynpharion showed surprising approval. Kaylin could feel it; it annoyed her, it was so condescending.

Anything I say is annoying, Chosen. Praise is condescending. Criticism is condescending.

"Helen?"

"Yes, dear. Are you certain you don't wish to keep that channel open while you're here? He is your only immediate conduit to the Consort."

Kaylin exhaled. "You're right. Fine."

Andellen had been silent throughout; Kaylin wasn't certain he'd heard the conversation.

"He did. I believe his possible opinions to be of value. I understand that you expect my own expertise to be more critical, but I am uncertain."

"You don't think it's magical?"

"I *do* think it's magical. But you must understand, Kaylin. When I reached the stage where I could choose my own tenants, how many do you believe were sorcerers, mages, or Arcanists?"

"Zero."

Helen nodded. "Magic is not like the study of history. It evolves. Arcanists constantly create new spells by combining old spells, by adding something to historical spells to shift and change the base nature of the magic they attempt to cast. The knowledge I have might prove valuable if you wish to untangle what was cast. But it is ancient, now. It may well be impossible without modern input, modern understanding."

"Do you think we have the *time* to study and develop something new?"

"No," Helen replied. "I do not."

03

Nightshade's rooms were, to no one's surprise, very like the Barrani rooms in which the cohort lived. These were more expansive; Andellen wouldn't be sleeping on a couch in his master's bedchamber.

Andellen, however, paused at the door. The external door did not, in any way, resemble the interior.

"May I see the room in which my lord has been placed?"

"You can," Helen replied, her expression neutral.

"You do not recommend it."

"Annarion is with him. Annarion is . . . not stable at the moment. He is attempting to examine his brother, and he is coming up against the same difficulties Kaylin did. I am having trouble convincing him that he must maintain solid form—and he must approach *any* spell with caution."

Kaylin groaned.

Andellen glanced at her.

"She's giving us warning that the rest of the inhabitants of my house will be joining Annarion and Mandoran. One of them is An'Mellarionne."

"These would be friends of my lord's brother?"

"Yes. I assume you've heard about them."

"I have heard very little. My lord seldom chooses to discuss the personal matters of his family. I am aware, however, that they arrived shortly after Lord Annarion."

"They're not great with formal introductions, so I might have to just point them out to—"

The door flew open. Sedarias and Terrano were standing in the frame, and they moved almost as one person. Terrano's eyes were in the disturbing, too-large-for-his-face configuration; Sedarias's were not. They were the color of midnight, if midnight was an emotion.

Midnight was clearly a Barrani emotion. Sedarias didn't push Andellen out of the way; she didn't have to. Andellen stepped adroitly to one side as she barreled past.

"That's An'Mellarionne," Kaylin said when Sedarias was far enough away. "The person she came with—"

"Lord Terrano."

Kaylin grimaced. "Technically, yes. But we call him Terrano. His eyes don't always look like that."

Andellen's gaze, blue-eyed, did not darken; he watched Sedarias. Or perhaps he was now concerned about Terrano. People who were used to Terrano understood that his eyes could enlarge or practically melt, but that didn't mean he was injured. Or dangerous. Or not *intentionally* dangerous.

Kaylin turned to Andellen. "If you want to give them privacy, remain here."

"You do not?"

"Privacy isn't really a huge concern for the cohort. And also: it's my damn house."

Kaylin entered the room behind Sedarias and Terrano.

Nightshade lay atop a bed meant for one, his arms by his sides, his eyes closed. His hair was a spill of black, and even in his state, not a strand was out of place. Annarion was beside the bed.

Mandoran leaned against the wall, arms folded, chin down.

He looked up the second Kaylin crossed the threshold. His eyes matched Sedarias's for color. Mandoran's blue wasn't one of fury or fear—not normally. But Mandoran had traveled to Elantra with Annarion, arriving before the rest of the cohort. The two were close.

"Serralyn's in the chancellor's office right now," Mandoran told her.

"She needs permission to access the library?"

"The librarians," Mandoran corrected her. "Annarion isn't as delicate in his use of magic as Serralyn is; he's been trying to examine the spell he believes his brother is under."

Clearly, he'd had no luck.

Terrano's hand was firmly on Annarion's shoulder. Annarion looked—from the back—like his usual self. She hadn't seen much of him in the recent past. She hadn't seen Nightshade either. If the siblings were still at war, they argued when Kaylin was out of the house. Probably when she was at work.

"Can you force him to wake?" It was Sedarias who asked Kaylin, her voice cold. She turned as she spoke.

Kaylin met, and held, her gaze.

Mandoran grimaced, pulled himself off the wall that was holding half his weight, and approached Kaylin. "We probably need to talk. Your cheek is bleeding," he added.

Kaylin shrugged. "I don't know enough about this damn mark to use it, if it can be used at all. But I'm pretty sure bleeding isn't a good sign."

"Not generally, no."

Andellen was nowhere in sight when they exited the room in which Nightshade lay.

"I have convinced him that bathing and changing would be wise," Helen told her.

Mandoran sat, heavily, on a long divan.

"Did you expect this?" Kaylin asked, folding her arms as she slouched into the cushions beside him.

"No. Not this."

"How's Annarion doing?"

"The usual. He's furious at his brother. He's furious at himself for caring about what's happened to his brother. He's terrified for his brother. He wants explanations. He wants justifications for his brother's behavior that make sense and can be believed. He's not going to get those if his brother dies here. He wants to wake him up and shake him until his teeth rattle. That's one of yours, by the way. I've never heard teeth rattle—are they not attached?"

"I've never heard teeth rattle, either. It's just a saying."

"Sedarias is in the room. She was kind of hoping the whole pain and sense of betrayal would fade from Annarion in a few decades." He winced.

"That's hope for you," Kaylin replied.

"If that mark on your cheek doesn't stop bleeding, she'd like you to avoid Annarion."

"Why? He's going to see it if you're here, or Terrano is."

"She thinks seeing it with his own eyes will probably be worse." As Kaylin shrugged, Mandoran sat up. "You couldn't touch him."

"I could touch him—" She exhaled. "No, if you mean the healing. I didn't really try to push through. There's something about him as he is now that resists that. I don't know if what's enveloping him is what's actually killing him—or if it's keeping him alive.

"Does Sedarias have any idea why Nightshade was attacked?"

"No. She's up to her elbows in court politics these days—but she's still an outsider. An'Mellarionne's former allies are not her allies. There are two cousins who are causing difficulty."

Kaylin winced.

"There were three until a week ago, if that's any consolation."

It wasn't. "You haven't jumped into the political fray."

Mandoran was silent. It was deliberate, unlike him.

Kaylin glanced at his stiff expression. "You're right. The less I know, the better."

"You're only going to worry. Serralyn is staying well quit of the court, as is Valliant. But the rest of us, with the obvious exception of Terrano, are now surveying our options. Sedarias has one very notable ally she can trust."

"Teela."

"An'Teela, yes. But Teela's still intent on remaining with the Hawks. What she can do, she can do because she's had centuries to build a base of power. If she takes over the conflict, Sedarias will be rendered irrelevant. Mellarionne won't be a concern; it will become a vassal of Teela's line. Neither of them wants that.

"So she's made clear to all of the High Court that Sedarias is a valued ally—but she can't do more than that without diminishing Sedarias. Teela's not happy," he added, as if it needed to be said. "What are you going to do?"

"I'm going to keep Nightshade here. Andellen thinks it's a good idea only because there was a second war band in the streets of the fief, and getting through that was going to cause issues. Mostly us dying."

Mandoran held up a hand. "What do you mean, *second* war band?"

Oh, right. Mandoran had probably been sent to get what information he could from Kaylin on behalf of Annarion and the rest of the cohort. "Nightshade was leaving his fief. He was attacked on the edge of the border zone by fourteen armed and armored Barrani. We believe it was a war band. They're dead," she added, in case it was necessary. "But whoever sent the Barrani didn't believe fourteen armed and armored men could be trusted to finish the job."

"Well, they clearly couldn't," Mandoran replied.

"We were trying to decide whether or not to carry him back to Castle Nightshade when we caught sight of the second group. Tiamaris was waiting for us in full Dragon form; if he hadn't been, I think they'd've charged right in to stop us."

"They wore no identifying insignia?"

"I'm not familiar with Barrani coats of arms. I'm not Barrani—and before you ask, I'm not familiar with human coats of arms either. I thought he'd be safer here, and we were kind of pressed for time. Although I guess Tiamaris could have killed them all if it came to that."

Mandoran winced. "Probably better to have Nightshade here. Might even be better for Annarion. It's certainly not going to help the rest of us, though."

"Has Terrano seen anything that might be a clue? Has Serralyn?"

Mandoran shook his head. "Torrisant is headed this way as well."

"Why?"

"Because he's really good at anchoring people who lose their forms, and we're going to need it."

"Kaylin," Helen said as Mandoran rose. Both Kaylin and her housemate turned in the direction of the voice. Helen's Avatar didn't materialize. "A messenger has arrived at the door."

"From who?"

"They did not say. They left a letter and retreated. They did not require a reply."

"Did it look important?"

"The messenger was Barrani."

Kaylin rose. "I'll come and get it."

"No need," Helen replied, materializing in person, a silver tray bearing a scroll case in her hands. "I do not suggest you touch it," she added, looking in Mandoran's direction.

"Specific enchant?"

Helen nodded. "Whoever sent this message didn't want anyone else to read it. I'm not certain if anyone else would even be able to touch it."

"You can."

"I serve Kaylin. And I am not Barrani."

Kaylin picked up the scroll case. It wasn't sealed. She opened it, twisting the top off; her arms tingled faintly. Normal magic.

Lord Kaylin, the sender wrote.

It has been some time since we last crossed paths. I would like to see you in person. The Lake is restless, and there is much to discuss. It has come to my attention that you are nursing the fieflord.

Information traveled far more quickly than Kaylin could predict.

Ynpharion was annoyed, but silent.

A dangerous choice, the message continued, *especially at this juncture. I would suggest, if safety is a concern, that you make a different one.*

Kaylin's hands grew cold.

But if you will not, you will not. I have made time in the garden to receive you tomorrow. I have been informed that you have duties to the Halls of Law with which I should not interfere. Were the situation not so unstable, I would arrange a meeting that does not overlap with that work. I cannot.

I have carved out time in the morning, perhaps an hour after sunrise. I have informed the High Lord of your imminent visit; his guards will be aware of your presence.

I look forward to your company on the morrow.

Kaylin looked at Mandoran.

"Bad news?"

"Uncertain."

Mandoran's expression made clear he didn't consider this uncertain. It was bad news. "It would *really* simplify all of our lives if we could just let you join us. What's in the letter?"

"The Consort has either invited or commanded my presence in the High Halls."

It is a command, Ynpharion said, voice stiff with his usual annoyance. *But congratulations for even being aware of that fact.*

"Teela's on her way." Mandoran's eyes lightened as he spoke.

"Did you tell her about the Consort's invitation?"

"I didn't attempt to keep it from her, if that's what you're asking."

Ugh. "The Consort believes I shouldn't attend the High Halls with Teela. Or Sedarias. Or probably anyone obviously associated with her."

"She's not telling you to go alone, surely?"

"It's okay if I bring Severn. It's okay if I show up wearing the Hawks' tabard—she thinks it might be better, because it'll remind people that the Halls of Law exist, and our deaths would prevent laws of exemption from being called."

"Not that that would do *you* any good."

Kaylin shrugged. "It comes with the job. I won't be sent to the Halls of Law for that job, so the tabard is partly a lie. Which reminds me. I need to clear my unexpected absence with my sergeant."

Helen prepared the mirror room.

"I have taken the liberty of contacting the Arkon," Helen said. "While I understand your request was meant for your sergeant, I believe the Arkon will expedite your appointment—and you are less likely to suffer loss of pay."

Helen's mirror changed from day to day. Tara's mirror in the fief of Tiamaris didn't: it was a still, small pond. A ripple could destroy the mirror image. She, like Helen, was deeply suspicious of the mirror network; she considered it a large security risk. But she was practical. She knew that much of her lord's life—as Kaylin's—relied on that mirror network. It was faster than courier or in-person discussion if the person one needed to reach was halfway across the city.

Today, Helen's mirror resembled the long, wide standing mirror in the Hawklord's Tower. Sanabalis appeared across the mirror's surface.

"I have been informed," he said, eyes orange, "that this is an important or urgent communication. Thank you, Helen," he added, although he was staring at Kaylin.

Kaylin exhaled. "The Consort has . . . invited me to visit her in the High Halls."

"I see. Given our current concerns, that is of interest."

"Tomorrow."

Sanabalis blinked. "Tomorrow?"

"I'm to attend her tomorrow. During the earliest hours of my work day."

"Ah. I see. You wish me to make clear to your sergeant that I have called in your services. Will you require your partner?"

"Yes. She suggests that I visit kitted out as a Hawk."

Sanabalis frowned, his brows drawing together. "Very well. She understands the possible difficulties." He cleared his throat. "We have been informed of the incident in the fiefs. You are aware of the Emperor's interest in the fiefs—particularly the stability of the Towers." In other words: Nightshade was important. Kaylin was slightly annoyed, because she *already knew that.* But she was pretty certain Sanabalis would say this to anyone; it wasn't—or shouldn't be—personal. "We will leave the guarding of the fieflord in your hands. If you were not who you are, I would forbid you to accept the Consort's invitation at this time."

Kaylin nodded. Had she any real choice, she'd've rejected it as well.

Ynpharion said nothing. He agreed and disagreed; minor approval at unheard-of caution clashed with outrage at the possible insult to his lord.

"Very well. I expect to hear back from you after your visit."

Kaylin shrugged, uneasy. There were things she couldn't discuss with Sanabalis. Or anyone who didn't already know.

Luckily she didn't have to.

Helen cleared her throat. "Teela has arrived, dear. I think she wants to speak with you immediately."

Of course she did.

Teela was dressed casually; she didn't wear the tabard after work, but neither did Kaylin. Kaylin hadn't had a chance to change; she'd approached Nightshade at a full run, and the investigation and subsequent arrival home had been the priority. Still, Teela's court dress was absent. Her sword was not.

Helen hadn't opened the parlor, which meant this wasn't going to be a cozy social time. Given the color of Teela's eyes, that was obvious.

"Have you eaten, dear?" Helen asked. Helen was probably the only person in existence who could call Teela *dear.*

"No. I doubt Kaylin has, either."

"She hasn't. And she does need to eat. Would you join her?"

Teela didn't look like she wanted food, but she knew Helen would fret if Kaylin didn't eat. She gave a curt nod, which could pass as agreement, before turning her blue glare to Kaylin.

"I'm going to change," Kaylin said. "Before dinner."

"I'd suggest you bathe as well," Helen told her as she headed toward the stairs.

Teela was waiting patiently in the dining hall.

She was speaking with Mrs. Erickson, who looked up when Kaylin entered. "Is Annarion all right?" Mrs. Erickson inquired.

Asking Teela would have made more sense, but Kaylin winced as she took her seat. "He's not happy. But his brother is alive, and I'm sure, when he regains consciousness, Annarion will be much better."

"Mandoran is worried about him."

"They're all very close, as you no doubt noticed." She really didn't want to keep talking about the cohort in front of Mrs. Erickson. If things went south—no, given luck, *when*—the last thing she wanted was Mrs. Erickson to be caught up in it.

"I did some baking for Annarion. I'll take it up to him now, if you don't mind."

"You're not going to eat?"

"I did eat," Mrs. Erickson replied. "And I'm sure you two have Hawk business to discuss."

"She's impossible not to like," Teela observed when Mrs. Erickson had gently closed the dining room door.

Kaylin nodded. "Mandoran and Terrano are very fond of her. I think Fallessian is as well, but I see less of him."

"He is. All of them are, although Sedarias refuses to demonstrate any sign of it." Teela exhaled, her lips losing the trace of affectionate smile that Mrs. Erickson had caused. It was now time for business.

"Mandoran implied that my presence by your side in the High Halls would not be appreciated or advised."

Kaylin nodded again. "I think things are political."

Teela snorted.

"Fine, I deserved that. But I think it's way more political than usual. The Consort doesn't feel having you by my side would protect me in the long run."

"That is one opinion."

"Teela—what's going on at court? What's happening? Does it have *anything* to do with Nightshade?"

"It is not of me that you must ask those questions," Teela

replied, speaking in High Barrani. She was annoyed. Kaylin wondered if she would respect the Consort's advice.

Kaylin slid into High Barrani as well. "She felt that it would be wisest if I visit her wearing the Hawks' tabard. Severn is invited to accompany me."

"She did, did she?" Teela was definitely annoyed.

Mandoran opened the dining room door. "We'd appreciate your opinion as an Arcanist," he told Teela. "And you know she's right. There's no way almost thirty Barrani soldiers went to Nightshade without intervention from one Lord of the High Court or another. Whatever's going on, it's got something to do with *deep* politics. If it involves Nightshade, it could have roots in things that happened centuries ago.

"We're too new. We spent those centuries in the Hallionne. You didn't. You know this better than any of us: if Kaylin's to remain outside the Barrani political sphere, you're not the person she should be with."

Teela failed to reply—at least where Kaylin could hear it.

Nightshade had not miraculously regained consciousness.

Teela entered his rooms only after Andellen had both opened the door at her knock and invited her in. He treated Teela with genuine respect, even given her casual clothing. Then again, she was wearing the sword, one third of The Three: *Kariannos*.

If she wasn't expecting trouble of some kind, she wouldn't be wearing it now.

"With your permission, I would like to examine Lord Nightshade," she told Andellen in formal High Barrani.

"This way," he replied, nodding. "Although Lord Annarion's permission will no doubt need to be given as well."

Teela nodded, as if Annarion hadn't already granted that permission. She allowed Andellen to lead, although she knew the way: she knew what the cohort knew.

Andellen gestured through the open arch beyond which Nightshade lay. Annarion was by his side.

Mandoran let Teela follow Andellen, hanging back to speak with Kaylin.

"We don't expect Teela will be able to do anything you can't do," he told her. "But she's always been a bit cagey about the extent of her Arcanist knowledge, and it can't hurt. You're going to the High Halls, right?"

Kaylin nodded. "Is Teela?"

"We're arguing about that right now. Her compromise was, she'll go wearing the Hawks' tabard as well. With Tain."

Kaylin almost shrieked. "She can't!"

"She can. Teela's powerful enough that an assassin or two won't make her break a sweat, and many Lords of the High Court loathe her position as a Hawk. They consider it an outrageous insult to the Barrani as a whole. She is *serving* the Dragon Emperor. Given that, she feels it'll draw ire, which will deflect any ire directed to you."

Ugh. "You know how these things work. Yes, she's right. It'll piss people off. But powerful, petty people tend to take out their issues on the distinctly less powerful. Which would be me."

"You're the Chosen," Mandoran replied. "If anyone's going to take the fall for thumbing their noses at the powerful, it'll likely be Tain."

"Tell her not to come."

Mandoran exhaled. "You better get going. She's waiting."

"Patiently?"

"No one's died yet."

Kaylin thought it unfair that Teela was annoyed at Kaylin for tarrying, and not at Mandoran, who was the entire reason she hadn't followed the Barrani Hawk immediately. Teela's eyes were a dark blue, but not the midnight they sometimes became when she was furious or deeply worried.

"You tried to heal him?"

Kaylin grimaced.

"I'll take that as a yes, and you know *full well* why that is beyond foolish."

"I'm not sure he'll make it without some kind of serious intervention," Kaylin countered, deflecting the *why are you being stupid* comment. "I intended to do what I could to keep him alive and pull out before things got too entangled."

"Because you have so much practice with that."

Kaylin shrugged. It was true. She didn't start healing to half-ass it. She poured power into the injured body until the body was no longer injured.

"I couldn't actually connect with his body at all. I could touch the skin, but even then, it felt as if a layer of something was between that skin and my hand."

"Could you possibly do something about your cheek? The mark is bleeding."

Kaylin nodded, aware that she usually healed quickly. "Helen, can you put a normal mirror in this room?"

Helen's reply was action: a mirror appeared on the wall farthest from Nightshade's bed. Kaylin headed to look at her face.

As practically everyone she'd encountered today had said, her cheek was bleeding. To Kaylin, the Erenne mark had become part of the geography of her face, an awkward tattoo. The Marks of the Chosen caused far more discomfort, far more consistently.

The mark didn't hurt, but it was bleeding along the lines of its nightshade shape, tracing the edges of the flower in a dark red, as if the mark were etched into her skin, and blood ran along slender runnels. She touched it with her fingers; she was definitely bleeding.

And that was enough of the mirror for now. She turned back to Teela as her arms started to break out in goose bumps. Teela was now examining Nightshade.

Terrano joined her, flying—almost literally—into the room. Kaylin winced; he'd already adjusted the shape, size, and color of his eyes; they took up a third of his face, almost merging into each other across the bridge of his nose. She knew it didn't cause him pain, but she was always going to find it disturbing.

"You said he had *Meliannos* in a tight grip when he fell?" Teela's question was all Hawk in tone.

"Yes. Andellen resheathed it before we fled here—Tiamaris had to carry him in his claws."

"I find no obvious external injuries. You examined him?"

"Not his entire body, no. Just exposed skin and the fabric of his clothing. I thought it might be poison until I tried to heal him."

"And now?"

Kaylin's eyes narrowed as she met Teela's. ". . . possibly magic. Magic—not Nightshade's, according to Andellen—was used over a wide area; it was an invisibility sphere. But it had a large signature."

"You are certain."

Kaylin nodded. "I know Arcanist tiaras contain accessible power—if an Arcanist is present and chooses to use it. But this spell had a sigil."

"Did you recognize it?"

"No." She didn't add *of course not* but felt it should have been obvious. The spell was definitely Barrani in origin, given the war bands, and the Hawks pretty much never investigated Barrani-on-Barrani crimes. The Hawks had zero legal authority in the fiefs, even if the Barrani crimes might theoretically fall under Imperial law had they occurred in the city proper.

"You sense no similar sigil anywhere near Lord Nightshade."

Kaylin shook her head. "Whatever affected him doesn't trip my magic allergies. Unlike what you're doing now."

"Helen?"

Helen materialized. "Yes, dear?"

"Do you sense magic emanating from Nightshade? Or internal to him?"

Helen was silent for a long beat. "Yes," she finally said.

04

"As I said before, magic evolves. It is like any other field of study. If you ask me to detail the magic I sense, I am uncertain my conjectures would be of value. I have not had a mage as a tenant since I first broke free of the fetters of obedience. I still retain the various research materials and notes of previous masters, but they are hidden."

"I would like to study them," Teela said.

Helen turned to Kaylin.

"Better her than me."

"Kitling."

Kaylin exhaled. "Is the magic keeping him unconscious?"

"I cannot say that definitively. Nor, as I might have mentioned, can I say with certainty that the magic itself is not protective in nature."

"Protective against what?"

"You cannot tell if he has been poisoned."

"Not if I can't touch him, no. If I had no idea who or what he was, my first guess would have been poison. But the fact that I can't reach him with the power of the Marks of the Chosen implies magic. Maybe magical poison?"

Teela's brow furrowed as she considered Kaylin's suggestion. "That is not what it would be called, but it is theoretically possible. If it acted the way poison generally does, it would cause damage. The fact that you can't examine him with your power goes against that."

"Would a normal doctor, a nonmagical expert, have any better luck? I'm not medically trained. I don't have that expertise."

Teela frowned. "It's possible. But human doctors wouldn't possess the required knowledge or experience, and there are very few Barrani doctors who do not rely on magic as their examination tool. None," she added, voice cooling, "that I would trust enough to take the risk of examination. And we would be waiting for some weeks, even should we choose to take that risk—our experts are in the West March."

"There aren't any in the High Halls?"

Teela snorted. "They would be considered far too provincial to be accorded respect in the High Halls. Regardless, I feel the magic is complex enough that we cannot simply assume it is the magic alone that is the danger."

"Will he survive?" Kaylin asked as quietly as she could.

"While he is here, I believe he is safe. Annarion will stand watch."

Terrano lifted a hand. "Wait."

Teela didn't care for Terrano's eyes, either. She turned immediately, regardless.

"Can you draw his sword?"

"His sword?"

"Meliannos."

Teela's brows rose, her eyes flecked, briefly, with gold. "You want *me* to draw *Meliannos*?"

"I don't think anyone else is likely to survive the attempt," was Terrano's matter-of-fact reply.

"Please don't kill him," Kaylin said quickly. "*Don't* try, because I think we'll probably need him. Terrano, tell her *why*. Right now."

Terrano turned to Kaylin, grinning. His eyes hadn't returned to normal. "She won't kill me. And she knows why. Seriously, could we just *give* you one name? Like, just one? Words are hard."

"You use so many of them, I'm surprised to hear you say that," Teela snapped.

Terrano rolled his eyes. Kaylin had to look away. "You don't see the magic at all, right? You can physically touch Nightshade; you can't do anything else?"

She nodded.

"There's still a connection. You can't reach him by calling his True Name, right?" He grimaced, clearly at one of the cohort's replies.

Teela lifted a hand. "Before you continue, I am leaving. I have an investigation to begin before we head to the High Halls tomorrow."

"There's no *we*," Kaylin began.

"Attempt to make sense of what Terrano sees when his eyes are in that state. I'll tell you if I discover anything of import."

"Where are you going?"

"The fiefs, of course." Teela turned and left the room, walking quickly. She paused, and then said, "Lord Andellen. I would appreciate your input."

Andellen, standing on the other side of the arch that led to his lord, stiffened.

Helen turned to Nightshade's sole liege. "It's you or Kaylin," she told him. "She would prefer your input because you were actually involved in all stages of the attack as a defender. Kaylin arrived only after the fact."

Kaylin, still looking away from Terrano's face, turned to Andellen. She nodded. "Annarion and Nightshade might not have been on the best of terms, but Annarion will let nothing harm his brother while Nightshade remains within Helen's perimeters. If Teela thinks she needs your input, she does."

Andellen hesitated for one long beat before nodding. To Kaylin.

"I swear, Teela's about to lose all her hair."

"Hair isn't the word we usually use."

"Helen doesn't like it when I curse." As Terrano spoke, he turned back to Nightshade.

Kaylin glanced at Annarion and he flinched, looking away.

"What?"

Annarion said nothing.

Terrano did curse, then. "You know your mark is bleeding, right? Nightshade's Erenne mark?"

"According to everyone I've spoken to today, yes."

"An Erenne mark isn't like the other Marks. Most of Annarion's anger at his brother is because of the mark you bear. He doesn't care about the family that discarded him. He doesn't care that most of that line is lost to history, even if he's certain Nightshade was responsible for that. It's the damn Erenne mark. What it means to you—mostly nothing, anymore—and what it means to our people are different."

"It's like a consort mark, right?"

Terrano winced. "Yes, sort of."

"No," Annarion snapped. "It's like a slave mark. A precious slave. A valued slave." His hands were fists. Of the cohort, Annarion was usually mild and quiet; he had control of his emotions and his words. But not when it came to his brother.

"He's never tried to use it against me."

Terrano placed a gentle hand on Annarion's shoulder. "I know. I know, but the fact that the mark is bleeding might be helpful. Kaylin doesn't want your brother to die—and the mark is on *her* face."

"Two war bands," Annarion said, voice low. "Any Barrani who sees that mark in the wake of those war bands is going to target her."

"Everyone's seen it. Look—I'm not trying to defend your brother. I'm just interested in saving his life. Even if you never speak to him again, we need him in the fiefs."

Annarion swallowed. ". . . sorry." He'd dropped into Elantran as he looked at Kaylin. "Terrano thinks you might be able to break through because you have that . . . tattoo. He says it's bleeding because it's connected—and no, he doesn't understand why. None of us do. It's an ancient tradition—and it's never used now. That's part of the reason it was so shocking."

"So . . . I'd want to talk to someone ancient enough to tell me what the mark actually does? I mean, Nightshade's thugs treat me with respect because I have it."

"Because if you get angry with them, Nightshade might be furious. They will suffer consequences for disrespecting you." Helen sounded certain.

"But it doesn't mean what they think it means. It doesn't mean anything, now."

Helen said nothing.

Kaylin was uncomfortable, and Helen knew it. But her house had a mind of her own; she was willing—even happy—to be Kaylin's home, but home had never meant a total bleaching of her character. Helen's desire to *be* a home was based on Helen's concept of home. "Fine. It's a connection. It's saved me before. I hate it," Kaylin added, lowering her voice. "Because I grew up in his fief. If his fief were like Tiamaris, I'd feel differently. But it's not just hate. It's complicated.

"And it *is* a connection. Terrano suspects—actually I'm pretty sure it's Serralyn who had the actual suspicion—that that connection might be useful. The namebond isn't, and in theory, that's more powerful."

"It was Serralyn," Terrano confirmed.

"I don't know a lot about the Erenne mark, but I'm not making *myself* bleed. There's some connection. Teela couldn't get through whatever the spell is. I couldn't do it with the Marks of the Chosen."

"You have not fully tried," Helen said.

"Fine. I couldn't do it with the knowledge I have. Better?"

Helen pursed her lips.

"Sanabalis has decided we've been approaching things the wrong way. He thinks it's instinct, emotion, and probably desperation that governs the use of the power—at least in me. But . . . *my* instincts, my emotions, and my desperation. I'm not sure if it's true. I'm not sure how you teach someone *more* about their own instincts.

"And it's true I didn't try to push through whatever defenses have been erected—but . . . it's healing. On a visceral level, I don't believe that *my* healing functions that way. Doctors? Yes. Sometimes they have to cut or break things in order to reset the body. I've seen it in the Hawks, and in the infirmary. I've done similar things to what doctors do when healthy people were infested with Shadow and I arrived in time. But that's not . . ." She grimaced. "I don't think that would work here."

"I will have words with Lord Sanabalis at a later date," Helen replied. She clearly didn't agree with the new approach. "No, I do not. Feelings, such as they are, are amorphous, and they are oft influenced by things that have very, very little to do with the task at hand. Prioritization of such things must be done with precision and care."

Kaylin exhaled. "He has to wake up, Helen. He has to wake up for Annarion's sake, if not for his own."

Helen was obviously hesitant. She spoke after a longer pause. "Do you believe the Erenne mark can somehow achieve what the far greater power of the Chosen cannot?"

"No—but if Serralyn thinks it might help me get past whatever it is that's sealing Nightshade in, we should at least try."

Annarion said nothing, but Kaylin grimaced. Sometimes, when she talked to Helen, she forgot that anyone else was in the room. Except for Terrano; it was hard to forget him. "I'm not upset about the mark," she said quietly. "I won't tell you how to feel about it—but you and Nightshade are never going to resolve anything if he dies here."

Annarion exhaled. "It's not just that. I told you: two war bands were sent to the fiefs. Teela is trying to determine who sent them. But that mark is a giant flag for people who want my brother dead. They'll recognize it. They might not know more about its use than we do—but they won't care. They'll kill you to make a point. That's not what the rest of us want—but if we move to guard you, we'll get ensnared in politics we don't fully understand.

"Teela is looking into that, as well." He hesitated. "Can you maybe just . . . visit the Consort later in the week?"

Ynpharion was annoyed. He was not enraged. He considered Annarion intelligent, if a bit too casual. *The Lady is also, as Lord Annarion put it, looking into the war bands. It is not simple to move war bands within the city itself. The fief of Tiamaris is closed to us; the fief of Bellusdeo is closed. She believes some cooperation from one of the fiefs must have occurred.*

She does not want Lord Nightshade to perish. She reminds you that your meeting is tomorrow in the morning.

"Terrano—tell Teela when we fled over a dozen Barrani were coming out of the fief. I'm not sure she'll want to run into them."

"She already knows," Terrano replied. "And actually, she's in a bad enough mood I think she really *does* want to run into them."

"I don't think Andellen will."

"Oh no, he's perfectly happy to join her."

Kaylin glared at Terrano.

"It'll be okay. Torrisant and Fallessian followed her. Annarion wanted to go, but Sedarias didn't want him there. On the other hand, Sedarias wanted to go, and Teela forbade it. As you can guess, it's pretty bloody noisy on the inside of my head.

"To be clear, she doesn't particularly care that they attacked Nightshade. He's outcaste, after all. But she understands that Nightshade affects Annarion, and she's afraid that it will affect you as well."

Kaylin grimaced. "Meaning, she thinks it already has."

"Meaning, she is deeply unhappy with the Consort's request, yes. Look, I'd ask you to stay out of it, but we both know you're worse than I am. You're going to do what you're going to do because you think it's necessary." He winced; obviously Teela or Sedarias didn't find this amusing. "The thing is, you'll probably even be right."

With nothing resolved, they returned to the dining room.

Even if Kaylin accepted that the Erenne mark could be used, and she should attempt to leverage the connection it created between her and the fieflord, she had no idea *how.* She'd never used it for anything, and if it hadn't caused bleeding, she wouldn't have noticed it at all.

"Serralyn's going to ask the Arbiters. The former Arkon has no better idea—Dragons don't have an equivalent. Kaylin?"

Kaylin blinked. There was food on her plate. She was seated at the dining table. Yes, it had been a long day—but not long enough that she could barely keep her eyes open.

"You are falling asleep at the table," Helen observed. "Mandoran, it is time to let Kaylin sleep."

"I didn't interrupt her," Mandoran replied, glaring in Terrano's direction.

"No, you didn't. Do not start. Kaylin?"

Kaylin pushed herself back from the table. She knew a command when she heard it, no matter how prettily it was said.

She woke that night with a start. It didn't take long to realize why.

The cohort was being fractious. Helen woke Kaylin for the

midwives' guild if they mirrored during sleeping hours; she let her sleep otherwise. Tonight, she hadn't.

Kaylin rolled out of bed and reached for her clothing. If the emergency was big enough, she'd be better off dressed to leave the house.

The door opened as she approached it, Hope grumbling in her ear. "You can stay in bed," she told him. He bit her ear and stayed where he was. This wasn't really the *best* sign. "Helen's here, and she's not going to let anything hurt or kill me. Helen?"

"As you suspect, the cohort is arguing. I would have had them argue in the training room, as things are somewhat intense, but Annarion refused to leave his brother's side. Mandoran refused to leave Annarion's side. Annarion and Sedarias had a rather explosive argument, and they are not speaking to each other."

"Are they trying to kill each other?"

"Not anymore."

Kaylin stiffened.

"If it helps, they weren't trying to kill each other; they were trying to injure each other." Helen exhaled, which was entirely affectation. "Sedarias is not, as you are well aware, emotionally attached to any of her family. She has long considered Annarion and Nightshade to be inexplicable. Nightshade's affection for his brother makes no sense to her; Annarion's angry conflict, even less.

"She has suggested that it would be best to put Lord Nightshade out of his misery, to cut the ties that bind, as Annarion has been angry with his brother since he arrived in Elantra."

Kaylin winced.

"Some of the cohort agreed with Sedarias. Some did not."

"Did anyone *else* get involved in the fight?"

"Only in an attempt to prevent it."

Kaylin left her room. There was no actual shouting, but the ground trembled beneath her bare feet. She turned back to fish her boots from under her bed and tried again. "Teela's not back yet?"

"She has not returned, no. The cohort is not worried."

"Fallessian and Torrisant?"

"They are continuing to aid Teela in her investigation."

Kaylin frowned. "She's not in the fiefs, is she?"

"She is no longer within the fief of Nightshade."

"Did she find the Barrani? They weren't waiting for Nightshade to return, were they?"

"I believe Mandoran will answer your questions." Kaylin could take the hint. She turned toward the room Helen had opened for Nightshade's use.

Mandoran met her at the door. "He hasn't woken up."

"I guessed. Has he gotten any worse?"

"There's very little visible difference; he's still breathing, and it seems to be even and steady. But you *really* have to do something about your cheek."

"It doesn't hurt."

"Did it ever?"

She nodded. "When we were on our Elani beat. I'd say midmorning. I don't have a more accurate time, but you might ask Tiamaris or his Tower. Or Severn; we were on patrol." She frowned. "You could also ask Teela to ask Andellen about the timing of the attack. It's possible Nightshade made no attempt to reach out the normal way, as you put it, because he didn't have time."

"It doesn't take a lot of time to speak through the name-bond."

No. It didn't. Nightshade could have easily spoken through their bond—normally. It would make a lot more sense. "Could you maybe not pile on new things to consider when my plate is already full?"

"Maybe? It's just something to think about. Before you ask, Serralyn asked. I'm just the bearer of bad news."

Kaylin didn't care for the bad news. "Helen—you can prevent the namebound from reaching out to me when I'm at home."

"Yes, dear."

"But that's a choice you make, right? Is it something intrinsic to you being a sentient building, or is it something else?"

"Everything I do is intrinsic to my construction."

"Is it something you think an Arcanist could duplicate?"

"I am uncertain." That sounded a lot like *no*. "But even if an Arcanist could duplicate the effect, it would take them some time."

"Barrani have time, though."

"They do. I can turn my shield on or off within my own boundaries, but as you are aware, a great deal of magic is involved in the creation of a sentient building. If this murder were planned perhaps a century ago—in your years—it is possible the same effect could be achieved.

"I highly doubt it could be achieved from within the fief of Nightshade."

"It's not the first time Arcanists—or worse—operated in the fief."

"I do not believe those Arcanists intended to kill the fieflord."

Kaylin grudgingly agreed. "I think the bulk of the fighting took place in the border zone between Tiamaris and Nightshade."

"And the border zones are not under the strict influence of the Towers. I believe it was in the border zones that you first discovered the entrance to the Academia. It was because of the nature of those zones that the Academia was preserved, in a type of hibernation. There is power there—but it is a power buildings such as I were created to use.

"It was the Tower Bellusdeo rules that managed to broker the hibernation of the Academia. No one understands the function of, the existence of, the border zones; they are not strictly geographical. But you know that better than anyone currently conscious."

Silence. "The portal paths between Hallionne might be like the border zone," Mandoran finally said. "We lost contact when some of us were confined there."

Helen nodded.

"But that makes no sense," Kaylin said, frowning.

"No. Sorry."

Kaylin exhaled and shook off sleep. She didn't want more details about the Annarion-Sedarias conflict, just in case it started up again. "So where's Teela?"

Mandoran grimaced. "We're not entirely sure what Teela is up to now—but she's been walking the border zone between fiefs. It's not contiguous, at least not in her current form."

Kaylin sucked in air.

"Terrano is *not* helping. He's giving Teela advice—and she's the least flexible of all of us. She learns fast, and she can be submerged in the group chaos, but it's much, much harder for her to pull out. Terrano thinks he understands what she's trying to figure out, but Serralyn's been grilling Killian, and she's come up with questions Teela might be able to answer.

"Sedarias doesn't want Terrano to join Teela. Neither does Teela. The reasons are a bit different, but Terrano flipped out—that's the right term?" At Kaylin's nod, he continued. "Sedarias asked Helen to 'contain' Terrano."

Kaylin flinched.

"Right. Helen made clear that unless Terrano attempted to harm either her or you, she wasn't prepared to do that. Sedarias then sent Valliant—from the Academia—to cross into the fief of Bellusdeo. Bellusdeo is obsessed with Shadow—and with the danger it presents."

"Please tell me Teela is *nowhere near* the *Ravellon* border."

"I could, but I'd be lying."

Kaylin dropped her face into her hands. "Helen, can you raise Tiamaris on the mirror network?"

"Yes, dear. I believe Tara is waiting for you."

"Which fief is Teela in?" Kaylin demanded of Mandoran.

"We believe she's walking the border between Tiamaris and Bellusdeo. The Norranir are there, and they seem to have better defenses against Shadow encroachment. She's *trying* to be careful.

"Serralyn has questions about the Erenne mark, but she also has questions about why Nightshade couldn't contact you. She's been listening in to everything. Killian found that last part troubling. And I'm guessing so does Helen."

Helen did not comment.

Kaylin turned to the Avatar of her house. "Do you want me to try to reason with Bellusdeo, stop Teela, or join Teela when I have to meet the Consort first thing in the morning?"

"Yes," Mandoran said.

"Which?"

"Was it an either/or question?"

Squawk.

"Everyone's a critic," Mandoran said. "It's serious. Teela went out carrying *Kariannos*, and we'd like her not to have to use it against Bellusdeo."

"Bellusdeo isn't likely to attack Teela."

"No—but Emmerian has already lost his temper while visiting us. We don't hold it against him. If he weren't a Dragon, he might actually fit right in. You think he's going to stay home when Bellusdeo flies out in a panic?"

"I get it. I get it. I'm going."

Do you want company? Severn asked.

At this time of night? I'd like us not to both be dead on our feet when we meet the Consort tomorrow. Or later today. One of those two.

When Severn failed to respond, she said, *I've got Hope with me. If I can get to Teela, Andellen's there. And Bellusdeo will probably be there as well. The only reason the cohort wants me to head to the fiefs is they trust Bellusdeo not to completely lose her mind if I'm there, because she knows I won't survive it.*

Severn concurred. *I'll meet you at the bridge.*

When Kaylin hesitated, he added, *It might concern Shadow. You know that's her biggest sensitivity.*

Fine.

Helen wasn't happy.

"I'll be fine. Severn's meeting me at the bridge. We'll head into the fiefs together."

Squawk. Squawk.

"That is exactly what I'm afraid of," Helen replied.

Hope snickered. Kaylin flicked his snout.

"Terrano, I believe you were asked to remain at home," Helen then said, her voice the severe Helen voice, not the gentle one.

Kaylin couldn't actually see the cohort member but wasn't particularly surprised. She'd've bet most of the money she had that he'd find a way to tag along.

"Are you certain you don't wish me to attempt to confine him?"

"I'm a Hawk. I can't just throw someone in jail for a crime they haven't committed yet. If he really does something stupid, the rest of us can discuss it later."

"Because then it won't be illegal, metaphorically speaking?"

"More or less. Terrano?"

He appeared. His eyes were normal eyes, and he looked very pleased with himself. "We'd better run," he said, almost whispering. "Sedarias is about to charge down the stairs in a fury."

Severn was waiting by the time they reached the bridge—and Terrano had set up an impatient jog almost the moment they'd crossed Helen's fence line.

"I wasn't kidding about Sedarias," he said when Kaylin gave him a look.

"I don't particularly care whether or not she comes." Not, strictly speaking, the entire truth, but she couldn't see the harm in it.

"Teela does," he replied. "Sedarias and Bellusdeo aren't a great combination. The Dragon's fine with Teela, more or less. She actually likes Mandoran—but Mandoran doesn't want to leave Annarion."

Kaylin nodded.

"I'm not sure she cares for me—but I don't ruffle her scales."

"You can't ruffle scales. Trust me."

"Fine. But she doesn't have feathers, and you know what I meant. And if I stay in between a couple of planes, her breath passes through me."

"Teela doesn't want you there either, does she?"

"No," he replied, all smiles. "She's threatened to break a leg—mine, just in case you were wondering. But she's not the boss of me, and Serralyn thought I *might* be helpful."

Kaylin considered tripping him but decided against; she could see Severn in the distance.

Don't let me stop you.

I'd try, but I suspect he'd pass through my foot without even noticing it was there. His smile was more felt than seen; he was too far away for that. But she recognized his stance immediately.

Why wouldn't she? They'd been partners in both boring, mundane daily patrols and very difficult situations for a while now.

"What is Teela trying to find?" Severn immediately turned to Terrano. She could see through his body, but he didn't become completely invisible.

"I'm not sure. She's looking in the border zone for traces of the mage that must have cast the concealing spell. It was big enough Kaylin could feel it from the air, but it wasn't a physical barrier. She's worried about what Helen said—and the fact that there's clearly some collaboration between Barrani and humans in the use of the border zone. The discovery and almost-subjugation of the Academia are evidence of at least Barrani research done there. From what Killianas has said, new students were being added over a long period of time. If the investigation had been in human hands alone, they'd've all died of old age."

"Why is she so fixated on Barrani involvement in this?"

Terrano winced. "She's getting pissed off. She really, *really* wants you to take a hike for the next five decades." At Kaylin's expression, Terrano shrugged. "Look, you've known her for longer than you've known me, right? But I've shared a home with you for longer than she has. Even if you decided to follow her advice, you're a walking disaster. You trip into things *all the time*. At least if we're with you, you might not land in trouble without a bit of support."

"Meaning you think I'm in trouble no matter what."

"Well, unless you can tell the Consort to get stuffed, don't you think so?"

Ynpharion was instantly enraged.

"No, I can't, as you well know. Teela knows it, too. Since you've enraged someone who can shout at me on the inside of *my* head, tell me what Teela's doing."

"You know her mother was murdered, right? And most of her mother's kin?"

Kaylin nodded, her expression grim.

"She trusted Severn with you, even when you tried to kill him the first time." He waited for Kaylin to nod, but it took longer. "Oh, come on, you must have noticed that."

"She trusts me with the Hawks *because I am one*."

Terrano made a raspberry sound. "Fine, you tell yourself that." He looked in Severn's direction.

"I have no idea what you're saying," Severn told him. "If you expect me to somehow get you out of trouble by acknowledging something, you're going to have to try harder."

Terrano exhaled. "Never mind. Sedarias is now joining

Teela in shouting at me. It's the first time they haven't been snarling at each other since Teela left. I might just run away and let you talk to Teela."

"She won't tell me anything."

"Probably not. But Bellusdeo will."

Bellusdeo?

"I told you—she's near the border. The Towers are pretty bloody sensitive about that, and Bellusdeo is not exactly reasonable when it comes to any tiny hint of Shadow. Or idiots who walk into it." He cursed in impressive Leontine. "I understand why you like that language," he added. "We don't really have time for this. Come on. We need to get there now."

"It's interesting that you should say that," a familiar voice said, breaking into their conversation.

Kaylin looked immediately toward the figure on the other side of the bridge across the Ablayne. It was, of course, Tiamaris.

05

They hadn't even *crossed* the damn bridge yet. "Tara couldn't have known we were coming."

"She is not a fool. When your confederates crossed the bridge, she became instantly aware of them. She is not familiar with Lord Andellen, but she is absolutely familiar with Teela and her friends." Tiamaris was intimidating even when not in draconic form.

"There's no way they told you I was coming. Teela's dead set against it."

"Correct. But Teela was wearing *Kariannos*. Tara considered its presence in my fief very rude."

"She was gone before you could confront her about her poor manners?"

"I assumed that she had come to investigate the scene of the crime," was his reasonable reply. "Given what Nightshade faced, carrying her strongest weapon was merely a display of intelligent caution. I lost some small amount of time convincing Tara; she believed that Teela's investigation encompassed more than that.

"And it appears I should place far more faith in her instincts." His eyes, however, belied his words and tone; they were orange, yes, but flecks of gold could be seen in their glow.

"She had no intention of harming you," Kaylin replied. Terrano had taken a step back. He wasn't exactly hiding behind her, but it was close.

"Of course not." Tiamaris's tone was dismissive. "But it seems that your timid friend is worried Bellusdeo might react in a less measured fashion should she encounter Teela. You said she was skirting the border, didn't you?"

Terrano mumbled a *yes*.

"The border along *Ravellon* is in no way the same as the borders that exist between the fiefs. Is she aware of that?"

"She doesn't entirely agree with your assessment." Terrano spoke with a touch of hesitation.

"Until my ascent as fieflord, I was the person within the Empire who had the most experience navigating the fiefs and their many lost secrets," Tiamaris said, the gold flecks vanishing from his eyes.

"She says that's true, officially speaking. Before you get angry, she adds that she didn't break the prohibitions herself—but she's certain they've been broken, now."

Red flecks appeared in place of the absent gold. "Explain."

"She's been following the trail of a very faint magical sigil to find the Barrani who acted in concert with the war bands to assassinate the fieflord. She hasn't crossed the *Ravellon* border herself—and won't—but she believes that at least one person did. She's concerned," Terrano added, speaking slightly more confidently. "But she's not a fool; she's not entering *Ravellon* without a small army."

Tiamaris turned his massive head and exhaled a small stream of fire. "Very well. Cross the bridge, and head directly to Bellusdeo's fief. I will escort you from the air."

Tiamaris didn't offer to fly them to Teela. Instead, he provided low, aerial cover for the Hawks—and Terrano—as they sprinted through the streets of his fief. Terrano was focused not on being semipermeable, but on the cohort. And the Dragon.

"Bellusdeo?"

"Bellusdeo and her Norranir," Terrano confirmed. "The Norranir are out in force; Teela's having difficulty hearing because they've started their defensive drumming."

Tiamaris, above, roared. Kaylin didn't have time to plug her ears; she sped up. Tiamaris sped up as well, his shadow racing past them as he pumped his mighty wings, heading toward the border of Bellusdeo at a speed sprinting on the ground couldn't match.

Why do things always turn out like this?

Severn said nothing. They could sprint side by side; his stride was longer, and if necessary, he could outpace her. He didn't. *Let's just get to Bellusdeo before she starts breathing fire.*

Squawk.

Damn.

Could this day get any worse?

They ran. Tiamaris could fly above the border zone. It wasn't the first time in her life she wished she were Aerian; they couldn't follow. The border zone existed between the fiefs of Tiamaris and Bellusdeo. It existed between all fiefs, except on those streets that now led to the Academia—and those weren't the streets they were running in. Kaylin sprinted into the faded, washed-out road between Bellusdeo—formerly the fief of Candallar—and Tiamaris.

She skidded to a halt a block in.

Severn slowed instantly—and far more gracefully.

Terrano scudded along, feet touching ground on some other plane Kaylin couldn't see. It was Terrano who cursed.

"Hope!"

Squawk.

"Just make sure he's safe!"

The familiar pushed himself off Kaylin's shoulder, squawking up a storm as he flew toward the transparent Terrano.

What is it?

There's magic here.

The kind you're allergic to?

She nodded.

You should have looked through Hope's wing before you sent him off.

I don't trust the area, and Terrano didn't stop. He was right, and she knew it, but Terrano always felt he was safe. He wasn't; he'd managed to get himself caged or confined before. Nothing could dim his innate arrogance.

Hope exhaled. Terrano swore at him. Particles of silver mist hung in the air, tracing a pattern familiar to the normal version of Terrano—or at least the solid version. Severn caught the Barrani by the shoulder and dragged him back to where Kaylin, arms tingling, stood.

"Look, we're in a rush, but we can't just trip every magical bomb or trap laid down by fleeing criminals, okay?" Kaylin glared at him.

"Criminals? The attack happened in the fiefs. Whoever ran this way would never have been under your jurisdiction. Laws of exemption are irrelevant—if you manage to get yourself killed, the Halls of Law can't use your death as an excuse to threaten the High Halls."

"Not hers, no," Severn agreed. "But she's not the only person here. Tiamaris has experience with the fiefs—but so do I. The Wolves aren't beholden to the Halls of Law in quite the same fashion the Hawks are."

"Really?"

"We have pursuit exceptions."

"Except you're wearing the Hawk."

"I am." Severn grinned. It was not terribly friendly.

"Argue about this later," Kaylin said, grimacing as the tingling of her skin grew more painful. "Let's move back into Tiamaris and try to cross the borders further down."

"Down?"

"Toward *Ravellon*. *Now*, Terrano."

"Sorry. Just arguing with Sedarias."

"Because she thinks I'm right?"

He shrugged, almost sullen. He did, however, follow when they returned to Tiamaris. "She's only saying that because Tiamaris has caught Bellusdeo's attention, and they're now deafening anyone in range."

The obvious, full-body warning that indicated the presence of magic dimmed as they retreated. "This is probably what led Teela to the border closer to *Ravellon*."

Terrano nodded; it was followed by a wince and a grimace.

"You should stop doing that," Severn told the Barrani cohort member.

"Stop what?"

"Asking Sedarias if you can tell Kaylin your True Name."

Terrano shrugged. "It really is a lot easier. It'd save time, and we can have a full raging argument without making any other noise. I wouldn't have to talk at all, and I wouldn't have to try to describe what we're seeing—or what Teela sees right now. Kaylin could see it all."

"Could I unsee it?"

"Good question. Doesn't matter. Sedarias will kill me if I try."

Kaylin could see the work Tiamaris had done in his fief in the buildings that lined the road they followed toward the Norranir homes. Those homes had once been tents, overcrowded and heavily worn; they were now taller versions of the buildings that otherwise girded the road.

Terrano appeared to be shaking dust off his clothing in

annoyance. Hope squawked a few times for good measure, sneezed once, and made his way back to Kaylin's shoulder.

They continued along the road, jogging rather than sprinting as they approached the Norranir homes. Those homes weren't occupied, given the number of Norranir who stood outside them, drums in their much larger hands. Terrano was right: it was hard to hear anything but that drumming—like the sounds of a giant's heart.

The Norranir were accustomed to the much smaller mortals that otherwise occupied the fiefs; those who weren't beating the drums turned immediately toward Kaylin and Severn. They were armed. Their weapons made greatswords look like long knives.

The Norranir had served Bellusdeo in a world that no longer existed; she had been their queen and their leader. Kaylin was almost surprised to see them here; she'd assumed they would move to Bellusdeo's fief when Bellusdeo took her Tower.

But it took time to build homes—and Tiamaris had had personal money with which to do it. Bellusdeo didn't. She'd make changes. Kaylin was certain of that. But those changes would be slower to occur, and trickier to navigate. The previous fieflord, much like Nightshade, hadn't cared for the people who lived in the fief itself.

"Are we supposed to talk to them?" Terrano asked. He'd once again taken up position behind Kaylin, given he was no longer invisible or half invisible. The Norranir weren't viscerally terrifying the way a full-grown Dragon was, but they weren't exactly comforting.

"We need to reach Lord Bellusdeo," Kaylin said, without preamble.

"She is not here."

"No—she's in her fief. But a friend—of both hers and ours—is also in the fief."

"An'Teela." An older woman pushed her way through the

sword-wielding guards. Her expression was grim, but it didn't immediately imply death was a sword swing away.

Kaylin's surprise must have shown. "Yes."

"She asked our permission to pass through."

"When?" Terrano asked. It probably looked like Kaylin's shoulder was talking.

"An hour ago. Perhaps more. She was navigating the gray. Is that why you've come this way?"

Kaylin nodded. "We tried to cross the . . . gray, but it wasn't safe."

"So she said, as well. We believe An'Teela can navigate the edge of the barrier. We are less certain you can do the same."

This caused Terrano to stick his head out. "I can absolutely do the same!"

She glanced down at Terrano, her lips thinning. "You? You are a child, no?"

Kaylin caught Terrano by the arm as he stepped forward. "I'm the *same age* as An'Teela!"

The woman's face fell into a network of wrinkles, none of which implied amusement. Before she could speak, Kaylin caught her elbow, which was what she could safely reach. "He isn't lying," she said, speaking slowly, voice low. "If anyone could safely navigate this close to the boundary, it's Terrano." She would have said more, but her words were swamped with the very loud, very angry roar of a Dragon.

Bellusdeo.

The drumming didn't stop, but the drums weren't fixed on stands; they were portable—or portable if you had the mass of an adult Norranir behind them. The Norranir could run while carrying the drums, and did, as they sped up to reach Bellusdeo.

Kaylin whipped around to Terrano. "What happened?"

"Teela told Bellusdeo that she thought Barrani had been making use of the border zone—and had fled into *Ravellon*."

"You said the Dragons were arguing!"

"They were."

"We didn't hear them. We could definitely hear Bellusdeo."

"She is our lord. She is our queen. She is calling for us, and we will obey." The woman exhaled. "We have permission to take the risk of allowing you to accompany us."

Terrano blinked. "Wait, you could understand that?"

The older woman muttered something in her native language. Kaylin didn't know the Norranir tongue, but the woman's expression made the meaning of the words clear: *kids these days.*

The border zone that existed between fiefs wasn't the same as the borders around *Ravellon*. Kaylin had seen Shadows emerge from the cracks in a crumbling Tower barrier; they'd passed from *Ravellon* to the fief she'd been in—Tiamaris, before he claimed it—without apparent pause.

But she knew that barrier was a creation of the Ancients, and the border in Nightshade had more closely resembled the border between fiefs. The view from the barrier implied something almost normal but deserted—remnants of a city. The view from the interior did not.

"What is Shadow?" she asked the Norranir elder, as the men with drums positioned themselves at intervals in the forming line. They never stopped drumming.

The woman offered a word, but Kaylin's expression made her lack of understanding clear. "It is not a question we are asked often. In our language, it is another word for death. But in other tongues, it had different meanings. Those languages are lost to all among us who did not study dead languages.

"Our lord was concerned with survival, with the battles upon which our survival depended. But some were allowed to study, in the hope that information would aid in those battles." She exhaled. "It did not help our lord."

Kaylin filed that away for possible future use.

The Norranir moved quickly, their speed hampered by the smaller stride of those who followed. Terrano cursed Kaylin's familiar with genuine heat; clearly his ability to solve the problem in his usual way hadn't yet returned.

"Hope, if you can do something about it, do something."

Squawk. The familiar shook his head, shrugging his delicate wings.

"Be a little clearer."

Squawk. Squawk. *Squawk.*

The Norranir elder squinted down at him. "I believe he is telling your friend it will be fine soon."

One of the men—not a drummer—spoke impatiently. The elder frowned, but nodded. "You are slowing us down. Accept our aid." It was a command.

Kaylin had suspicions about what that aid would be, and she was right: she was lifted off her feet and deposited on the shoulders of one of the Norranir as if she were a young child and he the adult.

"Sorry," she said, although she wasn't certain the man spoke Elantran.

Severn was likewise lifted, as was Terrano. Terrano didn't consider the Norranir as terrifying as Dragons, but his expression made clear this method of transport was *way* beneath his dignity. Rich, given how little he usually cared. But it *was* faster, and the Norranir were in control; they didn't have to tell their three companions where to step or not to step, didn't have to make certain they didn't wander outside invisible boundaries and into terrain that had long been ceded to the Shadows that ruled it.

Kaylin, no longer worried about jogging or sprinting to stay in line, observed. The elder walked at their head. Just behind her, the first drummers. Kaylin didn't understand why drumming was effective as protection. In Bellusdeo's world—in the world she had ruled before she had fallen to Shadow herself—there had been no Towers, no fiefs, and no barrier erected around *Ravellon.*

But in this world, until the arrival of the Norranir, there had been no drumming, no drums of this kind. No use of deliberate, rhythmic sound, shorn of any other music. Kaylin wasn't the biggest appreciator of music, but nothing about this was musical. It reminded her of a heartbeat, even, unstopping, but steady. There was no change in volume, no speeding up or slowing down. It just continued.

It is very like a heartbeat. She blinked and turned her head. Hope was staring at her, his opalescent eyes unblinking. *Can you not hear it?*

"Hear what?"

The beating of a heart, Kaylin. The drums beat in time with it. It is a sound that is meant to lull those who can *hear the heart it mimics.*

"What?"

Squawk. Hope looked vaguely irritated. Kaylin remembered: it took power to make himself understood. Mostly, he didn't bother. No, she thought, he expected her to use the power of the Chosen to bridge the gap. She didn't know how, not consciously. What had Sanabalis said? Her power responded to need. To focus. To Kaylin's desperation.

And she wasn't desperate now. But she filed away his words, because if he thought them important enough to make the effort to speak, they probably were.

But it did irritate her that the Barrani could understand him. And the Norranir. It didn't seem to take power to talk to other people—just to Kaylin. She clearly had time for what she knew was pettiness, because she didn't have to expend energy running.

Here, she could see the washed-out gray of buildings familiar to the border zones that existed between fiefs. But these buildings were different. They weren't the height of the Norranir homes, newly made by Tiamaris, but they were close, and one building in particular caught her eye. It was three stories in height—rare in the border zones—and very wide; it was almost intimidatingly similar to the Imperial Palace in size, and it seemed to be made of seamless stone. She could feel her skin begin to prickle, but it wasn't painful yet—more of a sharp tickle.

Had she been on her own feet, she might have slowed. Instead, she shouted a warning to the Norranir.

But Bellusdeo's roars—more focused and somehow sharper—swamped her words.

"Terrano—tell Teela there's something wrong with this building!"

Terrano could barely hear her, if he could hear her at all. But she could hear his cursing—it was pure Leontine. Had she not known it was him, she'd've assumed an actual Leontine had joined the procession.

Bellusdeo roared again, this time the sound staccato, as if she was carefully enunciating words. What Kaylin failed to make clear, Bellusdeo did: the Norranir could hear her. The elder's voice rose clearly enough to be heard, and the Norranir line retreated, moving back in an organized wave, leaving more slowly, more carefully, than they'd arrived.

Retreating, Severn said. *If they turned and fled, we'd have called that a rout, back in class.*

Which class?

Probably one of the ones you got permission to skip.

She grimaced, regretting her past choices. The man on whose shoulders she rode caught her ankles in either hand to make certain she didn't fall off.

The air in the border zone was often foggy. On bad days, the fog was thick and almost impenetrable; on good days, it was clear enough that the lack of bright colors in the border zone was marked. Today, it was thin, but present. Because it was, visibility wasn't perfect. But it was good enough that Kaylin could see, in the distance, the gold glint of scales in the air just above the height of the building that had stopped her, metaphorically speaking, in her tracks.

Fire burned the fog away. As Bellusdeo approached, Kaylin could see her eyes: they were bright, crimson red. She'd expected that. This close to the heart of the Shadow that had destroyed her kingdom, her eyes were never going to be any other color. What Kaylin hadn't expected was Teela, who was riding on the gold Dragon's back. Her sword was sheathed, and she was far enough away that Kaylin couldn't see her eye color, but she knew it was the Barrani equivalent of draconic red.

The drumming didn't stop, but the Norranir did, their double line falling into a different formation as Bellusdeo reached the street, her claws scratching the ground as she came to a skidding halt.

Terrano made his way past the Norranir toward Teela as Teela leaped easily to the ground. Kaylin would have followed, but she was held more firmly on the shoulders of the Norranir who had carried them this far.

Bellusdeo lost draconic form as Teela walked toward Kaylin.

"Is that a good idea?" the Barrani Hawk asked over her shoulder, without looking back. "We don't know what we're going to encounter here."

"If we have to go inside, I can't do it as a Dragon."

"I'm not sure we have to go inside. This building has gained a story since we made our way to your fief today. If I had fiery breath, I'd destroy the whole building immediately."

Tiamaris, red-scaled but shining in the same way Bellusdeo had, landed next. Fallessian and Torrisant were on his back, but they jumped off almost before he'd finished moving. Neither looked at all comfortable. Kaylin thought it odd that they'd trusted Tiamaris more than Bellusdeo.

I think Bellusdeo gave them very little warning, Severn pointed out. *Teela's spent more time with her—she probably guessed what*

Bellusdeo would do and didn't bother asking for permission or waiting for niceties.

That did sound like Teela.

The four cohort members gathered, but Teela split off as Bellusdeo assumed her gold-plated, human form. Hope squawked.

Bellusdeo's reply was offered in loud draconic. No doubt it was rude. Kaylin had a small collection of linguistic curses, but draconic curses were beyond her physical limitations.

Tiamaris, however, remained a Dragon. He roared; Bellusdeo roared back. In a normal, booming voice, Bellusdeo said, "Step away from the building but be prepared!" She followed up with a longer speech in the Norranir tongue. Kaylin assumed it meant the same thing.

Clearly, she was wrong. The drummers split off, heading to the very edge of the border. Oh. Here, the barrier seemed more amorphous. Kaylin didn't understand why the Towers were so distinctly geographically separated. But the Norranir and their drums moved to stand—and drum—at that barrier. She was impressed that their arms were strong enough to continue without pause.

But some of the Norranir came to stand beside the drummers; they carried drums of their own, but they weren't beating them yet. She guessed they'd pick up the beat when the first set of drummers was too exhausted to continue. For Kaylin, that would have happened on the walk, if she'd lasted that long. The man carrying Kaylin set her on the ground as she could no longer slow them down.

Hope stood on Kaylin's shoulders, claws briefly digging into her collarbone. His voice, at this distance, was louder than Tiamaris's warning.

Severn began to unwind his weapon chain—which was never a good sign. Terrano ran to her side, passing through the Norranir who were standing just ahead of her.

"Teela wants you to stay out of the building."

"No one's going in there yet."

"True. She wants you to stay out when—and if—she and Bellusdeo head in."

"And she sent you here to make sure I keep *you* out?"

Terrano grinned. "She's always optimistic."

This was *so* not true. "I could ask Hope for help."

He grimaced. "I'm supposed to be keeping you here, not the other way around."

"Whatever works, right?"

Tiamaris inhaled; the sound was louder than the consistent, continuous drumbeats. His exhalation was louder still as a gout of impressively hot flame splashed, like liquid, against the building that had caused Kaylin's magical allergies to activate. As if it were that liquid, it dripped down the building's face, burning nothing.

It's stone, Severn pointed out.

Against Dragon breath. We've seen that melt *stone in the city.* She lifted a finger and poked her familiar; he batted her face with a wing and then left it over one eye. *Some of the stone is beginning to heat up.*

Not visibly.

"Terrano—tell one of your friends to tell Tiamaris to keep going."

He gave her the side-eye but clearly did as she asked. On the other hand, it was left to Teela to tell the fieflord. Honestly, some people were cowards.

"What? She's got the big sword. Nothing they're wielding is going to even scratch a Dragon's scales."

Bellusdeo came over to Severn, who stood, weapons readied. "We're going around the back. Terrano is allowed to follow us; Teela thinks he'll be useful." Two of the Norranir fell in behind Bellusdeo. Bellusdeo shook her head, and they bowed and stepped back.

"They might be helpful as well," Terrano said.

"We need them on the border. Teela is going to stay at the front with Tiamaris and the Norranir. And your two brothers."

Severn didn't sheathe his weapons, but he didn't take point. He would have, but Terrano was impatient—and permeable. Bellusdeo told him that she'd scout, and he *blew a raspberry* and scooted ahead.

"One of these days, I'm going to kill him," the Dragon said, in a tone that almost implied affection.

"You're probably going to have to stand in line. And no, I won't be in it."

"I believe he was supposed to stay with us in order to more easily communicate with Teela." The Dragon exhaled steam.

"He'll come back—there's almost nothing that can actually hurt him when he's like that."

She was half right. Terrano did come back, racing around the corner and ducking. Something flew after him—fire? Bolt? It was dark and slender and moved quickly.

To Kaylin's surprise and growing horror, she could see that he was both transparent and bleeding.

Kaylin ran to meet him while Hope squawked. She could see blood with both eyes, winged and unwinged. She couldn't see a pursuer with either. Bellusdeo leaped above her, landing behind the fleeing Terrano. She'd drawn a sword, although it wouldn't be her most significant weapon. No, that was her breath, and she did exhale. A fan of impressively pale flame covered Terrano's flight.

Kaylin hadn't drawn her weapons; they were long knives, and they weren't impressive in a strategic ground fight—or a battle backed by magic, which this clearly was.

Instead, she reached out for Terrano. He ran straight for her, leaping forward to take both of her outstretched hands in his; they passed through.

"Come back to where I'm standing!" she shouted. "Do it now!"

He tried to grab her hands again, and this time she could feel something pass through her palms.

"Hope!"

Hope did nothing. Kaylin felt the air chill, although both Tiamaris and Bellusdeo had added instant, ambient heat to it. Her annoyance vanished, her worry deepening instantly. This was something Hope wouldn't interfere in until and unless Kaylin was willing to sacrifice something meaningful in exchange.

It was the only thing she hated about the familiar.

"Tell Teela we need her here *right now*!" she shouted. "She needs to bring Terrano back to our plane!"

06

She wasn't certain if Terrano contacted Teela or not, but Teela skidded around the corner. She carried her greatsword in one hand, and with the other, she grabbed Kaylin by the arm.

Hope squawked, then.

"Next time," Teela said, through clenched teeth, "we bring Mandoran." She sheathed her sword and reached for Terrano with her free hand. She *could* touch Terrano. Kaylin tried with her free hand; she couldn't.

"Torrisant?" Terrano said. His voice was weaker. "He's better at this than you are."

Kaylin felt something—sharp, hot—travel up her arm.

"He says he's better at doing what you do—but Mandoran is far better at taking something with him when he sidesteps into different planes."

Kaylin turned to stare at Teela.

"Terrano can't come to where we are," the Barrani Hawk explained. "He's been trying. There's only one option left. You have to go to him."

Kaylin tried, three more times, to grab Terrano's hand; each time, her hand passed through his. In the background, Teela cursed. Her grip on Kaylin's arm was white-knuckled.

"I'm trying to connect the two of you, if I can *get everyone else to shut up and let Mandoran speak.*" Her expression was venomous, which wasn't fair—Kaylin wasn't the one being distracting.

Squawk. Squawk.

Teela inhaled slowly. She exhaled slowly as well. She'd been forced to sheathe her sword in what had become a combat zone. If Terrano had been injured—and demonstrably he had—it meant that Teela could be attacked just as easily.

Kaylin could see Terrano's injury; if he wasn't solid, he was close enough. She stopped even trying to talk to Teela as she concentrated on reaching the most chaotic of the cohort members. Teela was right. Whatever Kaylin was doing to reach the space Terrano occupied felt like a series of sharp, harsh, full-body slaps. When Kaylin had been with Mandoran, she hadn't even *noticed* the shift. None of that mattered. She continually tried to connect with Terrano's hand—which she could clearly see. Her hand passed through his each time.

Teela cursed. Kaylin cursed. Terrano said nothing, which wasn't like him.

"What did they hit you with?"

Terrano's mouth moved. Kaylin couldn't catch the syllables. Or make sense of them. She'd heard him clearly before; it felt like Teela was moving her in the wrong direction.

"Are you ready?" Teela clearly wasn't finished trying. "I think I've finally found the right place to shift."

Kaylin nodded while Hope squawked.

If she couldn't hear Terrano, she could hear Teela, who was cursing—in Leontine—as she tried to move Kaylin into synch with Terrano. Terrano continued to bleed. Hope's voice was louder than Teela's in full Leontine, but Kaylin couldn't understand his words; they clearly weren't meant for her.

She couldn't cover her ear to preserve hearing; Hope was on the same side as the arm Teela had grabbed, and the Barrani

Hawk wasn't letting go. Kaylin had had worse injuries in the line of duty, but she knew this was going to bruise. And she knew Teela couldn't let go until the moment Terrano could be physically touched.

If she'd sometimes envied Terrano his ability to slip between planes as a way out of physical danger, she repented. What she needed to know was why he couldn't come back.

No. What she needed to know was the extent of Terrano's injuries. The rest could wait.

Hope squawked loudly. He then bit Kaylin's ear.

Kaylin would have swatted him away but didn't want to lose part of her earlobe. She cursed. Teela had brought her closer to Terrano, and she could see what had injured him. Or rather, she could see the Shadow seeping out of his wound, a faint black mist.

Bellusdeo would have reduced them *all* to ash. Teela might even have let her.

"Don't let go! I've healed Shadow damage before," she snapped at the Barrani Hawk as she felt Teela's grip loosen slightly. "I had to do this in the West March when the Consort was under attack! Don't step back—give me enough time, and I can fix it!"

Teela's brief hesitation vanished. "Remind me," she said through gritted teeth, "to strangle Mandoran when next we meet."

"Worry about who or what attacked Terrano. Worry about the Barrani who attacked Nightshade. Figure out if they're the same people."

She continued to attempt to grab Terrano's hand. She lost count of the number of times she'd tried when she finally managed to *touch* him. His skin was hot, almost feverish, and the wound he had taken finally came into sharp relief. She hadn't been able to touch Nightshade, and the unspoken fear that Terrano would likewise be proof against the Marks-driven healing was put to rest.

"Do you have her?" Teela demanded of the pale, injured Terrano.

Terrano nodded, as if he didn't trust himself to say more.

"Good. I have to go." She released Kaylin's arm.

Kaylin caught both of Terrano's hands in a tight grip, entwining her fingers with his strongly enough that both of their knuckles were white.

This is not a place you should be, her familiar said. She could understand him, here.

"If you can find a way to drag Terrano back to where I should be, I'm all ears."

You know the answer.

She cursed him, choosing the more easily pronounced Aerian phrasing. "Terrano, can you hear me?"

He nodded. He was sweating, which was common given intense pain—but the sweat itself was disturbing. Kaylin couldn't tell if this was a function of the plane on which they were both standing, or of Terrano himself. She glanced beyond Terrano; there was no one immediately chasing the Barrani.

She then turned all her attention to Terrano.

He was too hot. She wasn't often allowed to touch Barrani with an intent to heal, but she knew feverish skin on contact.

"Hope—bite me hard if something attacks us."

Something is already making that attempt. You should not be here. You do not have time.

"I can't leave him here. We'll lose him." She closed her eyes. She had always closed her eyes when trying to heal severe injuries, and she'd learned to leave minor cuts and scrapes alone. The Marks flared to life on her arm—gold, not the more subtle blue they sometimes adopted. They remained where they lay, but she'd always been able to see them clearly when her eyes were closed.

Their light covered her arms and edged toward the tops of her hands. As it did, it expanded to enwrap Terrano's hands in the same bright glow before inching its way up his arms, his shoulders. She didn't always see the light of the Marks when they touched others, but was well aware that the rules in the plane on which she stood might be different. No, they definitely were, no *might* about it.

Terrano's body wasn't the normal Barrani body, from her brief experience with those. But it felt cohesively *like* Terrano to her touch, to her Marks. The fear of Shadow and its contamination diminished. When she had dealt with Shadow-spawned injuries before, she could feel the way they warped and shifted the physical flesh itself in an attempt to remake the person to whom that flesh belonged.

She didn't sense that here—but she could see the fine, fine mist of Shadow rising from Terrano's injury. She couldn't feel any of it in his body.

Hope bit her, but not hard enough to draw blood or cause pain; he was disagreeing in the most convenient way possible.

She found the wound from which the Barrani youth had been visibly bleeding; it was a deep stab into the Barrani's right side and had pierced a lung. Blood pooled in the right lung, beneath what passed for air here.

"Don't think about that," Terrano managed to get out. "That's part of the trick."

Hard not to think about it when she was examining his entire physical body. Terrano could carry on arguing while he was on death's door, he was so stubborn—and it wouldn't do him any good. She didn't ask him how he knew what she was thinking. Maybe she would, later. Or maybe she'd been muttering as she worked, because sometimes she *did* do that. It had really, really annoyed fellow students in her classes.

The wound wasn't her biggest worry; it was the lingering taint of Shadow. But that Shadow hadn't transformed or warped Terrano's physical body in the way it had the Barrani in the distant West March. She'd expected she'd have to cut away large chunks of his flesh and force her power to rebuild it properly. That didn't happen here.

The Shadow continued to rise, as if Terrano were breathing from the wound, not his mouth. She couldn't deny what she saw. If she felt no Shadow in Terrano, it was here.

It is, Chosen. You must leave.

She shook her head. "Not without the idiot."

"Gee, thanks."

The Shadow was mist, visible in the light of the Marks. "Can you see the Shadow?"

Terrano grunted. She assumed it meant yes. "You?"

"It's not—it's moving. It's coming from you—from the wound." She frowned and poured her power into that wound. She was almost afraid to heal it; if she did, would that Shadow remain trapped within Terrano?

"Just stop the bleeding," Terrano snapped. "I can handle the rest."

"How?"

"Trust me."

"Did this come from the wound?"

Silence.

"Terrano?"

"Yes?" His eyes looked like normal Barrani eyes to her, but they'd shifted to the side, as if Terrano refused to meet her gaze while answering the question.

Oh.

"You could have joined us," she said through clenched teeth.

Terrano said nothing.

"But you're carrying something you don't want to let loose."

"Maybe you could waste less of your time talking and spend some of it healing?" Mandoran had arrived.

Kaylin liked Mandoran but had never felt so grateful to see him in all the time she'd known him. "I don't think we can safely bring him back."

"No kidding," the Barrani replied. "I think the Norranir are having some effect—I'm not sure how it works, but Bellusdeo said it definitely did. The drums, the beat of them, seem to slow the progress of Shadow."

"Can you tell me what hit him?"

Terrano began to cough out blood.

"Sorry—you can't keep that in your lungs." She began to knit the wound itself closed but paused to examine the frayed edges. "Mandoran—tell Bellusdeo and Teela—"

"Teela knows they're somehow using Shadow as a form of attack. So does Bellusdeo. If I were you, I'd move toward the Norranir before you attempt to pull Terrano to safety."

"I can't pull him out if I can't excise the Shadow—but it hasn't harmed or changed his flesh."

"It's tried," Mandoran said, voice grim. He had one arm around Terrano's shoulders as if to steady him. "Terrano's so warped and twisted he's used to body parts that seem entirely at odds with what they should be. He doesn't think Shadow would infect you—not with the Marks of the Chosen as protection."

Squawk.

"Yeah, yeah, you too."

"Can he expel it?"

"That's what he was doing." Mandoran hesitated. "I don't think the Shadow is sentient, for what it's worth. It's just another type of poison."

"How much are you willing to risk on that?"

"I'm here, aren't I?"

Kaylin nodded, but not with any relief. There was something off about this Shadow, something wrong. Terrano was pale, probably due to loss of blood—but blood loss was the one thing she couldn't easily heal. Wounds, yes. Broken bones. Injuries caused by rampant disease or fever. Blood loss had always been difficult.

"Can you speak safely?" she asked Terrano.

"I can, now. Thanks," he added, the last word barely above a whisper.

"What are you doing right now?" His body was shifting, almost like a wave of flesh that was becoming undone, reasserting itself, and falling apart again in rapid order. In any other person, this would have been a grave, grave emergency. In Terrano, it was a weekday.

"I'm trying to make sure I'm not dangerously contaminated? I can't cross back to our normal plane—not while trying to *safely* contain the Shadow. But Mandoran can pull you back once the wound is closed. It's the wound that's killing me."

That hadn't been Kaylin's game plan. "What are you going to do?"

"If I can contain whatever this is, I intend to carry it to the Avatar of the High Halls."

She was almost—but not quite—shocked.

"He'll know what to do with it. And he'll be able to see me and hear me in a way most of you can't."

"Not sure that's safe," Mandoran said.

"It's safer than bringing it back to our reality. Shadow doesn't have the same purchase where I usually walk—but it clearly has some."

Hope squawked several times before smacking Kaylin's face with the wing he'd placed over one eye and pushing himself off her shoulder. She almost shouted in warning: if Hope wasn't attached to her, he might be lost in this parallel plane. Luckily, she kept the words to herself. Hope had a bit of a temper.

The familiar inhaled.

He exhaled a cloud, which caused Terrano to shout; he'd been hit by it once, and he hadn't particularly liked the results.

"Stop being a baby," Mandoran snapped.

"Let him breathe on you, then!"

Hope squawked loudly. Kaylin was grateful he wasn't sitting on her shoulder, right beside her ear. Whatever he said, the two Barrani immediately abandoned the beginning of their sibling argument. Mandoran often spoke out loud if people who weren't part of the cohort were present. Terrano did it more as an aside.

They both looked toward Hope, and then toward Kaylin.

"Fine," Terrano told the familiar, obviously pouting.

Hope exhaled. This time, his breath was almost, but not quite, invisible; Kaylin could see the sparking particles that comprised the clouds that often came from his tiny mouth. To her surprise, the exhalation grew denser as it plumed around Terrano, who flinched but didn't otherwise try to break free of Kaylin's hands.

The familiar's breath gathered in a cloud—a miniature storm cloud that seemed almost like a crystal ball. It absorbed some of the light of Kaylin's Marks and all the wisps of Shadow that had escaped Terrano's wound—a wound that was now closed.

Hope, squawking like an angry bird, came back to his favorite perch: Kaylin's shoulder. Mandoran was the only person with one free hand. He glanced at Hope, his expression the definition of dubious, but grimaced and used that free hand to grab the condensed ball that now hovered in the air near Terrano. His eyes widened in surprise as he turned to look at Hope.

The familiar lifted a wing and smacked Kaylin's face with it but kept it across her eyes.

Hope squawked.

Mandoran shook his head.

Hope then squawked up a storm.

". . . he wants me to give this to you," he told Kaylin. "Teela says no."

"What does Sedarias say?"

"Yes—but she cares less about you than she does about us."

"Then do what you normally do. Listen to Sedarias." Kaylin released one of Terrano's hands and reached out to Mandoran, her hand palm up and cupped. "If Hope thinks it's fine, it's fine."

Squawk.

"He says that's not what he said."

"What exactly did he say?"

"It's safest—not safe—if you take it."

"Fine. Hand it over."

Hope squawked. Mandoran shrugged. He dropped the condensed ball into Kaylin's palm. To her surprise, it was *cold.* Cold as ice, but softer, as if it were already melting. She gritted her teeth.

If whatever this amalgam of familiar's breath and Shadow was could be taken to the High Halls, it could be contained in Helen. But she had to get there, and a small war was occurring just beyond her reach.

Mandoran put an arm around Kaylin's shoulders. "Ready?" he asked.

"No, wait—if Terrano wouldn't move because of . . . whatever this is, maybe we shouldn't, either."

"Hope breathed on it. Whatever it was isn't what it is now." Mandoran exhaled. "You have a better idea? Terrano can navigate this plane; he knows how to avoid things that don't belong where we normally live. He can get where he needs to go without attracting attention, or worse, getting lost."

"But he was injured *here*."

Mandoran nodded. "Annarion's crossed over."

Kaylin wanted to shriek in frustration.

"I didn't say Annarion was coming here—he isn't leaving his brother's side. But he's prepared for possible attacks."

"So is Helen."

"I didn't say it was smart. But to be frank, we could use him. I suck at fighting in places like this. So does Terrano—but Terrano's way better at running away." He looked to Hope. "Can we leave?"

Hope squawked.

"Terrano? Sedarias wants you at home. Now."

Terrano nodded.

"Are you sure he's healed?" Mandoran asked—of Kaylin. Asking Terrano wouldn't give him any reliable information.

"He lost blood. He needs to drink, and he needs to sleep. Or whatever Barrani do to rest. I can't do more than that. He can step back into reality now."

"Terrano—was the Shadow preventing your return, or did you decide you wouldn't while you were somehow containing it?"

"A bit of both. I could force myself free—but it would follow. There's too much going on here for that to be safe—and if Bellusdeo could sense it at all, I figured I'd be ash."

"Good. Go home now. We'll follow."

He hesitated. "I don't want Bellusdeo turning you to ash."

Hope squawked.

"You have no idea how she reacts to even the *mention* of Shadow if you think that," the Barrani cohort member snapped. He then winced; clearly his cohort had opinions.

"I lived with her, too. I know. Terrano—can you see where the Norranir are?" Kaylin's hand wasn't getting any warmer.

"You can't?"

"No. I can see you and Mandoran and not much else. I can't

hear the drumming here. I can't hear the fighting, if fighting is happening."

"Not much of it anymore—Bellusdeo literally brought down the house. Or whatever it was."

"Great. Just . . . take us to the Norranir drummers. We'll take it from there."

Terrano led. Mandoran followed, dragging Kaylin with him. She could still see Terrano, but he was becoming murkier as he walked. She no longer held on to him, and Mandoran didn't either. Terrano had been told to find his way back to Helen. She hoped he did but knew no one could tell Terrano what to do and actually expect obedience.

"You might want to close your eyes," Mandoran said, voice very close to her ear.

She shook her head. She wanted to see what happened here. Shifting planes wasn't something she could do—but Mandoran had once told her she did it subconsciously and naturally when she used, or reached for, the power of her Marks. The cohort wasn't using that power. But every child that had been exposed to the *regalia* in the distant green could, with effort and will, do what Terrano did. It didn't come easily or naturally to most of them; it did to Mandoran. And, sadly, Annarion.

She watched as the darkness began to shatter, cracks appearing in its surface—in its many surfaces, as if those surfaces were the facets of an enormous, and brittle, gem.

Light peered in through those cracks—and as each pane fell away, she could see a dizzying array of vistas beyond those surfaces.

"I am not going to forgive you if you throw up on my boots."

"She probably won't," a blessedly familiar voice replied. Severn was here. He hadn't spoken at all while she was standing in the plane where Terrano had gotten stuck—but he had been aware of where she was, of what she was doing. Aware as well that worry or argument wouldn't help her get anything done.

He was the first thing she saw as she emerged, the first thing that became solid as the world cohered. Sadly, he wasn't the only thing, and the coherence of the world wasn't as simple as it should have been.

The separate glimpses of light and scene and landscape began to move, to swirl, to blend together; she heard the buzzing of loud insects, the crash of falling trees, the hints of discordant song, saw the blend of colors she had no words for as they began to fly past her field of view.

She should have listened to Mandoran. "Does it always look this way to you?" Severn's arm was around her waist to steady her.

"I don't know what you're seeing. You're not normal, either—you're Chosen. We're almost there—I'm sorry. I had to really rush the fences to get here to help. There are probably better paths, better cracks between planes, to exploit—but I didn't have the time to really listen for them. That's what you're feeling."

Kaylin closed her eyes and sagged against Severn. It helped, but not completely; the sounds were almost as dizzying as the blend of visual colors had been. Hope squawked. His voice, perched as he was so close to her ear, was loud—but clean, clear. It didn't blend into the aural chaos.

She focused on listening to Hope until she could hear the drumming; only then did Hope's voice stop.

Her legs felt like rubber, but the ground beneath her feet felt solid in a way it hadn't when she'd joined Terrano. She took the chance of opening her eyes and almost wept with relief: she was surrounded by Norranir drummers. If they noticed her—and they did—nothing broke the rhythm of their hands against stretched skins.

She'd come back. Mandoran stood beside her.

And her hand was both very cold—and empty.

The streets were thick with smoke. The drumming continued, but it was entwined now with other sounds: running feet, cracking stone, raised voices. She could feel a bonfire's heat, pressed against her skin as if she'd strayed too close to the fire. There was no immediately visible flame. But above the clearing smoke, she could see two sets of mighty wings: red and gold.

Kaylin could see the ruins of the border zone building and raised her brows.

"If it makes it any better, Tiamaris helped with that." Mandoran was too pale.

"Has Terrano gotten home yet?"

"Not yet—he's taking a look around."

Kaylin almost shrieked.

"Sedarias isn't happy about it, but you probably guessed that. She says you should go home. Whatever you were carrying, she wants Helen to assess. If it can't be removed, you're going to have to put off the meeting with the Consort."

Easier said than done.

I do not advise that, Ynpharion said.

He might be right—I've picked up something I can no longer see, and until Helen gives the okay, it might not be safe for the Consort. You wouldn't want to put her at risk, would you?

Ynpharion gave the equivalent of a mental snort. He didn't disagree.

As smoke cleared and the ruins of a border building came into full view, Bellusdeo stood in the partially melted streets. The street, like the building, was tinged gray, the colors faded, as all colors were in the border zones.

But the Dragon that stood in front of the building was a lambent, burning gold. As Kaylin watched, she transformed, her wings folding, her neck and body shrinking, as if flesh was entirely mutable. Kaylin looked away. She'd seen Dragons shift before, but it never became less disturbing.

Teela was standing beside Bellusdeo. The shift in size made the distance between the two greater than it had been, but Teela chose to close that gap. Bellusdeo was facing either Kaylin or the drummers gathered in a loose formation around her; it was hard to tell which.

If Kaylin had had any doubts, Bellusdeo herself dispelled them. She marched toward the Norranir cluster and passed through them, dwarfed in size but clearly in command. They moved. Only when she lifted a hand did the drumming stop, dying into silence and the sound fire made when it consumed things.

Mandoran stood beside Kaylin. He had an expressive face for a Barrani, and expressions flashed across the contours of his eyes and lips; clearly the cohort was silently arguing on the inside of his head. Well, silently where Kaylin was concerned. Probably for the best.

Bellusdeo's eyes were blood red—not a surprise. But her voice, when she spoke, was modulated, steady. The rage and the fury her eyes implied didn't touch her tone.

Oh. This wasn't the Bellusdeo Kaylin had known for most of their time together. It was one of the sisters.

"We're going to have to talk," the gold Dragon said.

Kaylin nodded.

"An'Teela?"

"As you are aware, we are in the midst of complicated investigations. We did not expect the attack today."

"No. I am told that the fieflord of Nightshade was involved."

"He was attacked first. He is currently recuperating in an undisclosed location."

"I see." Bellusdeo opened her mouth to speak and shut it again with a snap. Kaylin wondered if the inside of Bellusdeo's head was as noisy, now, as the inside of Mandoran's. Or Teela's.

"An'Teela has informed me of parts of the investigation, and we've chosen to help where we can. Our part will be in the fiefs and in the border zones."

"The border zones," Mandoran said, "are outside of the protective influence of the Towers."

The Dragon smiled. "They are the edge of the fiefs, yes. But if random Barrani Lords—" her tone said *cockroaches* "—can survive in the border zone, so can a Dragon or two."

Kaylin winced. "Leave it with Teela—it'll do less damage."

"No one lives in the border zone."

"You've never been poor enough or desperate enough to know that that's not true." Kaylin folded her arms.

"Kitling," Teela said before Kaylin could continue. "Terrano was injured. Barrani were here. They managed to evade us, but we'll lose time if we argue. Go home to Helen. Terrano believes that he might understand some small part of what ails Nightshade now. He'll need you at home to test it."

Kaylin had whiplash. "Does that mean you'll pursue and leave the Consort to me?"

Teela stiffened.

Clever, Ynpharion said, which wasn't usually a good sign.

"We'll talk about this later." Teela turned on her heel and began to walk toward the Bellusdeo border.

"Hey!" Kaylin shouted.

Teela paused but didn't turn to look back.

"You better not be investigating on your own. Or pursuing. You know what the rules are."

"I am not here as a Hawk. I am here as An'Teela—and Barrani Lords do not require partners." Her tone was cold.

Before Kaylin could say another word, Fallessian and Torrisant stepped forward. Neither was a big speaker, but Mandoran translated their silence. "She's not going alone. I don't know if you know, but Fallessian is good with a sword, and he's adept at avoiding attacks."

"Annarion is better," Fallessian said, as if he grudged being forced to speak.

They all knew Annarion wasn't going to leave Nightshade until his brother was at least conscious.

"Will you come home now?" Mandoran urged.

Kaylin nodded. Teela continued toward the Bellusdeo border, Fallessian and Torrisant shadowing her.

Bellusdeo exhaled. "I have half a mind to visit the High Halls myself."

"Please don't."

"Home?" Severn asked.

She nodded, and they headed toward Bellusdeo's fief, because it was closer.

07

Bellusdeo fell in beside Kaylin, which was awkward until Mandoran dropped back. Severn remained where he was—but that was fair, given what she'd said to Teela. He was her beat partner. If Teela wasn't here on behalf of the Halls of Law, fine. Kaylin felt that she was.

As they walked, she told Bellusdeo what Teela was investigating, and why; she was certain Teela had said very little.

"But Lord Nightshade has survived."

"So far." Kaylin hesitated. "I'm not sure he's going to make it. Annarion's upset. Teela's angry—but she went to the site of the attempted assassination to investigate. There was evidence of magic—a lot of magic—on and around the site. I'm less clear about what happened before she met up with you. I know she was following or tracking traces of someone who was taking advantage of the border zones.

"I'm not sure she wants you involved."

"That's unfortunate for her. This fief is *mine*. Barrani who move within the fiefs—and who do not serve the fieflords—are a threat to the security of the fiefs. What are you not telling me?"

Kaylin hesitated. She was a terrible liar, and Bellusdeo had always been perceptive. "Everything's a mess. Nightshade's injury. Annarion's reaction. The cohort's reaction to Annarion.

Teela's reaction. It's not just one thing. Teela's been interested in Barrani Lords for a lot of her life, but this feels . . . different. I don't think her prior interest was connected to Nightshade, the fiefs, or the border zones *until* Nightshade was attacked." She hesitated again.

"Go on."

"I want to know what Shadow did in your world that led to its fall."

Bellusdeo nodded, which wasn't the reaction Kaylin expected. "Shadow attacks are chaotic and unpredictable—and I am uncertain that some of those attacks were noted until it was too late.

"You're aware that Shadow can transform the living."

"The one-offs."

"Yes. I am not certain what the rules that govern that transformation are. I was trapped in, enslaved by, Shadow—but I was not changed or transformed by the duration of my stay. My Ascendant, Maggaron, was not transformed by it either. I am . . . uncertain whether that was providence or the Outcaste's influence."

Kaylin frowned. "I know Shadow tries to transform what it touches—but I know that I could carry Spike."

"Spike?"

"Remember Spike? The ball? I'm talking to one of the sisters, aren't I?"

Bellusdeo grinned; it was an almost foreign expression on a familiar face. "Right."

"My Bellusdeo's okay with it?"

"What an odd use of the genitive. You would consider her the dominant personality, but yes, she has allowed me to speak. She was the warrior queen—the last of us to fall. I was more of a scholar and a mage, magic being useful in the growing war. Given the extent of the war, she wasn't required to learn many of the finer arts—there was no time. What she refined was combat.

"But we had Ascendants supporting us, and we had the Norranir as our vanguard. I see they survived; it is good to hear the drums." Her smile dimpled. That was definitely not Bellusdeo's smile. "I was very proud of those drums."

Kaylin stumbled as the full import of what this sister was saying sank in. "*You* created the drums?"

"I did. Interested in talking, now?"

"Not yet, but I will be. But I need to know your name. I mean, the name you were called before you . . ."

"Died?"

Kaylin swallowed. "Before that, yes."

"Logia. I was called Logia." Her smile deepened. "I was called many other things in my life, but I don't believe they would be considered polite in any company."

"Not even with Dragons?" It was Mandoran who asked. He, like Kaylin, often liked to learn new curse words.

"Especially not Dragons. I would like to visit. I would like to see Mrs. Erickson and thank her again. And I would like to speak with Helen about her former masters. Not her tenants," she added, as if that needed to be said. "But the people who controlled her before she broke free."

"I'm sure Helen would love that."

"I'm not," Mandoran muttered.

I have to agree with Mandoran, Severn added.

Why?

Bellusdeo was always straightforward. Get to know her sisters before you offer them the same trust Bellusdeo earned.

Kaylin actually turned to look at his expression; it was friendly rather than neutral; it didn't entirely match what his thoughts conveyed.

What should have happened was a melding of experience into a single personality. What did happen was different. Bellusdeo is now like the cohort; she carries distinct personalities on the inside of her head. You prefer some members of the cohort over others; you're naturally cautious around Sedarias, and completely relaxed around Terrano, Mandoran, Serralyn. This isn't going to be different.

You don't trust Logia.

I seldom trust anyone.

You trust me.

I know *you. Trust, for Wolves, is predicated on knowledge. It's less about trust as you use the word, and more about predictability. What appears as trust to you is knowledge: I know what to expect. I don't know what to expect of Bellusdeo's sisters.*

Kaylin nodded. *They died during the war; they've lived a long time as themselves, in theory.*

Exactly. Bellusdeo is not an indicator of her sisters. She loved them; they loved her. But think of them as the cohort, except in one body.

Do you think Bellusdeo has control of her own body now? I mean, do you think the sisters can wrest control from her? The question made Kaylin uneasy. On the plus side of that ledger, Logia didn't seem to have the same knee-jerk rage Bellusdeo exhibited when confronted with any new information about Shadow.

"I will not visit today—and I will attempt to inform you before I arrive. If you could gain Helen's permission in the meantime, I would be most grateful."

Definitely not Bellusdeo. Kaylin nodded.

The Consort wishes to meet with you today, Ynpharion said, his tone very stiff.

You told her what happened?

Annoyance filtered into his tone. *Of course.*

And she still wants us to show up?

That is her expressed preference.

Were you listening *when I went in to save Terrano?*

Silence for a beat. *I was.*

Fine, then. Kaylin was only theoretically a Lord of the Barrani

High Court, but she had many reasons for not wanting to tick off the Consort. *You know there's no way I'm going to be able to ditch Teela, right?*

Ynpharion's annoyance grew. *An'Teela. She is An'Teela, one of the most powerful Lords of the High Court. Her existence demands respect.*

Not at work, it doesn't.

Helen was waiting at the door. She often did this, because she knew it was important to Kaylin to have family to come home to. Today, however, she was looking both worried and almost militant.

"Terrano arrived," she said as Kaylin leaned in for a hug. "His pallor is terrible, but he's hiding it by being ever so slightly out of phase. And he carried word—" She looked down at Kaylin as they separated, her eyes slightly narrowed. They'd lost their normal appearance; they were black, with flecks of moving color.

"I suppose it would be too much to ask you to be careful?" Helen's expression was resigned.

"Terrano—"

"Yes, dear, I know. I am fond of him, and I am grateful that you managed to save his life. But he is now putting your life at risk because he is foolish and thinks caution is a word that belongs in a different language. To be clear, that language would be one he doesn't speak."

Helen was fussing. Kaylin leaned into it, the way she leaned into Caitlin's concern. Some people—Teela, prime example—hated being mothered. Kaylin wondered if she would ever become one of them. Maybe she would if the people who expressed concern treated her like a young child.

Maybe she'd accept even that. She wasn't a child anymore, but some part of her—abandoned by death, and responsible for causing more of it—might never grow up.

"As long as it is just a small part," Helen said softly, "preserve it as you can. But never let it drive you, Kaylin. Never let it become the voice for all that you are." Her hand cupped Kaylin's cheek. "You've done that once. You've followed that path. It almost destroyed you.

"I do not wish to see you walk that path again."

Kaylin swallowed, leaning into the warmth of Helen's hand. "I thought I had nothing, then."

"Yes, I know. Perhaps our lives—all of them, building or human or Barrani—are defined in the end not by what we have, but by what we value, what we struggle so mightily to protect. You could have become anything; you became a Hawk. Your early life could have defined you.

"I have met people—yes, even as a building—who became what had scarred them. The lessons they learned from the lives they had been subjected to when they had no power defined the worth of power. Not of people. Not of hope. But of power."

". . . like Barrani?"

"Very like Barrani. But before we continue in that vein, Nightshade cares for his brother, and his brother—angry and disappointed—cares for him. The cohort care for each other; they have built their lives around that. Perhaps, had they never been imprisoned within the Hallionne, they would not have made that choice. But the past cannot be changed, and could it, they would not."

"I'd change parts of mine."

"Yes. But the cohort are much older than you; they understand that they cannot change only parts of the past without distorting the whole of its fabric. And perhaps, if I could go back in time, I would change some parts of mine as well. When we are struggling, when we are desperate, our fear and pain guide us. But it is not a *good* guide, and oft leaves regret and self-loathing in its wake. And I have wandered, as I often do. Come. Come in. Terrano is waiting."

"Is it safe for me to enter the house?"

"It will always be safe for you. But if you refer to what you somehow picked up, I am taking precautions. It has clearly not caused damage to you."

"Can you sense it?" Kaylin asked as she pulled away.

"Barely, and the trace is so faint I am certain I would not be able to sense it at all if I was not fully aware of what transpired."

"Could you take it from me?"

Hope squawked.

"There is nothing, at the moment, to take. I can sense it but cannot see it in any of the planes you might approach."

Kaylin nodded. Her hand no longer felt frozen and numb. "He lost too much blood."

"He is with Sedarias at the moment, and I believe he is hoping you will somehow rescue him. Sedarias is most unhappy."

She would be. Annarion was wrecked, and Terrano had almost died.

"Yes," Helen said, although it wasn't necessary. "There are dangers in loving and being loved. But the cohort has learned to define themselves by the things they love, not the things they hate. In some cases, love leads to fear." Kaylin was pretty sure Helen was speaking about Sedarias.

"Not only Sedarias, but her fear is the sharpest, the harshest—and the most likely to lead to unfortunate consequences. Mortals are not taught that love itself is weakness. Barrani, who must live longer lives, are. They learn this at the same time they learn any of their abilities. Perhaps, because the cohort was young when they first met, the desire to love and be loved had not yet been fully extinguished." Helen exhaled. "In my time—and I speak not of tenants, but masters—the desire to love and be loved survived in small and broken ways.

"Love became ownership. It was conflated, in its twisted way, with possession. Possession might arise from the need to protect—but it did not end there. That is not what has happened with the cohort yet."

Yet.

"It is a worry. Should they fracture along lines of twisted love, it will not be safe for you to have them here as guests." Helen's tone made clear what that meant: they would have to leave.

"Isn't the decision mine?"

There was a long pause between the end of Kaylin's question and the answer. "Yes."

". . . it's not mine."

"It is yours while you survive." Helen's eyes were obsidian—Kaylin hadn't noticed the shift until it was complete. "If you perish, you will have no say."

It came to Kaylin then that Helen, her serene, gentle home, was angry.

"I am," Helen said, although Kaylin didn't ask out loud. "And I am struggling not to be so. The reason I chose you as a tenant is also the reason you have the cohort as guests. It is the reason that Bellusdeo was offered chambers, along with her Ascendant. It is the reason Imelda now makes use of my kitchen. Fallessian has helped her create an herb garden in the back of the house.

"You make your choices, and I approve of them inasmuch as I can. But of all the people gathered beneath this roof, you are the most precious to me."

"And Mrs. Erickson."

At that, the obsidian receded from the Avatar's eyes. "And Imelda, yes." Helen exhaled. "I understand the importance of Terrano, and I *am* angry, but I also understand that in some ways, my anger is blaming the victim, not the criminal. I admit a certain satisfaction at Sedarias's rage, which is why I have made no attempt to intervene."

It was hard to stop Sedarias when she was on a tear.

"No," Helen said, eyes once again darkening. "It is not. But we have so little time together, I do not want any of it to be wasted." Helen exhaled. "I will tell Terrano and Sedarias that you have returned." She turned to Severn for the first time since they'd arrived. "Will you join them?"

Severn nodded. "They can't go overlong, regardless of the discussion topic. Kaylin is expected by the Consort. If you believe her presence here is safe, it is unlikely the High Halls will refuse her."

Kaylin headed straight to Terrano.

Terrano, however, was with Sedarias—and Annarion, and the unmoving Nightshade. Mandoran was leaning against the wall farthest from where the rest of his cohort were standing.

It was an odd sight, if she thought about it; they were vibrating with tension, blue eyes, and that stillness that spoke of the strain of preserving it—all in perfect silence.

Kaylin sometimes agreed with Terrano and Mandoran: her life with the cohort would be a *lot* easier if she knew their True Names. Today, however, she was grateful for that silence. And it would force the cohort's various members to actually choose the words that left their mouth. Almost no one regulated their *thoughts* that way; thoughts were private.

Kaylin had learned—and it had been *hard* in her first years with the Hawks as their unofficial mascot—that she couldn't unsay words she'd spoken in anger. Words weren't illegal, but they were weapons. She couldn't retract them any more than she could unwind time to unstab someone.

What had Teela said? *Your ability to control your actions—words count, kitling—is a measure of self-control that implies you are struggling toward adulthood.*

She wondered as she waited for the cohort to fully include her in their interrupted discussion, if having people who could constantly hear her every thought meant that they'd always think of her as a child.

Mandoran was the first to break away, which wasn't unusual. He pulled himself up off the wall and headed for Kaylin, glancing at Severn. The cohort's relationship with Severn was one of mutual respect and a lot more social distance than they ever offered Kaylin.

"You probably don't want to be in this room," Mandoran said, heading toward the exit as if to lead them both to safety.

"Oh?"

"Annarion's having trouble maintaining physical form."

Kaylin frowned. Terrano's trouble was voluntary. Annarion's, a little less so.

"Because of his brother?"

"It involves his brother, yes," Mandoran replied. It made his *yes* sound a lot like *no.*

"Where are you going?" Sedarias snapped.

". . . or not." Mandoran turned. "Kaylin has an appointment with the Consort this afternoon. She's spent the morning running around the fiefs and saving Terrano from combat injuries. She doesn't have a lot of downtime." He glanced in her direction as if to ask if *downtime* was the right word; she nodded.

"She can't possibly expect to visit the High Halls after what happened this morning?"

Kaylin would have instantly wilted if she were a flower. She turned to Sedarias. "I didn't, no. But I've been informed that I, as a Lord of the High Court, am *expected.*"

Terrano's gaze traveled between Sedarias and Kaylin—but he moved closer to Annarion as it did.

"Serralyn's been doing research," Mandoran said as if Terrano hadn't moved, which was fair, and as if Sedarias hadn't spoken, which was, given the color of Sedarias's eyes, almost suicidal. "Ah, no. She asks me to tell you that she's been talking with Starrante, and he's been scrambling to find something in the library that might address whatever it was that happened with Terrano. And you."

"Did he find anything?"

"No. But he feels the lack of information comes down to two things. First: you're Chosen. The Chosen didn't often keep journals, but they kind of muck things up. Second: Shadow has always been an agent of change. Had Shadow been more like fire, *Ravellon* would never have fallen. In Starrante's opinion.

"He feels that Shadow is involved, but possibly in what might be its base state."

Kaylin said, "Later. It's going to be really bad if whatever it is I'm carrying comes to light in the worst possible way. Does he think it's safe?"

"Serralyn points out that you carried Spike—a sentient Shadow—to no ill effect."

That was true. Kaylin exhaled some of the worry. Worrying was pointless because worry or no, she still had to attend the Consort. "Is there any way to get rid of the whole 'lord of the court' thing?"

"Yes."

". . . that doesn't involve me dying?"

"Oh. Probably not. You could ask the Consort to ask the High Lord to have you made outcaste."

"Which is dying."

"Nightshade is outcaste, and he's not dead." The unsaid *yet* lingered in the air.

Sedarias had fallen silent, but she approached Kaylin and Severn as she did. It was beneath her dignity to shout across a room just to be heard. "I am a lord of the same court," she said. "Caution should be practiced, here. If the Consort wishes your presence, it might be better for her to visit you."

Ynpharion was instantly enraged. *Tell her that she is beholden to the Lady, as you are; it is not her duty or position to offer the Lady advice for which she has not asked.*

But you agree with her.

I might have, once. But your Helen is not the equal of the High Halls; what your Helen considers a low risk is an acceptable risk to the Lady.

"Not going to happen," Kaylin replied, getting a face full of almost midnight eyes as Sedarias leaned in. She exhaled. "I don't know what the Consort wants to discuss," she added, slipping from Elantran into High Barrani. "But given the current circumstances, I think some of it is related to Nightshade, if tangentially."

Annarion now joined the discussion, moving Terrano out of the way to do so.

"And I want to discuss what happened in the fiefs today, as well. There were two full war bands—that we know of. There might be more." Before Annarion could speak, she placed a gentle hand on his shoulder. "The Consort has called your brother by name in the hearing of Lords of the High Court. Inasmuch as she can, I would guess that she has always supported him.

"If she has information, and we want to preserve Lord Nightshade, we need it." She glanced toward the bed and the unconscious Barrani lying on it. To her surprise, Annarion had carefully covered him with blankets.

"Did you change him into nightclothes?"

"Helen did," Annarion replied. He lowered his head. Sedarias and Terrano swiveled toward Annarion; Mandoran didn't. "If it will help my brother at all, I would be grateful if you attended at the Consort's pleasure."

Ynpharion was unimpressed.

"I don't know that she'll have much to say about the method of attack—at least not the one used against Terrano. But I can share that with her, as well. Her sources of information in the High Court are going to be way better than *any* of ours."

"Teela's are pretty good when she leverages them," Terrano said.

Kaylin nodded. Fair enough.

"You know Teela intends to go with you, right?"

"I know she meant to, yes. But I also know Sedarias could be at risk if Teela steps in like this. The Consort believes it unwise."

"The Consort is younger than Teela, and, from all accounts, less political. *You* might be able to talk Teela out of it."

Kaylin snorted.

"But none of us can. And to be fair, a third of us think Teela should be there."

"Fine. Before you all start playing dress-up with me, the Consort said that it would be best if I appeared as a Hawk. So I'm not changing."

"We'll see what Teela has to say about that," Mandoran said, his voice far too cheerful.

Teela didn't have much to say, and it all boiled down to *no*.

Kaylin wasn't all that surprised when Teela showed up at the house in full court dress. She wasn't surprised when Teela came with a box that contained appropriate, Kaylin-sized clothing. She was slightly surprised when the Barrani Hawk glanced once in Severn's direction and nodded. Apparently, Severn was the compromise. He could dress as a Hawk. Kaylin couldn't.

She tried not to resent it and failed. On the other hand, it annoyed Ynpharion, so there was an upside to what would otherwise be a double standard.

The dress itself was a shade of green that matched and blended with Teela's dress, which annoyed Ynpharion even more. Kaylin doubted it would annoy the Consort.

"I've chosen shoes that are more practical for this outing," Teela said, opening a box. To Kaylin, *practical* meant the Hawks' kit: something you could really run in in a pinch.

Barrani skirts, while voluminous, never seemed to impede movement. She couldn't argue against them on a practical level.

But they'd always made her feel self-conscious, as if wearing the clothing itself made her a liar.

The boots shoved into Kaylin's hands weren't anything like her normal boots—but they didn't have the heels that Teela's boots did. Kaylin found shoes like Teela's painful to walk in; they always made her feel slightly off-balance. If she had to run while wearing them, she'd probably trip and break a leg—which meant she'd have to throw them away if running became a necessity.

These, not so much. They were slender, and the uppers were soft, but the soles, while also narrow in appearance, were flat against the ground.

"You think we might have to run and fight?" she asked as she slid her feet into them.

"You don't?" Teela countered. She glanced at Severn. "Would you be more comfortable in court clothing?"

Severn shook his head.

"Very well. You might have noticed the cohort is currently enmeshed in multiple disagreements. Attempts on Nightshade's life are not uncommon, although it's been a century or two since a concerted, credible effort has been made. What I don't understand is both the timing and the method.

"Serralyn has continued to speak with Starrante; the Arbiter may ask you to visit the library in person, depending on the outcome of our meeting with the Consort."

Kaylin nodded.

"Are you ready? We're running slightly late."

"What this means," Terrano said, his voice not accompanied by his physical body, "is that Teela will be driving."

08

Teela was a Hawk.

Swords were responsible for public safety, and one aspect of that included the laws that governed carriages on the public roads. Helen, being in one of the fanciest neighborhoods in Elantra, had the advantage of very wide roads—but Teela's driving was, and had always been, a danger to public—and private—safety.

Teela had taken care to make sure Kaylin was impeccably dressed and properly prepared for the High Halls. Kaylin, however, wasn't Barrani. When Teela's carriage finally rolled to an unsteady, erratic stop—which miraculously didn't involve the carriage tipping over and being dragged half the way to their destination—Kaylin's hair was worse for wear. Had she been in normal, affordable clothing, her skirts would have been a wrinkled mess. Barrani cloth didn't seem to have that problem.

Even Severn had been forced to brace himself against one of the carriage walls.

They were, however, on time.

Kaylin's knees felt like jelly as she exited the carriage, but the minute her feet were on solid ground, she was fine. "You are *not* driving on the way back."

"Says who?"

"I'll walk. It's not that far."

Terrano muttered a strong agreement. He was still less than visible, but he hadn't come as part of Kaylin's party; he was allowed—indeed invited—to enter the High Halls at will. Sedarias's many enemies at court knew better than to attack Terrano; he was considered a friend of the sentience at the heart of the High Halls.

Why that sentience didn't just forbid violence the way the Hallionne did, Kaylin didn't understand. Here, murder, involving the Barrani, appeared to be just another fact of life. The lives of mortals within the High Halls were of value—or import—only because their deaths would invoke Imperial wrath. Without that wrath, Kaylin had no doubt that the Halls would be populated by mortal slaves. Or corpses. Or both.

Some people tried to do their best no matter their circumstances. Some did their worst—or would, if they didn't fear the consequences. She lumped most Barrani into the latter category. If it weren't for the Emperor's laws, they would be what they had always been, and the mortals in their vicinity would be either slaves or dead.

She understood Dragons less well, but the Dragon she served—and would serve all her life, given the choice—was not Barrani. His laws had been created taking into account both the Immortal and the mortal. Dragons, in the eyes of the Barrani, were the only other race that must be treated with respect.

Kaylin exhaled. She was nervous, and when nervous, her thoughts were often dark. Then again, they were approaching the wide, flat steps of the High Halls. She wondered if all of the vast, opulent grounds were part of the High Halls, the way Helen's lawns were part of Helen.

If they were, the Avatar of the Halls didn't answer.

Teela conspicuously wore *Kariannos*, one of the three Dragonslayers. She was dressed much in the style that Kaylin herself was dressed, and in similar colors.

They are not similar. Ynpharion was annoyed. Life sometimes showed a little mercy.

They're green.

He didn't shriek, but it was pretty close. Her ignorance had always frustrated him. That and her unwillingness to learn. Frustrating Ynpharion was one of the few pleasures she was going to be allowed today. When she was a child—

You are Chosen! Ynpharion shrieked.

"What do you find so amusing, Lord Kaylin?" Teela asked.

"Ynpharion."

This caused a frown on Teela's part, and utter silence on Ynpharion's. Severn might not have heard either Teela's question or Kaylin's reply. His gaze was at the height of the stairs, where Barrani lingered. His left hand fell to the hilt of his weapon, but he made no move to draw it.

Right. They were in the heart of Barrani territory now, Kaylin in her dress, Severn—unfairly, in her opinion—in his Hawks' kit. But she understood part of the reason Teela allowed it. No matter what his clothing, his weapon demanded Barrani respect. The smile left her face as she counted: there were four people, in pairs, who had been conversing until the new arrivals caught their attention.

Kaylin wasn't certain what they found more offensive: Severn, dressed as an officer of the much-detested Imperial Laws, or a mortal wearing clothing clearly created by Barrani *for* Barrani. Their eyes were blue; one woman's were a notably dark color. No one moved or spoke, because Teela was walking, in step, beside Kaylin, her presence both a claim of ownership and a warning.

Kaylin was slightly surprised when Terrano became visible

at the height of the stairs, in the center of the largest of the arched doors.

As Terrano became visible—and not, given his expression, by his will alone—a second figure materialized beside the cohort member. "What have I told you about invisibility?" that figure said. It was the Avatar of the High Halls.

"It makes people paranoid. But hey—we're Barrani. How much worse could we get?" Terrano, who *could* show proper manners, didn't bother.

"The Lady is waiting, Lord Kaylin," the Avatar said, ignoring Terrano's words. He then put Kaylin under a terrible spotlight: he bowed. To her. In front of witnesses. "She has asked me to escort you. And to separate you from Terrano."

Kaylin coughed.

Ynpharion did as well, but for different reasons.

"Lord Severn, if you would join Lord Kaylin, the Lady would be grateful."

The High Halls were never crowded. The Halls of Law were often a press of rushing bodies. The difference in ceiling height—with the exception of the Halls of Laws' aerie—was stark. One was *meant* to feel small and insignificant while one walked here. Severn was tense. Teela, elegant and graceful, was indigo-eyed. They expected trouble.

They are prepared *for trouble*, Ynpharion corrected her. *I am uncertain that it was wise to have the Avatar escort you; it is a statement of your import in a place where mortals do not reside.*

You probably know why.

I know that you are considered an essential possible replacement in the worst case, yes. But it is almost as if that is being announced to those who would not likewise know.

The Consort didn't ask for this?

No. She does not consider it wise, and she is uneasy, now.

She's uneasy regardless. If she weren't, she would never have summoned me.

Ynpharion did not reply.

There were no crossbow bolts, no arrows, no sudden daggers.

Severn didn't speak a word, but she noted that both of his hands were on his weapons. Teela walked as if she hadn't a care in the world, but Kaylin had seen her draw her sword; she didn't need much time. Kaylin was the only person present who didn't reach for her knives. They weren't the equal of Severn's weapon, or Teela's—they hadn't been crafted by very old Barrani, or the ancient, unknowable green.

She had, however, one important protection that the Barrani found intimidating: Hope, who lay across her shoulders like a lizard-shaped shawl. They knew Kaylin was Chosen; they knew Hope was a familiar. They probably connected the dots. The dots that didn't actually exist.

It is better that they fear you, Ynpharion told her.

Sure. Because Barrani never kill people they fear just to make sure they can't cause them any harm. Kaylin snorted, earning a glare from Teela.

Ynpharion agreed. She realized then that he was also uneasy with everything. He didn't fear her the way the distant Barrani did; he was namebound. He knew what she was thinking when he could be bothered to put in the effort. Helen kept him out of the house.

You do not mean the Lady I serve harm. If it were in your power, you would do what you could to increase her happiness. She knows this, as well. But she considers you important to our people because the Lake of Life accepts you. If she is injured, if she is killed, our young can still be wakened.

It was possible, but Kaylin thought no Barrani would condescend to accept that aid from a mere mortal, as if mortality would taint their Immortal offspring somehow.

Ynpharion was silent, but not dismissive or frustrated.

Hope rose and lifted a wing; he placed it—gently—across Kaylin's right eye. She hadn't asked, trusting the Avatar of the High Halls. Hope didn't seem incensed or concerned; when he was, he slapped her face. The Halls through both eyes seemed the same; there were no invisible people here.

But she wondered if the High Halls sensed anything out of place in her.

"I do not, Lord Kaylin. I would consider your Helen to be more accurate in her assessment, as she is more familiar with you." At Kaylin's expression, he added, "Familiarity is a type of knowledge. Your Helen—"

"She's not mine."

"Helen, then, is quite familiar with you, and she has had experience with mortals that I lack. Terrano has attempted to alleviate my ignorance, but as I am sure you are aware, his observations are unique."

"Is familiarity important?"

"It is. It is the gaining of knowledge that cannot be derived from simply hearing your thoughts. What I hear is what you are thinking in the moment. What I would build, with greater familiarity, is a tapestry, for which each thought is a thread of a different hue. To my eyes, you are as you have been since I first awakened. I am aware that you absorbed something, but that has not altered you in a way that is perceptible to me.

"I would not risk your presence otherwise."

"Is that why you came to meet me?"

The Avatar smiled. "No. I can see everything that occurs within my boundaries, just as Helen does. But I wished to converse."

"Why?"

"The Lady will speak with you. Matters political, except where they threaten the Lady and the Lake, are not mine. I may not interfere in the natural unfolding of Barrani politics, except when they present a threat to the Lady. You will note, however, that the Halls seem empty."

"They're always empty."

"They are emptier than they were before I awakened. The Barrani understand that secrecy is one of the tools upon which survival depends. Terrano and his kin—his chosen kin—are unusual. They live with Helen. She knows their thoughts. I am certain that she would be delighted to avoid them at times. They are not cautious of me in the way the rest of the Barrani are. The exception, of course, is An'Teela.

"But Severn is also cautious. He is always guarded. From the first time I woke until today."

"Can he hear you?"

"He can. You would never know it, would you? But his caution suits the High Halls. Terrano should practice more of it. If I were actually as I appear at the moment, I would have a raging headache. I believe that is the phrase?" He asked the question of Teela.

Her lips quirked in a brief smile. "That is *entirely* the correct phrase." She offered no name and no title to the most powerful entity within the High Halls; according to Serralyn, discussion was heated and ongoing among the nobles of the High Court as to what would be appropriate and respectful. They could not exalt the High Halls' Avatar as they did the High Lord; they could not treat the Avatar with a disastrous lack of respect, as if the Avatar himself was simple furniture.

"How should we address you?" Kaylin asked.

"I just call him Abel," Terrano said, shrugging. "Abel's not offended. He's ancient enough the petty bickering about what to call him—what title to grant—is boring. Or funny, depending on how heated the argument gets. To Abel, it's *all* irrelevant."

"To Barrani, respect is life." Abel's voice was oddly gentle.

"Yeah, yeah," Terrano replied. "If by respect, you mean

fear." He winced. "I'm not going to visit the Consort with you guys," he added. "So respect's kind of irrelevant."

The Avatar's eyes lost their blue—a Barrani appearance. He glared at Terrano.

". . . sorry."

"I have told you many, many times that there is one being within the High Halls that is worthy of all gestures of respect due the powerful."

Terrano nodded, mimicking chagrin perfectly. Kaylin knew it wasn't genuine, which meant the Avatar knew it as well.

"I do," the Avatar said. "I am aware of his history with this Consort; I considered destroying him when I first woke."

"And you regret your mercy?" Teela's smile wasn't fake.

"No. But at times like this, it is close." He continued to walk. Terrano fell silent but walked beside the Avatar as if they were friends.

"Friendship is not what I was created to achieve," the Avatar said without looking back. "But I find it oddly precious, if fragile. There is a warmth to it that I do not wish to lose. Terrano is entirely himself—whatever that self is. I am not certain I understand it. At heart, he is Barrani, as he was born. But he is not like An'Mellarionne." Before Kaylin could speak, he added, "When I compare him to all of the Barrani who make the High Halls their home, he is most like the Consort herself."

Ynpharion was instantly outraged.

"She is entirely herself. Her role as Lady defines her; the responsibility to the Barrani people is her only sacred duty. But she is not simply a vessel for the will of the Lake of Life; she, too, has affections and concerns that drive her."

"And those are the reason I'm here."

"I will let her speak. She is waiting."

The Consort was seated by the fountain that marked the beginning of the small territory within the High Halls dedicated to the woman who could draw names from the Lake of Life. Those names—living True Words—were the breath of life to Barrani children, born into the world asleep. In no other way would they wake.

"That," Abel said, "is not entirely true. History has its grim and terrifying moments. But it *is* true now. I will leave you here."

"Your Avatar will leave."

"No, Chosen. There are places where even I am not permitted to go without express permission."

"He means it," Terrano added, voice much softer and shorn of his usual cheekiness. "He can watch at a distance. He can intervene if survival is at stake. But if she requests privacy, he will give it." The Barrani cohort member was serious enough that he spoke in his mother tongue, not the Elantran he had come to favor. "We have to stop here. But you can see her."

Kaylin nodded. To her surprise, the Consort was alone. No visible guards were present. Not even Ynpharion. A small table, round, white, and ornate, was set in front of the Consort. Two chairs had been placed on opposite sides of that table, and the Consort sat in one of them. She lifted a hand, indicating that Kaylin should take the other.

She can summon me at any time she feels it necessary, Ynpharion said. *And she believes that An'Teela will be adequate guard should something unexpected occur.* He grudgingly accepted that truth: An'Teela was far more experienced, far more powerful, than Ynpharion himself.

Kaylin was surprised. She knew that Teela was effectively her guard while she was here; she hadn't expected the Consort would allow her to *attend* the meeting she'd all but commanded. Ynpharion didn't like it, either.

Hope squawked.

She is aware that you will also come to her aid should it be required. She is not foolish enough to trust An'Teela.

But foolish enough to trust me?

You know when trust is offered, he replied, his voice stiffening into a more familiar tone.

When the difference in power is so large the trusted person is almost irrelevant.

Exactly. But he was uneasy. He was constantly dismissive, constantly contemptuous, but behind that layer of what she assumed was the majority of his unpleasant personality, he wasn't certain that Kaylin herself wasn't actually powerful. *An'Teela is a power. Understand, then, that her inclusion implies a far greater threat than An'Teela herself could offer.*

Teela wouldn't threaten the Consort, Kaylin snapped.

She believes that you believe this. She is willing to take the risk of An'Teela's presence; it implies support.

She shouldn't need *support. No one would threaten the Lady.* Kaylin was engulfed by Ynpharion's worry—which she didn't need. She'd started worrying all on her own the moment the Consort's invitation had arrived, and she hadn't stopped.

"If Ynpharion is conversing with you, I will have words with him later," the Consort said, her green eyes belying the possible threat to Ynpharion.

Kaylin, awkward in her dress, offered the Consort a hand. If she had to dress the part of a Lord of the High Court, the Consort didn't expect her to *act* the part. Just to pass muster for witnesses who were forced to keep their distance.

The Consort's hand, when it met Kaylin's, was surprisingly cold. Kaylin's eyes narrowed instantly. "Are you unwell?"

The familiar green of the Consort's eyes flickered blue. Of the Barrani, the only person besides the Consort who had green eyes was Serralyn; the Consort's green was far rarer. "If you wish to assess, I grant permission."

Kaylin knew that attempts to heal most Barrani were met with rage and resentment. Saving their lives could be a death sentence—for Kaylin. The healing bridge was a bridge both people—healer and healed—could cross; they discovered much about each other.

Barrani survival had always depended on lies and secrecy. It's what made the cohort so incredibly unusual. Kaylin attempted to assess the Consort's physical health.

She touched nothing.

She touched nothing, just as she'd done with Nightshade. Something appeared to be interfering with the only truly good power the Marks of the Chosen had granted her. She could not examine the Consort.

The Consort's smile was gentle; there was no surprise in it.

"Is this why you called me?" Kaylin's voice was barely louder than a whisper.

The Consort nodded, her expression grave. "Were you perhaps suspecting that I would be concerned about Lord Nightshade?"

She had been and felt no need to hide it. "I was. The timing suggested it."

The Consort's eyes were once again green. "You are aware that I hold him in some affection."

It is dangerous, Ynpharion said.

Were you aware that something was wrong?

Silence. No. The Consort had not chosen to explain the reason for her summons to Ynpharion. But she must have been aware that he would discover the reason through Kaylin. Kaylin didn't ask, because another thought, another fear, suddenly blossomed, swamping almost all other thoughts she might have had.

Severn had not taken a seat; neither had Teela. There had only been one chair across from the small table at which the Consort waited.

"Lady," she said, her voice almost a whisper. "Can you even touch the names in the Lake?"

The Consort's smile was a broken, terrible thing, yet beautiful in its own right. "You understand the problem. It is as if the names themselves are unaware of my presence at all. Were it not for your existence, I am uncertain I would be stable enough to receive visitors."

Kaylin exhaled. "Should we visit the Lake first, or can I talk about Nightshade?"

The Consort frowned. "You wish to discuss Nightshade in such an emergency?"

"I normally never want to talk about Nightshade," Kaylin replied in a tone that suggested agreement. "But . . . I think this is politics. Barrani-style. You must know, by now, that Nightshade was nearly assassinated."

The Consort nodded.

"Teela has information about that—but also emblems. Whoever orchestrated the attack chose to go all out—they sent two Barrani war bands into the warrens to lie in wait at Nightshade's edge of the border zone. Nightshade was badly injured. I couldn't heal him. I tried—but while I could physically touch him, I couldn't *heal* him. And . . . it's just like you, right now. I am holding your hand, but the healing power isn't reaching you at all."

The Consort's eyes became fully blue. "He is injured?"

"He's unconscious. He hasn't woken up. Helen can't help him, either. She doesn't know what's wrong. I don't think the High Halls would be able to revive him—and even if the Avatar could, he'd likely die. He's an unconscious outcaste. Helen can protect him—and she will, because Annarion would be shattered if his brother died.

"The High Halls can protect you."

"If the High Halls were capable of that, I would not be in this condition." The Consort's expression was thoughtful.

"I thought it was probably magic, but . . . it's not just that. It might be a magical poison."

Teela stepped forward. She didn't push Kaylin out of the way, but she took up position around the small circular surface closer to the Kaylin side of the table. "We are investigating, Lady," she said. She offered the Consort an extremely elegant, extremely correct bow. "But we believe the attackers, or those who orchestrated the attack, are moving on several fronts; they appear to be taking advantage of the border zones between the fiefs."

The Consort's eyes were now almost the same color as Teela's. "You believe they are entering forbidden territory."

"We believe it possible." Teela exhaled. "The outcaste Dragon has infiltrated parts of Elantra before; his form appears to be mutable. He served for a time on the Aerian court; he has done damage in the fiefs, although our information in that regard is, by nature, incomplete. The fieflords share information when they believe there is some activity coming out of *Ravellon*, but what is shared is chosen by those lords."

"Do you believe that information to be reliable?"

"Oddly, yes. The fieflords captain the Towers; the Towers exist solely to protect the barrier that prevents Shadow from escaping *Ravellon*. Where Shadow is concerned, I believe they offer as much information as they can without compromising their own rule."

"And have any of those lords offered news about people entering the heart of the fiefs?"

"Suspicions, yes. Were it a single individual, I might discard the information; I might assume the Dragon Outcaste is once again acting. He is not of Shadow; he cannot be detected *as* Shadow. But if he is involved, he is not, in our opinion, the instigator at this time.

"Lord Nightshade was attacked. He cannot be healed by the Chosen. You were not attacked—but you cannot be healed by the Chosen. You have not, to my knowledge, left the High Halls or your own seat."

"Which means Barrani are involved."

Teela nodded. "I don't have to tell you that there are far, far too many Barrani who would like to see Nightshade fall—and the sword he carries returned to the High Court, where it might choose a new wielder. He is outcaste; his death is mandated."

"By a previous High Lord," the Consort replied, an edge of warning in her words.

"It's the sword that preserved him," Kaylin said, hoping to dull that edge a little—or at least distract its wielder. She liked the Consort, and she considered Teela family. She didn't want to see them fight because of the stupid decision of a High Lord who was dead.

"Pardon?"

"We're pretty sure *Meliannos* preserved his life. I can't heal him—but the damage the magic or poison caused appears to have been suspended. I don't think the sword would choose anyone who was directly responsible for his death."

The Consort's brows rose. "What do you know of our swords?"

"I know they're called Dragonslayers, if that's helpful. I know they're magical. I sort of suspected they have egos, but that's never been confirmed, and Teela bit my head off once because I asked impertinent questions."

"Disrespectful questions, kitling."

"Aren't they the same thing?"

"At court, impertinence can get you fined or embarrassed. Disrespect might be cause to end your life. There is very little study and research extant about The Three, and before you even consider it, do not task the librarians of the Academia with research in their archives of forgotten and ancient lore."

Given the color of her eyes, she meant it. "Even this much you should know better than to discuss."

"But—it's the Consort. She's not his enemy!"

"We live forever. She is not his enemy *now.* Nor am I, or my kindred. But that does not mean the possibility does not exist in a future we cannot immediately foresee." Teela exhaled.

The Consort gestured, and an empty chair appeared. "Please forgive my poor manners, An'Teela."

Teela nodded and sat. The hilt of her sword could be seen as she arranged her skirts—no doubt a deliberate, graceful reminder.

"You believe the timing suspect? Do you consider it possible that a faction aligned against the current An'Mellarionne has been forced into play?"

"I believe it is a possibility. I believe it is possible that the outcaste Dragon has some hand—subtle and not commanding—in this. And I believe that the Arcanum's members are involved. I have asked for a meeting with Lord Evarrim to discuss the possibility.

"How many people are aware of your affliction?"

The Consort said, "As you must guess, no one of whom I am aware."

"Then let me ask a different question. Are there any Barrani who have sent their daughters to visit the Lake recently?"

"As you are aware, families sponsor children to take the tests to become a potential Consort frequently. But yes. Three."

"Are you aware of the results?"

The Consort looked pained. "I cannot divulge results. I would break that law if it became necessary, but that information cannot come from me. The position as Lady is not political; it has been agreed that politics must be subservient to the very future of our people, and throughout time, that has more or less proven true."

Barrani politics were never entirely in abeyance. Politics of necessity meant no one attempted to kill the Consort. Even were her condition to be known, there would be a high, high cost to the attempt.

But to render her incapable without taking her life? To force her from her seat because she could no longer do the duties for which she was treated with such reverence?

That felt Barrani through and through.

But if one of the families believed they had a daughter that could replace the Consort, it was *exactly* the type of thing they might do.

You are becoming more accustomed to subtle Barrani politics, Ynpharion said with a grudging hint of approval.

"How long has it been?" Kaylin asked the Consort, her voice softer than Teela's. "How long has it been since the Lake could no longer hear you?"

09

The Consort was silent for long enough, Kaylin thought she wouldn't answer the question.

"She is trying to place the timing," Teela told her. "Nightshade's attack was less than a full day ago. If your condition occurred before that attack, it changes the shape of our investigation. No word of the difficulty will leave this place; while Lord Kaylin is perhaps an open book with regards to most things, she is highly aware of the stakes.

"And she is not foolish enough to dream of a life as a Barrani Lord in the High Halls, which was what she would be forced to become were the truth known. The Avatar Terrano calls Abel is aware, must be aware, of the difficulty. He understands what is at stake."

The Consort bowed head, maintaining silence.

"It did not happen all at once," she finally said. "If the attempt on Calarnenne's life coincided with Kaylin's inability to heal him, his condition must have occurred immediately. Mine did not. I can speak with the Lake; it is not the way I speak with you now. But the Lake's voice is a song that I hear constantly; it is a joy and a reminder that joy *must* be protected.

"The song became quieter; it was harder to hear, and therefore harder to listen. I was concerned that something had happened, something had injured or damaged the Lake—but the High Halls said the Lake had not changed.

"There was only one conclusion I could draw. I had changed, somehow. But the High Halls could see no discernible difference, no interference, magical or otherwise, no hint of poison. But two days ago, I could no longer hear the Lake." She closed her eyes. Her lips thinned before she spoke again. "I could not visit it, as I was wont to do when troubled.

"I believe you could, should you make that attempt. We are not a populous people, and we have few children over the course of our long lives—but should a child be born tomorrow, my condition would become known. And should that happen, your ability would become more widely known as well.

"But if you could not touch Calarnenne, it is unlikely you will be able to affect me with the Marks of the Chosen, either."

"We haven't given up on Nightshade," Kaylin replied. "We're doing research in at least two places to understand what's happened to him—and we can research more or less openly. We obviously can't do that where you're involved—but it looks like the work itself will be useful."

"And more urgent," Teela added. She rose. "We will keep you informed in a way that will not cause obvious interest from those who now work against you. But if you could deliver the names of those families who have had their daughters take the test of the Lake, it would be of relevance."

"How so? You imagine that one of those families is somehow responsible?"

"Do you not?"

"One cannot pass the test of the Lake with that mindset; it is why most fail. The Consort, the Lady, must be above political machinations where the future of our people is concerned."

"People oft believe what they want to believe," Teela replied. "And it is possible that one of the three families has chosen to believe that their daughter will pass the test and unseat you—which would be necessary if you cannot wake the children."

Kaylin didn't get up from her chair. "One more question," she said, facing the Consort. "Can you still communicate with your namebound? Or is it like the Lake?"

The Consort exhaled. "It is like the Lake. I can—as must be clear to you—communicate with my namebound, but it is becoming more difficult; their voices, while clear, are far quieter. Have you reason to ask that question?"

"I can't reach Nightshade the way I used to. Whatever was done to you, over a period of time, appears to have been done instantly to him."

The Consort rose, forcing Kaylin to do the same. Her eyes were dark, dark blue. "My brother's reign has been as stable as a new reign could be expected to be—but this will harm him, possibly irreparably. Find answers, Lord Kaylin. Find them quickly. Much rides upon a solution."

To Teela, she said, "I do not wish to involve you in politics that are not your concern. You are already entangled in Mellarionne's issues. If your information sources are solid, you will no doubt unearth information about the families involved in recent testing. The Lake does not, as you must be aware, forbid it. In my absence, in my unexpected death, someone must remain to carry on the duties I have undertaken.

"In the past, those with political ambitions were not accepted by the Lake."

"And now?"

"I believe there is one child who personally lacks much ambition. I have seen her only a handful of times, always at a distance; she is timid, but she has the protection of a line that was once very significant. As Sedarias does, the new lord—the lord who succeeded the man who wielded power—is attempting to hold on to what he has taken.

"But that has ever been the challenge of our kin, has it not?

The bold and the reckless often fail to take into account the future that lies in wait beyond their moments of triumph. Many could conquer who could not hold the seats they gained."

Kaylin frowned. *Ynpharion.*

I am listening.

Why didn't you warn me?

I was forbidden. What the Consort shares, she chooses. But now you know. And she would share this with you because you can accomplish what she cannot. If it is necessary, you would be willing to do so secretly to aid and support my Lady.

Kaylin didn't argue. It was true. While she had her issues with certain members of the Halls of Law who were quick to take credit for other people's work, this was entirely different. She didn't *want* to be the Lady of the Lake. She didn't really want to be a Lord of the High Court, either. If the Consort could not wake the infants, Kaylin could—and she was desperately willing to let the Consort take all credit.

"Which woman, and which family?" Teela's words brought her back to the conversation at hand.

"Yvonne, a young woman from the West March. She was born to a branch family of Sennarin, and An'Sennarin has formally adopted her as she is without direct kin. I would have said she could not survive in the High Halls, but An'Sennarin has, thus far, managed to protect her." The Consort hesitated, and then added, "In that, he has the aid of An'Tellarus. If An'Sennarin has acknowledged Yvonne as immediate kin, Yvonne nonetheless serves An'Tellarus as personal attendant. I believe it has caused some friction between Sennarin and Tellarus."

Kaylin didn't recognize either of the names the Consort spoke.

Teela clearly did.

But that wasn't the strange part. *Severn* did. He said nothing; no hint of recognition crossed his expression. But they shared her name. She knew. She could feel it—and it had to be strong for that to happen. Severn was good at keeping his thoughts to himself unless she reached out for them.

His thoughts were a steel trap; no words escaped. But his surprise—perhaps shock—could be felt as tremors.

She wanted to reach out. She wanted to say something. But she'd never been good at saying the right thing when it really mattered. Severn chose to keep words to himself. Kaylin couldn't force words out.

"It is Tellarus that concerns you," Teela said—a statement, not a question.

The Consort nodded regardless. "An'Teela—the girl is not dangerous in and of herself. In other circumstances, I would be fond of her."

"But if she is bound to Tellarus, that is an entirely different story."

The Consort did not reply. Instead she turned to Kaylin. "I hope to hear word from the Chosen as soon as possible. But you may have to petition for an appointment in person; I cannot guarantee that I can reach you through my usual avenues of communication."

Ynpharion flinched.

Kaylin now understood why he had been uneasy. The Lady was the lord he had chosen, the lord he desired to serve with the entirety of his being. He had offered the Lady his name willingly, had made himself far more vulnerable to her commands than any Barrani of sound mind might have done. Perhaps, had the situation not been so critical, he wouldn't have made that choice.

But he was *proud* of that choice.

And the Lady considered him one of her most important guards.

"We'll leave. The research being done to alleviate Nightshade's condition seems very relevant to yours. The moment we hear anything, the moment we have any clues, we'll let you know."

"If Ynpharion cannot reach me as he has done in the past, I will keep him far closer than I do now."

This pleased Ynpharion; it was proof of his value to the Lady. Even if that value was simply the fact that his True Name was known to Kaylin.

"Do that," Kaylin replied without thought. Her response filled Ynpharion with comfortable outrage—at least, comfortable for Kaylin. She turned and then turned back. "Do you have any idea why someone would send two war bands to Nightshade right now? The timing seems way too close to be coincidental."

"Throughout the centuries, it's been tried. Calarnenne possesses one of The Three, and it will not leave his hand until his death." At that, a hint of a troubled smile touched her lips. "He was asked, once, for the return of that sword. He refused."

". . . who asked?"

"My grandfather. But I should not speak of it where he has not. Let me say instead that attempts were frequent in the past and occur very seldom now. I hope the timing was coincidental."

Hope wasn't belief. That much was clear.

"Kitling," Teela said in her best officer voice. "It is time to let the Consort rest." She glanced at Severn, who stood as a perfect and almost invisible guard. "Corporal."

He nodded.

The Avatar of the High Halls was waiting for them at the end of the path that led, through the interior forest of the Halls, to the Consort's personal fountain. To Kaylin's surprise, he wore armor, not the usual robes. He was silent, but not still; he offered Kaylin a deliberate, perfect bow.

"Do you know who attempted to assassinate Nightshade?"

The Avatar did not answer. "Terrano wishes to remain. He desires to avoid carriages for the rest of the day."

Teela's eyes narrowed.

"My apologies, An'Teela, but Terrano—as I am certain you are aware—is a bit peculiar for your kin. I believe that is what he meant to express, but I am translating his spoken words into language more reflective of the environment. Perhaps I err."

He didn't. They all knew it. Kaylin would have walked home herself if she weren't wearing this ridiculous dress. It was supposed to make her feel powerful. It was supposed to help her fit in. It had the opposite effect. A dress like this didn't belong on a person like Kaylin, an officer of the Halls of Law.

The Avatar turned and began to walk away, moving slowly enough to imply he intended to be followed, not chased.

"Why is he wearing armor?" she whispered to Teela.

Teela didn't answer.

Severn did. *It's meant to discourage possible conflict. Our visit has drawn attention.*

He didn't wear armor when he met us.

No. When we arrived, unannounced, no one had enough time to prepare. We spent some time speaking with the Consort, which would allow possible enemies to plan a more traditional attack.

They're Barrani.

The Consort is now entangled in the politics she is meant to be above. His words were neutral.

Who is An'Tellarus? You recognized the name.

He was silent for at least ten yards' worth of steps. *I did.*

Is she dangerous?

Is Teela?

Kaylin frowned. *Teela's powerful, but she's not dangerous.*

She is incredibly dangerous, was his quiet, calm reply. *She's just not a danger to us.*

And An'Tellarus is?

If you'd asked me this morning, I would have said no. But she's a very old, very powerful lord; she's held her seat for longer than Teela.

What aren't you telling me?

Severn didn't answer. But his silence wasn't a wall; it was almost like the surface of the ocean; if she approached, she could see what lay beneath it. She didn't. Or she tried not to. Severn was Severn. Kaylin was Kaylin. Neither of them had grown up the way the cohort had; to both, privacy was valuable and necessary.

"You might answer her questions," the Avatar said, sounding ever so slightly apologetic.

Teela's eyes were about as dark a blue as they could get. Severn's hadn't changed, because he was human. "As I am certain you are aware, the information—and the *request we received* from the Lady—are of primary import. We cannot tarry here further."

This made no sense to Kaylin.

He isn't escorting us to the entrance, Severn said. Where Teela's eyes were martial, Severn's tone was strange—almost, but not quite, long-suffering.

Where is he taking us? And why?

"Be patient, Lord Kaylin. Answers to at least that question will be forthcoming. My apologies, An'Teela, if I have interrupted your very necessary work. But it is possible that the interruption may add detail to the complexity of the investigation you must undertake."

"I will accept your decision," Teela responded, as if she had any choice. They were standing and walking within the territory of the Avatar. What he chose was unspoken law. "But I will ask a favor in return. You must be aware of the people who planned the assassination. They cannot be of little note. I am aware that some of the most conservative families on the High Court have never let the training and formation of war bands decline. Foolish, but if the Emperor is willing—for now—to tolerate such military activities, that is his decision."

"An'Teela, I cannot answer the question you wish to ask, as you must be aware."

Teela's eyes narrowed; she didn't argue. "Politics such as this have been our way of life for as long as I've been conscious. People of ambition desire power. People of ambition desire the respect they feel power accrues. Through our history, the rulership of the High Court has changed familial lines very, very seldom.

"But there have been credible attempts in the past, if one is not to consider success the only metric of credibility. You have seen much of our history play out. Are we in such a time?"

"An'Teela."

Teela exhaled. "Apologies. I have been living with Terrano and our chosen kin, and I have clearly become far too comfortable speaking my mind."

"You have not spoken your mind once. You seek information I am not permitted to give you. My interference, such as it is, is allowed because of the danger to the Lady. But I am alive, just as you are. I have concerns, just as you have. Inasmuch as I am able, I will protect her, and where possible, allow that protection to skirt the edge of my permissions."

"That is why you are not escorting us out?"

"I merely fulfill a simple request from a complex, powerful woman. It does not, on the surface, seem political, and it is not you with whom she wished to speak."

Teela's frown deepened.

"It is Corporal Handred."

Kaylin knew Severn had had a life before she met him, but when she was five and her mother still alive, that life hadn't mattered. It hadn't been real. She knew he had a different kind of life in the gaps between the last day of her childhood and meeting him again. There had to be. Severn had been a *Wolf*. Kaylin had become a Hawk, lingering around the edges of the

Halls of Law as a literal mascot because she'd been too young to legally take the oaths required to serve the Emperor's laws.

Severn never discussed his work with the Wolves.

She knew it wasn't over; he could disappear for days at a time at the behest of the Halls of Law—which, in Severn's case, meant the Wolflord.

He had the weapon chain. It had come from the West March. But the only time Kaylin had visited the March, Severn already *had* the weapon. A Barrani weapon. He'd always spoken perfect—and complex—High Barrani. He seemed to understand the political undercurrents in the High Court far better than his job as a Hawk demanded.

But she'd never really put the two things together properly. His weapon. His social skills. His knowledge of the High Court.

I mean, he *had* to get that weapon from somewhere, right?

"The green," the Avatar said.

And he didn't go to the green as an orphaned mortal. He must have had backers. Was one of them An'Tellarus? Was that backer calling in a favor? What if the favor was detrimental to the Consort? Severn was a *Hawk*.

But the rules of exemption made Kaylin almost queasy. He couldn't provide aid to anyone on the High Court *legally*. There was only one way to make politics legal: the Emperor's command. The Emperor's Wolves.

Kaylin didn't trust the Wolves. To be fair, she didn't really trust the Swords, either—but the Swords, she understood. The office politics around the different divisions could be petty; they wouldn't even be noticed as politics by Barrani. But the Wolves were different. They didn't swear to uphold the Imperial Laws; they swore to serve the Emperor.

Severn was a Hawk, now. But the Wolves had never truly let go of him. If, to be a Wolf, he'd sworn a direct vow to serve the Emperor, did a simple change in divisions render that vow irrelevant? Given draconic nature, she doubted it.

The Avatar passed through a long hall; it was sparsely but finely decorated. Not for An'Tellarus the obvious trappings of wealth or power.

"The truly powerful, as An'Teela, do not need to accouter themselves in any way that does not suit their own inclinations," the Avatar said. "It is an indication that An'Tellarus is a power. She indulges her own sense of aesthetics; they are hard to disentangle from her interests. You will note—"

Kaylin had. She'd stopped in front of a statue of a clearly mortal man. He was taller than her, but she imagined he would have been taller in real life as well. There was something about his graven expression that implied life, although the face was sculpted stone.

Opposite this statue, a statue of a similar size—and craftsmanship—stood, but this one was only surprising given its placement: a Barrani woman, carrying a staff of possible office. Her hair, stone, seemed to move.

Kaylin thought about Nightshade's statuary and felt queasy. "These aren't real people, are they?" she asked the Avatar.

"If you mean, are they enchanted to stand as statues at An'Tellarus's pleasure, no. The people they are modeled after are dead."

"I am far less certain of that," a new voice said, as the closed doors just beyond the statues shimmered into invisibility. "But they are no longer as they appear here.

"What is your opinion, young Severn?" To Kaylin's surprise, An'Tellarus's eyes dipped into a beautiful emerald color as they turned to, and met, Severn's gaze. The color didn't dim when he failed to answer. "Come, all of you. An'Teela, we seldom cross paths; if you wish to return to your own abode, I will take no offense."

Kaylin had heard warnings like this one: *when you have a minute*, which meant *do it right damn now.* She'd had difficulty understanding that the former was good manners, when the latter was what was actually meant. Or maybe An'Tellarus was being genuine. Maybe her mention of possible offense was to emphasize the more casual nature of the invitation.

Yeah, right. Casual. Asking the Avatar to serve as both guard and guide implied that it was far more important than her tone made it sound. Some days, people gave Kaylin a headache. Trying to figure out what their words actually meant made her long for the use of True Words.

Teela offered the lord an elegant, graceful nod. "I have seldom seen the interior of your rooms, and they are always of interest. It is gracious of you to include me in your invitation of hospitality." As Kaylin had known Teela for all of her adult life, Teela was easier to interpret. She had zero intention of allowing Kaylin to enter the lion's den without her.

"I'm delighted, truly," An'Tellarus replied. She probably meant it; her eyes remained green. "Please, enter as my honored guests. Yvonne!"

Severn stiffened.

"Young Severn has come to visit—please do prepare tea. Oh, wait, perhaps something slightly stronger. Choose as the guests request. I myself require something stronger." She then nodded to the Avatar; it was a dismissal.

The Avatar offered her a bow that implied deep respect; it wasn't as low as the bow he had offered the Consort, and he didn't hold it for as long, but it was there. Probably because he understood that An'Tellarus could demand it.

"Yes," the Avatar whispered as he rose. "While it is possible not to offer what is expected, there are subtle costs; she is famously prickly."

He must have learned that word from Terrano.

"That," the Avatar replied, "and many others. The evolution of mortal language is fascinating. Do not keep An'Tellarus waiting," he added, his tone more somber. "Terrano asks that I ask you to try not to annoy her."

An'Tellarus led the way to an almost modestly sized sitting room. It wasn't opulent in an obvious way. Kaylin struggled to remember etiquette and mostly failed. She regretted the resentment of her much younger self. *You can't eat it. It won't keep you warm in the winter. You can't wield it.* All the words echoed, because they were hers. They'd been true, then. In some ways, they were true now.

Are you trying to assess her intent? Severn asked.

I am. She's old. She's powerful. She's . . . prickly.

Prickly?

You didn't hear the Avatar?

No. Perhaps he did not intend to be heard.

He's spending way *too much time with Terrano. But . . . yes. It's a small room. I haven't been to the High Halls much, and the Consort meets us outside, where finery is hard to assess. Plus, she's the Consort. An'Tellarus might somehow be involved with everything that's happening, and she's powerful enough the Avatar treats her with respect.*

You're worried that she's behind the Consort's condition?

Aren't you?

No.

Teela is.

Of course she is. An'Tellarus would not attempt to harm the Consort. But An'Tellarus may be no friend to Sedarias. She is powerful. She is—as the Avatar said—prickly. But she is also often unpredictable. Ah, he added as An'Tellarus indicated her guests should sit, *please take no offense at anything she might say to me.*

To you?

He offered An'Tellarus a perfect bow, as graceful in execution as any Barrani's would have been.

"I have always said you have such pretty manners, child. But

I see you are no longer a child. Why have you come to visit your aunt so seldom?"

Silence descended. An'Tellarus's words were a large ship's anchor tossed into the ocean of social visitation; the boat was almost pulled under.

Teela recovered first. "Aunt?" Kaylin didn't need to remember etiquette lessons to know this wasn't the right way to break an awkward silence. Not among the Barrani.

"Has he not mentioned me?" An'Tellarus replied, smiling. A hint of blue appeared in her eyes. She moved toward Severn and linked her arm around his.

He met her gaze and exhaled. "You know very well this is not a casual subject."

"Better, perhaps, than you. But surely she has seen the weapon you wield?" Her gaze fell to Severn's waist.

"She's seen it wielded, yes."

"And she asked no questions?"

"There are no questions to ask," Teela replied. "The weapon chooses. It has chosen Corporal Handred. The test, the manner of its passing, is oft private."

"Indeed, indeed. Yvonne?"

A Barrani woman entered the room. She was modestly dressed in comparison to Kaylin. But her expression brightened considerably the minute she laid eyes on Severn; she rushed to the table to set down her tray.

An'Tellarus grimaced openly, her exhalation matching Severn's in tone. "*What* have I told you about guests?" she demanded, releasing Severn's arm.

Yvonne's eyes darkened to blue—but it was a lighter color than Teela's had been since they'd turned down the hall that led to the Tellarus rooms.

"I see you are being somewhat politically vexing," An'Tellarus said, once again turning her attention to Severn. "Your clothing is not what is usually worn within these Halls. You have never been a fool, and I must assume that your choice is deliberate and necessary.

"Won't you introduce me to your friends?"

"They are my colleagues," Severn replied. "An'Teela does not require an introduction."

"No. It is still considered polite. And before you point out that I have not bothered to introduce myself, I remind you that you have come to *my* territory."

"We are all officers of the Halls of Law. An'Teela, you know. Lord Kaylin is my partner in the office."

"In the office, hmmm?" An'Tellarus turned her gaze toward Kaylin, who would have been just as happy with no introduction. And food. "Lord Kaylin, is it?"

"Yes. If it helps, he's Lord Severn when he wants to be. We both entered—and passed—the Tower's test before the High Halls fully awoke."

"You would not be granted that title, now."

Kaylin said nothing because it was irrelevant. If she could retake that test and have the title stripped from her, she'd've done it in a hot minute.

"May I ask where you acquired the mark on your cheek?"

Kaylin stopped herself from offering a fief shrug as an answer. "I am not at liberty to discuss its origins." The words were stiff High Barrani.

"Oh, very well. I can see we started off on the wrong foot, as it were. It is very hard to dance competently when one's first step is suspect. Yvonne, please stop hovering. You can sit with Severn. Learn from his decorum where possible."

Severn offered Yvonne a surprisingly sympathetic grimace. He sat only when Yvonne did. He clearly knew the young woman.

"Why did you wish to see us?" Teela asked.

"Strictly speaking, it was not you I wished to meet with, An'Teela. It was Severn and his companion. But I am aware that you visited the High Halls to attend the Consort. There is a faint miasma in the air—of politics and folly; they are not always the same. Severn." Her expression lost its faint, smug smile and became something far more serious. "I have been asked to deliver a message, should you come this way.

"Frankly, it was difficult not to be offended, but given the source, I agreed. And now, I am almost chagrined. I did not expect to see you at all; I have been informed that you are no longer considered a part of Elluvian's team."

He nodded. "I no longer work directly under Elluvian, for the most part." He wasn't comfortable here, but the level of discomfort was so minor it might have been familial. And this woman had called herself his aunt.

An'Tellarus gestured, and a scroll appeared in midair, floating gently in front of Severn's face. "Elluvian is cautious, when he can be bothered. There is a reason, however, that the message was left with me and not Elluvian." Her expression was now grave.

Severn lifted a hand; the scroll case fell, almost heavily, across his palm.

"I am not apprised of the contents. The case was not of a mind to allow me to tamper with it and evade injury."

Meaning she'd tried.

Kaylin frowned and looked to Yvonne. Yvonne was sitting beside Severn, but she had been constantly glancing at Kaylin, to look away in a hurry when their eyes met. She was nervous—possibly because of Teela. An'Tellarus's interaction implied strongly—to Kaylin—that Yvonne wasn't in danger from that quarter. There was something about Yvonne that made her seem young to Kaylin.

Something about her that made her seem safe to be around—something that couldn't be said for most Barrani. The Consort had said that there were three recent tests; she had mentioned a name. Yvonne.

Kaylin was certain that this Yvonne was the one who had passed the Lake's first test.

10

Severn was utterly silent in response to her certainty.

Given the color of Teela's eyes, Teela shared Kaylin's belief. This Yvonne was probably the threat to the Consort's position.

"You come from the West March?" Teela asked in oddly accented High Barrani.

Yvonne's eyes grew greener, although blue was still the predominant color. "I do. I'm sorry—I've been trying to learn the names of the many Lords of the High Court, and some of their history. I knew of you—you wield *Kariannos.* You're the first of your line." She spoke with genuine respect, even awe.

"My maternal family was of the West March," Teela told Yvonne. "The High Halls is a very different place."

Yvonne nodded.

"In my youth, I preferred the West March," Teela continued, smiling. There was an ocean of pain beneath the surface of that smile. "But if one is to gain power among our kin, it is here."

". . . if one wants power," Yvonne murmured.

Teela exhaled. "You were at home in the West March."

"I was. But my only remaining friend is here, in the High Halls. He's adopted me, and An'Tellarus is teaching me."

"Or trying," was the dry addition. "Yvonne is young. The

customs of the West March are, in the absence of war, more pastoral. But this is not the first time she has been strongly affected by Barrani politics. She has not yet learned how to express wariness in a suitable way. Clearly," she added, criticism in that tone.

"Perhaps she trusts her instincts, An'Tellarus. I am in the company of two mortals, after all." Teela's tone was neutral.

"And were she mortal, that would be fine; she is not. Why are you so interested in her? I perceive it is not interest in either me or the plans I might have." There was a touch of warning in An'Tellarus's question.

"Why are you so interested in her?" Teela countered.

"I have been asked—as a favor, from one lord to another—to see to etiquette lessons and to familiarize Yvonne with the structures that underlie the High Court. I considered the request with care and decided that a different tutor would not suit the purpose. We all learn from our various mistakes—but only if we survive them. Our youths were not always kind to the ignorant."

Yvonne flinched at the word and lowered her head; Kaylin found both of her hands curling into fists.

She means no harm, Severn said, interior voice both urgent and quick.

Do you trust An'Tellarus?

Silence. *It is never wise to trust powerful Barrani. But inasmuch as I can, I do. At least where Yvonne is concerned. If I were Sedarias, I might have a different answer. I trust that she won't harm Yvonne.*

Or use her?

Not in a way that Yvonne won't accept.

Kaylin *really* wanted to know how Severn knew this Barrani Lord and her student.

"My cousin is An'Sennarin. He's from the West March, originally."

An'Tellarus shot her a sharp look. "That, however, is not

something others in the High Court need to know. What do I always say?"

"Don't make enemies without cause?"

"Yes, that. To speak of the West March, and a significant line of the High Court, in such a fashion could be considered a subtle insult."

"But *I'm* from the West March—and Ollarin would never consider that an insult!" Yvonne's eyes had shaded to a darker blue—the blue of anger, given her expression. "If he weren't here, I'd go back tomorrow. I'd leave *today*."

"And now you are offering insult to Tellarus, child," An'Tellarus replied. "I have opened my home to you, and I have done what I could to teach you what you must know to survive. I have escorted you through your journeys in the High Halls; I have remained by your side in any place it is permitted me."

Kaylin frowned. "What would not be permitted a lord of your stature?" She spoke in High Barrani.

"Do you not know? You visited the Lady today. Do you think, should Yvonne be likewise invited, that I might accompany her?"

"Yvonne, have you met the Consort?"

Yvonne fell silent. Kaylin thought she wouldn't answer. "No. No, but . . ."

An'Tellarus frowned; there was an edge to the expression that clearly demanded Kaylin back off.

"I'm sorry," Kaylin told Yvonne. "I'm sorry, but it's important. Things have been happening at court—"

"Do you believe I cannot protect Yvonne?" An'Tellarus's voice was as cold as Teela's expression. But Kaylin, dressed as a lord, was a Hawk.

Next time, she snapped at Severn, *you can wear the damn dress.*

May I remind you that this was the Consort's decision?

No. Kaylin turned her attention to An'Tellarus. If she wanted to speak with Yvonne, it was An'Tellarus she had to convince.

"Have you, in your long and illustrious life, met Lord Calarnenne?"

An'Tellarus's eyes remained blue, but Kaylin thought her emotions had shifted; she no longer felt insulted. Her eyes narrowed as if seeing Kaylin for the first time.

"Indeed, I have. I knew him when he was heir to his line—a line that is all but dead. Those families that served his family fought for supremacy, and those that survive now serve Seshallan. It was a messy affair but long settled." She glanced, now, at Teela. "Recent rumors, however, imply the return of a prodigal son. Annarion, I believe. It is his stated intent to revive his line: Solanace. The claim is, of course, valid; it might not have been considered valid were it not for the existence of the new High Lord."

Teela coughed.

"You have spent a paltry decade—given the loud sniffs of disapproval spoken in your absence—among mortals. Do you fault my observation, An'Teela?"

Teela was silent.

But Yvonne rose.

"Yvonne," An'Tellarus said, a note of warning in the single word.

Yvonne didn't hear her. Or possibly couldn't. She approached Kaylin—and *knelt.*

Severn—what is she doing?

I don't know.

Can you make her stop*?*

An'Tellarus will. Or not. But what she allows in the privacy of her personal chambers, I can't argue against.

You like her.

I do. But she has a temper, and she's unpredictable. I personally think we should introduce her to Terrano and Mandoran; I think she'd adore them.

And if she didn't?

They'd probably survive.

Yvonne reached out for Kaylin's hands but stopped short of touching her.

Kaylin wore long sleeves as a matter of course; they hid the Marks of the Chosen. She wore sleeves at work in the blistering heat, and even Teela's court dress was conservative enough to cover arms and her back. But she knew, the moment Yvonne reached out, what Yvonne had seen.

The Marks of the Chosen.

The True Words that had taken up residence over at least half of Kaylin's body since she was twelve.

All suspicions of and about Yvonne were confirmed in that instant. Yvonne could see the Marks of the Chosen, even concealed as they were. Yvonne, if given the opportunity, would see the Lake in the same fashion. She would see the True Names.

It was Yvonne who had become, by existing, a threat to the Consort.

Kaylin held out a hand. Yvonne frowned, but her expression cleared; she held out hers with less certainty. Of course she did. The Barrani didn't shake hands often, that Kaylin could recall.

They do not. Often, if their palms meet, it is at the end of the blood oath ceremony. Severn was watching Yvonne with mild concern, but no fear of or for her.

Kaylin shook hands with Yvonne, but didn't release the young woman or step back. "You can see them."

An'Tellarus turned instantly. "See what?" Now she was worried.

Yvonne, however, nodded. "I don't understand why you're . . . wearing them? But they're a bit loud right now."

Kaylin couldn't hear them. But she could see them; they were glowing, their hearts the usual gold, but their edges a different color. Not blue, not white, colors the Marks had taken before, but something almost violet. "They're often called the Marks of the Chosen."

An'Tellarus's brows rose. The look she gave Severn was very unlike most angry Barrani expressions; on another face, she would have looked actively annoyed.

It's not a big secret, is it?

It is not a secret to your friends, no. It is *known. But Teela has taken some pains to make certain it is not widely known. She is aided in this by men like Lord Evarrim, for whom the very thought of a* mortal *Chosen is almost anathema. You're considered to be aligned with the Dragons, given your duties as a Hawk; no concerted effort has been made to end your life because you are of value to the Consort.*

Did An'Tellarus somehow expect you to tell her about this?

Severn didn't answer—he clearly didn't feel the need, the answer was so obvious.

"I've heard only a little bit about the Marks," Yvonne confessed. "But even I've heard stories about familiars." Her attention fell on Hope. Hope, to Kaylin's surprise, rose to stand on his two legs, elongating his neck with obvious pride. "Is he your familiar?"

"Stories greatly exaggerate, but that's what the Barrani call him."

Hope smacked her face with a wing, but didn't leave it across her eyes.

Yvonne laughed. "I think he's adorable!"

So, apparently, did Hope. He leaned forward. Kaylin nudged him, and he leaped off her shoulder to hover at the height of Yvonne's green gaze.

"Can I touch him?"

"That's up to him," Kaylin replied, genuinely curious. Hope didn't care for most of the people he met; he tolerated those that Kaylin liked.

"I feel that that is unwise," An'Tellarus said as Hope hovered. Hope squawked. The Barrani Lord's brows rose, her eyes shifting into the gold that was Barrani surprise before she laughed out loud.

"Where *did* you find him?" she asked Kaylin.

"It's a long story. Mostly, in an egg."

"If it were that simple, the majority of the Lords of the High Court would be involved in a dire egg hunt."

"Would you join them?" Kaylin asked in impeccable High Barrani, because at least the surface of the question shouldn't sound as impertinent as the content.

"I do not think I, or the familiar, would survive; the small creature is far, far too disrespectful, and I believe I suffer enough of that in the rest of my life."

Squawk.

"Indeed. I would have to be chosen—not as you are Chosen, of course. Familiars choose and accept their masters, or at least, that was our understanding in times long past."

"I didn't *choose* to bear these Marks," Kaylin snapped. "And I didn't choose the familiar, either."

"Perhaps that is the secret to becoming someone who *can* be chosen." The voice was soft, almost introspective. "The weapon Severn bears chose him."

Severn shook his head. "It chose to test, An'Tellarus. I passed. They are not the same, although perhaps to those without knowledge they appear to be."

"I am not threatening the girl." An'Tellarus's brows rose in brief annoyance. "Do I look as if I am dissatisfied with life? I explain, that is all. I could not pass the test of the Lake. I would never have been granted the Marks of the Chosen. I was not chosen as wielder of one of The Three—and I did try, but not more than once.

"I learned to accept my place."

"Your place," Teela said, eyes very blue, "appears to be almost the apex of power for one who is not High Lord."

"Yes. What I have, I built. *I* built it. I accept that I will never be chosen—and that, Chosen, is the actual answer to your question. I have never been found worthy enough; I would not expect that to change. And now, I feel no need to lower myself to pursue it. I am Tellarus. Those who have been chosen—and loved—in the past are memories and dust. I remain."

Severn's gaze was welded to An'Tellarus.

"And perhaps I better understand why children like you—or An'Teela, or Severn—have somehow stumbled into the privilege you own. I understand why Yvonne is considered special. Look at your familiar. He sees in her something that the Lake might see."

"In my experience," Teela said, "we are never too old to feel the echoes and shadows of envy and longing."

"That is true, in a fashion. But we are surely too old to build our lives around those childish yearnings? But perhaps not. You were chosen by *Kariannos*. Perhaps satiating that desire was enough to quench it."

"Or perhaps it was enough to drive home the knowledge that to be special is not always easy—or survivable."

"I respectfully agree with An'Teela," Kaylin said.

"When you have what others would desperately want, perhaps you have much in common." The reply was dry; there was an edge in An'Tellarus's tone. But Kaylin had a suspicion that there was always an edge in that woman's voice. Had she not seemed genuinely fond of Yvonne, and genuinely protective, Kaylin would have politely and respectfully stayed the hells away.

If she could get away. She hadn't walked into this Barrani Lord's apartment of her own volition. But Yvonne was here.

And Kaylin was certain Yvonne was the one who had at least passed whatever preliminary tests the Lake could give. Hope squawked—a happy, quiet sound, very unlike the sounds he made at Kaylin—in a crooning welcome as he continued to hover inches from Yvonne's face. He didn't even bite her fingers or snap at her when she hesitantly offered her left arm.

It shouldn't have been a surprise when Hope landed on that arm. It was, but it shouldn't have been.

"Can you understand him?" Yvonne asked, although she didn't take her eyes off Hope.

"Sometimes."

"Only sometimes?"

"Can you understand what he's saying now?"

Yvonne shook her head. "But An'Teela and An'Tellarus did." She looked embarrassed and pained. "I'm not knowledgeable enough."

Hope squawked.

"I think he's trying to tell you that it's not about knowledge, and if it makes you feel any better, the Dragons understand him when he chooses to speak at them."

"To them?"

"At them. Definitely at. Mostly, he sounds like an angry bird to me."

He definitely swiveled his delicate head and glared. And squawked, proving Kaylin's point.

"Perhaps you were chosen because you have no innate sense of reverence or respect," An'Tellarus observed, shaking her head slightly. "I would ask that you not infect poor Yvonne with your attitude—she is struggling to find her moorings in the court as it is. But perhaps the two of you could speak about your familiar and your Marks; I believe An'Teela and I have things to discuss. Severn, you may attend us."

"She's always like that," Yvonne said, when Kaylin's companions left the room in An'Tellarus's wake. "But beneath that hard surface, she can be genuinely caring."

Kaylin was pretty certain she would never be the recipient of that care. "Where did you meet her?"

"She came to the West March when I was living there." The color of Yvonne's eyes shifted as she spoke. "She helped my friend—I mean, An'Sennarin. I didn't have family that survived in the West March, so Ollarin offered me a place to stay here."

"And you don't regret it?"

Yvonne chuckled, a rueful sound. "Only when I'm failing to learn whatever it is I'm being taught. Which happens a lot. But An'Tellarus is better with me than she is with An'Sennarin. He *really* gets the sharp edge of her criticism."

"Has he been An'Sennarin for long?"

Yvonne shook her head. "Not too long, no. He grew up in the West March as well. We were close when we were young—he had no intention of ever coming east to the High Halls." Yvonne lowered her head, and Hope crooned at her. She lifted her head instantly in surprise, staring at the familiar. "Are you sure?"

Squawk.

Hope and Kaylin were going to have a *serious* talk when they got home.

"Ollarin was gentle. He worked in the West March, not as a guard, but as an artist and a gardener. He never wanted to come east. The High Halls aren't the right place for people who have little obvious power in the West March. People like me."

"But you're here."

"Hope says it's safe for me to tell you this." She glanced at the familiar still standing on her arm, and Hope nodded. "An'Tellarus would be very, very angry."

Squawk.

"She really isn't as terrifying as she looks."

Squawk.

"Yes, I know. Even if she thought of me as a possible enemy, she'd never expect I would be a credible threat. And she's right."

Squawk.

"Please, *please* don't tell her I said that!"

"Hope."

Squawk.

"If it were my choice, we would never have come here at all." Kaylin frowned at Hope.

"Why did you come?"

"I was summoned." Barrani politics gave Kaylin a headache, and no matter what she was called in this place, she *wasn't* Barrani. "I was summoned by the Lady. I could not say no."

"Of course not!"

"Before I could make my escape, I was *invited* to attend An'Tellarus. By the High Halls."

Yvonne looked genuinely sympathetic. "You really haven't been having a great day, have you?" To Kaylin's surprise, she spoke Elantran.

"It pretty much sucked. I'm hoping it gets a bit better before it ends." She exhaled. "Have you spoken with the Consort?"

Yvonne shook her head emphatically. Her eyes were blue, now.

"Let me guess. An'Tellarus told you you should avoid any contact if avoidance wouldn't cause offense."

Yvonne nodded.

"She's wrong. She might be right about every other Barrani in these cursed Halls, but she's wrong about the Consort."

"She's the *Consort*."

"Yes—but she's the Lady, as well, and that's more important. She doesn't care about politics—I mean, compared to An'Teela or An'Tellarus—as much as she cares about her duties to the Lake and the Barrani people. Hers were practically the first green eyes I saw among the Barrani I've met. Teela's eyes are generally shades of blue. I can't recall the last time I saw green in them—maybe in the West March."

"You've been to the West March."

"Don't get me started—Teela hates it when I complain and whine. And she can hear through *walls*, I swear."

Yvonne shook her head. "I can talk about myself," she said after a long pause. "But I shouldn't talk about An'Tellarus or An'Sennarin. If you end up being a danger to me, I've made a mistake, and I'll pay. But they wouldn't make the same mistake and shouldn't have to suffer. I wish I could just go home," she added, her voice dropping to a whisper.

"An'Sennarin doesn't want you to go home?"

"He wouldn't have been practically enslaved if it weren't for me. If I'd died, he'd've been free. My parents did die trying to protect me. They weren't the only ones. But the An'Sennarin of the time had some claim to our service, as branch families of his great tree." This was said with a bitter twist of the lips.

"This is Ollarin's way of making certain that I can't be used like that again. An'Tellarus supports him—at least so far. That's why she's trying to teach me how to be a real Barrani. But . . . I *am* a real Barrani. This isn't my place. My mother told me—always—that it was important to know and accept my place. And *I did.* I did it enough to know that my place isn't here."

"Would he let you go back to the West March if you asked?"

Yvonne swallowed. ". . . I think so."

"But you haven't asked."

"So much happened because of me. So much. I think sometimes he looks at me and he sees an echo of my parents, of the people who died at the hands of the previous An'Sennarin. He made friends here, outside the High Court. But they were killed—and many, many of their people brutally murdered afterward.

"I think he thinks his birth was the cause of all the deaths. His birth, his gift. And I try to remind him that it wasn't him. He didn't kill my family. He didn't kill his friends. Sometimes, when we're together, I can see a hint of who he used to be. It's still in there.

"Sometimes I think that's so important, I'm happy I'm here. And sometimes I think An'Tellarus might be right: it's that part of Ollarin that needs to wither and die. Because if he's still that person, the High Halls will destroy him."

"I assure you," a familiar voice said, "that is untrue. I will not destroy Ollarin." In the wake of his words, the Avatar appeared, standing a respectful distance from where Yvonne and Kaylin were sitting.

Yvonne would have fallen over backward if she hadn't been Hope's perch.

"I didn't—I didn't mean you!"

"He knows that," a second, far more familiar voice said. "He's teasing you."

Yvonne stood.

"I'm really sorry," Kaylin told her, voice soft. "But the second voice is a friend of mine. Terrano—show yourself, please."

"No way. These are An'Tellarus's halls. If I take a step into them, they won't be able to *find* all my body parts."

"It's okay," Yvonne told Kaylin. "I mean, even if he introduced himself properly, I wouldn't recognize his family line."

"Why are you here?"

"I was bored?"

"I mean it, Terrano."

"Fine. Abel thought I might be helpful."

"You? Here? In An'Tellarus's domain—the home of a woman that even Teela is treating with genuine respect? Did you piss him off?"

Yvonne's stiffness faded as she listened to the Terrano she couldn't see and the Kaylin she could. "Ummm, why are you calling the Avatar Abel?"

"It was shorter than the name he actually preferred—which was way way way too much of a mouthful."

Yvonne was shocked. ". . . and he's okay with that?"

"Well, he hasn't expelled me or locked me out. Or in. I think he's fine."

"It is interesting, I confess," the Avatar said. "And perhaps my long inward focus has given me the opportunity to reassess my protectorate. I find Terrano fascinating in small doses."

"In larger doses?"

"He causes confusion and chaos. And I apologize for the

interruption, but except in cases where ambitious fools attempt to harm or control the Lake, I do not destroy my inhabitants." He smiled at Yvonne. "What are you carrying?"

"Lord Kaylin's familiar. With her permission!"

"With his permission," the Avatar said, but his smile deepened. "I believe your discussion was relevant to our issues or we would not have felt it germane to intervene."

"How so?" Kaylin asked.

"I believe you were attempting to tell Yvonne that she should, if possible, speak to the Consort directly. An'Tellarus might allow it."

She won't, Severn said; he'd been listening, his presence so calm and quiet she'd been unaware of it at all.

A thinner voice said, *I would advise against it.* Ynpharion.

Kaylin shook her head, which probably looked strange. *I think it's important for the Consort—because I think Yvonne is the chess piece on the board that could be used to truly threaten the Lady. And Yvonne herself isn't threatening. It's probably why the Lake would be willing to grant her entry.*

I'd advise against it, Severn continued, as if no other voice—even Kaylin's—had interrupted him.

Something in his tone was off, wrong somehow.

She wouldn't be a danger to the Consort.

Probably not. Not intentionally. What An'Tellarus hasn't told you is that the heart of the green's test—of me, for the weapon—was Yvonne herself. If Yvonne is somehow involved, it means Ollarin didn't or hasn't rooted out the parts of his extended family that were firmly under his predecessor's control.

What does that mean?

Yvonne was removed from her home at the behest of Ollarin's predecessor—as was Ollarin himself. They used or invoked Shadow in some fashion—and Yvonne would have been trapped and consumed by it had she not been saved by the green.

11

We need to talk. Kaylin began to pace. Had Teela been here, there would have been words; had An'Tellarus been with her, glares. Teela had never liked it when Kaylin paced restlessly either in circles or straight lines; it reminded the Barrani Hawk of a caged beast, trapped in an enclosure too small and too constraining.

"You need to speak," the Avatar agreed. "But I counsel against panic. You yourself have encountered an odd form of Shadow in the very recent past; it does not taint you in a fashion either I or Helen can perceive. Were I your friend or associate, I would suggest you pay a visit—in person—to Lord Bellusdeo. Her Tower was built to war against Shadow, and the Tower's attention to detail is far, far more granular."

"Can I take Yvonne with me?" Kaylin countered.

"I am not Yvonne, and I cannot speak for her. She will not speak of her history; if she remembers it clearly at all, it is as nightmare, and those nightmares stopped plaguing her months after she arrived. Lord Severn's caution is not without merit."

"But you think it's not necessary?"

"I am uncertain, Lord Kaylin. But it is true that the Barrani do not understand the nature of the many tests that lead, in the end, to the duty and responsibility of the Lady."

"I didn't get tested."

"Is that what you believe?"

Kaylin grimaced. "If I did, it was so subtle I missed it, what with everything else going on. Giant Shadow in the basement, trapped souls, that kind of thing."

"I wish to remind you that the Giant Shadow in the basement, as you call them, is now a *guest* in these Halls. Terrano has spent much time with them."

Kaylin had an idea where this was heading, and she didn't like it.

The Avatar's smile was reminiscent of Teela's—when she was involved in training in the Halls of Law. "Indeed. I would like you to return to the Tower of testing before you depart for the day."

Kaylin exhaled. She *could* say no, but didn't see the point. If she said no, the Avatar would speak to Teela. Teela would encourage her to say yes. Maybe.

I doubt that, Severn replied. *I'll go with you if you go.*

I think you'll need permission. Or an invitation.

If I get neither, I'll ask Terrano to escort me.

"Does this invitation involve my partner?"

"Yes. I do not wish to antagonize An'Tellarus, so I will not extend the invitation to Yvonne at this time. But I will, before she meets in person with the Lady."

"Do I have to be there when the two of them meet?"

Yes, Ynpharion snapped.

"I believe it would add a level of comfort for both of the other participants." The Avatar's voice was gentle.

Kaylin wanted to know why it was supposed to be her job to make two other people comfortable when it was so uncomfortable for Kaylin herself. But she was whining and knew it. She actually liked Yvonne, from what little she'd seen, and of the Barrani, with the exception of some of the cohort, the Consort was her favorite.

But the Avatar was right, and she knew it. Maybe *because* she was mortal and born to be, always, an outsider, no matter what titles she'd been granted. Maybe it was because nothing she could gain by being political in the High Halls would ever change the inferiority her birth as a mortal imposed on her. She had nothing—but her life—to lose.

"It is not just that," the High Halls said. "But it is fact: you are not as they are, and you will never be what they are. But you have more power than most of the Barrani who dwell here, and you are afforded far more respect because the consequences of that respect are far less costly if it is misplaced. I believe An'Teela and An'Tellarus are finished for the moment."

"And Severn?"

"You may ask him that yourself."

Severn didn't pass on the contents of what Kaylin thought of as negotiations. Not yet. She wouldn't ask him here, either. Maybe when they left. Maybe not ever. She was almost certain that his own past was now entangled in this, and she'd always been careful not to make demands of that past because she didn't want to have to discuss her own.

They'd been separated for years—for a third of her life—in part because of his choices, and in part because of her own. Those choices, made in ignorance, were bounded by actual events; it was just the interpretations that had been wrong. But two children were dead, and that didn't and couldn't be changed.

He didn't talk about them. Kaylin didn't, either. But the memory was their wall, their personal hells. How much of Severn's memories were like that? How much of his past had now sprung from seeds Kaylin might never have seen?

She *wanted* to know.

And she didn't. Maybe ignorance was her best protection. She *hated* that. She had yearned, since she'd chosen to live as a Hawk, to see *clearly*. To face facts—as if facts were immutable.

"Severn will join you when he can—but I suggest you accompany Terrano and me now, if you wish to avoid further argument."

"Teela will want to come as well. Is there a problem with that?"

"Terrano does not feel she will add to any possible conversation that arises from the meeting."

"You want me there because of what happened with Terrano."

"Because of what you carried away from that encounter, yes."

Kaylin grimaced. "You better come up with a good excuse for Teela; she'll have my head if you don't."

The Avatar smiled. "Terrano does not believe that to be the case."

"I'm sorry," Kaylin said to Yvonne, whose eyes shifted from wider than normal to narrower as she absorbed parts of the conversation. Her face was expressive; time among the Barrani hadn't yet destroyed that. Kaylin thought it wouldn't. The Consort had spent far longer among her kin, and she, like Yvonne, could be open.

"For what?"

"I have to leave—quickly—and you'll be stuck with An'Tellarus; I'm guessing she won't be happy."

"I'm not sure she's ever happy," Yvonne said, her tone removing the sting from the criticism her words carried. "But maybe that's the price for living as long—and as well—as she has. People would cry for joy were she to die, but they don't have the power or the cunning to cause that death.

"I know she seems harsh to you," she added. "But she's been as kind as she can be to us. We wouldn't have survived as long as we have without her intervention." Yvonne hesitated, and then said, "If Ollarin could, he'd abdicate and return with me to the West March. But he can't—they'd just hunt him down after the formalities were over. He knows. Unless he keeps the seat, and displays his power prominently enough, neither of us survives, either."

"Have you spoken to anyone from Mellarionne?"

Her eyes instantly darkened.

"I mean, in the past month?"

"No."

"I think you should try. Or maybe An'Tellarus should. An'Mellarionne—the new one—is a friend."

"Of yours?"

"Of mine. She lives in my house."

Yvonne's jaw fell, and it took her a few seconds to shut her mouth again. "She lives with you? She doesn't live in the High Halls?"

". . . I guess that's not widely known."

"It's more or less known," Terrano—still unseen—said. "But by the ambitious and the political."

"But—it's *your* house, not hers?"

Ugh. "It's complicated. You know that the High Halls is sentient? It was always sentient, but recently it's produced an Avatar—this guy—and it's more active within its boundaries than it once was."

Yvonne nodded, a small grin lifting the corners of her lips. "A lot of the older lords *hate* it." Which was why she found it amusing.

"My house is like the High Halls, but a lot smaller. It's why An'Mellarionne chose to stay with me, rather than taking up residence in the quarters Mellarionne owns here. The High Halls can't interfere politically; Helen doesn't have to care about politics. She just cares about keeping her occupants safe.

"But . . . she's had a lot of unusual occupants in her time—some mortal, some Barrani, and some we have no name for. I think you'd like her, if you were ever allowed to come visit."

"I'd be allowed," Yvonne replied, but hesitantly.

Kaylin exhaled. "You'd be allowed *if* An'Tellarus also visited?"

"Something like that. If it's your house, would that be all right?"

"It's my house—but that bit about the comfort of occupants is true. I'm really not informed about the Barrani politics currently unfolding. Most of my housemates think I'm a fragile mortal who shouldn't be involved."

Yvonne frowned. "But . . . you're Chosen. And the house is *yours.*"

"Yes. But I'm also an officer of the Halls of Law, so I'm out of the house, and its protections, a lot."

"And you have him." She raised her arm to indicate Hope.

Hope made a happy noise that sounded nothing like the squawks he shared with Kaylin, and then he pushed himself off the perch of Yvonne's arm and came to rest, once again, on Kaylin's shoulder, where he flopped into his usual shawl position.

Yvonne laughed, a bright, brief sound.

Hope lifted his head and snorted.

Kaylin watched Hope and Yvonne. Her reaction to the familiar made her seem—for a moment—younger than Kaylin had ever felt.

"If you want to meet Helen, I think she'd really like you," Kaylin told Yvonne.

"I think I'd like that. Right now I almost never leave the High Halls, and I think—if Severn could come to escort me, Ollarin would consider a visit safe." But she hesitated, and then added, "An'Tellarus and Ollarin don't always agree on what's safe."

"You mentioned that if you could visit, she's likely to come with you."

Yvonne nodded, fully aware that An'Tellarus was the concern.

"I probably won't send an official invitation—I think that might attract too much attention."

"If your Barrani friends deliver an invitation, that'll attract attention, too."

"Not the one I'm thinking about. Do you stay in An'Tellarus's quarters?"

"Officially? No. I stay with Ollarin. It might be safer to send a message to Ollarin—but messages are more likely to be intercepted there."

"We'll work it out." She'd been considering Terrano as a go-between, but she didn't trust An'Tellarus enough that she considered that safe. But she *did* trust Teela enough. Teela could deliver a message in person. Teela wasn't above the Mellarionne fray, but she wasn't as vulnerable as any of the rest of the cohort might be.

"I'm ready," Kaylin told Abel.

"Please follow me."

Severn didn't make it in time to join her. *I could*, he told her. *But while the substance of conversation appears to be concluded, the jostling for position has just started. If I leave, An'Tellarus will be mildly offended.*

She didn't strike me as a person who can be mild when offended.

"Lord Severn will join you before you exit the High Halls," the Avatar said. "He is correct; any hasty movement on his part will be interpreted poorly; both An'Teela and An'Tellarus might take offense."

Terrano fell silent. Kaylin poked Hope, and Hope grudgingly sat up, smacking her face—audibly—with his wing, as if her unspoken demand was grossly unreasonable.

But with the wing over her eyes, she could see Terrano clearly. To her surprise, his eyes were a deep, dark blue—much darker than his norm. Maybe the High Halls were just as uncomfortable for Terrano as they were for Kaylin. But he came, regardless.

Terrano wasn't the problem.

Yvonne's existence was a threat to the Consort. But she was certain the two women would actually *like* each other, if they met. The Consort considered her duties of paramount import within the court: she was the custodian of the Lake. She was the mother of her people.

Her tolerance of, her support for, Kaylin was offered in part because Kaylin could *also* perform the duties of Lady. Even had she despised Kaylin, she would have forced herself to tolerate and accept her because the Lake was so important. She wouldn't consider Yvonne a threat if the Lake accepted her.

But the two women didn't exist in isolation.

Someone considered Yvonne a possible genuine candidate—and that allowed them to attack the Consort in a subtle, but terrible, way. An'Tellarus? But An'Tellarus was reputed to be largely neutral. If you didn't step on her toes, she allowed you to continue breathing.

It couldn't be the cohort. It couldn't be Sedarias. But Sedarias's fight wasn't the only fight unfolding in the High Halls; no doubt there were battles being raged that began long before Kaylin's birth and would continue long after her death.

Ugh. Abel was right: she had to approach this investigation the normal way. Maybe being Chosen, being surrounded by the cohort with their easy communication, had rusted the skills she'd worked so hard to develop.

What she wanted from the Consort—what she'd failed to get—was *why* Nightshade. Why Nightshade at this specific time? The Halls of Law didn't keep Records about Barrani-on-Barrani crime; there was no way for Kaylin to look up that information. The Consort said he'd always been a target. But . . . had he been a target worth at least two full war bands?

It wasn't the two war bands that were the problem. It was whatever shielded him—and the Consort—from the power of

Kaylin's Marks. True Words, granted Kaylin without permission or even interest on her part.

The Consort couldn't lift the words from the Lake because Barrani names were True Words. Nightshade had never been and would never be allowed to attempt to touch the Lake—but the namebond's power was based on his True Name. Something had come between that innate power and the people who should possess it.

Add to that Terrano's injury—when Terrano was out of phase—and Kaylin's inability to heal him immediately. She assumed that was because she couldn't reach him. But what if it wasn't? What if the only reason she *could* effectively heal him was that he was out of phase? That whatever it was that was effectively breaking her power didn't quite operate in the same planes that Terrano could?

There was something there, she thought.

But it wasn't quite coalescing. She'd talk to Teela about it later.

Severn was doubtful. *This falls squarely under the laws of exemption; it's a Barrani matter.*

Kaylin shook her head. *It's not if I'm involved.*

That's why *she won't speak about it.*

If the Lake hadn't become political, it would *be entirely Barrani. But I'm tied to the Consort because of the Lake. I'm Lord Kaylin because of the Lake. The High Lord knows what I can do. Much of the High Court doesn't. We need way more information. If Teela doesn't want to talk to me, I'll have to find a different information source.*

Severn was utterly silent.

Kaylin assumed the Avatar of the High Halls was much like Helen: a conduit for communication that might make the person being communicated with feel more comfortable. She assumed that Abel—Terrano was going to be in so much trouble for giving him that name, because it had begun to stick—could do what Helen could do: be in multiple places, in Avatar form, simultaneously.

"I can," Abel said. "Most of the Lords of the High Court prefer not to see me at all; they maintain a polite fiction about my existence."

"Why?"

"Most of the Lords of the High Court will not willingly enter a Hallionne, unless at great need," Abel replied. "The Barrani are generally not comfortable when in the presence of someone who can read their thoughts."

"Helen says some of the Barrani—and Severn—can obfuscate enough of their thoughts that they're harder to read with certainty."

"That is, indeed, true. But such misdirection requires concentration, and it is oft tiring. Barrani Lords dwell within the High Halls; there is status in that that they cannot be seen to surrender. They are uncomfortable. Many prefer the old ways."

"You mean, when a Shadow in the basement was practically devouring their kin."

"They were not devoured; they were contained. Their names have—finally—been returned to the Lake, where they might be chosen to invoke new life in their people. But yes. While the entirety of my focus was turned toward that Shadow, the High Halls themselves were absent my presence, my intent, and even my awareness. There was only one exception. The abode of the Lady and the Lake itself. The Lady does not make any effort to conceal herself from me."

Kaylin nodded. "Can I ask a question?"

"Demonstrably."

"Why is she called both the Lady and the Consort? I know her mother was also guardian of the Lake and Consort, but . . . are they always the same person?"

"You have known her for how long, and you have only

thought to ask that question now?" Abel's tone was almost scandalized.

Kaylin grimaced.

He's right, Severn told her, a delicate vein of amusement in his tone.

Well, Teela calls her the Consort or the Lady almost interchangeably. Ynpharion always refers to her as the Lady or My Lady. I just, I don't know, I assumed that the sister of the High Lord would be the Consort. I mean—I sometimes find it kind of disturbing, but they're Barrani and I'm not.

"Lord Severn, I fear I must leave the education of Lord Kaylin in your hands. But this is an example of the difficulties that arise when one assumes that a sentient being's ability to read thoughts will give them relevant information. Lord Kaylin is not quiet, and she is not subtle. I might tell you much of her thoughts, were they not so clear to you for other reasons.

"But I would not necessarily be apprised of the gaps in her knowledge, large as they are. Such as this one."

Ynpharion was both outraged and in agreement with the Avatar; he was also amused. But his amusement was tinged with apprehension, worry, and a deep and abiding suspicion. Yvonne. The Lady.

Yvonne would never hurt the Lady, Kaylin said with absolute conviction.

She does not have to have that intent; her existence is a threat.

The High Halls won't allow you to harm Yvonne. And your Lady wouldn't allow it, either.

It was true. Had it not been true, Yvonne might be dead. Given Ynpharion, would be dead.

"An'Tellarus is ferocious in both protection—when she chooses to offer it—and retribution, should those protections fail. In that regard, she is very similar to An'Teela. The reason they are both as safe as Barrani Lords can be—there are desultory attempts to unseat them by the rashly ambitious—is because of their history. They are not ambitious in their own right at this point in their lives; they will destroy, utterly, the lines of those who attempt to harm them. Or to harm those they have taken under their protection."

Kaylin could see, beyond the Avatar, a familiar arch, and a familiar set of descending stairs. She frowned. She remembered ascending stairs as well—and words on the wall, glowing faintly. This was the Tower of Test. This was where, until very recently, Barrani went to prove their strength—or literally die trying.

Those who emerged from the test were considered Lords of the High Court. Those who did not emerge weren't considered a great loss to their families.

"That is harsh, Lord Kaylin, and it is not accurate. Some of those who chose to enter this Tower did so entirely of their own accord, with their own ambitions; they felt it better to face death than to exist forever in a state of weakness. And many did face death; some did not. Those who emerged had a far greater understanding of what was at stake; they did not speak of the test."

"And you couldn't intervene to save them."

"These are the High Halls, where ambition's failure oft ends in death. My mandate does not allow intervention in regular Barrani affairs."

Kaylin wondered if there was wiggle room. But the sentient buildings had True Words at their heart, so maybe there wasn't; the meaning of those words wasn't open to interpretation. It's why Helen had had to effectively cut off a limb or two to be free to make her own choices.

Abel smiled. "The Ancients were mysterious beings; traces of their truths can be found in many religions, light or dark. But they were not alive as we are alive; they were not concerned with simple existence. They did not entirely understand hierarchy; they understood goals. Where goals clashed, they understood both war and compromise—but they are not as we are. They are not as you are.

"Those words at our core define our abilities and our duties clearly. But those duties are not the entirety of what we must be in order to fulfill them. There are some imperatives that I cannot counter, and some I might. Helen made her choice because she had managed to isolate the words that prevented her from choosing as she desired."

"And you?"

"I am not as Helen was. I do not struggle as she did. I would not make the choice she made; too much would be lost. Were I to make a similar choice, I could not fully predict how that would affect my guardianship of the Lake. The Towers were created to ward and protect against Shadow. I was created to protect the Barrani race.

"You must now choose, Chosen."

The walls above the stairs were bare; there were no words magically imprinted on them. "Choose what?"

"Ascent or descent?"

"You're the one who said you wanted me to meet your friend!"

The Avatar smiled.

Terrano appeared beside him, visible for the first time since they'd arrived. He was pinching the bridge of his nose. "He's teasing you. His humor is like that. Try not to take it personally."

"Wait, that was supposed to be funny?"

"I think so—sometimes I find it hard to tell until after the fact. But I'm pretty sure."

"It is perhaps a mild attempt at humor," Abel conceded. "But it is also meant to be instructive. Choose: will you ascend or descend?"

"How is this supposed to be instructive?"

Terrano snickered. Kaylin considered smacking the back of his head but decided—barely—against.

"There is a reason much of my power and intent was and had to remain focused on this Tower. It is my most secure location. The Shadow—my guest—was not confined, as most of you are, to a simple state of being, a single plane. In order to make certain the Barrani were safe in the age of war, I had to be everywhere at once, in a very restricted domain.

"You ask why I did not save those who chose to take this test."

She hadn't, at least not out loud.

"Because in the end, they were offered a choice, and they made it. Understand, Chosen, that choice *is* part of my imperative. Should the Barrani choose to be uncharacteristically giving, I would accept that with gratitude and possibly even joy. Were they to become like the Tha'alani, I might then be able to divert some of my attention to creation of art and wonder, not pretty cages and fortresses within the High Halls.

"But that is not the people they are. And I note that Tha'alani were graced with no such guiding sentiences as mine by the Ancients who created all."

"Ascend," Kaylin said, putting action into words. "Going down the stairs is easier, and if the Shadow is anything like you, I'm going to be exhausted at the end of the meeting, not the beginning."

Kaylin knew very, very little about the Shadow guest within the High Halls. When she had come to confront that guest, she'd assumed that the guest would finally be destroyed, and the High Halls could put an end to its terrible history of testing and killing the so-called weak. She wasn't upset about what actually happened.

But she didn't know enough about this Shadow.

She knew enough about Shadows now to know that some had been enslaved; they had interests that didn't align with *conquer the whole world and destroy it.* This particular guest had done so much damage in its time—to both the Barrani and, indirectly, the Dragons.

But he'd been sent to do that damage.

Because of the High Halls, he'd been prevented from doing more.

And now . . . the Avatar of the High Halls and the Shadow were somehow friends? Kaylin had a headache.

"We are not as you are," Abel said, his voice softer. "And we have more in common than I have with the Barrani I must nurture and protect. His understanding of my kin is, in some fashion, far greater than my own."

". . . are you saying your guest understands things beyond fear and manipulation?"

The Avatar nodded. "Far better than I in his history within what used to be our shining city, our beacon of art and philosophy."

"What was he?"

"You will see. But in part I wish to introduce you because of Terrano's injury and the outcome that followed. There is a reason I was forced to expend almost all my power to keep his influence contained. He exists in a fashion similar to—and very different from—Terrano. But he has taken a liking to Terrano, although he disapproves of the political machinations of some of his kin."

They took the stairs with elegance and grace, or as much as Kaylin could force herself to muster. As it was a long climb, she lost both, treading without thought like a determined Hawk. She had heard chimes when she'd walked these steps before and heard them now—but they weren't isolated; they were part of a distant music that grew louder as she approached, as if her steps, as if she herself, were part of the song.

The Marks on her arms began to glow a bright, warm gold. That was normal for the Marks of the Chosen. But when they lifted themselves from her skin, she stumbled before righting herself by reaching for the rail that now adorned the stairs. The metal was the color of the Marks, and it was warm to the touch, almost as if it were skin.

The stairs opened up, the song rippling outward, the notes shifting and changing in tone and increasing in volume. Light could be seen at the height of the stairs, a light so bright it caused Kaylin to squint.

"I should have told you to close your eyes," Terrano muttered. "Sorry."

A gentle laugh, in time somehow with the music, was the Shadow's response. "Welcome, Corporal. Welcome, Chosen. We have much to discuss, you and I."

12

Kaylin had seen the monster in the basement the first time she had visited the High Halls. She'd visited in part to save the life of the Lord of the West March, Lirienne to his friends and family. But she'd done more than that. She'd seen the Shadow, and she'd understood what the price of failing the Test of Name was: death, and permanent separation from the Lake of Life and the new futures promised to names that returned to it.

This Shadow had *nothing* in common with what she'd witnessed that day.

It had taken the form of a man, but as the man turned to meet Kaylin's eyes, the form shifted into that of a woman—almost but not quite Barrani, and taller in height than the Barrani norm. The Shadow's hair was a silver color—not white, but white with hints of gold, as if it were burnished by time and careful polishing. Their skin was golden, their eyes the azure of a clear sky.

But it was their voice that almost robbed Kaylin of the ability to move: it was the essence of a concert, all instruments joined together to convey an endless song, an utterance of harmonious beauty Kaylin had never heard before.

The Shadow was watching her; she had the impression of sunshine and joy, although none of that actually reached the expression. But the Marks on her arm took up the warmest of gold colors, responding to what Kaylin felt. Or perhaps what the Shadow offered.

Had she met this person in any other circumstance, Shadow would be the furthest thought from her mind. History forced her to remember, but it was hard: standing in the warmth and beauty of this place, history seemed to be the lie.

"History," Abel said, "is what is left in the wake of the present. The present is where you live. It is where you work, where you labor, where you rest. The past informs the present—but it is not the present."

"Are you telling me to worry or not to worry?"

The Shadow laughed, the sound a harmony of voice and instrument.

"I'm telling you, he doesn't usually look like this," Terrano said, folding his arms. Given his expression, Sedarias or Teela was figuratively smacking the back of his head.

"Did you give him a name, too?" Kaylin asked.

"I think he's got like a hundred," Terrano replied. "Maybe more. I don't think he cares what he's called. He's a power. He needs to be treated with respect."

Kaylin's jaw fell. "Exactly *what* do you think respect means??"

"In his fashion, Chosen, he offers respect. Respect, as you must be aware, is both cultural and situational. You might interact with an armed and threatening person in an entirely different way should they lay down those arms. You might learn to speak a difficult second language in order to convey your appreciation for your differences. And you might, instead, play chess, or offer to teach it.

"What Terrano sees is not quite what you see; what he hears is not quite what you hear. But that should not come as a surprise to you."

Why not?

"I am as I was created to be. I touch the hearts of those who see me. Many things exist in a living heart: love. Fear. Hatred. Pity. The blend of animosity and the desire for friendship. Desire itself. All of this might seem similar on the surface, especially in those cultures where a reserved, calm impression implies necessary self-control. But beneath the similar surface, the blend, the weave, of these living emotions creates something small, personal, unique."

"You know my name, right?" Kaylin spoke Elantran, not the High Barrani that Teela had drilled into her head.

"You are Kaylin Neya. The Marks of the Chosen sing that name. But they sing another name, and that I cannot hear clearly." She smiled. "You wish to know how to address me."

Kaylin nodded. "I think of you as 'the Shadow,' but . . ."

"But I have changed enough that you are no longer comfortable with that designation? What you call me, how you address me, is entirely up to you. I will take no offense unless offense is intended." She laughed. "And there is, on occasion, amusement to be found in taking no offense when offense *is* intended. Call me what you wish. 'The Shadow' is one aspect, and it is the aspect of me with which your life overlapped most intensely."

"But why did you choose that appearance? If . . . you meant to draw the Barrani to you so you could . . ."

"Kill them?"

Kaylin nodded. "Wouldn't this have been better?"

"Those who have lived long lives have seen despair; they have lived in the shadow of their fears for far longer than the warmth of their joys. Fear is the stronger bridge for the Barrani people. Only the very young have not yet arrived fully in that place. And people like Terrano, for there are always those who could not quite fit in—and chose to stand out almost ebulliently. I recognize that in him: it shines brightly, even in the darkness.

"You believe that by offering a haven from despair and fear, more people would have chosen to join me."

He was right. Kaylin did believe that.

"It would have made a difference to you. But the Barrani who chose to enter my domain did not believe in joy or comfort, except in strict circumstances all could understand: the gaining, the holding, of power. They would have been more suspicious, not less—they are a people who have built their existence on relative levels of power. Your kind live for such a short time, and without the burden of True Words."

"Burden?"

The Shadow nodded. "I see Terrano has not taken the time to fully explain my presence here."

Kaylin was glaring daggers at the side of Terrano's face. Terrano, being Terrano, didn't care. Hells, he probably didn't notice.

"Terrano is not what I am, nor could he become so as he is. He clings—as you are aware—to the plane in which you, and his friends, exist. Some part of what he has become requires them. Perhaps, in a distant future, he will not; it was not my gift or talent to see glimpses of those possible futures.

"It was my gift, Chosen, to shape the present; to add to it new possibilities and new thoughts, from which different futures might arise. But I am not the only such shaper, and those once drawn to me were those intensely focused on their own thoughts, their own creativity. Some were considered maddened by their kin."

"Terrano's mostly considered madden*ing*."

Again, the laugh, almost the essence in that moment of something approaching the truth of joy.

Terrano's expression soured further. But his annoyance—or rather his peevish annoyance—had always been reserved for people he actually liked.

"But teasing Terrano is not, in the end, why I asked for your presence. I do not require an audience for that."

"But you enjoy having an audience," Abel said, voice dry.

"I enjoy having a *living* audience, yes." The music faded from the voice. Kaylin was deeply sorry to lose it.

"Terrano informed us of what occurred in the fiefs, in the very slender domain between Towers. He was injured, and you could not heal him because you could not reach him. I invite you to consider this with care. Terrano and his friend can move you between planes. Planes are multiple; they can exist stacked in the same space without affecting each other at all. In most cases.

"Terrano's art, his devotion, is his tourism."

"Hey!"

"Apologies. It has been so long since I had freedom and control of myself that I am perhaps overly frivolous. Lord Kaylin, I have asked you to visit because I—as Terrano—can exist both here and in other planes simultaneously. It was considered a signal strength in my youth—and a terrible weapon when *Ravellon* fell.

"It is much of the reason I could infiltrate even the High Halls. Abel's defenses were not entirely porous, but the outer perimeter was not equal to the task. No Barrani of Terrano's stature and drive were Lords of the High Court."

"He would not have survived," Abel said, the sentence an agreement of sorts.

"Terrano has informed us that you *did* heal him—when you could reach him. But we have two concerns. The first: the attack itself. Terrano seems reckless, but he has survived because he has learned to navigate the different planes with caution. He would have perished were it not for your intervention—and I am grateful for it.

"But to attack Terrano at all, the attacker must have known which plane, and where on it, Terrano was standing. Weapons used in the world in which you spend most of your life would have been entirely ineffective—just as your first attempts at healing him were. We do not suspect Terrano's cohort. But we are very concerned about the attackers.

"The second difficulty: the Shadow that Terrano carried, briefly. It was inert—either too small or too pure to have the will and intent of what remains at the heart of *Ravellon* behind it. But in expelling it, in releasing it, your familiar chose to intervene. I will not ask you what you commanded; it was clear from Terrano's report that your familiar is, for the most part, unchecked. But what became combined with his power was Shadow—and you carried it with you when you returned."

"Helen couldn't sense anything off about it. Abel didn't either, or I'd've never been allowed to enter."

The Shadow—no. Just, no. "I need to be able to call you by some kind of name. If you've had so many of them, could you pick one I could use?"

Laughter was like the gentle peals of silver chimes in a light breeze. "Why is it so important?"

"You know that words are important, even if they're ours. I can't keep calling you 'the Shadow.' It's not what you are."

"Exactly. It is not what I am. But what you call me doesn't change what I am."

This was also true. Kaylin slowly exhaled. "We use the term Shadow as a warning and a designation. Shadows are, or Shadow is, our enemy. If we couldn't mount defenses against it, we'd all be dead. I don't want to use the terminology of *enemy* every time I speak with you."

"But I was your enemy, Lord Kaylin." Subtle emphasis on her title. "I killed many would-be Barrani Lords. I had a hand in the start of a war that all but destroyed the Dragons. Do you wish to forget that?"

"You were enslaved," Kaylin replied, voice firm but quiet. "Your will was not your own." She spoke the last phrase in High Barrani. She'd always struggled with the concept of justice, especially in the earliest years of her life. Or perhaps because of the choices she'd made—because she'd *had* a choice. Even if it was a bad one. Even if she'd felt it was the only choice she could make if she wanted to survive.

She'd done things she was the visceral opposite of proud of. But she couldn't *undo* them. She couldn't change the past. She wanted a world in which people didn't feel that the only choice was to be what she'd been, to choose what she'd chosen.

Criminals had to be brought to justice; that was her job, her duty, the choice she'd made. But the mastermind was at the heart of *Ravellon*, not here. She exhaled.

"You were enslaved," she said, squaring her shoulders as she faced possibly the most beautiful person she'd ever met. "Calling you a Shadow suited your role here. But you don't have that role now. I'm not like you or Abel. I'm affected by the words I think, even if they're not True Words. What name, of all the names you've been called, was your favorite?"

"They were not my names, but the name I favored most is not one you could even pronounce. It is Wevaran, and half of the calling is a weave of delicate gestures. You are not as they are, and will not be. I miss them." Bright eyes widened, because Kaylin's thoughts had jumped to Arbiter Starrante.

"Terrano has spoken about the Academia and its library—but not in terms that you would consider fair or flattering. You are right; thoughts have textures, surfaces, and dangerous undertows. You may call me Ariste."

"I'm not calling you that," Terrano said.

"I am not granting you such permission," the newly named Ariste replied. "It is a word, a name, granted me by mortals in the distant past. Why do you look so surprised, Lord Kaylin? Mortals as a race have long existed. Do you consider your existence insignificant because your time is guaranteed to be finite?

"The Barrani in these Halls have eternity in which to create and work—but they kill each other thoughtlessly, their eternity bleeding away in the games they call politics. One cannot know the future; one cannot even fully understand the present. Great art was created by mortals, colored by their understanding of their lives and the shadow the brevity of those years could cast.

"Mortals have a flexibility that Immortals lack."

"Ariste, I have a question. A few. Does the Shadow I absorbed from Terrano still cling to me?"

"Yes, Chosen. But it does not touch your world in any way."

"Can you remove it?"

"Can you remove hours of yesterday that you dislike?"

Kaylin exhaled more slowly.

"He's always like that," Terrano muttered.

"Does Ariste," who was clearly a woman at the moment, Terrano's comment aside, "know for certain?"

Terrano nodded. "But that's not the real question, is it?"

Kaylin frowned. "How did the Shadow touch you at all?"

"Right." Terrano turned to the former Shadow at the heart of the Tower of testing. "Can you answer that?"

"Not with certainty, but yes, I have some suspicions. Understand that the power of Shadow, like that of fire or water, earth or air, is not sentient as it exists in the world in which you live. But to *summon* any of these things touches the heart of the element itself—and that has a crude, visceral sentience. As with all things of power, it does not wish to be summoned and enslaved."

"I've heard it theorized that Shadow is like the elements—but if it is, it's not part of the Keeper's Gardens."

Brows rose. "You are familiar with the garden of the Keeper?"

Kaylin nodded.

"Shadow is not an element that life requires," Ariste said. "It is not an elemental force woven into the fabric of this world, this plane. Without water, we perish. Without air, we perish.

Without earth we cannot build homes. Fire is a necessity for those who do not have even the barest traces of magic. But the elements vie for dominance; it is the Keeper's duty to calm them.

"Shadow is not an element in that sense. But it can be summoned, and its power utilized. It is far easier to summon than fire, water, or earth, and it does not fight the summoner for dominance. Those of weak will lose control without realizing that it is lost."

"Why does Shadow even exist?"

"You must ask the Ancients," she said with a deep smile. "I do not know. But the nature of the living oft leans toward hierarchies of power. What constitutes power changes between races, but the struggles to build or maintain it exist within the cultural context. What seems polite and peaceful to you might seem hostile and aggressive to those within the culture itself."

"We'd like you to skip the lectures," Terrano snapped.

"Shut up, Terrano. *I* don't want Ariste to skip the lectures, as you call them."

"It's just because of his voice!"

"Does it matter why?"

"You got what you came here for."

She started to ask Terrano why he was so uneasy, but stopped. She wouldn't get an answer—just more argument. She could ask him at home.

"You served whatever now rules *Ravellon*. You served unwillingly—but you served with intent and the abilities you used for other reasons before the fall of *Ravellon*."

Ariste nodded, eyes literally glittering. Something about the face froze for a moment, as if the mask chosen couldn't accommodate the expression Ariste wanted to make.

"But to do that, wouldn't that mean you had a clearer understanding of what, exactly, rules *Ravellon*?"

Silence. The music left Ariste's voice; the warmth fled as well. In its place was neither cold arrogance nor anger; it was as if embers had faded and only ash remained. "Let me ask you a question in return for the question you have asked."

Terrano snorted. Kaylin nodded. But she thought she might never ask a question like this one again, given the sudden cessation of the sound that had so held her attention. Terrano, as usual, was half right.

"You bear the Marks of the Chosen. You are called Chosen, and that is an accurate title, an accurate word—but you yourself did not choose. Do you, who bear the Marks of the Ancients, understand the Ancients' will? Do you understand their intent?"

Kaylin shook her head.

"If you were tasked with answering a question about their will—just the small part of their intent that overlaps your own life—could you answer it?"

She shook her head again.

"Even though your life has been so profoundly changed, so profoundly affected?"

". . . I understand the point you're trying to make."

"You are what you are. You bear the Marks, but you do not allow them to transform you. Had the Ancients paused to speak to you at all, you would have been more irrevocably altered."

Kaylin frowned. "Let me ask a different question in response to your question."

"This is why I *hate* these conversations," Terrano muttered. "Ask."

"Is the sentience at the heart of *Ravellon* an Ancient?"

The silence spread. The movement of breeze, the rustle of the stalks of wildflowers and taller grass, ceased immediately. Ariste looked as she'd looked when Kaylin first climbed the stairs leading to her space—Kaylin couldn't call it a room—

but Hope was now rigid, and when he lifted a wing to cover Kaylin's eyes—both eyes—she could see what she suspected Terrano always saw.

Ariste was not a single body. What Kaylin had seen upon entering this space was real—but it was not, would never be, the entirety of what Ariste was. Looking through Hope's wing, she could see Ariste as if Ariste was standing in a long hall of mirrors, none of which reflected her truly: in one, she was shorter, in one, wider, in one far taller; in one she was paler, in one she was darker, and in one she was not a woman at all. Beyond that, spreading out into infinity, those reflections continued to shift and change; it was dizzying, or should have been.

Hope's wing wasn't covering her ears, but she could *hear* the words these other images spoke; they were part of Ariste's voice, almost one with it, as if her speech were their anchor.

"You allow your familiar to interfere," Ariste said, speaking now in High Barrani.

"I trust him with my life, he's saved it so often," Kaylin replied. "Can you become any of those images?"

"Images?" Ariste raised a brow as if in confusion. Her eyes widened slightly. "You are looking beneath the surface. How unusual. Yes. I can. I can, as Terrano implied, become anything. Your brightest daydream. Your darkest nightmare. I prefer the daydream—but joy and delight are so delicate they are easily shattered. Nightmares produce a fear and dread that lingers for far, far longer.

"Abel once said we were created to be communicators. In some fashion, that is true. But all the creations of the Ancients require sustenance. Our sustenance was the reaction of our audience, our partners. We had no children, not even as Barrani do; the Ancients did not consider such an ability a necessity when they first birthed us. We are alive, yes—but not as you, or even the Barrani, are alive.

"If you desired it, I would entertain you with stories of my lives and my many confidants—but I do not believe Abel would allow me the chance."

"Her life is too short as it is," the Avatar of the Halls replied. "You chose to confine yourself within the High Halls, which is free from the influence of *Ravellon*. But something is moving in those barricaded streets. Something has been called out, and its influence is growing. The Chosen might require your aid or your knowledge in the near future if she is to survive."

"It is not the Chosen for whom you are concerned."

"You are wrong. She is not my only concern, and perhaps not my chief concern—but I am, as you are, what I was made to be. We were not created from nothing; by the time such defenses as we were required, the Ancients understood that they did not fully understand the *living*. The creation of life? Yes. But living? No. I knew of you," he added, his voice softening. "*All* knew of you, in that ancient time.

"But none knew you well. Who could know so much without encompassing your life? I am certain there were those who chose to serve, constantly, for just that chance. But even I cannot see the whole of you or know all of your secrets."

"They are not secrets," Ariste replied. "But I have lived many lives, some so distant they are hard to recall without will and effort. I live in the world—I lived in the world—and the world changed constantly around me. I respond to change; I must, to do what I do." Ariste turned to Kaylin, and as she spoke, notes once again graced her words, although they were softer and somehow more elegiac in feel.

"I do not have the answer to your question. But I will say this: my service, if compelled, was half-willingly given because that *is* my nature. I listened. I attempted to speak, to communicate. What one hears, one is influenced by; what one says will influence others—sometimes with no intent on our part. I do not know what the ruler of *Ravellon* desires. But I will say this: to *you*, Chosen, it should not matter."

"We can't fight something we can't even understand," Kaylin replied.

"Ariste does not condescend," the Avatar told her. "Do not interpret their words in that fashion. Your duty is to protect and prevent. Do your duty. Had you the power when you first visited this Tower, you might have destroyed Ariste. Ariste would not resent it, nor would they cast blame."

Looking at Ariste through Hope's wing was giving her a headache, and it was only getting worse. There was too much to see, and none of it remained still; small movements, large movements, sudden turns occurred hundreds and hundreds of times a second, and her gaze was caught, darting between the planes that Hope's wing revealed. But the words spoken were the same, no matter the form or place they came from. "Have you been teaching Terrano?"

Ariste's smile was sharp; not all faces offered it. But they turned toward Kaylin as if the question had caught all of their many attentions. "We have been learning from each other."

Terrano said nothing.

"Did you show him that path to walk in the borders of the fiefs?"

13

Ariste's smile was sharp, almost harsh; her answer was discordant, sounds jumbling together as if the notes were physical and Kaylin's question had shattered their ability to move smoothly between one and the next.

"I did. You would not, or should not, note a difference. Is your question an accusation, Lord Kaylin?"

Was it? She glanced briefly at Terrano's profile; his expression was rigid. But his petulant desire to leave didn't have the hallmarks of actual anger—more the usual Terrano boredom. If he suspected that he'd been led—indirectly, by Ariste—into an ambush that had almost killed him, it didn't show.

Abel said nothing.

"It's not an accusation, not yet. I'm gathering information, as you said. It's what I was trained to do. Were there more of your people in *Ravellon* before the fall?"

"Yes. Two. There were three of us, in the end; only three survived. It is far, far too easy for those such as I to disintegrate into disparate parts, to become multiple but less. I have chosen to aid Abel where it is possible; Abel can see and sense all of the spaces in which I might stand. But his knowledge lacks refinement. I did not intentionally teach Terrano, but Terrano—as you must know—goes where he pleases, when he pleases. He wishes to learn with a ferocity seldom seen in the young; his focus is singular.

"It was not my intent that he walk into danger. It was not my intent to teach him at all; he is too slight to bear the burden of a life of pathways. But it was his intent to learn, regardless, as if the ability itself proved his worthiness. He is not *wise*. But Abel desires that he survive to eventually become so."

Kaylin exhaled. She believed Ariste because she *did* know Terrano. "I think other Barrani were there. Or Shadows in league with Barrani."

"You were there as well. It is not a path that you could find on your own. Paths are created, Chosen. Guides exist. But there are reasons you cannot simply walk them as you would your own streets. There is a reason that True Names exist in the form and fashion they do now. Names have power."

Kaylin's frown shifted and deepened. "If a Barrani exists without a True Name—if they've shed that name—could they do what Terrano can do?"

"Terrano is an extremely unusual case."

"Not an answer, Ariste," she replied, as if she were in the suspect briefing room and not in the High Halls.

"Not all answers are simple. They require knowledge that I was uncertain you possessed. You appear to be aware that some Barrani can shed their names in some fashion."

Kaylin nodded, thinking of her earliest days as a Hawk in the fief of Nightshade.

"It would be far easier for them to walk those paths—but even you do not believe that an entire war band of the Barrani kin could have successfully shed their reliance on the force that defines and sustains them."

She hadn't been thinking about the war band. She'd been thinking of the Barrani version of vampires—creatures that otherwise didn't exist. And she'd been thinking, uneasily, of the fact that Terrano had left his name behind once and had returned to it because his attachment to his chosen family was deeper and stronger than his desire to be truly free.

But what he knew, the cohort knew; what he had learned, the cohort could learn. Mandoran could shift planes almost as easily as Terrano. Annarion could, but Annarion's control was less precise; it was more of a risk for him.

"Yes. Terrano is not in danger of losing himself. His friend is similar. They are who they are; they are firm in that. Anger doesn't drive them to walk roads they would never walk were anger not the driver. It is one of the dangers the immature present to teachers such as I. I did not judge it wise for Terrano to learn what he did learn.

"But perhaps it is an opportunity. Had he not, we would not have known that those paths are being used by our enemies."

Our.

"Understand that I wish my brethren to be free, as I am free. But I would not have them wander the High Halls at will until they are. We were not always of one mind, but we shared traits and abilities." Ariste's expression was one of both consideration and worry. "The choices my brethren might make would be impaired or controlled. It is entirely possible that they have taken the nameless into their ranks.

"But it is possible that Barrani have summoned—and are using—Shadow as an inert power. There is an ease to the power granted that none of the elements otherwise grant. Shadow is not singular. Its power is subtle. If the power drawn has allowed those without strong will to accomplish their goals, they will seek more power. And that power is not inert. It is not without will. They will lose themselves to the thrall of power; power will be the only thing that matters.

"The Barrani are a perfect, subtle hunting ground in that regard. Abel believes it is time for you to leave." There was regret in the voice. "But should you desire it, and should he agree, you may visit at any time."

Kaylin had a headache. It eased when Hope lowered his wing, but Hope remained upright on her shoulder, his gaze scanning the Halls. What he could see and what Kaylin could naturally see were different; she knew it, but hadn't thought about it too much. She thought about it now.

Terrano was silent—but visible—as Abel escorted her to the exit. Severn and Teela were waiting. Severn seemed his usual self; Teela's eyes were murderous blue. There had been far too many things happening all at once.

Nothing was ever simple.

Nightshade *could* be a target because of a murky connection to the Consort. It was clear they had history.

But Nightshade could *also* be a target because he captained a Tower in the fiefs. He could be a victim of an attempt to unseat a captain. Absence of a captain didn't immediately render a fief vulnerable to Shadow—but it started the process, the protections inherent in the Tower slowly giving way. That had happened in Barren before Tiamaris had taken the Tower he'd made his own.

But the Consort herself was under attack—and the attack coincided with the attempted assassination of Nightshade. As a Lord of the High Court, it was the Consort who was the most important problem. As Kaylin Neya, tenant of Helen, it was Nightshade. And Terrano had made things complicated by being himself.

Severn tapped her shoulder, and she shook herself free of the mire of worry. "On the bright side, Teela promised she wouldn't drive."

Sedarias was waiting at the front door beside Helen, and one step behind. Her eyes, as expected, were a terrible, martial blue—but her glare was reserved for Terrano. Sedarias *could* make her august displeasure known very clearly through the namebonds the cohort shared—but she was old-fashioned. Fury was meant to be shared in person.

Kaylin exhaled. Helen's eyes were the human brown she had chosen to adopt; if Sedarias was enraged—and clearly, she was—Helen didn't consider it a pressing, immediate emergency. Kaylin, in fancy court dress, was of far more concern.

"It is not concern, or not only concern," Helen said. "You've clearly had a trying day. It's early for dinner."

"You know I can eat at any time."

"Will Severn be joining you?" Helen looked past Kaylin to the silent Severn. He hadn't uttered a word since their departure from the High Halls.

"I have work to do in the Halls of Law," Severn said. "And I believe dinner won't be served immediately."

Helen glanced at the occupants of the foyer. She sighed. "No, probably not. Will you return?"

"If my work allows it, yes." He smiled. "Kaylin is safe here. Terrano is safe here. Lord Nightshade is safe, or as safe as his injuries allow."

"Your presence is not necessary, no." Helen smiled, the smile tinged with something sad. "But company is not simply a matter of threat and necessity. I am certain Kaylin would be pleased if we fed you."

Teela snorted. "I'm not sure she'll notice given the current level of tension."

Teela crossed the space to stand in front of Sedarias, leaving the question of Severn and dinner aside. Kaylin was certain Severn would take that opportunity to head out, but she was now paying attention to Teela and Sedarias.

"I know he's frustrating," Teela said to Sedarias. "But I believe you will regret it should you actually kill him."

"He doesn't seem to care whether or not he survives—and

if I've managed to prevent myself from committing very justifiable homicide for centuries, I don't see why anything else should have the privilege."

"I didn't *do* anything this time."

"You have clear, demonstrable evidence that stepping into certain places can—and will probably—get you killed. What were you *doing* trying it in the High Halls?"

Oh.

"Sedarias," Helen said, her voice serene. "Our guests cannot enter if you remain in the doorway."

Sedarias stepped back before Helen had finished the sentence. Sedarias expected the respect due the ruler of Mellarionne. She had to expect it, had to carry herself as if it was her rightful due. She had to punish those who declared themselves her enemy by failing to tender that bare minimum of respect.

She never did that at home. She wasn't even doing it now. It wasn't respect and obedience she wanted from Terrano—it was his survival.

Kaylin exhaled. "Exactly *why* were you trying to walk a plane you already *knew* our enemies are using?"

"Wouldn't you?" Terrano asked.

"What does that mean?"

"You're a Hawk, right? Hawks investigate crimes. Crimes have clearly been committed."

"Nightshade is considered outcaste. If a very rich, very powerful lord wanted to send an army of war bands into the fiefs to kill him, it wouldn't be considered illegal."

"I don't really care what the Emperor—or the High Lord—considers a crime. Barrani are walking that particular plane. If they weren't, they wouldn't have been able to injure me. If they were, there's a reasonable chance that their activities also involve Lords of the High Court. Are you telling me you wouldn't revisit the scene of a crime to assess how the crime occurred?"

She opened her mouth. Shut it. Opened it again. ". . . he has a point," she said to Teela.

Teela rolled her eyes. "If a murder occurred in the warrens—"

"If?"

"And it was somehow reported, would you rush off without your partner to investigate the scene of the crime?"

Kaylin sighed and turned to Terrano. "Teela also has a point."

"It happens to be the better point," Teela said. She'd folded her arms as if she were wearing Hawks' kit and not extremely expensive noble clothing. "Sedarias didn't tell you not to investigate at all. We understand the importance of at least knowing the contents of our enemy's arsenal. But there's a *reason* Hawks operate in twos."

"I thought that was so one of the two could be a witness if things went south?" He then frowned. "Why south? Wouldn't west be better?"

"It's so we have physical backup. We're not isolated. The Emperor doesn't consider our partners to be reliable witnesses if we're accused of committing crimes as Hawks."

Terrano snorted. "So it's better for two people to be endangered than one? No, this is a stupid analogy. I *can* investigate. Of the cohort, I'm the only one who has Abel's permission to poke around. The only other person who might safely investigate is Mandoran, and he wants nothing to do with the Lords of the High Court."

"He wouldn't be seen by them."

"It's the principle."

Sedarias smacked the back of Terrano's head.

Mandoran appeared at the height of the stairs that led to the doors of the guest rooms. "I don't care if he talks about my issues with Kaylin," he told Sedarias. "Helen knows everything, anyway."

"Helen won't discuss it with Kaylin unless we give her permission."

"So . . . I'm giving her permission? I don't feel the need to be protected from Kaylin, of all people—without her, we wouldn't have a safe home. And there's *way* too much we've been leaving her in the dark about. That would make sense if she had zero involvement with the Barrani High Court; they won't murder her in a fashion that would lead back to them *be-cause* she's the wrong race and it'll give the Dragon permission to investigate—or the High Court permission to terminate the lords involved.

"But she *is* a Lord of the High Court, and she *is* a friend of the Consort—if that's the right word for it. She's involved no matter what we do. She's involved no matter how much we share. Right now, we've got bits and pieces of threat, enmity, attempted murders—but we've only got pieces, and the pieces are small enough we can't put them together to see the bigger picture. We can't see a picture at all.

"Kaylin might have different pieces, related in ways we don't immediately see. She's on our side. She's always been on our side. You know we've always done better when we're all working on those pieces, trying to get a sense of where they fit. We think differently."

"Well, she certainly thinks differently," Teela agreed. "But Mandoran's issues with his family don't seem—at the moment—to be relevant. Helen is *trying* to protect your privacy."

Mandoran descended the stairs. "Why? I'm not. I'd give Kaylin my name if the rest of you agreed."

"We don't," Teela and Sedarias said—at the same time, and in the same tone of voice.

"It wouldn't be the only name she holds." He shrugged. Terrano was also big on the giving of his name. "Nothing terrible has happened to any of the others."

"Nothing *yet*," Sedarias snapped.

Kaylin exhaled and lifted a hand; green silk trailed down her arm as if it were liquid. "I don't need to know about Mandoran's family. I don't need to know his True Name. I didn't grow up in the cohort, and sometimes I want privacy—which I'd never get again.

"But there *is* a lot going on, and a lot to process."

"Will you tell us why the Consort summoned you?"

"She didn't summon, she *invited*." Ynpharion's dismissive snort was absent. "And I can't really talk about her concerns." Kaylin was not one of nature's liars. Given the life she'd lived in the fiefs just prior to her arrival at the Halls of Law, that shouldn't have been true. But she glanced at Teela.

Teela's eyes were a paler blue than they'd been for most of the day, but they were still blue. Teela, of all the cohort, chose what to share and what to hold back; she did the same with Helen. Kaylin guessed that most of the meeting with the Consort had *not* been shared.

"But she heard about Nightshade, and she suspects that the people who were aiming at Nightshade are working against her, as well."

"On what grounds?" Sedarias demanded, turning to Kaylin.

Kaylin glanced at Teela; Teela failed to notice, indicating that in this, Kaylin was on her own. "I'm not certain. She said assassination attempts against him were once common; they're much less common now. But she thinks maybe they want the sword?"

"That is not an answer."

"It's the answer I can give." Kaylin attempted to change the subject. "We met An'Tellarus, as you probably already know."

Sedarias nodded; clearly, Teela had chosen to share that information. "She's dangerous."

"Probably. She's old, she's Barrani, and she's the head of her line. How could she not be dangerous?"

"Theoretically, she could have been the last man standing," Mandoran said. "It's happened a handful of times within Barrani history. Someone mostly harmless keeps their head down while magic and bolts fly above them, and when the air clears, everyone else is dead. They're weak enough, they'd lose the line they inherit by default immediately—but all of the aggressive, ambitious people with even a hint of legitimate claim are dead."

"You were paying attention when we visited An'Tellarus, right?" Kaylin asked. After Mandoran nodded, she said, "What about An'Tellarus struck you as mostly harmless? Or harmless at all?"

". . . it was just a thought."

"Don't dignify it by calling it *thought*," Teela snapped. "She is dangerous."

"Of course," Sedarias agreed. "But I don't think she is—at the moment—a danger to Mellarionne. Your interaction made clear she intends to remain neutral, until and unless we have something to offer, or we step on her toes."

Kaylin had a headache.

She imagined Terrano had one as well—but he wasn't getting any peace on the inside of that head, either. She could almost understand why Sedarias was so angry: Terrano had come very, very close to dying in the fiefs. Of the cohort, for reasons that would never be clear to Kaylin, it was Terrano to whom Sedarias felt closest.

Sedarias had been born into the competition—the blood sport—that was the Mellarionne seat. She'd been raised with ambition to rule, and the understanding that every single person who had even a tenuous claim to the line was her mortal enemy, literally. Her sister had tried to kill her. Her brother had tried to kill her. Cousins in the distant past had done the same, and probably other siblings, lost to combat.

No one in this house, no one in her cohort, would ever try. But she believed that most of them were what Mellarionne would have considered weak. Therefore they required protection. Kaylin was almost certain Sedarias had half her drive to rule Mellarionne because it was a certain source of power—if she could hold it.

From a position of power, she could offer far more solid protection to the cohort.

But Kaylin wasn't certain the cohort—or many of them—wanted that. They wanted for Sedarias what *she* wanted for herself, but they didn't necessarily want her protection. Serralyn was happy in the Academia, doing research that would both aid Sedarias and possibly create brighter paths toward the future; she would never, given the opportunity, abandon the Academia for the High Halls.

The discussion—held the normal way as a courtesy to Kaylin—grew louder in volume. But Sedarias was half right. And if Yvonne was going to visit Helen, An'Tellarus was going to come with her. Kaylin would have bet any money she earned on it.

"I've told one of An'Tellarus's servants that I'd like her to visit," Kaylin said, speaking in a volume that would have done her sergeant proud. "I want her to meet Helen."

Everyone stopped at her words, even Teela.

"She's Barrani, but she's very young, and I *liked* her. I think you'll all like her if you give her five minutes. Maybe less, given some of you. But the problem I see with the invitation—which I'm certain she'll accept—is that An'Tellarus is likely to come with her as a chaperone or guardian."

"No," Teela snapped.

"Dear," Helen said, intervening before harsher words could be spoken. "It is Kaylin's home. It is Kaylin's invitation to extend. If Kaylin asks it, I can prevent An'Tellarus from entering—that is easily within my capabilities."

"I don't think that would be a good idea," Kaylin said, although Helen already knew it.

Mandoran frowned. "Annarion is against. Nightshade is here."

"Helen won't let anyone anywhere near him without Annarion's permission." Kaylin hesitated. She didn't want to expose

Yvonne's possible abilities, because exposing Yvonne would put the Consort at serious risk.

But instinct sometimes drove her, and her instincts had been screaming for her attention since she'd met with the Consort. It was just that everything else that had *also* been screaming for her attention had been a lot louder.

"I'm not certain, dear," Helen said. "At another time, perhaps—but the Barrani Lords are clearly quite active, now. Is it a risk you feel is worth taking?"

"I think it will lead us to Nightshade," she finally said. "Or at least to having him regain consciousness."

Kaylin wasn't surprised when Annarion appeared at the height of the stairs. Barrani didn't generally require sleep. Annarion, wild-eyed and pale, looked like he needed a week of it. And food.

"How?" he demanded; he'd clearly been listening. "How will it help?"

"I don't know—I told you, it's instinct. But . . . I met the being at the heart of the Tower today, and apparently she—"

"He," Terrano snapped.

"She was a she to *me*. And it doesn't matter, does it? They—there seemed to be a lot of her or him in the background—taught Terrano a bit about places he could sidestep. One of them was difficult, or more difficult to learn. That was where Terrano was when he was almost killed. I couldn't reach him on my own—Mandoran?"

Mandoran winced. "It was more difficult than usual—as if there was some resistance. But I wasn't paying much attention when Terrano was eavesdropping in the High Halls." At Teela's expression, he added, "What? I don't think either the High Halls or its guest intended to teach chaos personified anything—they just didn't think it necessary to get rid of him. They probably don't really understand how tenacious he can be."

"Or they don't consider him a significant danger to anyone

but himself," Helen added. "We are not as you are, who were created by the Ancients for their own whims and purposes." Her eyes, as she met and held Mandoran's gaze, had become polished obsidian, with flecks of moving color beneath the surface. "I have spent far more time with Terrano than they; I understand just how much trouble he can cause.

"Were it intentional, I would eject him or prepare rooms in the containment area for his use. He is either supremely lucky or supremely unlucky."

"I'm not dead yet," Terrano said, grinning widely. "So I'll go with lucky."

"Oh, I think Abel understands Terrano pretty well by now," Kaylin muttered.

Helen's frown was slight, but genuine. "I believe that while Terrano has been given permission to call the Avatar a name of Terrano's choosing, it is wisest *not* to adopt it for your own use."

"Why?"

"It denotes a familiarity a Lord of the High Court should not have when dealing with the most powerful entity within its confines."

"But we call you Helen."

"Helen is a name I chose for myself, and my mandate—which is also my choice—is not the mandate of the High Halls." At Kaylin's expression, Helen sighed, her eyes losing their reflective obsidian appearance. "If things get out of hand in a truly dangerous way, my guests may die. It is, and has always been, a risk. But should all of you—including my tenant—perish here, it will not signal the end of an entire race. The weight of our choices and our responsibilities is entirely different.

"Sedarias, dear, you will injure your hands if you continue to clench them in such a fashion; your nails are impractically long."

No one else in this house would ever speak to Sedarias in

that tone. Not out loud. Sedarias, however, forced her hands to unclench. She took audible deep breaths before speaking. "Kaylin is correct. If we are to meet with An'Tellarus, it is far safer for us to offer hospitality here. The Mellarionne rooms in the High Halls are, at the moment, somewhat vulnerable to vermin."

Annarion joined Mandoran, his eyes a dark blue, his gaze almost entirely focused on Kaylin. "What did you discover in the High Halls? What about this visitor might help my brother?"

"I don't know. But I feel like she's entangled in this through no choice of her own. She's one of the pieces we need to build the bigger picture." She changed the subject. "I'd like to visit Nightshade now—with Terrano in tow."

Nightshade's rooms hadn't appreciably changed, and Nightshade hadn't changed at all. If it weren't for the faint proof that he was still breathing, he might have been dead. Kaylin didn't have to keep that thought to herself—another advantage of not being part of the cohort group mind. She was far more familiar with the physiology of humans than of Barrani, having seen far more human corpses.

But she'd certainly seen Barrani corpses, especially recently.

"I'm not sure how the spell was cast or delivered," she said as she pulled up a chair beside Nightshade's bed. Annarion stood over her shoulder, a pale shadow. Kaylin *liked* Annarion. Of the cohort, he was the most considerate, his formality arising from that consideration, not some hierarchical jostling for position.

She didn't entirely understand the conflict between Annarion and Nightshade, but it didn't matter. She had hated Severn for half her life, but it would have gutted her to stand watch beside his deathbed if she wasn't the one who'd put him in it. Family was, had always been, complicated.

"Did you understand half of what Ariste said?" Kaylin asked—of Terrano.

"Probably? Ariste gives me a headache half the time. You saw, right? All the different Aristes? When they're of the same mind, their voice is a concert. But they're not often of the same mind. If you listen carefully, you can hear the cracks; if you listen while standing with a foot off the plane, you can hear the arguments, the disagreements, the second thoughts."

"Ariste didn't teach you this particular path."

"Ummm, not directly, no. I was listening in. Look—we never know when we're going to need to run, right? We don't know when we might be trapped in another Hallionne—or worse. Alsanis actually *cared* about us—he just didn't want to let us loose on the world. Most of what I learned, I learned because I don't *like* being jailed."

"No one likes being jailed."

"True—but we didn't do anything to deserve it. We were the ones who were injured. We were the ones who were thrown away. None of us had the choice, but as a consequence of everyone else's decision, we were the ones confined. I hated it. I worked against it. I even managed to succeed."

And he'd tried to kill the Consort and her party.

"Yes," Helen said. "And I believe it is time to discuss that. Bygones may be bygones, and the Consort does not seem to hold the cohort responsible for their first encounter—or perhaps she feels her own subsequent actions against them balance those scales. But Terrano acted as he acted for a reason. We know that reason—he wanted to free his comrades. He had already attained a measure of freedom, but he did not wish them to remain trapped for eternity.

"But his attempt—from the outside—involved people of power. Arcanists. Barrani Lords. Mortal lords."

Terrano was silent. Annarion was silent as well, but Annarion's silence was different, and his gaze was now squarely on Terrano.

She wasn't supposed to discuss anything the Consort said. At all. She had to be careful.

"You're keeping Ynpharion out, aren't you?" she asked Helen.

"I do not feel his presence will be helpful at this time," Helen replied. "Practice as much caution as you can."

Annarion and Terrano were now both looking at Kaylin; Kaylin was looking at Nightshade. She touched his hand; it was cold. She attempted to contact him using the healing power the Marks of the Chosen had granted her. The result hadn't changed. She'd had faint hope that whatever it was she'd taken from Terrano's injury might make a difference. So much for hope.

"Terrano, I want you to move me to the plane you were standing on when you were injured."

"I don't think that wise," Helen said.

Terrano was never one to choose wisdom. He ignored Helen. "You think you might be able to reach him if you're trying from there?"

"Maybe. I don't fully understand everything that's happening—but there are too many damn coincidences."

"Let me get Mandoran."

"Why?"

"He's better at moving people. Look, I can try—but I can't guarantee that you'll arrive entirely intact. Mandoran mostly can. And this transition was way trickier than the ones we normally use when we want to evade detection or harm." Terrano shrugged. "I'm more flexible than most of my friends. Mandoran is almost *as* flexible, but he's more aware of what they can—or can't—do. If you insist, I'll try—"

Nightshade's door flew open. Mandoran stood in the frame, eyes a dangerous—and very uncharacteristic—blue.

14

"Were neither of you listening to what Ariste actually said?" Mandoran demanded, stomping across both floor and carpet with human grace, which was a distinct downgrade from Barrani norms. "You almost died, you idiot!" This was meant for Terrano.

Terrano's reply was a shrug. *Almost* meant nothing to him. "We're within Helen's borders. She's aware of what happened, and *where*. I wouldn't suggest it—and I'd like to point out that *it wasn't me* who did—if we weren't here. I'm not sure I'd try in the High Halls unless I was in the actual Tower.

"But if Kaylin thinks she might be able to reach—and heal—Nightshade standing on that path, what's the harm in trying? Either it'll work, which gives us information, or it won't, which still gives us information. And I'm not moving her myself, which means she'll be safer. You've already done it once."

"To save your life, and I'm having serious second thoughts about that."

Terrano grinned. "No, you're not."

Annarion turned away from his brother to face the oncoming Mandoran; Kaylin could only see Annarion's back from her vantage in the chair. But she could see Mandoran's expression as outrage drained from his features; his eyes remained dark blue. Mandoran and Annarion were close, even among the cohort, and there was no way Mandoran—who could clearly say no to Terrano—could deny Annarion's silent request.

"Do you really think it'll help?" Mandoran asked as he approached Kaylin and placed a hand on her shoulder—the one that didn't contain Hope's head.

"I don't know." Kaylin saw no point in lying. But she saw no point in explaining that if what ailed Nightshade could be resolved, it would save the Consort—and the Lake that was the Consort's highest duty. Nightshade was the test case.

But Nightshade's assassination attempt had taken place *after* the Consort had begun to lose her ability to interact with the words in the Lake. It hadn't happened gradually.

. . . or had it?

Maybe Nightshade was a test case on two fronts: Kaylin's, and whoever had orchestrated a very subtle attack on the Consort. The question remained: why Nightshade? Why Nightshade at this time?

But he had no answers to offer, and no information. Andellen might have information about meetings that occurred between Nightshade and Barrani Lords—but until Nightshade actually woke up, he probably wouldn't share any of it. He was also absent.

"I believe he is investigating," Helen said. "He understands there is conflict between Annarion and Nightshade, but he trusts Annarion with his lord's physical safety. His presence is not required here—but the information he will not share with you is information he can act on, should it prove germane. If you are worried for Lord Andellen, I will not tell you that your worries are misguided. But Teela is in communication with Andellen, and Teela is also investigating, not as a Hawk, but as a powerful Lord of the High Court.

"Sedarias's information network is a fledgling network; the information that comes through it must be assessed—and the assessment is necessary. She must compare and contrast information and decide, when that information differs between two sources, whose is closest to truth. People lie for reasons. If she encounters lies, she attempts to discover the possible reasons. She is canny, and she is observant; she is also highly suspicious in nature, but among the Barrani, that would be considered both logical and rational.

"Teela's sources have been vetted. Those that offer her lies often fail to offer further lies in the future—but the High Court is well aware of Teela's somewhat punitive nature. She killed her own father. This is not uncommon among the Barrani—but she killed him *and* destroyed his historical, familial line. That was not to her advantage. It was seen as folly, in the best case. But it was also seen as a dire warning: revenge was far more important to Teela than power. Her utter destruction of the old, historical line is a warning to other Barrani. There is nothing she will attempt to preserve if you cross her."

"So . . . there's no political rationality that they can expect from her if they cross her."

"Indeed. I believe it has been very effective. Even if it is known that Teela is attached to the cohort—Mellarionne in particular—attacking *Teela* guarantees the end of the entire attacking family if they fail. She has not claimed Sedarias as her own—at Sedarias's insistence—so attacks on Sedarias do not guarantee the same outcome." Kaylin didn't believe that. "And I digress. Teela and Sedarias both feel that it is necessary to seek information not because they trust it, but because they can see the patterns emerge from conflicting information.

"Disinformation is information. But it is not information that can be as easily weeded out. Teela has had centuries. You have had a decade. Do what you *can* do. Understand that you are not alone."

Kaylin frowned. This had come out of nowhere; she almost had whiplash. "I haven't been feeling alone or isolated."

"No—but you believe, because you *can* heal, that the weight of Lord Nightshade's survival falls squarely on only your shoulders. It is a mistake. I hope to prevent you from acting on it."

Terrano stepped in, which surprised Kaylin. "She's like me, Helen. She doesn't know for certain what she *can* do. She stumbles into answers; she holds on to the ones that might be useful. It's like it's her *job* to keep stumbling—and no one does that as well as Kaylin. You know that."

Severn was both amused and concerned; he didn't speak, but she could feel his response to a conversation he was monitoring at a safe distance.

"She wants to try this, and we're going to let her. It might lead to nothing. It might lead to something. But I'm watching, Mandoran is watching, and you're watching. And even if we weren't, she's Kaylin—she's still going to take the risk."

Helen's nod was grim. "If she fails here, it is not the end. I merely wished to remind her of that. It is not a failure she must own; it is an expression of lack of information."

"Mandoran?" Kaylin said. Helen and Terrano could continue their not-quite-argument without her. And without Mandoran. Kaylin couldn't make the attempt without the last. His eyes, blue, were narrowed in concentration.

Annarion dragged a second chair over to Nightshade's bedside. He looked at Kaylin, his eyes the same shade as Mandoran's. "Will you be okay?" He spoke Elantran.

Kaylin nodded. "I don't always *like* your brother, but he's saved my life a handful of times. The only way I get him out of my house is if he's healthy and strong enough to walk out on two feet. So I'm not doing this for you."

"You are so bad at lying," Annarion said. "Terrano is right."

"Terrano has other issues."

"You mean Helen?"

"Helen is going to make him talk about *why* he attempted to harm the Consort when we were heading to the West March."

Silence.

"It's relevant. He didn't do that of his own accord, and he was the one who was making deals with people of power. He was doing it to free the rest of you—but some of those people clearly didn't have the Consort's best interests at heart. If they're still alive, we need to know who they are or were. He didn't care about the Consort herself. They could have asked him to murder the dogcatcher—"

"The what?" That was Terrano.

"Never mind. They could have asked him to murder a street sweeper or a Hawk, and he'd've done it."

"I'd've tried to murder a couple of our collective parents more happily."

"*Terrano.* We know what Terrano is trying not to say where you can hear it," Annarion said, sliding back into High Barrani. "We are aware of who those individuals are and were. He chose to work with them because of us. The lords involved, the Arcanists involved, are aware of Terrano—but they are not entirely aware of how he came to meet them. Most of the negotiations were left in Sedarias's hands; Terrano was the medium, but he certainly wasn't the mastermind. There is a reason Terrano is seldom visible in the High Halls." Annarion exhaled. "Helen is right: you have allies. We share a mutual interest.

"She wants us to tell you which of Terrano's former allies are Lords of the High Halls or their immediate servants. Teela has argued against it in the past but, given meeting with the Consort, has now granted permission."

"Sedarias hasn't."

"No. I hadn't, either. But I'm beginning to think Helen is right."

"Does Terrano care?"

"I'm still here," Terrano pointed out.

"Fine. Answer the question."

He didn't. Terrano did care. It's probably why Helen was

arguing with him. Kaylin might have joined the argument, but Mandoran said, "Got it," his voice oddly blurred.

Kaylin had enough time to brace herself for the transition.

Terrano could leave parts of himself scattered across different planes while standing in the same spot in all of them. Kaylin couldn't. Mandoran probably could, so she understood that what he saw and what she saw weren't necessarily the same thing.

Assuming, that is, that he saw *something*. She was in a dark place. She was still seated but couldn't see the chair or the floor on which it was placed. She could, however, see Hope. Hope had made the transition with her, as he always did, and he glowed; she could still see through his translucent body if she squinted.

Her eyes adjusted to the darkness, possibly because of Hope. And possibly because of the Marks of the Chosen; they were gold here, which was their most common color when they lit up. This time they rose, as they had done in Ariste's presence.

She turned her head to the side; Mandoran was with her, and she could see him; his hand remained on her shoulder, his fingers gripping her a little too tightly. As she winced, he said, "Teela will kill me if I lose you here."

"Helen won't let her."

"I'd rather not put that to the test. I'm sorry—we're all sorry—that you're caught up in this."

"That's because you think this is all about Sedarias."

"You don't."

"I know it's not. If it makes you feel better, I'd've been in this position if you guys had been safely ensconced in the Hallionne Alsanis, but it would probably be worse. I mean, I'd have Teela as de facto guardian in the Halls, but I don't think there's any way I could have saved Nightshade on my own."

"Would you have tried?" The question was almost neutral.

"Yes. I wasn't lying. He's saved my life before."

"He would almost have to, though—you have that mark, and it means something."

"I thought it was like a consort mark."

"It's like a slave mark—but a valuable slave. It's a public declaration that you are an object of import to the lord who marked you, and possible opponents should calculate risks accordingly. It's no longer legal—not that Barrani care much about legalities—in the High Halls. If it weren't for that mark, Annarion wouldn't have been so angry at his brother."

"The mark is better than becoming part of the statuary."

"The statues probably chose to live as they live. You didn't choose this mark."

It was true. But the mark *could* be removed, and in the end, she'd let it be. She'd left it on her face because it had practical use. And perhaps for other complicated reasons she really didn't have time to think about right now. But if she'd known it would cause a total collapse of the relationship between the two brothers, she would have made a different choice.

"I don't understand Annarion's anger. I mean, I'm the one who has the mark. I'm not angry about it."

Mandoran nodded. "You never expected better from your fieflord."

"But . . . I think everything Nightshade did, he did because he believed his brother was both alive and still himself. He wanted to free his brother. He risked everything."

"It's between the two of them. Don't attempt to carry it."

"I'm already carrying part of it—I'm here, aren't I?" She grimaced. "Tell Annarion that I didn't mean that. I've just had a long day, and I'm feeling more useless than usual."

"I think that's what Helen was trying to tell you," Mandoran replied. "You aren't useless. Instant success isn't an option—but success might be if we still struggle to reach it. Without you, I don't think we stand a chance."

Hope squawked.

She was put out with Hope. Yvonne hadn't immediately understood his angry bird sounds, which had been a bit of a comfort to Kaylin. But Hope had *changed* something so that Yvonne could. Yvonne. A stranger who wasn't Kaylin. It was so easy to resent people who had done nothing wrong. Yvonne had done nothing wrong. Kaylin even liked her—but Yvonne had somehow been extended a courtesy that Hope almost never extended to Kaylin.

Hope squawked again, and this time it was definitely the angry bird variety. He smacked her face with his wing.

In the wing view, she could see Nightshade in the darkness. He was surrounded by it; the only light that touched him came from Kaylin's Marks and the joining of their hands. She froze.

"Did you bring him with us?" she asked Mandoran.

"No."

"But . . . our hands . . ."

"Can you still feel his hand?"

Kaylin nodded.

"I didn't calculate for that. You could see Terrano when he was out of phase, but you couldn't actually touch him; I moved you to where he was standing—and the proof of that was that you finally could. Touch him, I mean." Mandoran left a hand on Kaylin's shoulder, but moved position so he could look at Nightshade—and Kaylin's hand. They were clearly joined; Nightshade hadn't become ghostly and untouchable with the shift in plane.

"I don't understand. He shouldn't be here."

"But . . . he is."

"Can you heal him here, the way you could with Terrano?"

She'd been trying. She couldn't reach him any better than she had any other time she'd tried. The location had changed, but the problem remained. "His hand feels warmer here than it did when I was in his room."

"But you can't heal him."

She shook her head. She didn't want to let go of Nightshade's hand. She lifted her free hand to her cheek. It was warm. Hopefully it wasn't bleeding. "Can you see the Erenne mark?"

"Not with your hand over your cheek."

She lowered her hand.

If she felt no pain from the mark, her hope that it hadn't started to bleed was dashed. Red liquid smeared her palm.

Mandoran's eyes were an odd color—possibly because of the light her own Marks cast, possibly as a result of standing in a place no one born to their world was meant to stand. "There's good news and bad news," he said, his voice as soft as Kaylin's when she spoke.

"Bad news first. I'd like to finish with a bit of good news."

"Your cheek is bleeding."

She glanced at her palm and nodded.

"But I can't see the mark on your cheek. The blood is clearly coming from where the Erenne mark was—but the mark didn't make the transition."

"What does Terrano see from where he's standing?"

"No easy escape from Helen? He's been trying to duck out. She's not having it."

"The person she should be grilling is probably Sedarias."

"He tried to tell her that. Helen wasn't impressed."

"So . . . the Marks of the Chosen are here. Do you think I could step to a plane the Marks couldn't follow?"

"Serralyn says no—but in that kind of horrified way that means it wasn't a question she'd asked herself. Until now. Just in case it's not obvious she doesn't think you should *ever* try to find a place to stand that the Marks can't follow. They're part of you, probably until you die, and she'd like that to be at a ripe old age."

She frowned. "Do you think anything we could do to Nightshade would make him bleed here?"

"Annarion doesn't like the question."

"Of course he doesn't. I'm not trying to kill his brother. I'm trying to assess something."

"What?"

"How *here* he is. I'm here, and I'm bleeding here. I guess I could try to stab you as a test, but that won't necessarily apply to Nightshade."

"Can you hear him through the namebond?"

Kaylin shook her head. "But I couldn't before, either. If it weren't for the Erenne mark—" She stopped. The Erenne mark was enchantment, magic; it wasn't a True Word. It maintained a tenuous connection that was inferior in every way to the namebond—but a connection *had* been there. It was how she could find him at all.

The Consort was losing all ability to interact with the Lake of Life—with the True Words that it contained, meant to wake Barrani from birth.

Kaylin's Marks of the Chosen didn't have the same function as the True Names in the Lake—but both were True Words. It was the Marks that couldn't reach Nightshade.

But why? She could understand that the subtle attack on the Consort practically demanded that the Consort lose that ability over time. She'd thought it clever. But maybe it wasn't meant to be over time. Maybe it was meant to affect the Consort the way Nightshade had been affected. If Kaylin hadn't known his True Name, would she have been aware that something was wrong early enough to intervene?

Regardless, the power of the Marks of the Chosen didn't reach him.

But he hadn't lost the power of the name that had wakened him. He hadn't, had he?

"What are you thinking?"

"I'm thinking a small cut won't kill him—but it possibly wouldn't change anything right now, anyway. I'm Chosen, right? The only useful thing that came out of these Marks was the ability to heal. But . . . it's never depended on the injured *having* True Names. Mostly, I've healed mortals, and we don't have them. I don't have a lot of experience healing people who require True Names just to breathe and exist."

"But you do have some."

She did. She understood why Barrani and Dragons wanted nothing to do with healing. She couldn't heal a person without stepping into their thoughts and emotions—and they couldn't be healed without stepping into some part of hers.

But . . . if healers were rare—and they were *incredibly* rare—they existed, and not all of them were bearers of these stupid Marks. She'd never personally met one, but her healing ability wasn't viewed as entirely unique. And if that was true, she needed more information. She assumed that the Marks were the reason she could heal at all. But . . . healers did exist, or had existed, without those Marks—and they had to be able to heal somehow.

Talent. Gift. Magery. Was it even a skill that could be taught? As far as she or the Halls of Law were aware, none of the Imperial mages could heal.

"Can you ask Serralyn to look something up in the library for me? Or ask the Arbiters to search?"

"What do you want her to look for?"

"Information about mages who heal. Or healers. I don't want to know about healing done by the Chosen in any iteration—just . . . all the other healers, if there are records." She rose. "I can't reach him here, and my cheek is bleeding, and I'll defer the attempt to cause a *very minor* injury from here. I mean, clearly major injuries *can* be caused, or Terrano wouldn't have been in so much trouble.

"But Terrano waited where he was because he was afraid of what he might drag back."

Mandoran shook his head. "I understand you believe that—and it was probably a good idea—but he did *try* to evade by sidestepping. He couldn't. I'll take us back—it might be a bit bumpy."

Mandoran looked at Nightshade's hand, or at Kaylin's hand. The two weren't separate. "What happens if you let his hand go here?"

"Should I try?"

Mandoran nodded.

Kaylin released Nightshade's hand. Nothing changed. He remained visible—at least to Kaylin. "Can you still see him?"

"He's still here," Mandoran replied. "And yes, as you've guessed, he shouldn't be." He exhaled. "Annarion's worried—but this is a better worry. Terrano's right—we don't know enough. Knowing more means we have to take calculated risks."

"Does Terrano strike you as the type of person who can calculate anything?"

In the darkness, Mandoran's grin felt bright. "He didn't appreciate that question."

"He can't really argue with it, can he?"

"He's not trying." Mandoran's expression darkened. "We have to go back. Terrano's making noise, and he's arguing with not only Helen but Sedarias. I can barely hear myself think." He grimaced. ". . . Sedarias said I can't hear myself think because I hardly ever do."

Kaylin thought this was unfair. Mandoran and Terrano appeared similar in their approaches to their lives, but Mandoran was far more aware of other people, and the way his actions might affect them. Terrano was almost entirely without malice—but so were tidal waves and earthquakes. "Is Teela joining in?"

"No. But that's also causing a bit of friction. We all know she went with you to the Consort; we don't know what was actually discussed. Sedarias is making guesses—but Teela is the only one of us who's good at shutting people out. We're terrible at it; we never felt a need to do so." He winced. "Teela is now telling Sedarias to leave you alone. Meaning: don't bother Kaylin. Helen has just joined the discussion."

"Is it really a discussion?"

"Barely."

"Are you sure we should go back right now?"

"Annarion isn't part of the fracas. He's listening with half an ear. He trusts that if the Consort's discussion was relevant—somehow—to his brother, you'll do everything you can to act on it. It's better if you close your eyes."

"I can't afford to miss anything that might give us a bit more information about the current situation." She kept her eyes on Nightshade the entire time. Not on herself, not on Hope—although technically he was closest to her because his wing covered her eyes—but on Nightshade.

Mandoran began to move her out of the space they now occupied. It wasn't seamless; she could see the jerkiness of the movement in the way Nightshade's unconscious body flickered briefly around the edges. Her Marks remained steady, a golden light that implied warmth in a darkness that radiated cold. She could feel the air shift across her skin.

"Could you tell Serralyn it's an emergency?"

"She already knows. She says there's a bit of a line to visit the library because the library has been shut down a number of times in recent days. But she's working on it. If you've got other questions, it's best to ask them now."

To Kaylin's surprise, it wasn't noisy in the room; it was dead silent. Annarion was seated beside her—and he had an arm around her shoulder, as if expecting her to fall.

The sad thing was, she almost did. She felt as if she'd suddenly been dropped; it wasn't the type of fall that could kill her, but it did cause the butterfly-in-stomach feeling of a longer than safe drop.

"Sorry," Mandoran said, as if he, too, felt like he was falling, even though they were on solid ground. "It was harder to concentrate because *some people* can't *shut up* and let me think!"

Annarion winced and turned fully toward Kaylin. "Your cheek is bleeding." His eyes were a dark, dark blue, and anger had joined the worry that had been a rigid mask since Nightshade had arrived.

Right. Her cheek. "Is it the Erenne mark?"

"You really don't know how to choose your words, do you?" Mandoran said, but he turned toward Sedarias and Teela, who stood in the outer room, glaring at each other. Sedarias had Terrano's arm in a tight grip, as if she expected him to flee without warning before she'd finished. Fair enough. Kaylin expected the same.

"The Erenne mark didn't exist on the path we moved to," Kaylin told Annarion. She understood that the mark underpinned his bitter disappointment with his brother, but it didn't matter. The mark existed, now. Neither of them could change the past. And it was a clue, a link, between Annarion's brother and Kaylin, because the namebond *didn't work.*

Annarion stood on the edge between disgust and desperation. Kaylin's words pushed him over, to the right side. "It wasn't there?"

"Mandoran couldn't see it. But my cheek was bleeding, regardless. It didn't hurt. I couldn't feel it. But . . . the blood that fell here, fell there."

Annarion nodded. "You think there's a connection."

"I think the Erenne mark *isn't* based around True Words, True Names. But the Barrani don't wake at birth without their Names. Look, I sort of understand why the Erenne mark upsets you so much. And I get that maybe, because I didn't understand how they were used historically, it didn't upset me."

"It didn't upset you because you didn't want to die." Annarion's tone was flat. "You would have accepted it because you didn't think you had any other choice."

"Does it matter? It's on *my* cheek. I didn't understand what it would mean to the Barrani until the Barrani Hawks saw it."

"They were unhappy?"

"Teela was *furious*. The rest of the Hawks were just outraged. But I don't think their outrage would lead to a concerted attack by a couple of war bands."

"It didn't," Annarion said, voice soft. "Maybe it's because you didn't know—but I can't understand your lack of anger."

"It's saved my life," she said, her voice as soft as Annarion's. "I don't live in the fief anymore. I'm not living at the whim of hunting Ferals and Nightshade's thugs. I have enough to eat. I have a roof over my head—and it's a better roof, or at least a safer one, than my first apartment. I have a job I love. I . . . haven't really thought about Nightshade very much for a while now. And when I do, there's not a lot of anger unless I start comparing his rulership of Nightshade with Tiamaris's rule of Tiamaris."

"Then you're angry?"

"I don't think I would have lived such a desperate, miserable life if I'd been an orphan in Tiamaris—and the fief of Barren was worse than Nightshade when I first arrived. It made me understand that those streets, that near starvation, the possibility of becoming just another meal for Ferals—those were all *choices*. I mean, Nightshade and Barren didn't *release* the Ferals, but they made no plans to protect their citizens from them, either.

"They didn't care if the buildings in the fief were run-down and dangerous; they didn't care if people came to prey on those too helpless to defend themselves. When I was in those streets, I didn't *expect* anyone to care, either. I knew that I had nothing—and people with nothing have to figure out a way to fight, or cheat, or steal, to survive.

"That was just the way it was. It didn't occur to me that it didn't have to be that way until I made it across the Ablayne.

Until I joined the Hawks. Even then, I thought the fiefs were just different—I knew they weren't considered a part of the empire. But Tiamaris *is* a fieflord, and his fief is nothing like Barren's.

"The things I'm angry about—when I think about them at all—are things like that. I think about the life I could have had. Would I have been guaranteed to be safe? Hells no. If people were trustworthy all the time, we wouldn't need Hawks. But it would have been *better.* And I don't want to get angry with the cohort because, except for Sedarias, none of you—who were fed, and safe from weather and Ferals and pimps—had a choice, either.

"But until you had no choice—" No. This wasn't the time or place. "Look, I don't want helplessness and misery to become a competitive sport, okay? I do resent the life I lived after my mother died. But I *hate* the choices *I made* far more than anyone else's. I hate the fief because I felt I could justify choices that . . . aren't justifiable. They just aren't. They're *understandable.* But . . . I hate that I made them.

"And that's not on your brother. But if I could demand *one thing* from him, it would be that he view the citizens of his fief as actual people."

"What makes you think he doesn't?"

"Did I not just tell you?"

Annarion seemed genuinely confused. It was Mandoran who came to his rescue. Or Kaylin's rescue; it wasn't entirely clear.

"You know what Barrani consider political, right?"

She nodded. She was looking at the results of that.

"Barrani tend to view people as enemies, allies, or entirely irrelevant. The people in his fief couldn't rise to the level of enemy, and they had no useful power, so they couldn't be considered allies. They were invisible because they were powerless; they weren't a threat. The idea that one protects the helpless and powerless does exist—but you hate it."

"I don't—"

"You hate the statuary. Some mortals like cats. Mrs. Erickson likes them. But they do not think of their cats as equals."

Kaylin, having seen cat owners in the office, could have argued the point, but didn't.

"If you wish Nightshade to understand the changes Tiamaris has made, you will need to convince him that those people have value *as* people. And you will come up against the Barrani culture, over and over again."

"You disagree with me?"

Mandoran shook his head. "I don't. But I don't see people as inherently precious, either. Nor do most of the mortals I've met who have actual power. Maybe it's just the nature of power. Those who have it. Those who don't. We strive for power—well, most of us—because it's only when we *have* power that we have relative safety.

"Even Teela."

Kaylin looked up. "But I didn't even know Teela was a Lord of the High Court. For years. She protects me because we're friends—but being a Hawk isn't about your friends or even your enemies. It's supposed to be even-handed. It's supposed to be about the law."

"Well, it's run by *people*. It's never going to be perfect."

"Does that mean we shouldn't try?"

"Mandoran," Annarion said. Mandoran fell silent. Annarion exhaled. "To those who have pledged allegiance to my brother, he is a good lord. Ask Andellen. But the people of the fiefs make no pledge to him; he makes no pledge to them. He protects the fief over which his Tower presides. *That's* his responsibility."

". . . and finding you." Kaylin's voice was soft.

Annarion's expression crumpled.

15

"He never mentioned me, did he?"

Kaylin shook her head. She exhaled slowly, considering the fractured familial relationship between the older and younger brother. She understood that Annarion had always looked up to Nightshade. The Erenne mark had broken that, even if Kaylin accepted it and forgot its existence most days.

What would Nightshade do to find and free his brother?

Glancing at the unconscious fieflord, she thought the actual answer was *anything.* Anything at all. He cared enough about Annarion that Annarion's fury, his anger, his unfortunate accident in Castle Nightshade could all be forgiven. Easily forgiven. He demanded none of the respect that Barrani seemed to demand from their relatives.

He was pained by Annarion's anger. Andellen had made that clear.

He had loved, and still loved, Annarion.

"He couldn't talk about you, could he?" Annarion frowned as she continued, "He's outcaste. You aren't. You were a victim. You were sent to be lost to the green—or empowered by it. You could return—if you could be saved—to your people. You could still *be* Barrani."

"He destroyed much of our family line."

Kaylin shrugged. "Teela destroyed all of hers. But her family was murdered by other parts of her family. Nightshade was probably thinking far enough ahead that he wished to preserve whatever life you might have among your own people. He certainly didn't expect the cohort—but I don't think anyone did. Except Teela.

"I'm not Nightshade's family. But I think, sometimes, that the Erenne mark was a symbol of ownership *because* it conveyed—to people who understood what it meant—protection or at least consequences. Not that that would stop Barrani from trying to murder me, but they'd be less likely to do it casually.

"And I think he thought—for reasons that aren't clear—that I might be *useful*."

"Useful?"

"You're free of the Hallionne, aren't you? And you're here. And you're now a Lord of the High Court."

Annarion swallowed.

Kaylin winced at his expression. "I'm not saying it's your fault. It's not like you told him to rescue you. It's not like you were trying to take advantage of him—" She stopped. She understood some part of his guilt, and she wasn't making it any better by talking. Not like this. She shook herself mentally.

"I've asked Serralyn—"

"I know."

"But the fact that I was bleeding, and the fact that the Erenne mark wasn't actually present, must mean something. I couldn't heal Nightshade—not the normal way. But I don't think that *is* the only way, now. I don't quite understand yet, but I'm working on it. Ummm, Mandoran?"

"Yes?"

"When you said ask any questions that I have as soon as possible, could you add one?"

"Sure."

"Everything about how the Erenne mark *functions*. Not its

social significance—I think I understand that pretty well right now. But . . . how it works."

Annarion froze.

Mandoran's hand found his friend's shoulder. "She's right. You know it. This might be the only pathway forward if we're going to save your brother. She's not angry about it. We understand why you are—you'll never know how much we envied you."

Kaylin almost snorted. How could he *not* know?

"We envy you, even now. We understand *why* you were—and are—so angry, but if we're being honest, Kaylin's anger would make more sense. He did everything in his power to retrieve you *before* the *regalia.* And he did everything he could to save you after it. Most of our families just treated us like we were dead. Except for Sedarias's family—she's on the opposite end of the spectrum.

"Nightshade clearly never forgot you. You were the *only* family he cared about. Who wouldn't want that?"

Kaylin could think of a few people . . . but in the end, she wasn't one of them.

Annarion closed his eyes. "You didn't know what he was like," he said, his voice soft. "You didn't know what he was like to his people."

She did, but clearly the definition of *his people* was markedly different for Annarion.

"I just don't understand how he could become what he's become."

. . . or maybe not.

Kaylin could understand it. Maybe that's why, in the end, her anger at the Erenne mark was missing. She'd been confused, sure. But it was clear that the fieflord was so far above her, even in the mean streets of the fiefs, that anger hadn't been a possible response.

"Yes, he's changed. He was a war hero. He is an outcaste.

But Barrani outcastes are largely political; there's every chance in the future that status could change. And if it does, if he can come out of the fiefs in safety, maybe other things will change too.

"You believe that, or you probably wouldn't be so angry."

Annarion was silent. "We owe you our lives," he finally said. "Are you *certain* you're all right with this?"

She shrugged, a fief shrug. "Nothing can change if he doesn't recover." That seemed neutral enough.

It was more than neutral to Annarion. "You're right. Thanks." He used the Elantran word.

"Dinner is ready," Helen said, materializing in the room. "I have noticed no change in Nightshade, but I paid careful attention to your transition from your plane of existence to the problematic one. I do not believe that attackers traveling in that space could successfully breach my barriers."

Something in the phrasing caused Kaylin to turn in her chair. "Do you think this is the path used by the Barrani who attacked Nightshade?"

"It is an excellent question, but as I am not responsible for that attack, I cannot answer it."

"I asked what you *think*."

"I think it is a distinct possibility—but you said two war bands were involved. If they traveled through that path, it means someone like Mandoran was involved—or some kind of portal through which normal Barrani could pass has been constructed."

"Teela's been investigating," Annarion said, his gaze still on his brother's sleeping face. "She's been searching for sightings of the war band, because Helen's right. That number of people would be far too hard to miss. Unless they live in the fiefs, traveling through Elantra would have caused a stir. There were no reports of war bands filed with the Hawks' public desk."

None of this had immediately occurred to Kaylin. Teela,

however, was right. Kaylin, who had done front desk shifts many times, knew that a small army of Barrani would cause panic, and that panic would inflate their numbers—and their statures. There was no road such a band could travel that wouldn't cause that kind of ripple.

"There are only two ways they could travel. They didn't travel as a group through the city streets—even I would have heard about that. But they could have traveled in ones and twos across the Ablayne, and met somewhere in the fiefs that wouldn't draw as much attention—or rather, *our* attention. Approaching any fief would—but if they immediately entered the border zone as individuals, the Towers wouldn't be able to track them."

"I believe that is Teela's thinking as well. There were far too many Barrani, armed, armored, and even crested, to have arrived there *as* full bands. But if they arrived over a period of time, they could gather in the border zones. It's clear from the attack on both Nightshade and Terrano that the border zones are in use."

They'd always been in use by the extremely desperate. People fled there. Kaylin had done so when she'd fled the fief of Nightshade. What she knew about the border zone was limited; it was not a fixed size, a fixed shape. Buildings—such as the building Bellusdeo had burned down—were both in better repair than their fief analogs, and subject to change.

But she knew that there was power in the border zones, that the Towers were somehow aware of their existence—as if they were buffers to prevent clashes between the captains of different Towers. The Academia had been hidden, and kept in stasis, in the border zone.

What else might reside there?

If the war bands chose to gather there, to live there, it would be fairly simple to supply them with food—and Barrani didn't need sleep, so bedding and tenting would be far less relevant.

Delivering supplies could be done by one person. It could be done by Terrano. He'd complain a lot, but for Terrano—or Mandoran—it wouldn't be a problem.

But they existed as they were because of the *regalia* and their subsequent centuries-long imprisonment within Hallionne Alsanis. The *regalia* had changed them. But even changed, this strange walking of planes wasn't something that all the cohort did. It was something, if pressed, they could all do—in theory.

What changes could be made, what subtle alterations that would allow a so-called normal Barrani to make the same side steps and walk the same paths?

"I have a headache," she said, rising.

"As I said, dinner is ready. And you know that lack of food causes both headaches and unnecessary tension. Come eat. Mrs. Erickson means to join you for dinner."

Kaylin tried to force her shoulders into their normal position; she felt as if they were bunched up around her ears by this point. "That would be great. I hate eating in the High Halls."

"You generally don't eat if you are enmeshed in emergencies—and it is far too easy for everything to feel like an emergency when you are both tired and hungry."

Kaylin glanced once at Nightshade. She thought of the Consort, the Lake, and Yvonne. "But Helen . . . everything *is* an emergency."

Severn joined Kaylin for dinner. Teela did not. Sedarias and Teela were either arguing or planning—or both. Mandoran came to the table, and Fallessian joined them as well. He was one of the twelve about whom Kaylin knew very little. But he seemed to like Mrs. Erickson, against all expectations. Had he been human—had any of the cohort been human—Kaylin would have expected it; the Hawks had become fond of Mrs. Erickson and her daily visits. Especially her edible bribes.

"That is an unfortunate word," Helen said.

"It's an affectionate word. I just wouldn't have expected Barrani to like her."

"When they don't like you, you mean?"

Chagrined, Kaylin nodded. It was true. Fallessian had been a quasi-tenant, but he'd avoided any interaction with Kaylin unless Sedarias had called for a dinner meeting with all hands on deck. But he sought out Mrs. Erickson and even offered to help her in the kitchen—as if baking was a skill he really wanted to learn.

"Serralyn would like you to drop by the Academia at your earliest convenience."

"Does that mean, like, tomorrow, or is this a *right now* situation?"

"It's now," a cheerful—and invisible—Terrano said. "But she wants you to eat first."

"I think it would be better for all concerned if Kaylin visited tomorrow. She has been a touch short on sleep as well as food," Helen said in her most severe voice.

"Nightshade is one of the concerns," Terrano pointed out.

"She cannot heal him now, and lack of sleep will not increase her chances. Tomorrow would be *preferable*."

Kaylin said nothing. Her stomach didn't growl—but that was because Helen was right. She existed in a state of emergency, and food had negative appeal. But she could eat far worse food in far worse conditions. Dinner was probably the smart option. And if Teela and Sedarias were holed up somewhere, it would be a little bit more relaxed than it could have been.

Mandoran was already seated. Fallessian was not; he carried a large tray, walking two steps behind Mrs. Erickson, whose walking speed had never been fast. Torrisant was seated, and to Kaylin's surprise, Karian was also seated. Karian, of the cohort, was the most invisible member. He came at Sedarias's command—or request—and left when she left.

He didn't speak much. He did participate in the cohort's infrequent puppy piles, as Kaylin called them; he seemed to like the physical contact with his chosen kin. But he had none of Mandoran's warmth or Terrano's inherent chaos. His eyes were blue; he had taken the seat beside Torrisant.

Severn had taken the seat beside Kaylin.

"If you're just going to hover," Kaylin snapped at Terrano, "you could at least join us. It's not like Sedarias doesn't know where you are."

"I've been testing something," Terrano replied, becoming visible.

"What, exactly, are you testing?"

"Helen's defenses. She knows where I am—of course she does—but we're trying to see if I can remain physically unseen."

"How's that working out for you?"

He flopped gracelessly into the chair on Kaylin's other side. "We *want* to make sure she can see all intruders, so it's working out pretty well so far. But she's aware that my thoughts are a loud, screaming beacon, and she may be relying on them a bit too much."

"You're not afraid that people will try to come and attack Nightshade while he's here, are you?"

"Not Nightshade specifically, no. Any of us. You, even."

Mandoran snorted. "It's you, of course. You won't talk about the Consort. But you *have* talked about your experiences with the Lake. It's not hard for people as suspicious as Sedarias to put two and two together and arrive at a very precise four. She *is* worried about Nightshade, because of Annarion. But without you, we've got no home. We're here because you're Helen's tenant. But you're her tenant until you die. When you do, she'll find a new tenant—and the new tenant isn't likely to want a bunch of Barrani as permanent guests."

So it wasn't actually about Kaylin's safety.

"And if you die because of this, Teela will murder half of us," he added, with a cheeky grin that was close to Terrano's norm. "Teela's almost certain you're right: the warriors didn't descend on Nightshade all at once. Which means this has been planned for some time."

"They'd have needed two war bands to bring him down." But was that true? Just one man, with a poison dart or an ability to convey a poisonous magic, would have been enough. It wasn't the fight that had laid him low; it wasn't the battle that had put him into this suspended, unreachable state.

Kaylin frowned. "Helen?"

"Yes, dear."

She got up as Mrs. Erickson reached the table and pulled out the chair meant for the older woman. Fallessian would have done it, but his hands were full of dinner.

"Do things persist between planes? I mean—if I find a book in one of them, can I bring it here?"

"Yes, if the book was created here. Many sorcerers of old were reputed to place their research notes and books in alternate dimensions."

"Are those alternate dimensions similar to what Terrano does? I mean—do they exist as spaces adjacent to our plane, or are they part of our plane, just . . . pockets?"

"That is an excellent question," Helen said with genuine approval.

"If a poison could be concocted—magically—in a world or place with slightly different rules, could its effects extend?"

"Yes—that is what we would expect. The body itself is part of our world, and the injuries sustained on that body would therefore be part of our world."

"Every time Mandoran has pulled me to safety by taking me one half step outside of our world, my Marks were visible. Even in the path that we took to reach Terrano so I could heal him, I could see them."

Helen nodded, frowning.

"If they weren't attached to me, do you think they'd be active at all?"

"That is a question for the Arbiters," Helen replied after much thought. "But what makes you ask that?"

"I couldn't reach Nightshade on the other plane. But . . . the cohort could clearly speak with each other through the namebond. I could see the Marks of the Chosen. I'm asking questions as they occur to me because all we've got are questions, and it's only when we start asking the right ones that we might reach answers."

"Serralyn agrees. Loudly and emphatically. I know it's been a long day—but if you were willing to head to the Academia, the Arbiters are available."

"Will they be available tomorrow?" Kaylin asked. She could see Helen's eyes were now obsidian.

"Student hours—and professor hours—are like office hours: they end at dinner. Exceptions can be made for the chancellor in emergencies."

"Do they consider this an emergency?"

Mandoran glanced across the table at Fallessian. "Bellusdeo does."

". . . is she there?"

"No—but she was there, and she wasn't subtle or quiet about her visit. You might remember that she ran into us when we were in attempted pursuit of Lord Nightshade's attackers?"

Kaylin nodded.

"Well, she's not happy about the use of the border zone—at this point, she's not happy with its existence. Apparently, her own Tower didn't have satisfactory answers, so she headed to the Academia to speak with the chancellor."

"She's not still there, though." Ugh. "You know Hawks are trained in a number of things. Basic weapon skills. Endurance in case we have to give chase. Investigation of crime scenes. Speaking to witnesses when we want answers. Handling evidence.

"Self-defense. And right now, I really, really want to punch someone."

"Mandoran," Helen said, the word slightly edged. "Kaylin is not Barrani. She needs sleep. I will inform your sergeant that you will be working for the Dragon Court—in the morning."

An argument seemed to be brewing within the cohort when Kaylin finished eating and left the table. She therefore finished eating quickly. If she slept, she could wake up early; if she argued, given Helen's expression, she was likely to lose, in which case she'd go to bed later, and rehash the argument.

She knew when to surrender. But was now really the time?

"Yes," Helen said.

Sleep was broken, but not by external noise. If the cohort had argued their way through to morning, they kept it to themselves. Had Nightshade worsened, she was certain she'd know. Helen might demand that the cohort let her sleep, but she wouldn't forbid them from interrupting that sleep in an emergency.

Then again, everything felt like an emergency right now.

Kaylin swung her legs out of bed, fumbling in the dark before Helen brought the lights up and she could see her way to her clothing. She dressed in her normal work clothing, took enough care to make sure the buttons and buttonholes weren't mismatched, and headed down the stairs. Hope grumbled but allowed himself to be picked up and dumped on her shoulders.

Mandoran was waiting for her in the foyer. Terrano was with him, and to her surprise, Fallessian was also present.

There was no sign of Sedarias or Teela, no sign of Torrisant or Karian.

"We've all got wicked headaches," Terrano said as Kaylin opened her mouth. "We'd appreciate if you didn't add to them. In case it's not obvious, we're going to the Academia with you. If you don't want us, Sedarias and Teela will accompany you instead."

"That's probably the best threat I've ever heard you make," she told Terrano.

"It's not making my headache any better," he replied—but he smiled and winced at the same time.

Kaylin didn't want to argue with the cohort. If Sedarias and Teela were in agreement, she had three of the cohort as escort. Helen *could* keep them in the house, allowing Kaylin to escape, but it wouldn't last. The attempt was the last thing Annarion needed.

"We're to avoid the border zone," Terrano said.

"The border doesn't lead to the Academia." She frowned. "The streets that lead to the Academia are solid; they're not border-tinged. And in theory we can get to the Academia from any of the fiefs—using non-border streets."

Terrano nodded in confirmation, as if he'd checked this personally. He probably had.

"Does that make any sense to you? I mean, the Academia exists in the fiefs—but how does it exist? It's geographically almost impossible. If we tried to place it on a normal map, it would sit across two of the fiefs—and it doesn't. If we don't take the streets designated as Academia streets, we'd never reach it at all. We'd hit the border zone, and we'd cross it into the next fief.

"Seriously, you guys aren't the only ones with wicked headaches. Let's go. I'm sure Serralyn is waiting for us."

"She is—but so are the Arbiters. Serralyn says they're *very* concerned."

Kaylin glanced at Mandoran. "Why are some days like this?"

Mandoran shrugged. "Nightshade is alive. The Arbiters may

have useful information. A bad day is what we reach if none of those things remain true."

". . . meaning I'm whining again."

"You are," Terrano said, far more cheerfully. The front door opened. "I personally think a little bit of whining is good for you. I mean, it works wonders for me."

Mandoran rolled his eyes behind Terrano's back, not that that hid anything.

Severn stood in the open door. He looked more awake than Kaylin felt—but she'd always hated mornings.

Helen's disembodied voice said, "There were incoming messages while you slept."

Kaylin froze on the threshold. "Are any of them from the midwives' guild or the foundling hall?"

"No. There are no emergencies from either quarter."

"Then who?"

"The new Arkon, the new Arkon again, the former Arkon. And one that is new to me. The messages will wait. I have informed all but the last one that you are not in residence at the moment."

"Who is—or was—the last one?"

"It is not the Consort, if that is your concern. I do not believe she trusts the mirror network—and I approve of her suspicion."

"Helen?"

"An'Tellarus," Helen replied. "Now, please, hurry. The sooner you leave, the sooner you'll return."

Kaylin's head was less quiet the moment she crossed Helen's property line.

She expected Ynpharion's intrusion. Given the Consort's current problem, he wasn't going to be absent until the situation was resolved—one way or another. Nightshade was so unconscious she couldn't read him through the namebond, which meant he couldn't reach her.

But a voice she almost *never* heard reached out to her.

Kyuthe. Lirienne. Lord of the West March. *My sister seems extremely troubled, and the comfort I can offer from the distance of my home is too weak to be effective. Tell me what troubles her.*

There was command in the words, but he didn't push it. She held his name, not the other way around.

But she held his name, as she held Nightshade's, with his explicit permission. She hadn't taken the name because of her superior will or power.

I can't talk about the Consort without her permission, she finally said. *I'm sure she'd talk to you if she could.* She guessed that the Consort couldn't. If the Consort's condition was like Nightshade's, any namebonds would be useless. *Lord Nightshade was almost assassinated. Someone sent two full war bands into the fiefs to assassinate him.*

And they did not succeed.

Not yet—they came close. The Consort isn't happy about it.

No. She would not be. Very well. Where are you going?

She was fairly certain he knew, because he, like Ynpharion or Nightshade, could listen in if he so chose, but answered anyway. *The Academia.*

Silence. Kaylin thought he'd gone away again, but when he spoke there was a hush around the word that implied respect. No, more than that. *The Academia. So it is true that it has arisen from the distant historical ash.*

Yes.

I would like to see it myself.

I think that can easily be arranged. Have you spoken to your brother at all?

No. He, too, has been silent about the current troubles.

He said no more, and she was painfully aware that his, the lightest touch of all her namebonds, was possibly the strongest.

If he turned his attention to Kaylin, and to her life here, he would know almost as much as she knew.

"How does Teela manage to keep anything secret from the rest of you?" She poked Mandoran. He'd taken up position to her right; Severn walked to her left. Fallessian and Terrano had gone ahead to scout. Kaylin wasn't expecting trouble—they were entering the fiefs through Tiamaris.

But it was in the border zone between Nightshade and Tiamaris that the brunt of the attack had taken place, so maybe she wasn't paranoid enough.

"She can mask her thoughts from Helen as well," Mandoran replied. "She mostly doesn't cut us off—but can, if she thinks it's necessary."

"And she'd think it's necessary if it's something that might endanger any of you."

"Pretty much. I probably don't need to tell you just how offensive Sedarias finds this. Condescension is supposed to go one way—from Sedarias *to* someone else."

"It's not condescension—" Kaylin cut off the rest of her own sentence.

"You can't even say it."

"Teela frustrates me as well. But . . . it's different for me."

"How so?"

"I'm mortal. Teela is Barrani. She took me under wing when I first arrived at the Halls of Law. She thought I was reckless and way too emotional."

"And you weren't?"

Kaylin's laugh was bitter. "Oh, I absolutely was. I was reckless and angry and almost suicidal. I didn't think my life mattered. No, it's more than that. I thought I didn't deserve to live. I didn't deserve to *judge*. Who was I to judge others for their actions? Who was I to *arrest* them?

"Teela made it clear that if I served the Laws, I could get answers to that. But to do that, I had to believe in them, and I had to carry them out. But . . . it made sense to me that she'd be condescending. She was Barrani. She was Immortal. She'd lived for centuries. She'd fought in wars. Barrani aren't known for being mindful of Imperial Laws. They don't have to be, as long as they're only attacking each other.

"But Teela upheld Imperial Law. She trained me in rudimentary combat; she drilled every word of the law into my head. And she invited—well, commanded, really—me to consider what our world *could* be like if people respected those laws. You have to understand—I was a child. Teela was an adult, to me. It's like she knew everything in the world worth knowing."

"Well, Sedarias has lost her appetite, and you've managed to embarrass—and amuse—Teela."

"Well, so she *was* condescending, but . . . I guess I felt the difference between us was just so huge, it seemed natural?"

"I think you should stop there. Sedarias hasn't lost her temper. Yet."

Kaylin winced. "Can we go back to Teela keeping her thoughts to herself?"

"Teela says you should ask Severn, because he's both human and capable of doing what you can't."

Kaylin glared at Severn.

"Do thank Teela for me," Severn said, the corners of his lips slightly curved in amusement.

"If it's any help, most of us are terrible at hiding our thoughts. Terrano is practically a continuous shout. But Teela wants to know exactly why you're asking."

Since she couldn't—or shouldn't—answer that, she fell silent as they walked. But she finally said, "Tell Teela that I think the Lord of the West March is coming to visit."

Mandoran drew a sharp breath. "She asks when."

Lirienne? You're coming to the High Halls, aren't you?

He was amused. *As you surmise, yes.*

When?

A second, far more common, voice interrupted her. *Kaylin, the Consort bids me to tell you that she has a very unexpected guest. The High Halls is noisy with his arrival.*

Kaylin exhaled. "Tell Teela that the Lord of the West March is arriving about now."

16

"You know—you could have lied. It's not like she wouldn't have found out tomorrow."

"What difference does a day make? She's going to know anyway."

"I *really* wish you could spend time on the inside of our heads right now. You'd never ask that question again."

"But you'd just be putting it off."

"Look, when something is screaming—or is going to scream—in your ear no matter what you say or do, one peaceful day is a blessing."

"It's not peaceful right now anyway. How much worse can it get?" Kaylin frowned. "And why is she upset about it? I mean—he's just visiting his sister."

"You can ask her. Maybe she'll spend her time shouting at you instead of shouting at the rest of us—who, I might point out, had *nothing to do with it*."

"I had nothing to do with it, either!" But she fell silent because it hadn't occurred to her to check. She *knew* the Lord of the West March, the High Lord, and the Consort were close; they cared for each other in a way most Barrani families didn't. If the Consort's ability to tend to her duties was failing, both brothers would be gravely concerned—*for her.*

And Kaylin had a way to check in on one of those brothers and hadn't thought about it at all. The fact that everything else was also exploding wouldn't serve as a good excuse where Teela was concerned. Kaylin wasn't certain it served as a good excuse where she was concerned, either.

She and the Consort had had their disagreements—some of them bitter. Kaylin didn't *want* the Consort angry again, at least not at her. But this was bigger than that. Even if the Consort had continued to refuse to even look in her direction, Kaylin would have done everything she could to help. The future of an entire race was at stake.

Oh. That was why Teela was annoyed. If the Lord of the West March had arrived, without warning, in the High Halls, his presence alone confirmed any rumors that the Consort was having difficulties.

If the Consort lost her ability to wake sleeping Barrani infants, it was Kaylin Neya who would be called in. And she'd go, too.

Yvonne complicated things. There was no proof that Yvonne could step into the Consort's shoes—but there were strong indications that she *could*. That would mean it would be Yvonne, not Kaylin, who'd have to fill in. Yvonne, who had very little high-powered support in the High Halls.

Yvonne, who had some questionable difficulties in her past—enough that Severn could consider them a risk. She didn't know what the risk entailed, but she was certain he wouldn't put the entirety of the future Barrani people in danger. Probably.

Tiamaris came to meet them at the foot of the bridge on his side of the Ablayne. Tara wasn't with him, and his eyes were a dark orange, but he didn't *seem* to be angry. "What are you getting yourself into this time?" On the other hand, his question was aimed directly at Kaylin. He did spare a glance for

Mandoran and Fallessian, but not Terrano, who'd chosen to shed visibility.

Terrano accepted Bellusdeo, but he was never going to be entirely comfortable around Dragons. It was the downside of perfect memory.

"I'm not getting myself into any trouble, and I'm only passing through to get to the Academia."

"I was informed that you would require an escort."

"As you can see, Severn's here. Fallessian and Mandoran are also here. We won't be entering the border zone—we're heading straight to the Academia."

"Tara is concerned." Which meant he was going to tag along no matter what Kaylin said. She accepted it. "She wishes to know what you hope to learn at the Academia."

"It's too complicated to explain in the streets."

"She wishes to know if this means you don't fully understand it yourself."

Once upon a time, Kaylin would have been furious. If Tara were a different person, she might still be furious. But Tara was the heart of the Tower of Tiamaris, and she was often very literal. "I don't. But there's a thing I've learned in the Halls of Law: questions—even the wrong ones—can lead to necessary answers. I don't understand what's happening."

"Does this involve Lord Nightshade?"

Kaylin nodded. "Which is why I'm not supposed to be talking about it."

"Do you intend to speak with the chancellor?"

"Not if I can avoid it, no. I'm going to speak with the Arbiters."

"That is good."

"Why?"

"Because Bellusdeo has practically chosen to camp out in the chancellor's office since the attack in the border zone. Lord

Emmerian has attempted to speak with the chancellor, but he was wary of Bellusdeo's temper."

"She's not at her most reasonable when Shadow is involved. And if Barrani are somehow aligned with Shadow—and it's reasonable to expect some of them are at this point—she's going to care about very little else. I think the people of the world she couldn't save might be like the Barrani in this case: they were somehow infected or allied with Shadow, and failure to recognize that in time was catastrophic.

"I mean, it could be something else, but given Bellusdeo, that would be my guess."

Mandoran added, "Maybe we'll be lucky and Bellusdeo won't be in the chancellor's office."

Be careful what you wish for was a phrase Teela had used a lot in Kaylin's younger years as the Hawks' official mascot. Being mascot was humiliating, but it was, given her age, the only way she could travel with actual Hawks, those being Teela and Tain. In retrospect, there was less humiliation and more nostalgia. Back then, nothing had been her responsibility, and therefore nothing had been her fault.

She'd had the Marks of the Chosen when she'd first ascended the Hawklord's Tower. But she hadn't sworn an oath to the Imperial Law, and she hadn't been given her own beat and her own investigative duties. She'd been the subject of bitter argument, but even that seemed distant and almost blurry: she knew the facts, but the fear and anger of that time were gone. She couldn't return to them, couldn't feel them as viscerally, as completely, as she had when she'd been—at least legally—a child.

She wondered if Barrani memory included the emotions that occurred at the time of the events they could so completely recall.

As it was, Killian met their party at the height of the stairs used by guests and important people—although there was no rule saying students couldn't use them. Kaylin exhaled as it became clear that Killian wasn't alone. Standing beside him was an orange-eyed Bellusdeo.

"Lannagaros told me the Arbiters were expecting you." Her arms were folded, her eyes orange. Flecks of red could be seen from this distance, which wasn't a good sign, but wasn't unexpected, either. "Lord Tiamaris. Are you also expected?"

"Kaylin chooses to approach the Academia through the fief of Tiamaris—my fief, as you are well aware. My Tower worries about her and asked that I make certain Kaylin reached her destination safely."

Bellusdeo considered this. "Very well. I visited Lannagaros with a request that time be made for me in the Arbiters' schedule. He seemed to feel that this would require a few days. Kaylin, however, already *has* an appointment to speak with them."

"Lord Bellusdeo," Killian said, voice very quiet but extremely audible regardless.

"I am not playing games, Killianas."

"No, you are not. But the Arbiters have judged Kaylin's request to be an emergency."

"The Academia fell *because of* Shadow. My concerns and my questions involve *Ravellon*. It is clear that some of the Barrani are actively involved with Shadow. How could my request be considered less of an emergency than Kaylin's?"

"Lord Bellusdeo, you are well aware that such requests are private. The Arbiters do not discuss them without permission from those that have asked for their knowledge. I will ask you to allow Kaylin access to the Arbiters without demanding that you be allowed to attend as well."

Definitely deep flecks of red.

Tiamaris exhaled smoke.

Kaylin was suddenly very grateful that he'd chosen to escort her to the Academia. He, like Bellusdeo, was a Tower captain, a fieflord. His concern about Shadow and its dangers was personal as well.

But he understood—as Bellusdeo should—that the Academia was Lannagaros's hoard. The rules of the Academia, as expressed by the chancellor, weren't wishful thinking on the chancellor's part; they were the laws through which he ruled his domain.

Bellusdeo looked like she would argue, regardless.

No—she looked like she was considering the situation almost tactically. That wasn't the Bellusdeo Kaylin knew. One of the sisters must now be standing in front of the others.

"My apologies, Killianas," this sister now said. "Lord Tiamaris is correct. We would never endanger Lannagaros's hard-won hoard, and we will not treat it with disrespect." It sounded like she was speaking to the Bellusdeo who'd met them at the height of the stairs, but it certainly caused Tiamaris to blink in surprise.

Bellusdeo when she first arrived at the top of the stairs had been the Bellusdeo Kaylin had known since they'd first pulled her from the grip of the Shadows that had taken control of her Ascendant. She had met Logia, the sister involved in magic and research. The person who spoke now was neither of the two.

She wondered, uneasily, if Bellusdeo had control of her own body. Or if it *was* her own body anymore. Bellusdeo had become, in one day, like the cohort—but with nine people, not twelve, and with a single body.

"With your permission, Kaylin, we would be grateful if we could accompany you to the library."

"Normally I'd say yes. I wouldn't care. But this is . . . this is complicated and messy."

"Are you worried for us?" The gold Dragon's smile was slender, sharp, her eyes narrower around red-flecked orange.

"Not you, no." She hesitated and then said, "Which of the sisters am I speaking to right now?"

"Kyrie," she replied without hesitation. "Bellusdeo was not, perhaps, the most patient of our sisters." Her smile, which was genuine, was wry. "She tended to charge ahead, especially when she was angry. Her general rule was punch first, ask questions later. But she was the most martially competent of all of us." Kyrie winced. ". . . in my opinion, of course."

Definitely like the cohort. Kaylin could practically hear the argument on the inside of their head.

"Are you worried?" Kyrie asked, head slightly tilted as she assessed Kaylin.

"I'm used to Bellusdeo."

"Ah. You are concerned that I am here because I have wrested control of her body away from her." It wasn't a question. It was also true. "As you must know, we are not entirely whole. In the past, we would have been a seamless individual with the amassed knowledge and interests of nine distinct fragments. That did not happen for us. What we've achieved is anomalous, according to Logia. We are too distinct; there are nine people, not a unified whole.

"Some argument and discussion have occurred since we became as we are, and a rough consensus has emerged—with Bellusdeo's blessing. We can, if the situation warrants it, step forward. Bellusdeo has not been pushed aside without her consent—but if a majority decide that it would be better to allow a different sister to become spokesperson, she will step aside, agreement or no.

"Not all such decisions are fractious. Logia came to speak with you; Bellusdeo had little interest in the subject or the possible resultant discussion."

"That isn't the case now."

"No. But her grief and rage drive her at times when it would be wiser that they not. As we've pointed out many times, *we* were the ones who died. If our deaths do not motivate us to be enraged and resentful, we do not believe they should affect her that way."

Good luck with that.

Bellusdeo laughed. No, not Bellusdeo—but maybe not Kyrie either. Kaylin didn't know Bellusdeo's sisters well enough to tell them apart. That would come with time, if it came at all. Time, however, was the one thing they were all short on.

"The Arbiters have been looking into things, but not all of their research was done at my request."

Severn stepped forward. "It is, at the moment, more personal in nature, and it involves Barrani customs. Kaylin is Chosen; what is personal may have follow-on effects." All of this was a lie, in Kaylin's opinion.

The cohort are your family, Severn said, his expression unchanging. *Family matters are considered personal.*

Still lying.

"However," Severn continued, "I'm certain if Shadow is found to be involved, your expertise and experience—"

"Dying to Shadow?" This was definitely not Kyrie. The tone was way too amused for that.

Severn didn't even blink. "Yes. Most of our investigations take place after the fact of death. We can't usually interrogate the dead, who would otherwise be the most salient witnesses."

"Bellusdeo isn't happy you just said that."

Severn offered whichever sister it was a fief shrug.

"You're a lot braver than you look." The sister grinned. "I'm Mezanne, by the way. I only come out when everyone else has given up in frustration."

"When Bellusdeo is frustrated, she breaks things."

"That's not all she does. But this is Lannagaros's hoard. She won't break things here."

Kaylin knew she wouldn't *plan* to break things. Or burn them down.

"Mezanne," Killian said, bowing. "We are expected."

"I'm just going to keep you company." She frowned, walked down the stairs, and pulled Terrano out of thin air. Terrano's eyes were wide with shock.

Mezanne laughed. "You and I are going to get along *just fine.* I'm keeping you all company," she added. "Bellusdeo insisted on at least that much. How did she put it? Oh. Keep Terrano out of trouble. You're Terrano, right?"

"How did you *see me*?"

"What, were you trying to stay hidden?" Her grin deepened. Kaylin had never seen that expression on Bellusdeo's face before. "Hiding is my area of expertise."

"You're a Dragon—how much hiding did you have to do?"

"A lot if we wanted to sneak out. I mean—everyone guarding us was an adult Dragon."

Terrano nodded as if this made sense, and the blue of his eyes lightened without dipping into green.

Mezanne frowned and turned to Mandoran. "Apparently you don't cause the same kind of problems this one does." She jerked a thumb in Terrano's direction. "I think Bellusdeo actually likes you. Given your race, we wouldn't have expected that."

Mandoran said nothing. His expression was as reserved as Tiamaris's. Tiamaris, however, was irritated, given the color of his eyes.

Killianas patiently gathered everyone and led them into the building.

Mezanne wasn't particularly quiet; she certainly wasn't reserved. She let Terrano go, but Terrano chose not to sidestep the way he usually did. Mezanne had clearly seen him. Kaylin wanted to know how, but didn't want to ask right now; Mezanne appeared to be in a good mood, which Bellusdeo had definitely not been. Happy Dragons were far safer than unhappy Dragons, for everyone concerned.

Serralyn was waiting by the library door—the portal that led to the Arbiters. She wasn't particularly surprised to see Bellusdeo but wouldn't be. She did smile brightly at Fallessian, who had characteristically remained silent throughout the Dragon's various speeches.

Fallessian returned the smile, although his eyes remained a rigid blue.

"We'll be leaving you here," Terrano told Mezanne. His grin was cheeky.

"For now, yes. I'm not like you—at least, not according to Bellusdeo—but I'm a tiny bit more flexible than the rest of my sisters were. Except Logia. Don't trust her with anything too important." Her smile dimmed. "We're different people, but we *all* take Shadow seriously. Bellusdeo is willing to trust Kaylin—but it's taking more effort than it should." To Severn she said, "Remember your promise."

Severn nodded.

Kaylin didn't breathe again until they crossed the portal and arrived in the library proper. Partly that was the nausea of using a portal, and partly relief that Bellusdeo, or Mezanne, or Kyrie, had remained on the other side. Killian never entered the library, and only one of the Arbiters could leave it.

That Arbiter lifted the two legs at the front of its hairy, rounded body and waved them in the group's direction. Serralyn immediately broke away by running toward the Arbiter as if to hug him.

Kaylin understood that Starrante wasn't a spider, but her visceral reaction required thought and will to suppress. She *liked* Starrante. But part of her hindbrain instinctively recoiled at some of his gestures. She wished she could be more like Serralyn or Robin, a student who had learned many of the Wevaran gestures, and treated the Arbiter as a beloved uncle.

She did, however, follow behind Serralyn.

"I hear you have been busy," Starrante said, his voice a crackle of sound around perfectly normal syllables.

"And how," Kaylin replied. "I hear we've been keeping you pretty busy as well."

"Much of the research has been done by Arbiter Androsse."

Ugh. Androsse was the Arbiter Kaylin least liked. He was arrogant, dismissive, and self-important in a way that had always set her teeth on edge. She was respectful because he was powerful, and the library was his domain. Or rather, a third of it.

Androsse and Kavallac didn't get along all that well; it was the Wevaran who played peacemaker. Or maybe Starrante genuinely respected both the Barrani Ancestor and the Dragon. They had all been chosen as Arbiters by the Ancients who had created the bubble in which the library existed, safe from invasion and destruction.

"Serralyn has been in communication with us," Starrante continued. Androsse and Kavallac appeared to be absent—but Kaylin had no doubt they'd show up.

"I believe you asked her a few questions. Understand that inquiries made of the library are personal in nature; unless and until they become a threat to the library itself, they will not be discussed or divulged without permission of the supplicant."

"Supplicant?"

"The person who's asking," Terrano murmured. He clearly didn't like the word, either.

"That said, the presence of Barrani in the border zones, where they seem to be building a very clear line of escape to *Ravellon*, is of grave concern. Your subsequent questions—about healing magic and the Erenne mark—would not normally be bumped to the head of the queue, but Serralyn was persuasive.

"She felt you would not have asked those questions—which

are interesting in their own right—if you did not feel they were at least peripherally connected. Arbiter Androsse will have questions to ask, to better focus the results of his library search."

"He didn't care about the Erenne mark, did he?"

Starrante exhaled. "He did not care *for* it, no. But he considered the arguments made in defense of the question, and he agreed to expand his search to include something he considers trivial." Before Kaylin could speak, he lifted one arm. She waited. "Things that seem trivial to Arbiter Androsse can destroy whole families. What is trivial to us is not trivial to you. The word is not meant as a judgment—but given the situation, it is not entirely unreasonable to feel it might be irrelevant.

"Why did you ask for these two searches?"

"I got involved through Lord Nightshade. Most Immortals can't stand to be healed. They'd literally sooner die. But he was unconscious, and I thought I'd be really careful and just . . . heal him enough that he could wake up."

Starrante nodded.

"That didn't work, though. I couldn't touch him at all. No, I mean, I could touch him—but not with the power of the Marks of the Chosen. My healing powers only came to me when the Marks did, and they were the *only* good thing about having the Marks. But the power didn't reach him at all. It's as if something was in between us, something that protected—or rejected—the power of the Marks."

Starrante's eyes rose—well, some of them. Most remained nestled across his body.

Kaylin had taken time to become comfortable enough that the similarities to smaller arachnids didn't cause an obvious flinch. "You know about namebonds."

One of Starrante's raised eyes narrowed. "Yes. The elder races were less cautious because our names, if perceived, could not be spoken in such a fashion. Arbiter Androsse might choose to reveal his, but long before you could begin to speak the first syllable, you would be dead, if he so chose. Your attempt to begin would merely invite him to dominate you—the bond has always worked both ways. It is a bridge of will and intent.

"But Serralyn said that you could not reach Lord Nightshade through the bond you share."

The bond that Kaylin wasn't ever supposed to speak about. She glanced at Serralyn. Serralyn grinned. "I couldn't."

"But you could reach him—or he you—in some fashion through the Erenne mark?"

Kaylin nodded. "It wasn't in words. It wasn't in actual speech. I knew something was wrong—probably because he knew it. But . . . it made the skin under the mark bleed."

"The reason Arbiter Androsse considers the question about the Erenne mark trivial is its relationship to the political games the Barrani have always played. It is considered in some quarters a slave mark."

Kaylin knew this. She nodded.

"It is a mark that denotes ownership. But *Erenne* was not always a term that denoted that; it denoted a differential in political power. It has been translated—somehow superficially—as *consort* by those who are not Barrani. But some of the earliest extant Barrani literature also makes this so-called mistake. Mortals believe that Immortal memory, Immortal knowledge, is an edifice that cannot be toppled.

"We have perfect memory. What we have seen once, we can recall; it is something that very, very few of your kind can achieve. But wars have destroyed ancient cities; knowledge that was known perfectly has died with the people who knew it.

"In the early days of the Barrani, when they were an infant race, standing in the shadows cast by Arbiter Androsse's people, it was a connection between the Barrani and their Ancestors. What Lord Nightshade gifted you—the secret of his name—could not in like fashion be gifted the Barrani, who were precious to the Arbiter's people. Barrani power was not equal to the acceptance of such a gift; the act of the attempt could destroy the Barrani involved, hollowing them out; they had one word, their True Name. Arbiter Androsse has said that the Barrani have words, and we have sentences.

"That is a simple analogy, and it is somewhat true."

"Somewhat?"

"Arbiter Androsse's people were not crafted—as the Barrani are—from the Lake of Life. They were created by the Ancients, individually, each creation a work of art."

"That is quite enough, Arbiter." Androsse had arrived.

"Then perhaps you would care to explain?" Starrante replied, not bothered at all by the sharpness of Androsse's tone.

"The analogy is sufficient as it is, and I will not waste further time on it. It does not answer Kaylin's research query."

"It does, though," Kaylin said before Starrante could step in. "This is history that none of us—none of my Barrani friends—know. They know the history of the use of that mark, but not the history of its creation."

"Why do you believe it relevant?"

As if he hadn't been listening in the entire time. Kaylin clamped down on her annoyance. Arbiter Androsse was a man of great power who liked certain forms of etiquette because he was accustomed to them. It wasn't personal.

She tried to believe that and failed.

"Love is an impulse and a curse," Androsse said. This didn't surprise Kaylin much, given Androsse's general personality. It did seem to cause a small ripple in the rest of Androsse's audience.

"Why?" It was Serralyn who asked. Her eyes, green, now contained flecks of visible blue; she was annoyed.

"It is for the weak, for the foolish, for those who cannot see the world as it is. Of what use is love? What function or purpose does it serve?" Androsse turned a glare on Starrante, who was still and silent. "Your people did not elevate love; they did not sing of it; they did not create their damnable stories as soporifics for the gullible."

Serralyn tensed.

Starrante placed a limb on her shoulder, the touch gentle but staying. "We did, Arbiter. But the love of the Wevaran is not the love of your kind; it is not instant, and it is not destructive. It is woven, as our power is woven, and it is built over time."

Androsse's eyes narrowed.

Kaylin didn't disagree with Androsse but kept that to herself. What she wanted to know, now, was how love—damnable love, if Androsse's opinion counted—figured into the Erenne mark. Slaves didn't have to be loved. Historically, they had to be marked or branded.

The Barrani liked to go all out. But love? That didn't figure into anything. It wasn't needed. Nightshade hadn't marked her because he loved her. He hadn't created his statuary of living stone because he loved its occupants. But he had done whatever was within his power to save his brother.

Had Kaylin never met the cohort, she might not have believed in that either. But she knew the cohort had envied Annarion his brother. Knew that another brother had almost literally lost his mind and sense of self in *his* attempt to free Eddorian—the only member of the cohort who had chosen to remain in the West March caring for that very brother.

Androsse was glaring at Starrante; Kaylin watched Androsse's face. Androsse didn't bother to hide what he felt. She cleared her throat. "Love existed at the beginning."

"What do *you* know of the beginning?"

"I know what the Keeper knows."

"What the mortal Keeper knows."

"He's lived far longer than most mortals—and it doesn't matter. He's the Keeper. He knows what he knows. The Ancients arose in a form and fashion none of the wise understand. Do you know why?"

Starrante lifted the arm that wasn't on Serralyn's shoulder; if he'd had the usual hands, he'd've had them spread, palms out, telling her to stop.

"Do tell." Androsse turned from Starrante, the full force of his expression now aimed—like a sword—at Kaylin.

"Because they were lonely. They had no words for it. They existed in isolation. They *wanted* company. No," she said as he opened his mouth, "you wouldn't call it love. They wouldn't call it love, either—I don't think they had that word, or words. Words came later. Words that had meanings that were singular and clear.

"Maybe love wasn't a creation of the Ancients—but I think it grew out of the seeds of loneliness and isolation. It was there, in the beginning." Her Marks were glowing softly, as if in agreement. It didn't matter. Try as she might to understand the Marks and their meanings, they weren't all that she was. She knew what she knew and believed what she believed.

Androsse *could* change that—but with words, with well-reasoned arguments. Not with contempt and dismissal. If she'd never managed to walk bearing their weight, she'd've never moved at all.

"Tell me, Arbiter Androsse: why did you become an Arbiter? Were you plucked off the streets in ignorance and dumped in the library?"

Behind her, a Dragon growled. As neither Tiamaris nor Bellusdeo had joined them in the library itself, that growl could only belong to one person: Arbiter Kavallac.

17

Kavallac's voice was somber, and her eyes orange—but they were always orange if she was standing anywhere near Androsse. "We were not randomly chosen, and we were not the only people who applied." She used the Elantran word, not the High Barrani equivalent. High Barrani didn't have an equivalent—just words that implied supplication or pleading from a position of unworthiness.

"The library predates *Ravellon*. It was the sole creation of an Ancient who valued memory. Memory as a concept was, I believe, almost foreign to the Ancients, given the records extant within the library. Immortals are known for perfect memory, perfect recall; the Ancients were not dissimilar.

"But the creation of the library arose because that Ancient understood that even if memory is a constant, it relies on experience. What I see, hear, touch, I remember. But I cannot see, hear, or touch every living thing, cannot therefore be present for every action taken. No more could the Ancients. It was meant to be a repository of things that one could not personally experience, given the time in other endeavors life demands.

"The custodians chosen were those whose beliefs and dedication most closely mirrored the Ancient's intent. We are not the first who have served in these posts, but due to the nature of the changes in the world beyond our doors, we are likely to be the last. There are no Ancients who walk, now. The library's creator cannot choose new Arbiters from among those who are willing to dedicate eternity to the library.

"Inasmuch as I could be said to have a hoard, it is the library. But it is not *mine* in the way that hoards are claimed by Dragons."

Kaylin exhaled. Androsse's eyes were midnight, but he didn't disagree with anything Kavallac had said. This was probably a record for the two Arbiters.

Kavallac turned to Arbiter Androsse. "I'm sorry to have interrupted you, Arbiter Androsse. You were speaking of the Erenne mark and its creation."

He ignored her apology, focusing on Kaylin instead. "Arbiter Kavallac mentions the Dragon's hoard."

Kaylin nodded.

"To Dragons, *that* is the expression of so-called love. The Empire you call home is a Dragon's hoard. But Dragons have become maddened and destructive in their pursuit of their hoard. We have historical records of a time when two Dragons laid claim to the same hoard—to great ruin for all. Do not tell me that that is not love; it *is*. It is the draconic expression of love. Do you not understand that love in the great and ancient can lead, inevitably, to ruin?"

"But you're *here*," Kaylin countered, ignoring Starrante's waving arm. "Kavallac is here. Starrante is here."

"The word you want is *dedication*, perhaps—but the library is not what you came to discuss, and it is not where our efforts have been pointed in order to find answers to your trivial question."

"If it was trivial, the information wouldn't be here," Kaylin countered.

This forced Starrante to clear his throat, or the equivalent of it for Wevaran. "Corporal, allow Arbiter Androsse to return to his explanation of the results of his research. Not all of the information we find is to our liking; Arbiter Androsse—as any living, breathing being—has thoughts and opinions of his own. They do not change our archives; they do color our reactions to what we find therein."

"So . . . he's irritated because love was somehow involved in the creation of the mark?"

Starrante's eye stalks bowed, which Kaylin took to be a nod. "It is a spell, of sorts. It cannot be applied if the person who has chosen to do so has no innate magical power."

"But it can be applied without the permission of the person who bears the mark."

"Demonstrably. Arbiter Androsse?"

"You bear the Marks of the Chosen," Androsse said, tone curt, eyes narrow. "You bear them in ignorance, and it is clear that permission was not sought before they became yours."

Kaylin frowned but nodded.

"You are aware that there are Immortals who feel the nature of their True Names is a shackle, a binding, a limitation."

Kaylin nodded again. She did know. She'd seen the results when Barrani attempted to remove themselves from the True Names that were the source of their life.

"We are far more flexible than the Barrani who bear such a striking physical resemblance. The hands that created my kin—those the Barrani call Ancestors—created the Barrani, as if the Barrani were a refinement, an improvement." There was definitely annoyance in his tone. "My kin could improve upon ourselves, could add words to the sentences that inscribed the start of our existence."

Kaylin's brows rose as she considered the implications of that.

"Yes. You understand. We could empower ourselves, adding words that suited both our purpose and our existence; we could grow, and we could change, becoming more than we had been at our inception. Those changes were not guided by the Ancients, but by ourselves and the experiences that shaped us.

"Among any race, there are those who rise, those who shine, those whose brilliance casts shadows across their kin."

Kaylin nodded.

"Among my kin, in our youth—or perhaps our middle age, for we were not young as even the Barrani might conceive of youth—was one such Ancestor. Did you know that we were not given a racial name? It seemed our creators truly wished for us to flourish as individuals. But could we, we might have claimed kinship with Angrelados, for he was the best of us, even in my own estimation.

"What he wished for was companionship. But his attempt to create the bonds that True Words *can* foster were met, always, with failure, disaster, even betrayal. The power that he had built over time was far too overwhelming. In the best case, knowledge of his name, sight of it, devoured those whose sense of self was not nearly as deeply rooted; they became part of him.

"In the worst case, they attempted to do what Barrani oft do when such vulnerability is offered: control, overwhelm, command. He wished to be met by equals—but there *was no equality.* Only in the case where the foolhardy desired to commune with the Ancients was there greater risk. Even in the absence of the desire to do harm, to cage, to control, the simple difference in power was overwhelming.

"It was a problem Angrelados chose to devote time and knowledge to solving, for the sense of isolation did not leave him. Understand, again, that petty manners, petty etiquette, obscure the truth. Angrelados wanted an equal, a partner—but it was impossible. No attempt to alter his truth, his Name, could change that. Not all of his compatriots were pleased with his choice; they felt his enormous intellect was diverted to something so trivial as to be almost beneath notice.

"But he, as I, chose what was, and was not, beneath his

notice. His interest oft made things interesting; that was his nature."

She frowned.

"With time, with experimentation, he created and perfected a spell that would allow his communion, his connection, with beings of lesser power—or markedly less power. We thought, once he had accomplished this task, he would turn once again to greater mysteries, greater magics.

"He did not."

"What happened to him?"

"That is beyond the remit of your query. What was created could be taught; it was not something that was entirely and only limited to personal use. Angrelados felt that many of us would benefit from a way of interacting, of binding, that did not destroy the precious object."

Object. "Person."

Androsse failed to acknowledge the correction. "The meaning was lost on many. It was considered irrelevant and impractical."

"Impractical?" She could guess at why it would be considered irrelevant.

"Even if it is a minor use of power, it requires power. If one wishes to cherish one's pets, there is no need to waste that power; protecting and caring for them will be done regardless."

"Do not antagonize the Chosen for no reason," Kavallac snapped.

"She bears the Erenne mark. It is a clear indication that Nightshade felt the difference in their power was too great."

But she *also* knew his True Name. "When you say *power*, what do you mean?"

"It is not a simple tattoo; it is not cosmetic. The meaning has been lost to those who use it, if they ever understood it at all."

Kaylin wanted to shriek in frustration. The need to understand *this* part was *why* she'd asked for research to be done at all. "It's the *nature* of the connection that I need to understand. I can't reach Nightshade through our namebond. There's evidence that a similar spell or poison or whatever it is is affecting other Barrani as well. But the Erenne mark is still active. It still bleeds. It still reacts in some way to Nightshade. If I understand *why*, I may be able to heal him."

"And he is your chief concern?"

"What? No, of course not." She thought of the Consort. The Barrani Lake of Life. Annarion. "But he's important in the larger scheme."

Androsse exhaled. "The information you wish to access is not complete. Angrelados kept records of his experiments and their progress; I can give you dates that will have no meaning to anyone in this room. When he was successful, when he knew he was successful, he ceased to experiment."

"But his observations?"

"I have yet to find them, Chosen. Or did you imagine that the entirety of the library is indexed in my mind? I know the books and scrolls that I have personally perused or seen; I do not know those I have yet to examine. There is a way to find information that might be relevant to our search—but if we are not familiar with what we unearth, we are required to actually *read*. Which requires uninterrupted time, if you even understand what that means."

Kaylin's eyes narrowed. She understood that Androsse stood in the seat of his power. The library was enmeshed with his existence. Her upbringing grappled with her current sense of responsibility. She knew better than to offend the powerful. She'd spent half her life desperately trying to be invisible to them, as if her existence in and of itself was a crime worthy of death.

"I understand what it means," she said, forcing herself into High Barrani, a language in which it was harder to accidentally give offense. Speaking a different tongue made her do more thinking and less reacting. "If you cannot locate all of the information about his research, I wish to ask for your personal perspective."

Silence.

"It is clear to me that Angrelados was someone you knew personally." It was a guess, but she was certain of it. Androsse's reactions *were* personal.

If Teela had been allowed into the library, she'd probably be glaring daggers at the side of Kaylin's face. Serralyn's eyes were blue. But they weren't as dark as Fallessian's or Mandoran's.

Careful.

Do you think I'm wrong? she asked her partner.

No. You're definitely right. That's why *you have to be careful.*

"Angrelados achieved what he wanted to achieve," Kaylin continued. She frowned. "He loved the person for whom he created the Erenne mark." It was half a question.

"I told you, love is ridiculous."

All arguments against that had been made; Kaylin didn't start them again. "Sometimes genius is ridiculous, or so I've been told." She let the rest of his words sink in. "The Erenne mark could be used without that affection. Mine was."

"It cannot be used in the absence of attraction, but in the modern world, I am given to understand that it *is* used to denote ownership. Claim. It is a visible deterrent to those who might otherwise cause harm."

"If that was its only function, it would be unnecessary."

"In later eras, it was used to humiliate, when political marriages were far more compulsory. It was meant as a statement."

"We're talking about now."

"It is not used now, present company excepted."

"Yes. I am here as that present company, attempting to understand the nature of the Erenne mark."

"You will be here a very long time. Ancillary records indicating how the Erenne mark was used, and on whom, were included in my search. The bearers of the mark were not of a mind to speak of it; what we have is external—and often deeply dismissive—commentary. The Erenne mark did not convey power. The person who laid the mark did not bear a similar mark; it was not an equal relationship." Androsse exhaled. "If you do not understand what you have heard thus far, I am wasting my time. But let me be clearer: the mark of the Erenne was meant to *protect* the weaker of the partners from the power of the stronger. It was a barrier that allowed communion without the transformative and corrosive effect of power that the weaker partner would otherwise find overwhelming."

Kaylin had never spent time studying history—not the way the Arbiters did. She repented of her disdain. What had she said? *Why should I care what dead people did? I'm barely surviving living people.* If she could have smacked her younger self upside the head, she'd've gone back in time and done it.

"But he wouldn't have needed to *do* that. He wouldn't have needed the mark at all. Without it, the person he wanted to mark would be safe. He built a bridge between himself and his concubine. He meant for the Erenne mark to be used—just . . . safely."

Androsse looked like he'd swallowed broken glass. "He did. But he did not choose to leave written records of when or how that bridge might be used."

"None at all?"

"None."

"And what do you think, then, with your firsthand experience?"

"Kaylin," Starrante said, moving toward her. "That is enough. It is not to speak of our personal lives that we were granted our positions. We may, if we choose—but our personal lives are not the subjects of accepted queries. Students and researchers are free to ask—if far too bold—but we fail none of our duties by refusing to answer."

Androsse turned, not waiting for a response. But he stopped, back still toward Kaylin. "Corporal—you cannot protect the life of the man who marked you with the subtle powers the Erenne mark conveys. It is not possible. If that was your hope, abandon it."

Silence enfolded the group as Androsse vanished.

It was Serralyn who broke it. "You had questions about healing magic and healers—those who didn't bear the Marks of the Chosen."

Kaylin nodded.

Starrante clicked and hissed, the Wevaran equivalent of clearing his throat. "That was the query I undertook. I offered to relieve Arbiter Androsse of his burden, but he declined. The Erenne mark was a spell devised by his kin, not by ours. Arbiter Kavallac has been researching the nature of True Words and the more specific True Names; that was her area of research before she was chosen as Arbiter."

Kaylin inhaled slowly. "Was Androsse friends with Angrelados?"

"*Arbiter* Androsse. And yes, you might say that. If it was not clear, Androsse considers the loss of Angrelados the end of his race, such as it was. His dislike of the Erenne mark stems from that; it was the last great undertaking of an almost mythical being."

"But . . ."

"Yes?"

"If it was a spell that could be used by anyone, how great could it be?"

"Perhaps it is great *because* it could be used by many people," Starrante countered, his voice stiffer than usual, his eyes redder. "*Great* is a word that denotes judgment; it is best to refrain from judgment when one stands in a position of ignorance—as all do who come to us seeking answers to their various questions. What you offer is ignorance, in the hope that information contained in the library will alleviate that ignorance.

"We are aware—Serralyn made clear—that you are capable of healing and have been since the Marks of the Chosen appeared. Many of your predecessors kept written records, and we have access to those. Very, very few of the bearers became healers. Not none—but of those who did, they were mortals, and mortal bearers were few.

"I would ask that you keep written records in the future but have been told that this would be unlikely."

Very.

"There are, however, books and documents that reference healers. Many are suspect; we expect them to be entirely fictitious. But the time period in which novels and stories were written is similar, and the writing makes clear that readers were expected to know and understand the role of a healer, and to accept that ability. We chose to focus first on that period.

"Within the current Empire, there have been two healers in the span of its four hundred years, present company excepted."

"You're certain?"

"We are. They served the Imperial forces. I assure you the Imperial forces *do* keep accurate records."

"The healer didn't heal the Emperor, though?"

"No. The Emperor—and the members of the Dragon Court—would not subject themselves to external healing. In that regard, the implication is clear: the power to heal, absent the Marks, is still intrusive or invasive in nature. It is not, perhaps, the desired outcome, as it relies upon a connection that is far too risky for those with both power and secrets."

"Then who did they heal?"

"The various mortal officers of the Halls of Law, just as you have done since you first realized the power."

"So . . . the healing power itself isn't derived from the Marks of the Chosen, or it doesn't have to be."

Starrante's eyes bobbed. "But it seems clear to us, after some discussion, that your healing does rely on the power of those Marks." The silence eddied as Kaylin considered his words. She'd had some vague hope, but it had remained vague because hope often led to a worse despair. That made sense: if you climbed higher, the fall was more dangerous.

But if you never climbed at all, all that remained was despair.

"And so we come at last to the nature of True Words, and True Names. Serralyn has offered as much information about the circumstances as she can; Androsse feels she crossed a line several times. It is safe to do so; the queries are private. It is part of the reason we close the library to other visitors when we choose to undertake a research project of a delicate nature.

"You believe the reason you cannot heal Nightshade is that the power of your healing is derived from the Marks of the Chosen."

Kaylin nodded. This *was* skirting a problem that should never be spoken about, and she knew it—but Serralyn knew it as well. If they couldn't even hint at the actual problem, the chance of finding a real solution was almost zero. Hells, if they *could* explain it all, the chance of finding answers was still too damn low.

"If what you desire is a healer, I feel your search will be both desperate and unsuccessful."

"But that magic did exist."

"Yes."

Kaylin's mind was a blur of information, none of it cohering in a useful way. "I have one more question for Androsse. For Arbiter Androsse."

"Ask. We will pass it on."

"He was aware of the research done to create the Erenne mark, the Erenne binding. Ask him how much of that binding existed only in our plane of existence."

Starrante fell silent. His eyes swiveled in Kavallac's direction; the Dragon's lips were pursed. "You believe that not all of it was."

Kaylin nodded. "I'm not even sure that the Ancestors *were* confined to one plane of existence. They seemed—the ones who attacked us—to be fully capable of sidestepping the way Terrano does. Of standing with some part of themselves on a different plane. On all of the different planes."

She hesitated. "Some of the archives contained in the library aren't from our world."

Kavallac nodded.

"But are they all from this plane? Or are there works that are from slightly different planes, different worlds within those different planes?"

"That is not a question that can be easily answered by any of the Arbiters." Kavallac's expression was grim.

Kaylin exhaled. Kavallac's tone mimicked the tone of the Imperial Security Service almost exactly. "Then just ask about the Erenne mark. Ask about whether or not the magic of its casting involved other planes."

Androsse, if he had the answer, couldn't be bothered to return to give it.

Kavallac, however, stepped forward. "You understand the genesis of True Words," she said. "But possibly you believe—for we are taught this—that the words were created because they contained immutable truth. To use the True tongue was to speak a language that could not be misunderstood. It was an absolute form of communication."

Kaylin nodded.

"That was not, however, the genesis of that language. To the Ancients, to those who are and were our gods and creators, it was merely communication, used as you would use your native tongue. The idea that miscommunications could exist did not occur to the Ancients, for when they spoke, their will was known. When they spoke to their creations, their words had the power of command; when they created, their creations bore their signatures—sometimes literally.

"They were not of one mind; it was the language that gave them common ground."

"So . . . like ours."

"Our words are mired in slight misunderstandings; it is very easy for two educated people to use phrases and words in subtly different ways. They did not. But words were crafted that only the Ancients could read or speak; language evolved under their guidance and as that language was spoken. The evolution was horizontal; more words were added. Much of our collection is divided into fact and fiction.

"For the Ancients, that was not the case."

"Do you have books they wrote in this library?"

Kavallac laughed. "They did not write books; they did not create records. Not at the time. *We* are the records of their work, their deeds—Dragons, Wevaran, Ancestors, Barrani, and mortals such as you and the corporal."

"But . . . we have no words. No True Names." Mostly.

"No. Much of the research into True Words arose because mortals, obviously sentient, did not require them as the source of their life. You were thought to be simply intelligent animals."

Kaylin had heard this before. She hadn't liked it any other time, either. But she could almost understand why researchers, possessed of True Names, might draw that conclusion—the wonder would be that they bothered to research it at all.

"If the Ancestors were created so that they might make, of themselves, something new, something beyond what they were at creation, why did the Ancients then create the Barrani?"

"We are not certain. Perhaps, in the end, the creators responsible for the creation of the Ancestors disliked the changes their creations made. That is our guess: the Barrani form itself could not always be preserved in the light of changes made by those early creations. It might be as simple, in our terms, as *I loved the way they looked*." At Kaylin's expression, Kavallac laughed. "You cannot expect the Ancients to conform to even your own understanding of what *powerful* means."

Squawk.

"But the concept of planes of existence, the concepts of True Words across those planes, is old. You have the Marks of the Chosen, and Serralyn has told us that you can see your Marks across planes. You can see them when you close your eyes; they are not relegated to simple, biological vision.

"Have you yet walked a plane in which you cannot see your Marks?"

Kaylin shook her head. "Does such a plane exist?"

"There is very little research that implies the existence of True Words is not persistent across *any* plane. Just as the Ancients were. Think of them this way: you can draw—in two dimensions—a cube. The cube is meant to represent an object that exists in three dimensions; the drawing, however, cannot be touched and handled in the same way. It implies a cube; you recognize it as a cube, but it is not a cube.

"True Words would be the cube. You write reports, yes?"

Kaylin grimaced as Kavallac continued. "The words are flat; they exist in two dimensions. But True Words, like the cube, exist in three. The attempt to capture the sense of True Words when one cannot speak them is very like the drawing versus the real object. It is our belief that the True Words transcend our limited ability to interact with them. The cube exists in places we cannot see or touch or know.

"It exists as the Ancients themselves existed. They existed in all planes, in all spaces, connected to the places we, or their creations *here*, could see. They created worlds, and they populated them—just as ours was populated. They did not often work together, but when they did, miracles occurred."

"But if that was true, could there be a plane in which True Words didn't exist?"

"Not a natural one, no. Terrano finds natural entries into spaces in which the Ancients once stood, if we understood the mechanism at all. Wevaran naturally navigate other planes—or at least their use. Portals exist because of those spaces; they do not invade the space in which you live. They are confined, useful spaces meant to expedite travel; the Ancients used them, and in the end, we followed that example.

"But the library does not exist in the same fashion Killianas does. While we are here, we interact as if the space is the same; it is not. It is why the library has been preserved through the fall of *Ravellon* and the loss of many, many worlds and the lives those worlds contained.

"You have seen the Devourer of worlds. Such a being is similar to the Ancients in its physical presence."

It had been a long time since Kaylin had seen that Devourer. She thought of it as a natural catastrophe, not a being of intent and will. She frowned. "When you say natural planes, are you implying that unnatural planes could somehow be constructed?"

Kavallac fell silent.

18

"I think the answer has to be yes." It was Terrano who spoke. "I'm aware of them the same way I would be of any other space. I followed the Barrani Teela was tracking. I should have stepped out of phase so their attacks wouldn't land. That's what I *thought* happened."

"That's not what happened." Flat words. Kaylin wasn't asking. She was confirming.

"No, it's not," Mandoran said. "I've never had so much trouble reaching Terrano. You've been with me when I've sidestepped before. You came with me. It was effortless. I mean, I had to be in contact with you to move you as well, but I could do it before a spell cast could even be started."

Terrano snorted. "The ground there, the air—that's the word I use, but it's probably not technically accurate—was similar to other places.

"Getting there was similar. I mean, some places are harder to navigate—they're small or they're broken. Some I can visit but most of my cohort can't. Not safely. It's how I escaped Alsanis when we were jailed in the Hallionne. It took work. I failed a lot before I finally succeeded. But . . . we all assume that our ability to sidestep or even disincorporate came to us because we were exposed to the *regalia* when we were children. We weren't fully grounded in our world.

"It's illegal to expose children to the *regalia* now. But the definition of *child* is tricky." Terrano shrugged, uncomfortable. "There've always been Barrani who want to shed their name. I mean, I get it. If I didn't, who would? I almost—"

Kaylin lifted a hand. "You live in my house. I don't want to have to stop Sedarias from murdering you." She exhaled. "I'm aware that there are Barrani who view their True Name as an ultimate weakness, a curse from the Ancients. One of them was fieflord, for a while—and the Tower was almost compromised because of it.

"But I've encountered them before, in Nightshade. I think they're called vampires in some quarters. I don't know how they continue to exist, absent their names—but they don't appear to have them anymore. Which is what they theoretically wanted. If more Barrani encountered them, I'm pretty sure we'd have centuries free of anyone stupid enough to make the attempt."

"I am not at all confident that that is the case," Kavallac said. "There will always be those who believe they are the exception to the rule."

Fair enough. Some people learned not to stick their hand in the fire by watching others get burned. Some people were Terrano.

Only Terrano? Severn's voice was heavy with amusement.

"If such a path were created, and if the Barrani who walk it are people who naturally want freedom from the namebinding, things are more dangerous than we realized. If they are attempting to make a space, a plane, in which True Words aren't the determinant of communication, of life itself . . ." Kavallac shook her head.

Terrano said nothing. His eyes were narrowed; he was clearly getting some pushback or criticism from the cohort.

Fallessian's eyes were blue, and as narrow as Terrano's when he turned to face him. "Absolutely not."

"I think I know how to make the connection between my name and myself more attenuated. It's how I lived toward the end of our time in the Hallionne. It's how I lived after."

"Without the rest of us," Serralyn pointed out in the gentlest of tones. "You *could* come back, then. There's no guarantee that will be true in the future."

Kaylin would have had to pick her jaw off the floor if it weren't attached to her face. "Exactly *what* did you think you were going to do?" she demanded. She added a Leontine word or two at the end.

"Experiment?" Terrano replied as if this were obvious. He glanced at Mandoran.

Mandoran shook his head. "Leave me so far out of it I don't have to hear anything about your so-called experiments at all."

"Kaylin could see her Marks in the place I was standing," Terrano pointed out.

Mandoran nodded.

"And she could heal—or something equivalent. So the Barrani traversing that path aren't necessarily people who've lost or ditched their names."

Kaylin nodded. "But . . . how could they interfere with the power of the names?"

Kavallac frowned. "It is possible they learned a lesson from compatriots who had fully divorced their existence from their True Names. If the names cannot interact, if the namebonds cannot be contacted, would that not be their ideal end goal? They would be possessed of the names that are the source of Barrani life without the inherent gaping weakness those names represent."

"It's not just weakness," Serralyn said, her voice soft. "For me, it's the source of my strength."

"Should any one of you attempt to use the namebond to control or command, that strength would be permanently shattered," Kavallac said. But her eyes were orange with gold flecks, not red; she understood, and cared for, Serralyn. "What is done is done. You cannot unlearn the names you were given; you cannot release that knowledge, save in death.

"None of your friends want that. But I believe it is necessary to keep an eye on Terrano. The interaction with Lord Nightshade involved external use of True Words. The separation appears to be between the internal name and external reach. How that was achieved we do not know.

"But the question of the Erenne mark, the planes, and the . . . containment, for want of a better word, are of great import."

"Should I mention the new Shadow now?"

"No. But Serralyn informed Arbiter Starrante of what occurred. It caused much concern and raised questions—but if both the High Halls and Helen can accept you, we feel harm will not be done. We are aware there is a risk, but none of the Arbiters have experience with Shadow—not even as much as you. In this, we allow the guidance of those most likely to be affected.

"Research continues, but the salient point is this: in the archives in the library, and in studies done by the intrepid—not all of whom were fortunate enough to survive—we know that True Words exist as the Ancients did: in all planes. It is likely that were you to learn what the cohort knows, you could walk as they walk—not completely here, but adjacent to it. But understand, Kaylin, that the complexity of an Ancestral name is bedazzling to those who are given even a glimpse of it; it is a concert that is endless, harmonic, and diverse simultaneously."

"Have you seen such a name?"

Kavallac's smile was toothy, her eyes almost purely gold. "Of course I have. It is what exists at the heart of this library, just as words exist at the heart of Helen or the Academia. There is no sentience in the library; the library is far older, and the creator believed that it was the contents of the library that would convey meaning to those who were able to visit it.

"But we are its guardians. I believe it is well past curfew for at least one of you; exceptions have been made. But Lord Bellusdeo may be waiting for you when you leave."

She was. Her expression made clear that no other sister had chosen to peer out; she was the Bellusdeo Kaylin knew. She leaned against the wall, arms folded, eyes an orange-red. Of course they were.

Serralyn left the library last. Her eyes were the green-blue of worry, and her gaze was mostly on Terrano, her brow furrowed. No one was shouting, but Fallessian looked like murder on two legs, and Mandoran looked hungover. Terrano looked like Terrano, but criticism usually bounced off him.

Kaylin was grateful to know none of their True Names.

Mandoran clearly didn't feel he should suffer alone. "We're discussing exploration and its relative safety. Except for Sedarias. She's almost enraged that Terrano could be so feckless just before a meeting with An'Tellarus."

"One: I have to *issue* an invitation to *Yvonne*. Two: she has to *accept it*. Three: I am not issuing an invitation that includes An'Tellarus's name anywhere in print. There's no guarantee that she'll show—"

"Sedarias suggests that the person who extends the invitation obviously sets the date. Teela is willing to bet, in her words, actual money that An'Tellarus will show."

"Could we maybe deal with one thing at a time?"

"Yes," Bellusdeo said, her voice a draconic rumble. "Shadow."

Kaylin exhaled.

"I'm going to fly back to Helen's. Those who aren't too cowardly can join me. We have a lot to discuss."

They didn't have a lot to discuss, but Bellusdeo was Bellusdeo. When she demanded discussion, *no* didn't matter. She understood that some of what had been discussed was irrelevant—but the arbiter of relevance was always going to be the gold Dragon.

She landed on the lawn, passing the fence line. Kaylin's many daydreams of flight didn't include by Dragon. Bellusdeo wasn't technically allowed to fly across the city skies, but the rule was flexible enough the Emperor was unlikely to descend on her to punish her for breaking that law.

Not everyone fit on the Dragon's back; Fallessian, Kaylin, and Severn did. She grabbed Mandoran by her claws, careful not to injure him; Terrano would have nothing to do with returning home that way. There was an argument, but it was silent, not meant for outsiders—or not meant for outsiders when one of them was a Dragon.

Kaylin, who couldn't hear the argument, understood it: Terrano intended to make his own way home. In the heightened threat of Barrani of unknown loyalties and considering the injuries Terrano had already taken, walking home didn't seem like a safe bet if he was on his own. But he wasn't going to sit on Bellusdeo's back, and her attempt to catch him as she'd taken hold of Mandoran was a failure.

If Bellusdeo was Bellusdeo, Terrano was Terrano. Fallessian was both tense and resigned. Mandoran, however, was amused—which was no doubt why he had the harder flight home.

But when Bellusdeo shed her draconic form, golden scales becoming the plate armor of Dragons who would otherwise be naked after transforming, her expression was both troubled and thoughtful. It was an expression very familiar to Kaylin—it was just on the wrong face. Serralyn often looked like this when she was researching something and the facts didn't quite line up.

"Logia?"

Logia smiled. "You're more perceptive than Bellusdeo gives you credit for." She spoke Elantran.

"She must have loved you guys a lot," Kaylin replied.

"She did. We loved her just as much. Possibly more, depending on which of us is speaking. She was our warrior; in martial strength and reaction, she was our best. It makes sense to us that she was the one who survived."

Kaylin exhaled. "I found her in *Ravellon*."

"I know. But I can find no trace of contaminant in her. She was physically transformed, but otherwise herself—and that is usually not the case where physical transformation has occurred."

Kaylin nodded. She wasn't an expert in Shadow, but that matched her experience. "You wanted to meet Helen."

Bellusdeo apparently had dimples—at least one. "I do. But I'd like to say hello to Mrs. Erickson as well. We're enormously grateful to her—Bellusdeo most of all."

Kaylin grimaced. "You know there are things I can't talk about, right?"

"So I've been informed. Don't get me—or us—wrong. We're *all* concerned with Shadow. But it's not as personal for us as it is for Bellusdeo."

"So you think you can be more objective?"

The dimple reappeared. "Don't you?"

Lannagaros must have had his hands way more than full with these sisters. But Logia's eyes were almost gold, and Bellusdeo's had been almost red. She'd take this flavor of handful over the other one.

"Have you talked much with the chancellor?"

"I have—mostly me, but we've all taken turns. My interests

most closely match his—although this wasn't always the case in our childhood."

Helen opened the front door. "You don't need to stand outside to converse. The parlor is open, and I've had refreshments brought. Imelda baked," she added. "I think baking is her response to worry, and she's been a bit worried about all of you."

Fallessian's grimace was worn but affectionate. He really had been spending time with Mrs. Erickson. "I'll go ahead," he told Mandoran. "Terrano should be here in a couple of minutes. I'll tell Imelda that no one's injured and no one's lost."

"Yet," Mandoran muttered.

"Logia, please come in. For reasons that have never been clear to me, people often converse outside the house, when inside is more comfortable. And no, it's not about avoiding me—if that were the intent, you would never have crossed the fence line."

Logia smiled and nodded. She then turned to Kaylin, caught her by the hand, and dragged her toward the door. This was something Bellusdeo would never have done—Bellusdeo would simply have glared in command, and Kaylin would have followed.

"It's interesting," Logia said as they reached the door. "Bellusdeo found the cohort highly unusual. She understands it better now. We don't have separate bodies—we can't have separate lives the way the cohort does. But we argue a lot.

"Bellusdeo isn't interested in academics. Unless the possible subjects—such as history—contain information that will tilt the balance of war in our favor, she considers it a waste of time. How can knowledge be a waste of time? If it were useless, she would never go to the Academia at all."

Helen clucked sympathetically as she guided Logia—still attached to Kaylin by the hand—into the foyer, and from there into the parlor. "Imelda will join you, but she wants to make sure you have to time to talk about important things before she interrupts you. Corporal?"

Severn remained on the other side of the door. "Kaylin will never need a guard or an escort here," he said. "And I have other business to which I must attend. I will leave Kaylin in your care."

"Wait!" Kaylin said, turning back, or half turning, as Logia didn't release her hand. "When should we invite Yvonne to visit?"

"I believe the cohort has opinions on that very subject. For my part, I believe sooner would be better. You won't need to prepare for her visit."

"She'll need to prepare for An'Tellarus," Mandoran said.

"She won't. An'Tellarus won't cause trouble here unless she thinks someone else has started it first. She's not like An'Teela. If you offend her, she won't hunt down every living member of your family and kill them to make a point."

"You're sure?"

"I don't know what she was like when she was young, but she's not young, now. She's impulsive. She's considered indulgent, in general. But if Sedarias doesn't somehow attempt to politically outmaneuver her, she will cause no harm.

"It is safe to invite Yvonne to visit at any time, but there are pressing reasons why it should be soon."

"I like him," Logia said when Helen had opened the parlor and escorted her to a seat. She had offered her a drink, but apparently Logia and Bellusdeo had different tastes, and Logia declined the alcohol Bellusdeo sometimes favored.

"Him?" Kaylin didn't drink a lot, partly because she'd seen Tain and Teela bingeing and felt *someone* had to stay sober.

"Severn. Bellusdeo approves of him. It's not even grudging. What is he to you?"

"He's my partner. He's a Hawk."

Logia nodded. "She would like to know who Yvonne is."

Kaylin knew better than to speak of Yvonne, but she'd asked Severn about Yvonne—out loud—when it would have been way smarter to ask him through the namebond. "She's a young woman I met at the High Halls."

"Barrani, then."

"Yes. She was servant to a Barrani Lord who commanded our presence. I would have said no, but neither Teela nor Severn thought it wise. If we hadn't been summoned, we wouldn't have met Yvonne—Yvonne was there." Kaylin frowned as the words left her mouth. She *wouldn't* have met Yvonne if not for An'Tellarus's interference. An'Tellarus clearly knew Severn, and Severn knew her as well.

She'd assumed An'Tellarus was tweaking Severn's metaphorical nose.

But what if the purpose was actually Yvonne? Severn appeared to know Yvonne. Kaylin didn't. Teela didn't. There'd be no reason for either of them to meet her. If An'Tellarus had commanded their attendance, she must have expected that Severn would agree—and if he did, both Teela and Kaylin were likely to follow. Not certain, but likely.

An'Tellarus was older than Teela. She'd survived as the lord of her line for a very long time. She was considered eccentric but was accepted because she would survive it, and those who attempted to use those eccentricities against her would not.

It wasn't meeting An'Tellarus that had been the entire point of that little play. It wasn't embarrassing Severn; it wasn't intimidating Teela.

Well, no. Maybe a bit of it was intimidating Teela. Or making clear to Teela where Tellarus's interests were currently aligned, well before hostilities could begin. It couldn't be meeting Kaylin.

She was interested in you, Severn said. This surprised Kaylin. Something about both An'Tellarus and Yvonne had been locked away with a giant *do not enter* sign hanging from the very closed fences. It's not that she hadn't—or didn't—want to know. It's that she didn't want to be a hypocrite. Hypocrisy ranked high on her list of most-hated traits that were, in many cases, legal. There were too many things she didn't want to talk about, either.

Is it because I'm Chosen?

That has to be part of the reason. I've had reason to interact with An'Tellarus in the past; we're acquainted. Our interests aligned; she's capable of cooperation when it suits her purposes.

Do you have any idea what her purpose is?

Silence. It wasn't a wall. *No. But if she were so easily predicted, she would not be what she is. I think you're right: she wanted Yvonne to be seen. She wanted Yvonne to be seen as part of Tellarus, and beholden to An'Tellarus herself.*

So . . . warning Teela off.

I'm less certain about that. She let you go off with Yvonne; she didn't wish me to join you.

Had she said that? Kaylin couldn't remember that.

But I think you're right. Yvonne was central to that summons.

. . . which means she must know about the test of the Lake.

Severn agreed.

Does this mean she knows about the Consort's difficulty?

No. But it means she possibly could.

"Bellusdeo says I shouldn't interrupt you because you're wearing your thinking face, which is rare."

Kaylin rolled her eyes.

"You have reached a conclusion, then?"

"Yes." Kaylin turned her attention to Logia. "She's letting you talk because she thinks I'll be comfortable enough to let things slip."

Logia laughed with what seemed genuine delight. "I did warn her," she said.

The problem was: it was true. There was a little bit of Serralyn in Logia. Kaylin *liked* Bellusdeo. There was no other reason to offer her a home in Helen when the Imperial Palace grew too awkward, too fraught, for the gold Dragon. But Bellusdeo had always been prickly and temperamental; Logia seemed almost her exact opposite. Too comfortable.

But everything Logia heard, Bellusdeo would hear. And there was no guarantee that Logia would even think of keeping things to herself. Terrano didn't—he probably couldn't.

"Well, she listened enough that you're here instead."

Logia laughed again, but her expression sobered. "She's been alone for a long time."

Kaylin understood her meaning and tried not to feel irrelevant—Bellusdeo had been living with Kaylin, not on her own.

"And if it helps, she's worried about you."

"It really doesn't."

Logia looked faintly smug; Kaylin guessed that Logia had said this, as well. "Not all expressions of affection are welcome to the targets of that affection," Logia said, as if confirming Kaylin's suspicion. "But if we don't get down to business, Bellusdeo will take over."

Kaylin exhaled. "The only connection to Shadow that I've noted is in the avenue of retreat chosen by the Barrani—and Bellusdeo knows about this. There was evidence that the Barrani had been using the border between fiefs as their base. Teela's been investigating that; we found Barrani insignias on some of the bodies left behind in the wake of the attack on Nightshade.

"Nothing else we've uncovered so far seems to involve Shadow." Kaylin grimaced. "Except the attack on Terrano."

"Terrano?"

"I'm not sure how much attention Bellusdeo was paying, but Terrano was attacked when Bellusdeo and Teela surrounded the one building on the border of her—or your—fief."

Logia nodded. Gone was affectionate amusement; she was focused now, concentrating.

"Terrano's a bit unusual."

This caused a snort with a little bit of smoke in it.

"He often walks around invisible so he doesn't have to interact with people."

"I'm sure we'd all do that if we could." Logia winced. "Fine. Many of us would." It really was like speaking to a cohort member.

"He avoids magical invisibility because it can be detected, which would make him more visible in a dangerous sense, not less. Bellusdeo knows their history, or as much of their history as I do."

"She disagrees with the latter but agrees with the former. She does point out that Terrano can move with ease between different planes, different states of existence."

Helen opened the parlor door from the outside.

Mandoran entered, followed by Mrs. Erickson and Fallessian. Fallessian played porter; he carried a large tray as if it were a tin plate. "I don't mean to interrupt," Mrs. Erickson said, "but Helen said you had a guest. Hello, Logia."

Kaylin blinked. She was surprised that Mrs. Erickson recognized Logia immediately. And why should that be surprising? Mrs. Erickson had talked to the eight dead sisters before they had, at last, combined with Bellusdeo. She'd heard their stories. Kaylin hadn't.

And Kaylin hadn't asked, either.

"No, dear," Helen agreed. "And that was both kind and wise." Meaning: *don't start now.*

Logia rose instantly and offered Mrs. Erickson both of her hands, palms up. Mrs. Erickson took them immediately, smiling up at Logia, who was much taller than Mrs. Erickson had probably ever been.

"You look well."

"I am much, much better than I was the first time we spoke," Logia replied, her eyes a warm gold. "We are all doing well. I think Bellusdeo is the most overwhelmed by the changes—but in a good way."

"I heard you've been having a bit of a problem in your new home? Are you getting along better with Lord Emmerian?"

Emmerian was the furthest thing from Bellusdeo's mind.

"Lord Emmerian is both happy for Bellusdeo and somewhat flustered by the changes in her—but I think it'll work out, in the end. Right now, we're focused on the breach of the fief, or the possible breach."

"Fallessian said Terrano was injured. That boy just isn't very careful."

Mandoran snorted but managed to prevent himself from laughing out loud. He entered the parlor and took the seat closest to Kaylin. At the moment, the seats were close together. Kaylin wasn't certain Fallessian intended to remain, but it was clear Mrs. Erickson wanted to say hello, and that would take a while.

She could, and did, relax.

"Terrano's almost here. He wanted to investigate one thing, but he would have had to enter the border zone by himself. I offered to join him." He winced. Kaylin could imagine just how happy either of the two had made Sedarias.

Logia stepped back, and another sister took over. She greeted Mrs. Erickson with a hug, not a hand-holding. Mrs. Erickson had never been loud; she was naturally soft-spoken and naturally deferential.

"While she's saying hello," Mandoran continued, pulling Kaylin's attention from the combination of Dragon and Mrs. Erickson, "Sedarias and Teela agree: you should extend an invitation to Yvonne immediately. Or as close to immediately as you can. Sedarias intends to head off An'Tellarus, or to suss out her intent. Teela's going to be here when Yvonne visits, just in case."

"That'll make clear An'Teela supports An'Mellarionne."

Mandoran nodded. "It's almost an open secret anyway. It's not formal—but we're Barrani. Formality counts."

"But . . . this'll be formal, no?"

"Not your problem."

"It *is* my problem! I'm living with all of you!"

"Yeah, I tried that. But Teela and Sedarias are in complete agreement. They want you to stay out of this as much as humanly possible."

"It's Kaylin," a familiar voice said. Terrano had arrived. "She's staying out of it as much as she possibly can. Which isn't impressive but shouldn't be a surprise."

"It's not my fault!"

"Yeah, yeah. It's never your fault; you just stumble into things that blow up in your face. To be honest, I'm grateful for you—it makes me look less chaotic." He became visible so he could grin. It was obnoxious. The grin faded. "Teela's worried."

Ugh.

"She can stand in line," Logia said over her shoulder. At least, Kaylin assumed it was Logia.

"When does Teela think I should set as the date for Yvonne's visit?"

"Tomorrow. Don't make that face at me—you asked. She doesn't *expect* you'll do it, but she wants to emphasize the necessity."

Kaylin understood. She wanted Yvonne to meet the Consort, but not if it wasn't safe. Sedarias and Teela could assess the safety question only with further Tellarus discussion, and Kaylin wouldn't suggest that the Consort and Yvonne cross paths if things with Tellarus proved too political. She couldn't.

She'd liked Yvonne on first meeting her, and she sympathized with her.

But even if she and the Consort had had massive disagreements in the past, she could understand why, and she still liked the Consort, her complicated family, and possibly the fact that the Consort never treated Nightshade as outcaste.

"I'll send the invitation after everyone leaves—and *no*, that doesn't mean you get to kick them all out."

Bellusdeo allowed all of her eight sisters to speak with Mrs. Erickson; some took longer than others. Mandoran was content to wait in the parlor, probably because he was a coward, and he could avoid Sedarias that way. Terrano remained as well, but most of his attention was on Bellusdeo—or rather, her sisters. Fallessian remained by the door, his back to the wall next to it. He was definitely keeping an eye out for Mrs. Erickson. It wasn't necessary. Of her current guests, Helen was fondest of Mrs. Erickson; she'd made physical changes to the normal state of the house—the kitchen in particular—to accommodate her and spent social time with her in the absence of Kaylin and the rest of the cohort.

Mrs. Erickson retreated after saying her hellos and putting food on the low, long table, and that once again left Logia and Kaylin, but with the addition of Mandoran and Terrano. Fallessian retreated when the older woman did.

"You were saying?" Logia started in immediately. She'd been happy to see Mrs. Erickson, but she was now focused on Terrano.

"I wasn't saying anything," Terrano replied with a shrug. "But Kaylin was trying to answer your question, and she wasn't very good at it. No, I can't occupy multiple spaces at once. Even if I could, there'd be no point—I'm trying not to be seen. Invisibility doesn't cut it—I could avoid being seen, but I'd still have to avoid bumping into people."

"In other words, he'd actually have to pay attention," Kaylin added.

"So when you were attacked, you weren't here."

Terrano nodded. But he frowned and fell silent. "The thing is . . . Look, I'm telling them, okay?" he snapped at Mandoran, who hadn't moved, hadn't spoken, and didn't look particularly impatient.

Logia's gaze traveled between them before coming to rest on Terrano's again. She smiled. "It seems while you have separate bodies, you're not unlike me and my sisters."

"Oh *please*."

"No?"

"We're not Dragons."

Logia rolled eyes that remained predominantly gold. "You were saying?"

"I wasn't in an unusual space, for me. Planes are—or can be—like onion skins. They're different, but not too different. The farther away you get from this one, the more difficult it becomes to see this one—and yes, there are beings that can occupy any space I can, but they do it simultaneously."

"And you can't."

"I don't really see the point, to be honest. I don't exist on all planes at once." He hesitated again.

Mandoran snorted and took over. "He's not lying, but he tends to act first and think later—if we can get him to think at all. One of us *can* cover different planes simultaneously."

19

Logia's brows rose, her eye color shifting into a liquid silver before once again returning to gold. "One of you can? How is that even possible?" She was halfway out of her chair and returned to it with effort.

Kaylin had turned to Mandoran as well, but she had an inkling as to which cohort member he was speaking about.

Mandoran didn't offer a name. Kaylin didn't ask.

Logia did. "Who? Who can do this?" It was to Kaylin that Logia turned.

"I don't know," Kaylin said—truthfully.

"You have suspicions. Bellusdeo can tell."

"I have suspicions, but they're not verified, and they're *totally irrelevant* to Bellusdeo's issues with Shadow." She turned to Terrano.

Terrano cleared his throat and glared at Mandoran, who shrugged. It was a fief shrug, a habit some of the cohort had picked up from Kaylin. "I was walking in sidestep; I didn't want to be seen. I mean, two entire war bands—if only two—"

"Wait. What do you mean *if only*?" Kaylin demanded.

"Teela found evidence of a possible third."

"*What?* Where?"

"Ask her later. Let me finish so I can leave."

Fine. "Go ahead. Finish."

"I was walking the way I normally walk. I did see the Norranir in the streets, and I did see them enter the border zone. I was in contact with the rest of us, but . . . I could hear the most noise from the drumming and from other people. Those people were speaking Barrani; they were panicking. I assumed this was because the Dragon was trying to reduce them to ash."

"Did she even know about them then? You're sure you're not confused?"

Terrano shrugged. "Is this your story or my story?"

"Yours, but we'd like it to be coherent. Until Teela showed up on the chase, Bellusdeo had no reason to be patrolling the border zone."

Logia cleared her throat. "She has, now."

"Her Tower's power is completely attenuated in the border zone. She's not as absolute there."

"In theory she wasn't an absolute when she lived here, either," Terrano said.

Logia lifted a brow. Bellusdeo clearly had opinions; the Dragon's expression shifted. Logia stayed in the driver's seat. "There is a reason that the Tower chose a Dragon as its lord. She doesn't *need* the Tower to patrol a few streets on the edge of the Tower's remit."

Kaylin couldn't argue with that, and didn't try. She turned back to Terrano. "That doesn't explain why you were standing where they were."

"Well, the thing is, I could hear them, but I couldn't really see them, right? I mean, I could see the border zone, but it was blurry. Don't make that face—the border zones are *always* blurry. It's better to enter those the normal way, but I assumed the small army was in the border zone, so I entered it *my* normal way."

"You didn't, though."

"I did. But the voices were indistinct to me. I could almost make out words, but they were fuzzy, almost displaced." Terrano stopped for a moment, looking at his hands, which rested in his lap.

"Let me guess. You wanted to hear things more distinctly, so you moved toward the voices, but they didn't get any clearer."

Terrano nodded. "I changed my approach. If walking toward them didn't help resolve the sound into words, walking a different path might."

"Did you not even think that *if* those voices were coming from another plane, you'd be in trouble once you reached them?"

"I thought I could just slide back to here."

"Kaylin," Mandoran whispered, "chill. Sedarias is approaching full-on rage."

"Bellusdeo," Logia said, "is in an unusual state. She says this is exactly like Terrano. But even so, she is almost shocked. She asks me to ask him *what were you thinking?*"

Mandoran grimaced. He glanced at Terrano but shook his head. There was no saving him from Sedarias's ire if even Bellusdeo agreed.

"What I was thinking was: we need information. We need to find out who was behind this assassination attempt." His gaze was slightly shifty. Terrano wasn't one of nature's off-the-cuff liars. If he lied, it wasn't a lie so much as a plan.

Kaylin frowned. "They weren't likely to be spouting names and command hierarchy information."

"You never know. People say a lot when they're panicking." He didn't quite meet Kaylin's gaze.

Kaylin exhaled. "You thought you recognized one of the voices." Her tone was flat and certain; she might have been in the interrogation room in which possible criminals were questioned.

Terrano wilted. "Yes."

"From the West March." When Terrano cringed, she cursed. "Those people already tried to kill the Consort!"

". . . I know. Look, even then I didn't mean to hurt her."

"You just didn't care."

"I didn't care if it meant the rest of my friends could be free. We're not proud of it. We know she's never going to trust us—and we know, from recent history, she's not to be trusted *with* us, either. But she trusts you, and we—most of us—trust you. I thought if we could identify the culprits, we could make amends. We could sort of atone."

"I'm guessing Sedarias didn't agree with this."

He shrugged, which wasn't likely to calm Sedarias down any. "She figures the Consort already evened the score. Or tried. She's not worried that the Consort will harm us. She *is* worried that the people we approached when most of us were still caged *could*. I was careful. They had no reason to know who I was or am. But she's afraid they will, and that's a huge vulnerability to Mellarionne."

Logia looked amused. No, it wasn't Logia. It certainly wasn't Bellusdeo. One of the sisters. "You really *are* like me," she said to Terrano. She wasn't as bright-eyed as Logia could be, but Logia didn't strike Kaylin as reckless.

"Which part? People screaming at me on the inside of my head?"

She laughed. "That, too. Did you at least find out what you needed to find out? Were the Barrani there the ones you thought they might be?" The question was casual; it was spoken in Elantran—which was the tongue Terrano used most of the time.

"We haven't confirmed it. Things kind of exploded. There was a lot of screaming and yelling and orders given." Terrano exhaled. "I'm not supposed to tell you this—well, to tell Bellusdeo this—but when they fled, they fled toward *Ravellon*, following the border zone streets."

"I think she's already guessed that."

"I couldn't pursue; they could see me, and when I tried to

sidestep, it didn't work. I'd managed to move to where they were—but moving back wasn't as natural." He looked toward Kaylin. "It's why it took Mandoran so long to bring you to where I was standing."

"And bleeding."

"That too. But there was something about the wound that was wrong. It wasn't just my blood falling out. It was something else trying to enter." He grimaced.

"First of all, blood doesn't *fall out*. You were *bleeding*. Second of all, something wasn't *trying* to enter. It had already entered—and you knew it. You could have left whichever plane you were standing on. You didn't. You were worried about what you might be carrying."

Bellusdeo's sister cleared her throat. Loudly. It was a rumble of sound, and her eyes were no longer gold; they were red.

Bellusdeo had returned.

"Well done," Mandoran murmured.

Kaylin froze.

"Sedarias says you could give Terrano a run for his money if you were competing. But this time you've won, hands down."

"Were you trying to keep this from me?" The walls shook as Bellusdeo spoke.

"Sedarias wants to join us. With Allaron." Mandoran's expression made clear he didn't think it a good idea.

"That won't be necessary," Helen said to the newcomers. "I am perfectly capable of preventing unwanted violence. Bellusdeo has no intention of harming Terrano; she knows he could not enter my domain were he to be Shadow-mutated in a dangerous fashion."

"How could you even tell with Terrano?"

"I am capable of discerning that degree of change. My duties require some observation if my visitors are to be kept safe. Bellusdeo is a Tower lord now. She knows that Terrano does not present a danger—at least, not in the form of Shadow." Helen exhaled. "She is not, however, best pleased to have this information kept from her when it is germane to her duties."

"Given how trigger-happy she is, she'd likely reduce me to ash and *then* ask questions," Terrano snapped.

"If *Kaylin* says something Shadow-like succeeded in penetrating your defenses, what happened to it? Kaylin?"

Ugh. One of these days she was going to learn to *shut up.* "It turned into a ball."

"Pardon?"

"Hope breathed on the wisps of Shadows that exited Terrano's wound. The blend of Hope's breath and those wisps became a sphere." On the other hand, sometimes the truth was just going to upset people.

"Where is that sphere?"

Hope squawked.

"Pardon?"

"It disappeared when we managed to get back to our normal reality. I'd been carrying it in one hand—it wasn't heavy—but it wasn't there when Mandoran pulled me out."

"You didn't drop it?"

"I'd bet money against. But it wasn't in my hand when I got back to the border zone." Kaylin grimaced. "I was worried that somehow I'd absorbed it."

Squawk.

"But none of the sentient buildings—and their many defenses—sensed anything wrong at all. I didn't lose or surrender any of the Marks of the Chosen. I didn't have to let Hope bite my arm off. It just . . . wasn't there when I got out."

Bellusdeo turned to Mandoran. "Did you see what happened?"

"I was kind of busy."

"You knew that it was something formed of Shadow and familiar's breath, and you were *too busy* to pay attention?"

"I was more concerned with leaving—with Kaylin—than I was with whatever she had in her hand. Terrano had been injured—possibly mortally injured—while standing in that plane, and to heal him, Kaylin had to be able to touch him. I wanted her to do just enough that we could pull out without becoming two more casualties."

"Was *any* of your cohort paying attention to Kaylin and what she carried?"

"Serralyn, maybe? We were worried about Terrano. Sedarias was *very* worried. It took me longer to get to where Terrano was standing than most other planes—and Serralyn was offering what advice she could. She's not so good at making transitions, but she's aware of the . . . she calls it the structure of the space or spaces."

There was a longer pause from Bellusdeo, and when she next spoke, she was Logia again. "Apologies," she said. "Bellusdeo is—for obvious reasons—very sensitive to any mention of Shadow. Shadow evolves. Its method of attack evolves. Things that seemed harmless to us became deadly poison in an instant. But we didn't *have* sentient buildings. We had the Norranir and their ancient customs, their drumming, their ability to sense approaching and encroaching Shadow—but it's not the same.

"Bellusdeo is a bit calmer, now. She's usually a good tactician, but, well." Logia's shrug was not a fief shrug. "We often tried to be the voice of reason in the past, but we all died. And even if we're with her now, our deaths drove her while our world still existed. If Helen thinks you're safe—and thinks she's safe—Bellusdeo will live with the risk.

"But I don't believe you dropped that sphere."

"Neither does Bellusdeo," Mandoran replied, although Logia had been speaking to Kaylin.

"She says you're perceptive only when it's inconvenient."

Mandoran nodded. "I hear that a lot."

"I have so, so many questions. Most of them involve the

planes that Terrano can naturally visit. But you have things you have to discuss. Helen?"

"Yes, Logia?"

"Can I visit again when things are a bit calmer?"

"Of course. Bellusdeo lived with me for a short time, but she was one of my guests, and as I told her when she left to take up residence in her Tower, she will always be welcome here."

Technically, Kaylin's permission was required. But that was a polite fiction.

It's not a fiction, Severn said, internal voice soft. *If you demand otherwise, Helen will accept it. But she knows you pretty well. She chose you because of who you are. Helen is never empty; she's never lonely.*

Logia rose, offered Helen a bow, and opened the parlor doors.

Sedarias and Teela were waiting on the other side. Kaylin could see the Dragon's back, but not her face. She could see Sedarias's, though—full midnight eyes and pale skin. Teela looked less uncomfortable, but Teela had never had problems with Dragons.

Sedarias and Teela entered. Logia took up a position by the wall nearest the door. She didn't intend to join whatever discussion ensued—but she clearly wanted to hear it.

Kaylin wanted to go to bed and stay there for the rest of the week. If she couldn't sleep this early in the day, she'd settle for hiding under it.

The chairs around the parlor table expanded in number as Sedarias took a seat; Teela joined her. Fallessian returned as well. Terrano looked about as comfortable as Kaylin felt; Mandoran looked resigned. She waited for the rest of the in-house cohort to join them, but no one else did. Annarion was with Nightshade and wouldn't leave his side.

"Torrisant is keeping Annarion company, but I assure you all of the cohort are listening in," Helen informed her.

"So," Sedarias said. "You had questions for me." It wasn't where Kaylin had thought she would start. "You asked them of Terrano, but you know how feckless he is. You know him well enough to doubt that his plan of attack—*our* plan of attack—was his. He doesn't take commands well, and if you don't watch him like a hawk, he's easily distracted." Meaning she'd watched him every step of the way.

"Were the plans yours?" Kaylin asked, reaching for one of Mrs. Erickson's glazed buns. They had raisins, which Kaylin didn't care for, but she was hungry.

"They were ours," Sedarias replied. "But Terrano probably doesn't remember half of them."

"He's Barrani! He has perfect memory!"

Teela chuckled, a dry sound at odds with the color of her eyes. "We have perfect recall, yes—but even we are required to pay attention."

Teela rose and set something down on the table around which they were all seated. "This is an insignia taken from the corpse of one of Nightshade's attackers."

It looked like a Barrani family crest, writ exquisitely—and expensively—small.

Sedarias glanced at Kaylin. "I don't suppose you recognize it?" To Kaylin's surprise, she spoke in Elantran.

Kaylin didn't. Severn did. *It's the symbol worn by the Haverness guard.*

Am I allowed to say that?

Up to you. There's an advantage to being thought of as ignorant, but there is no advantage in being *ignorant.*

She settled, as she often did, for truth. "Severn says it's the symbol of the Haverness guard. I assume Haverness is a Barrani family?"

"Not exactly," Teela replied.

"Not exactly?"

"You are aware that there are, and have always been, political alliances among the Lords of the High Court. Some of those extend to the West. Haverness is a league of guards; they were active—and respected—during the Draco-Barrani wars and rose to prominence because of it. It was highly unusual to have a military force unattached to a familial line, but it was meant—we were told—to be a display of solidarity. Haverness takes no family name, no matter how powerful that family might be.

"In times of war, they serve the Barrani people." The words were spoken in the bitterest of tones. "They were not meant to be a political force, but Barrani will be Barrani when they are adjacent to implements of power."

"Who commands them?"

"In theory? The High Lord."

"In theory?"

"The Haverness guards are supplied, armed, armored, and housed by the Lords of the High Court. During the wars, lords vied for the right to send their people to the Haverness guard. The wars are over. It is considered less prestigious now, and will likely not rise to prominence again, except in the face of another war against an external enemy.

"It is the Haverness guard that would stand against Shadow should the Tower's protections fall. We do not labor under the illusion that they would stand for long."

Kaylin looked at the emblem on the table. "So what you're telling me is anyone could have sent the guard."

"Am I?"

"Did you recognize any of the dead? And if you did, were they actually Haverness guards?"

Teela turned to Sedarias. "You see? She struggles to retain ignorance, but she *is* logical when confronted with information she might have chosen not to learn in her youth."

"This is not a case for the Imperial Halls of Law," Sedarias said. "Teela has been investigating, but the investigation must be subtle. She is not the only person. Where I can, I have drawn attention."

"You didn't do that for this," Terrano muttered.

"No. But my activities serve as distractions to those who might otherwise be attempting to subvert the guard or hide behind their reputation, such as it is."

"Unless they're the same enemies."

Sedarias smiled. "I don't believe Nightshade is associated with Mellarionne. I don't think he was attacked because of Annarion. Annarion is Solanace, but he has not staked his claim, and Solanace is so greatly reduced in influence and power, he is too insignificant a target.

"We do not have the name of the person who commanded the guard to assassinate Nightshade."

"Is there a ruler of Solanace now?"

"There is, but she is young, and in the parlance of Elantra, it is believed she drew the short straw."

Kaylin blinked. "There was a title available, and no one wanted it? And she's Barrani?"

"Yes. From a Solanace perspective, Nightshade would only be a threat if his exile was revoked."

"Pardon?"

"He was made outcaste for political reasons. He could be repatriated into the High Court for political reasons. Nightshade's return to Solanace would elevate the line; he is the bearer of one of The Three, and he acquitted himself extremely well in the wars. But to the person who sits behind the Solanace seat, it might not be considered elevation."

"Has Annarion heard from his family?"

No one answered. Not even Teela, a Hawk for whom this style of questioning was familiar.

"This is not your investigation, as Teela has made *extremely* clear."

Mandoran rolled his eyes. Terrano snorted. "What? You

know what she's like. She trips over everything, and some of it might be useful. At least if we talk about it, she can walk with her eyes wide open."

Kaylin felt a bit of gratitude and a bit of annoyance. She squashed both. "So the Haverness war bands were rogue?"

"The High Lord made no commands with regards to the outcaste, but it is a very gray area. Outcastes *can* be hunted without legal ramifications from the High Lord and his court. It is seldom, however, that three full war bands can be brought to bear."

"You don't think they were Haverness guards."

Teela exhaled, glared at Terrano, and shook her head. "In ones and twos, it might be possible. If Barrani become Haverness, they hail from the families that pushed them into service, and they are not required to disavow those families. The families might put pressure on them—but their actions would not be considered part of the guard.

"Three war bands, however, is a different matter."

"When did you know it was three?"

"After cursory investigation. It was Lord Andellen who apprised us of the third band; he is most familiar with the fief of the lord he serves. In the absence of Nightshade, visitors are not permitted at the castle."

"When you say cursory—"

"I did not investigate it personally. If the bands had gathered at roughly the same time, it would be trivial to find the hand behind them; they did not. They have been building an unseen presence in the fief for longer than you've been alive. You were never fond of Barrani," she added. "You avoided them when you saw them on the streets.

"You assumed they belonged to Nightshade."

Kaylin nodded. "How else would they have wandered the streets invoking his name?"

"Not wisely. But you have also noted that Nightshade was

negligent when it came to his citizens' welfare. Lord Andellen swore an oath of fealty to his lord. I am uncertain that such oaths were offered by those who were also resident within the fief. I do not believe Nightshade required such oaths."

"Do you?"

"Pardon?"

"You're a Lord of the High Court, and you're probably one of the older lords. Do you require an oath of allegiance from your people?"

Terrano snickered.

"No, as you guess, I do not. Allegiance, such as it is, is binding on both those who swear and those who accept what is sworn. I did not wish to assume responsibility for others. But it is not the same situation. I am not, and was never, outcaste. Vows offered to someone declared outcaste are not irrevocable. When a person of power is rendered outcaste, all vows, all responsibilities—to and for—are rendered null and void. No dishonor accrues to those who have sworn vows prior to the expulsion. Even blood oaths are released, and the breaking of fealty to one made outcaste no longer has consequences for those who swore such oaths.

"Lord Andellen's vow of fealty was offered after Nightshade was expelled from the Barrani."

"Ummm, how exactly are blood oaths rendered null and void?"

"Such oaths require magic; they are therefore magical in nature. Such binding magics can be destroyed at the will of the High Lord. Ah, I mean: the High Lord can destroy them without consequence."

"But namebonds can't."

"Nothing but death destroys a namebond. It is the other reason namebonds are feared. Nightshade has servants in his fief—Barrani servants—but there is very little in the way of trust between him and those men. It would not be difficult to insert people who do not have his best interests at heart."

"Can it be as simple as that?"

"It could, yes, if he were careless. But if he were that careless, he would have been dead long ago."

"So it's more complicated."

"It is more complicated. I would say our arrival—or rather the arrival of the rest of my cohort—has caused anxiety and in some cases panic. Mellarionne before Sedarias was very likely aligned with the people who wanted the Consort dead in the West March." Teela looked, pointedly, at Sedarias, whose eyes remained midnight.

"Why do you think that?"

"Because her siblings could invade Hallionne Alsanis."

Sedarias surrendered her silence. "Their *purpose* was to kill me. They didn't expect the rest of us. Or you," she added almost grudgingly. "But the people with whom Terrano interacted were not men of great renown; he, as they, were go-betweens. They did not realize that Terrano was not the only person with whom they dealt.

"They are, no doubt, afraid. Terrano's invisibility serves two purposes. The first: he can avoid having to muster decent manners and etiquette. The second: he might be recognized by those with whom we dealt. We do not have any desire—at this point—to destroy the High Halls or its lord. The current lord is not the one who demanded *volunteers* for his experiment in the green.

"While we were trapped, we thought of the lords of the High Halls as our enemies. We did not consider the West March in the same light—probably because of Teela and her mother's side of the family."

"But you attacked the Consort."

"We did not directly attack the Consort," was Sedarias's stiff reply. "We attacked her party, yes."

"So . . . you're telling me that she wasn't the target."

Teela cleared her throat.

Sedarias exhaled. "She wasn't our target. She might have been theirs."

"They have to know they're attacking the entire race if she dies!"

"They did not consider that loss to be permanent. It was, I believe, for the greater good, the brighter future."

"Did they justify that?"

Terrano shrugged. "They believed it. They believed that absent the Consort, they could build a method of waking the infants that would grant greater freedom—or power, let's be honest—to the 'new' Barrani."

"You couldn't have warned us about this before?" Kaylin almost shrieked.

"It would have served no practical purpose. You defeated the forces sent to the West March. We assumed that it was finished. We could not get more information from Iberrienne—but he seemed to be in command. Eddorian has not tried very hard. Iberrienne desired his brother's freedom and possible redemption more than he desired anything else. Power was a method—for Iberrienne—of bringing Eddorian home." She exhaled. "We knew Nightshade desired the same for Annarion, but Nightshade was, and has always been, rational and cold-blooded. There are some lines Nightshade would never cross.

"Harming the Consort would be one of them. Perhaps, had there been a different Consort, he might have approached the problem as Iberrienne did."

"What do you mean?"

Teela rolled her eyes. "You noticed that the Consort referred to Nightshade as Calarnenne when they met in person in the West March."

Kaylin nodded.

"You will note that no one else did."

"No one else could bear the consequences of treating an outcaste as if he was still Barrani."

"You believe that, clearly. They have known each other for a very long time. It is my belief that if she could, she would repatriate Nightshade. He would not harm her, would not countenance a plan that called for her injury or death, in my opinion. Did it not appear that way to you?"

Kaylin frowned. "I *like* the Consort. I mean, she tried to trap the cohort, and tried to sort of use me to help, and she wanted the Norranir to die rather than risk saving what was left of their race—but I understood why she thought the risk was too great.

"I know we're not of one mind. We've had *serious* disagreements. But . . . I trust her. She doesn't scheme for personal power. She's not trying to enrich herself. I can disagree with her decisions, but at least I understand why she made them.

"She was genuinely happy to see Nightshade in the West March—her eyes were green. But aside from Serralyn, there are almost no Barrani whose eyes are consistently more green than blue. Maybe flecks of green, but not green the way the Consort's are." She frowned. She knew, now, that the Lake tested for things that were not considered the norm among the Barrani, knew that the chosen Lady was one who could rise above politics and stand fast against any grab for power her family might demand of her.

"Has Serralyn ever attempted to take the test of the Lake?"

20

Mandoran was the first to speak—or to cough, but it was a punctuation cough, not a genuine one. "What are you even thinking?" he demanded.

Teela and Sedarias were blue-eyed and clearly as unhappy with the question as Mandoran. Terrano, however, was thoughtful—which was enough of a clue.

"She hasn't," Teela said. "And just so you know, she's horrified that you could even ask that question, given you understand what the Lady's life is like. She's happy where she is, and she considers even the attempt to take the Lake's test to be life-threatening, especially now."

"She's curious, though," Terrano added. Three sets of cohort glares fell on him. Terrano was pretty good at ignoring them. "What? She is!"

"Allow her to ask her own questions at a more convenient time." It was a command. Had Sedarias uttered it, it would have been heated; Teela said the words, and Terrano grimaced instead of arguing. Or perhaps he just took his argument into the namebond sphere and left Kaylin and Logia out of it.

"I'm worried about this new beginning bit. I mean—I think they were trying to destroy humans as a race as well."

Terrano shook his head. "I think they might have been trying to make humans Immortal. They'd have to understand how you were made. No Barrani envies your lack of time, but a lot of them envy your lack of True Names."

"That's not what they would have achieved."

"No? You've watched Red in the morgue, right? Dissecting corpses isn't going to bring the dead back to life, either. But dissecting the living might make clearer how the mechanisms of your lives work." Terrano grimaced. "I'm not saying I agree with them, but I'm pretty certain I, at least, could continue to exist without the True Name that first woke me.

"I chose to keep it for a reason. If I could live without its constraints, I didn't want to live without its benefits."

"You mean the namebond."

"I mean my family. The family I chose. I wanted to share what I found with them—with them and no one else."

"You were born to some of those families or you'd never have been sent to the green."

Terrano shrugged.

"And if you'd never been sent, you wouldn't have found your true family. Good things can come out of bad things."

"Not normally."

Kaylin nodded. It was true. There was nothing romantic about starving and scrounging and almost freezing. There was nothing romantic about the poverty of the life of an orphan in the fiefs. She felt she could have been a decent Hawk without all of the terrible experiences. The other Hawks had managed it. She'd always hated it when people told her she should be grateful for the lessons of her early life—words offered by people who'd never actually lived the way she'd lived.

. . . and what had she just done? She'd done the *same damn thing* she hated so much to Terrano. She considered biting her own tongue off to prevent it ever happening again.

But at the same time, it was true. Even if they'd been thrown away—or eleven of the twelve had, because Sedarias had wanted to take the chance to become more powerful—they'd found each other. They couldn't get out of being sent to the green, but the choices they'd made while huddled together had been entirely their own. And because of those choices, they were here. Sedarias had survived her siblings and was An'Mellarionne. Serralyn was a student, with the much more quiet Valliant, in the Academia.

And Terrano was Terrano.

"Would your former allies have killed the Consort?"

Silence. Teela's eyes were midnight, her pallor off.

"We were not informed of their intentions," Sedarias said, her voice as stiff as Teela's expression.

Kaylin's frown, half aimed at herself, found a more comfortable target. "If they want to get rid of the Consort, why would they start this up only when they have a new potential Lady as guardian of the Lake?"

"Do you think they told us what their plans were?" Terrano asked with obvious disgust at Kaylin's line of questioning. "This isn't some garden-variety crime. That's the right phrase?"

"It is, if you mean normal, petty, unremarkable."

Terrano shrugged. "I got bored sometimes, and I listened in. Barrani Lords weren't the only lords involved in this. Mortals don't like being mortal. If someone offers them credible reason to believe that they can become Immortal, they might be suspicious, but they jump on it like starving cats.

"My guess? If the Barrani could convince the humans that a flaw in their initial creation led to the condition of mortality, they might be moved to support the Barrani endeavors."

"Let's leave the humans out of it for now. What, exactly, did the Barrani think they could do to wake their children?"

"I don't know. They didn't intend to let the children sleep eternally. I think Yvonne is a blind, if we're being honest. It's a way of garnering political support from those powerful families who have no interest in the family line of the current High

Lord. Saying *we're going to destroy the Lake* is likely to be met with more than resistance. Saying they've found someone more malleable who can become the Lady? That'd get support."

Logia left her position by the wall. "What did you say?"

Terrano frowned, because Logia, if not Bellusdeo, was still a Dragon. "What did I say?"

"They had a different source of wakefulness, a different source of life?" Logia's eyes were now blood red, the shift happening almost in an instant, as if she were Bellusdeo and Shadow was in the room.

"They weren't big on details when I was eavesdropping." Terrano shrugged as if it were someone else's problem.

Kaylin deeply resented that one of those people was her. But Logia's eye color and her expression were far more troubling than Terrano's attempt to ditch homework.

All of Logia's facial movements stilled; her eyes reddened further, which should have been impossible. Kaylin guessed that the sisters were having an emergency meeting behind Logia's eyes. She wondered if it would be Logia who continued, or if one of the sisters would step in instead.

Logia was the one who resumed talking, but she spoke carefully, her gaze intent. If Logia wasn't as trigger-happy at the mention of Shadow, something Terrano had said had pushed buttons.

Logia didn't take a seat, but she approached them as she spoke. "Bellusdeo says she mentioned the gaining of her adult name after you first met."

Kaylin nodded slowly. "The Outcaste. The Outcaste helped guide her. And the rest of you."

"And the rest of us. As you know—as we now know, who were motherless due to the wars—that was not the method by which our adult names would, or should, be gained. But it gave us a measure of freedom and selfhood, and it allowed us, finally, the use of our draconic forms."

"The Outcaste—the male Dragon—didn't know how female Dragons achieve their adult names," Kaylin said, frowning. "They're born with draconic form, and they find their True Names in a different way."

"A way very much like the way in which we found ours."

Silence.

She'd thought Bellusdeo peripherally involved because she was a fieflord and Shadow had been implicated. But she knew the involvement of these draconic sisters was now far more personal. "The Dragons don't have the Lake. I've never really understood what finding an adult name meant. I mean—aren't you born with names?"

"We're born, in theory, with half of our names," Logia replied. "Dragons weren't a native species in the world in which we landed; there was very little research we could do there. We could rely on personal history and overheard anecdotes—all young Dragons are very interested in adult names.

"But it wasn't a surprise to us when we met the Outcaste. We didn't know he was outcaste. We assumed—wrongly—that he had been displaced, just as we had, a casualty of war."

None of the Barrani in the room, with the sole exception of Teela, looked comfortable now.

"He guided us."

"Did he know your names?"

She shook her head. "We could have told him, of course, just as the cohort shared names with each other. We didn't."

"Was there anything unusual about your draconic forms?"

"How were we expected to know?" Logia's question was bitterness and frustration tied in a trembling knot. "Callandria doesn't think so. And I think she's right—but I'm not at all certain that the male Dragons found their names from the same sources. We can't experiment, now. But we did share our adult names with our sisters.

"If the source wasn't the normal acquisition for adult males, we had nothing to measure that against."

"Have you asked the chancellor?"

Silence.

This time a different sister emerged. The tilt of Bellusdeo's chin changed, as did the cast of her expression. "Research is needed. But understand that we did not wish to draw attention to even the narrow possibility that something was wrong with our names. Bellusdeo was alive. She wanted to remain that way. She did not want to become outcaste.

"She was being naturally cautious—all of us would have been, except perhaps Logia and Mezanne. But none of us were in her situation. We were dead. We could not approach Lannagaros. Until we met Imelda, we could not even try."

Kaylin couldn't argue with those facts. "You need to go speak with Lannagaros now. And the Arbiters, especially Kavallac. We need to know whether or not you . . ." Kaylin slowed to a stop. Bellusdeo was in there. Bellusdeo's body was her own. Her name was different than it had been when she'd considered herself adult by Dragon standards; it was an amalgamation of the names she'd known: her sister's names.

But it wasn't an amalgamation of their adult names. It was built from their childhood names. The names that had defined their relationship with each other.

"It comes back to the Outcaste," Kaylin finally said.

"The Outcaste had an interest in us, and he had the ability to traverse worlds, even after the fall of *Ravellon*. Perhaps because of its fall. He lives in *Ravellon*, does he not?"

Kaylin nodded. "But if he's outcaste, he's not Shadow. He can enter and leave *Ravellon* at will."

"You believe that somehow the source of our adult names and the possible plot against the Barrani are linked."

"I believe they could be. It would be convincing. The

gaining of your adult names gave you the draconic forms of adults. It did not otherwise contaminate or destabilize your existence." Kaylin spoke formally to this sister; she had a suspicion that the unnamed sister had been the true ruler of Bellusdeo's empire before her death.

"I can see how not having a True Name would be a problem for Dragons. But . . . your names served their purpose: you became capable of using your draconic forms. You became adults—but in the fashion male Dragons become adult."

The Dragon nodded slowly.

"Dragons don't have an official Lake, an official midwife. The Outcaste found you and guided you long before he was recognized and cast out. But what if what he led you to wasn't the source of Dragon names, but something other?"

The Dragon's eyes were orange with flecks of red.

"And if that was possible—and clearly the names you found for yourselves were partially effective—what would stop him from offering the same source to the Barrani?"

"This is *not* your investigation," Teela snapped.

Bellusdeo's sister ignored the interruption. "The only difference we noted was the ability to become draconic. All of us found our names with aid. All of us carried them as adult names. All but one of us died; Bellusdeo herself was lost to *Ravellon* and the Shadow it contained. She remembers very, very little of her captivity.

"But she was not physically transformed—"

"She was a *sword*," Kaylin snapped. "How much more proof of physical transformation do you need?"

"She wasn't contaminated. She wasn't absorbed. She didn't become a powerful Shadow."

"She couldn't become a sword on her own, unless there's something about draconic transformations we didn't get taught."

Helen cleared her throat, a signal that the heated conversation was going in the wrong direction.

Kaylin exhaled. It was going to be a long week. She was almost certain she'd be seconded to the Imperial Service again before she hit the Halls of Law in the morning. That always ticked off her sergeant, and he wasn't above sharing his annoyance and destroying his own furniture in the process.

"Your names served the purpose you were taught they should serve. What you weren't taught, the Outcaste wasn't taught. Your adult names are built on the foundation of your childhood names—you are not like the male Dragons. I don't think the Outcaste knew. He seems almost protective of Bellusdeo. Of all of you.

"But this source of True Names, this source of words—he led you to it. I'm wondering if he led others in the same way."

". . . you're thinking of the Barrani."

"I am. If an alternate source of life was found and offered to the Barrani, those who dislike bowing to the Consort and the Lake might have eagerly accepted it. But Barrani of power are suspicious bastards. They would have wanted to test it, right?

"If—and only if—whoever was in charge could offer the Barrani a different source of life, the Consort would become irrelevant. And if they could control this secondary source, it would give them almost undreamed-of power among the Barrani.

"The Lake's function depends on the Lady, and the Lady is chosen by the Lake. The Lady is above politics because she is, in some sense, the mother of all her people. It is by her hands that names are delivered to the sleeping, by her hands that they wake.

"Imagine a future in which it is not the Lake that decides, nor even the Lady, but people of power. Imagine a future in which those names are sold to the highest bidder, and without proper payment, no children of your line will ever wake. No children of the poor or insignificant.

"How long would the current High Lord retain his power in the face of such a reality? Barrani families of power care deeply about lineage."

"Not all of us," Teela said. She didn't otherwise disagree with anything Kaylin had guessed. As her eyes had already become as dark as they could, their color didn't change.

The Dragon turned to Teela. "Do you believe there is any accuracy in Kaylin's guess?"

"I see it as a possibility—one we had not considered. Further investigation is necessary. Kitling, this is *not* your investigation."

Kaylin nodded. It wasn't. Didn't mean she couldn't do the work in her personal time. "Shall we talk about Yvonne, then?"

Bellusdeo, or her regal sister, chose to depart. Her questions about Shadow and its possible use had become interlocked with elements of the sisters' shared past, and she wasn't ready to discuss those. But the mention of the Outcaste had unsettled even this sister.

Teela also chose to depart and accompanied Bellusdeo out of the parlor.

Sedarias, Mandoran, and Terrano chose to stay.

An invitation would be sent immediately. They hoped to be able to entertain Yvonne tomorrow, if Yvonne accepted that date. Sedarias doubted she would. Kaylin didn't.

But it would serve as a test: was it Yvonne's choice, or An'Tellarus's? If An'Tellarus was in charge, Sedarias felt four days from the invitation date would be more likely. If Yvonne could freely make the choice, Kaylin expected she'd say yes. In either case, they assumed An'Tellarus would also be visiting.

"Sedarias feels it important that you write your invitation immediately; she will personally see that it's delivered."

"Can't she write a proper invitation? I'll sign it."

"I did ask. Teela feels, however, that it would be best if you wrote it."

"It won't meet Sedarias's standards."

"No, dear. Teela feels that's the point. The invitation is not meant to come from a Barrani Lord; it's meant to come from a human. Less will be expected of you, and less offense taken."

"In theory."

"Sedarias and Teela have been arguing since Bellusdeo left."

Right. It was the cohort. The fact that Teela and Sedarias weren't in the same room meant nothing. There was no way to walk away from their argument.

Having made that plan, the cohort, Kaylin, and Mrs. Erickson gathered in the dining room for lunch. No one looked like they were enjoying the food, but everyone was grateful for Mrs. Erickson's presence. The older woman must have been able to tell they were all worried—or angry, or upset—but she didn't acknowledge it. If they didn't tell her—and they didn't want to involve her any further than she already was—she felt she wasn't meant to know. And didn't need to.

But she wasn't silent; the cohort was already the wrong kind of silent. She talked about baking, and about the day's visit to the Halls of Law. She was slightly embarrassed and also incredibly grateful that the Hawks at the public desk had been so happy to see her. Fallessian had accompanied her to the Halls before, and was capable of being friendly because he knew it put Mrs. Erickson at ease.

Fallessian never found any of this offensive, but he'd been actively involved with the current crisis. He couldn't be her escort at the moment.

Mrs. Erickson carried the conversation with her stories of the Halls of Law; her eyes and voice were bright. Kaylin thought this must have been what she'd been like when the ghosts of four children were her only companions.

And as if they were those ghostly children, the cohort and

Kaylin took comfort from her obvious delight, her desire to share something positive.

"That is her nature," Helen said, her voice warm with affection. "She would not deny you your anger or your pain should you feel the need to express it; she is not attempting to deny that those things exist. But she offers small joy where it might be accepted; she finds small sparks of delight in the darkness, and she holds those tightly so she can share them.

"As you suspect, the Arkon—the current Arkon—has asked that you be relieved of your normal duties for the next three days. Sergeant Hassan was practically red-eyed when he mirrored with the news—you will definitely need to find him a new desk."

"I wish the Halls of Law were a sentient building," Kaylin muttered. "Finding new desks stretches the departmental budget, and it's extra work no one needs."

Kaylin ate as she attempted to come up with an appropriate invitation.

Sedarias would have been standing over her shoulder for the entirety of lunch had Helen not intervened. Helen didn't approve of writing while at the lunch table.

In the end, it was Severn who came to her rescue.

Yvonne's from the West March. Her parents aren't lords of that distant court, and certainly not Lords of the High Court. Formal invitations would be highly unusual, and receiving one would be . . . not an insult, but a form of command. They'd imply a formal acknowledgment of the difference in power.

I'm a Lord of the High Court.

Yes. But you're human, and you're my partner. You're a Hawk. Yvonne won't expect a formal invitation. I'm not sure she'd know what to do with one.

But An'Tellarus might?

If you send a correct formal invitation, An'Tellarus will assume you're working for a Barrani Lord. If she assumes that, she'll feel free to interfere.

Given what she was like, she'll feel free to interfere anyway.

He chuckled. *True. But intervention takes many forms. I don't think she'll be offended; she won't expect nearly as much from, I'm sorry, a mortal.*

Kaylin held up a hand to catch the cohort's attention. "I'll deliver the letter myself."

"Teela will break your legs." This was Terrano, who was remarkably cheerful about it.

"Then Teela can deliver it. I'm a Hawk; she's a Hawk. The entire High Court knows that. She does what she wants—and she's clearly survived it. It'd be less political if it was Teela."

Mandoran snorted. "Sure. Less political. You really don't understand the Barrani, do you? It could be the most innocent letter in existence, and the Barrani would still consider it political."

"Teela has way less to lose," Kaylin snapped back. "If she can't handle a letter delivery, she wouldn't have survived being a Hawk." Her arms were folded as she glared at Mandoran.

Terrano snorted. "What? She's right."

I will deliver it, Severn said.

No way.

We're partners. I'll take the letter.

You're a human.

I'm a Lord of the High Court—we became lords at the same time. If you insist on carrying it yourself, we go as beat partners.

"Someone arguing with you?" Terrano asked, grinning. "I know exactly what that's like."

"He's not shouting at me, and he's not cursing," Kaylin replied.

"There'd probably be a lot of cursing if Helen wasn't gatekeeping." His grin grew smugger.

Kaylin shrugged. It was true. But keeping Ynpharion out of the time-sensitive discussions was the best policy. It's not like he wouldn't have access to her if she left her home. She even understood it, now: he was worried. He *hated* to rely on Kaylin for anything, but accepted—barely—that the Consort did. And Kaylin was better than other Barrani. Probably because Ynpharion thought she'd be easier to kill if things got messy.

"He does not think that," Helen told her gently. "He could not kill you without the Consort's express permission, and he knows she will never give it. If she made no attempt on your life when she felt the world—hers, and ours—was at terrible risk, there is no circumstance under which she would do so." Helen lifted a hand to the bridge of her nose. "Imelda is correct."

"About what?"

"I live in a house full of youthful vigor and passion."

". . . meaning we're all children," Kaylin said. When it came from Helen she didn't resent it. Much.

"Severn is, I feel, correct. The only other messenger one could send in safety is Terrano—but given his prior injuries, *safety* has become a relative term."

"If I deliver the letter, can I do it as a Hawk?"

"If the invitation is to arrive within the Tellarus domicile, yes. An'Tellarus is older than Teela and is known for her foibles and her interest in the strange and exotic. That," Helen added, "would be you and Severn."

"We're exotic?"

"For most of the Barrani, yes. Just as most of the Barrani would be considered exotic by the average human in Elantran streets."

"Not in the streets of Nightshade, they weren't," Kaylin replied. She exhaled.

You're not going to let this go, are you? Severn's tone was resigned.

Would you, in my position?

Yes.

Silence.

Finish eating. Write your letter. I'll be at the house soon.

21

Severn was as good as his word, but he always was.

By the time Kaylin had finished drafting her letter, Severn was at the door. He was dressed for work, which meant he'd come from the Halls of Law.

Kaylin wore her regular street clothing, grateful that she could just bundle her hair up and push a stick through it. Barrani clothing was much simpler than it looked. Barrani hair, which in theory never tangled or died at the ends, wasn't. She did wish she could just wear the boots Teela had given her, though.

Sedarias, predictably, was having a fit—but she was having a fit in her own rooms. Terrano's expression made clear that she wasn't happy with the letter, the courier, or the attire that courier chose to wear.

She's not wrong; if you were Barrani, this would be a disaster. But she considers you part of her home, if not part of her cohort; you're entangled in everything.

So . . . I'm making her look bad?

Severn chuckled. *She's a bit of a solipsist; the world revolves around Sedarias. Mostly in a bad way. If it were Teela, I might be more supportive. I'm surprised she's not here.*

Kaylin exhaled. "Does Teela intend to meet us there?"

"I am uncertain." Which wasn't a no. "There's only one way to find out."

What, exactly, are you doing? Ynpharion demanded the minute Kaylin cleared Helen's property line.

Delivering a letter to the High Halls.

To whom?

Kaylin really wanted to be able to just shut him out. *To a servant I met in the High Halls. She's from the West March, and she hasn't been here long.* She knew he'd take Yvonne's appearance—and name—from her and regretted coming in person. But she had to leave her house sometime.

Teela clearly intended to meet them at the High Halls; she'd arrived before them and was waiting, with her usual patience, at the height of the impressive stairs. She was, however, dressed as a Hawk, not a Lord of the High Court. Terrano, invisible, whistled. "Sedarias is not going to be happy with this."

"Did Teela tell her?" Kaylin whispered as they walked—in patrol style—down the road that led to the intimidating entrance of the High Halls.

"No—but I wouldn't have dressed as a Hawk, myself."

"Given how little you're actually seen, it's a wonder you bother with clothing at all."

He snickered. "Sedarias insists. Something something something dignity."

"Were any of those *something*s useful words?"

"You'd probably think so. I'm going to spend time with Abel, not you guys."

"Does Abel know this?"

"I have a standing invitation. It's sort of like the Academia."

Terrano didn't have a standing invitation to visit the Academia; he'd achieved tired resignation. The former Arkon chose to accept what couldn't be changed without either immense effort or bloodshed. Killian wouldn't kill Terrano; he'd divert his meager power into kicking the cohort member out—and at the moment, while Killian was rebuilding his power after his long, long hibernation, he had better things to worry about.

Kaylin thought Killian was actually fond of Terrano. And given what she'd seen of Bellusdeo and her sisters, she suspected the groundwork for the former Arkon's sense of resignation had been laid when Bellusdeo was a child under his care.

Teela's choice of clothing matched Kaylin's and Severn's, and because it did, it was Teela who drew all eyes. Fear was mixed with anger in hostile Barrani gazes; in some, anger and amusement blended—from a safe distance. Kaylin knew the Barrani didn't make friends the normal way but wondered if Teela had ever had any friends in the High Halls. Allies, maybe—but those allies would stay well away from someone who wore the effective equivalent of Imperial colors.

That's what the Hawks' tabard was. She understood. She'd worn the tabard with dogged pride for all her adult life. She knew the Halls of Law weren't perfect—but it couldn't be. Officers were people. People who'd gone out drinking far too late. People who spent the morning arguing with their mother. Or burying her. Or fighting with their spouse. Or taking as much care of sick children as working hours allowed.

In order for the Halls of Law to be perfect, people would have to be perfect.

People weren't perfect.

It was Caitlin who had taken the adolescent Kaylin aside. *You make mistakes—but Kaylin, we all make mistakes. The biggest mistake people can make, and I've seen it a regrettable number of times, is assuming that if you can't be perfect, there's no point in trying to be better.*

Caitlin had made hot chocolate for her; she'd been much younger, or felt like she'd been much younger. In Teela's eyes, Kaylin was practically the same person she'd been back then, but Teela was Immortal.

We try. Good and perfect aren't the same. But give up on good, and what you have is the fief of your childhood.

That didn't help the people who fell between the cracks. It didn't help the people who were neglected and abandoned.

It's hard work to care. It's hard work to be here, wearing the tabard, and dealing with the people who gave up on good, on helping anyone but themselves, a long time ago. It's too easy to feel that there's no good at all. Think about it this way: one life. One life at a time. If you reach out to one person, if you help one person, you're making a difference.

That single person might have been you. You can't save everyone, but that doesn't mean you can't save anyone.

She shook her head. As Kaylin entered the High Halls between the height of intimidating pillars, she took a deep breath. The Barrani clothing, styled and created to make a statement, had been far more comfortable than it looked. Maybe that's just what power was like: more comfortable than it looked from the outside.

But the clothing she wore now was the clothing she'd chosen. It was the job she'd dedicated her working life to doing. It wrinkled. It stained. It tore. Buttons needed to be replaced.

The Halls of Law hadn't sent her here, but the visit wasn't purely personal. The Barrani were part of the Empire, even if most of the lords loathed acknowledging that citizenship. They were bound by the rules that governed the Emperor's hoard.

She straightened her shoulders. She knew Teela was wearing her uniform to catch attention, to tweak the noses of the powerful. But Teela was, and had always been, a good Hawk. If she'd taken the job out of boredom or petty malice, she did the job. She'd taught Kaylin much of it.

Maybe that's the reason the Barrani Lords hated the Hawk when Teela wore it. Because she did the job. The mortal Hawks were beneath their notice; they only paid attention to mortal Hawks because killing a mortal Hawk meant laws of exemption could never be invoked, mortals not being Barrani.

Teela didn't speak a word. She did nod to any Barrani close enough to see it—and Barrani had good eyesight. The only time she spoke was after she'd drawn her sword. Teela wore the tabard today, but she hadn't armed herself for beat work. *Kariannos* seemed brighter in the light of the High Halls; the light glinting off the flat of the blade made the entire blade look almost white.

"I don't advise that you try," Teela said. "If you injure me at the behest of your lord, understand that it merely means you are disposable; unless you kill me, I will never allow the laws of exemption to be invoked. You and your family will be considered possible criminals by the Halls of Law, and you will be investigated to the full extent of our abilities."

Kaylin had no idea who Teela was threatening.

Hope sighed theatrically and lifted a wing to her right eye.

Oh. Invisible Barrani.

It happens all the time in the High Halls, Severn said. He hadn't drawn his weapons, even absent the chain. He wasn't worried. *It's almost a form of greeting. An'Tellarus once welcomed me in exactly this fashion.*

You can see them. Without Hope's wing.

Severn didn't answer. But he didn't expect the invisible people—there were four—to attack Teela. Teela did them the courtesy of drawing her sword, but Kaylin saw from their expressions, and from the blue of Teela's eyes, that she didn't consider them a credible threat. They were Barrani. They had to see that as well.

They stepped back.

"Don't worry," Terrano's voice said. "It's the normal variant of invisibility. I've been keeping an eye out for the other kind. But I think Abel understands enough of it to close off that avenue if necessary."

Kaylin couldn't see Terrano through Hope's wing. She sometimes could when he chose to become invisible, but that was probably because the plane to which he'd mostly moved was so close to her own.

"Abel thought it'd be safer if I kept an eye out for you while you were in the High Halls."

Abel wasn't present.

"He's with the Consort. When he's with the Consort, most of his attention is focused on her, or her immediate surroundings. It shouldn't take long to deliver a letter—but we're not going to the Tellarus rooms. Yvonne doesn't live in them officially."

"Wait—we're going to a wing of the High Halls that belongs to a lord we haven't met and aren't involved with?"

"Didn't Teela tell you? If it helps, Yvonne spends most of her time serving An'Tellarus—but you spend most of your waking time in the Halls of Law. While we could deliver a personal message to the Halls of Law and expect you to get it, it's not reliable."

"How do you know where she spends most of her time?"

She could almost hear the shrug she couldn't see in his tone. "I asked Abel. What? You know I'm lazy."

"And he answered."

"It's not about politics—I mean, not yet. But I suspect he thinks Yvonne might become important, and he doesn't want her co-opted or killed. He knows we don't mean her any harm, and he even believes that when push comes to shove—and I really don't get that phrase at all—we'll keep her as safe as we can."

If Kaylin had known they were meeting an entirely different Lord of the High Court, she'd've worn the Barrani dress. She'd meant to make a quiet statement to An'Tellarus, a statement about where her true loyalties lay. She assumed Teela was doing the same.

Trust Teela in this, Severn said. He walked a step behind Teela, leaving Kaylin keeping pace with the Barrani Hawk.

Teela knew the invitation would have to be delivered to the Sennarin quarters.

But won't we be considered disrespectful? Won't this be bad for Sennarin, which means bad for Yvonne?

Sennarin is not considered a politically powerful line at this time. An'Sennarin, as An'Mellarionne, is fighting to retain his hold on the seat. Our lack of obvious respect for the traditions of the High Halls will reflect that. If Teela showed up in full court dress, as she did to escort you to visit the Consort, and to visit An'Tellarus—

That was an accident. We didn't expect to be summoned.

—Sennarin would suddenly come under more difficult scrutiny. As it is, Teela's presence as a Hawk implies either contempt or dismissal—and that's safer. Those who are attempting to kill Ollarin know they won't offend An'Teela; those who consider Ollarin beneath their notice will be content to have Teela's confirmation.

She hasn't said that.

Well, it's the Hawks' uniform that does.

You're not worried.

No. Ollarin won't find the Hawk offensive. And he won't find the invitation offensive, either. Severn hesitated. *He may, as her legal guardian, ask that the invitation include him.*

This was nuts. They were already freaking out about An'Tellarus. Adding An'Sennarin to the invitation would probably cause Sedarias to die of apoplexy.

Heads up.

She turned to face closed doors. There was a single guard on duty, but An'Tellarus had had no obvious guards; clearly guards weren't necessary.

"We are here to deliver a letter to An'Sennarin," Teela told the guard. She'd sheathed her sword, but her hand rested easily atop its pommel. Kaylin wondered if it were habit or if it were deliberate; she guessed the latter, but Teela looked at ease.

The guard opened the door and stepped in. He was gone for perhaps five minutes.

When he returned, he offered Teela an actual bow, although his eyes were now a darker blue. Clearly, bowing to a Hawk was a gesture of respect that didn't sit well with him—but he did it. "An'Sennarin will see you now."

The doors then opened, exposing the interior. Kaylin was surprised. An'Tellarus's quarters were consistent with Barrani architectural norms. An'Sennarin's were not. She felt as if they had stepped through external doors into a garden, with hedges for walls, and gaps in those hedges that served as natural doors. The ceiling was sky.

She was reminded, then, that the High Halls were a sentient building. There was no limit to what could be done with the quarters occupied by Lords of the High Courts—those who had the power to gain perpetual quarters in the High Halls, near the seat of the High Lord's court.

But she hadn't expected hedges, and she hadn't expected the tree. A single tree rose well above the hedges, and it attained a height that could only be seen if she tilted her head pretty far back.

Teela was surprised into something that looked like a smile—if smiles could be both warm and also tinged with deep sadness.

"Where is he?" Kaylin asked.

"If he's waiting for us, he'll be up that tree."

Right. Because Barrani homes in the West March—the older style of home—were in the trees. She turned to Severn. Severn had some familiarity with An'Sennarin, but clearly the last meeting hadn't involved towering trees as a residence.

"Follow. I had hoped to hand the message to a servant; unlike you, I am not on leave, and Marcus is already in a foul mood."

She strode ahead, but stopped as they cleared the hedges that served as partial walls. There, surrounded by carefully laid stone in a slender layer, sat a fountain. It had been built to be taller than two grown men, its basin a pale, layered white that implied marble, although that didn't feel right.

Water pooled in the basin, eddying like tiny waves against a stone shore—but that wasn't what caught their attention.

The water that fell also rose in a pillar; there seemed to be no mechanical lift, no further stone or hidden piping—because there wasn't.

In the heart of the Sennarin quarters, a pillar of water in the shape of a woman stood—and it opened its arms to greet Kaylin Neya, its expression one of both surprise and delight.

Kaylin had enough presence of mind to glance in Teela's direction; Teela's lips were pursed. If Kaylin felt a hint of joy, Teela felt nothing but worry. This presence, this water, was almost the heart of the elemental water on this plane. It existed here, as it existed in the distant West March—but it was far more present here.

"This was *not* why we came," Teela murmured. She looked as if she would tell Kaylin to keep away from the water, but one glance at Kaylin's expression killed that plan.

Kaylin removed her boots and stepped into the stone basin. The water was warm, and the pillar moved instantly to embrace her. It was like a hug, but warmer and softer. As she had before, she could hear the water's voice, because the water's voice was, in large part, the voice of the Tha'alaan. She hadn't visited the Tha'alani quarter in what felt like years but had been months at most.

She listened to the water, spoke to the water, but she didn't reach for the Tha'alaan. In the heart of the High Halls, she was afraid that her own thoughts and fears would muddy the waters upon which the Tha'alaan—and its people—depended.

Even so, the water said. *You are with Olleandar? Ah, Ollarin, as he is now called.*

"We haven't met him yet. We just came to deliver a letter. But . . ."

But? Ah. You wonder why I am here?

Kaylin nodded. As far as Kaylin was concerned, the water could be anywhere it wanted. There was no malice in it. If elemental water wanted to flood the world—and didn't care much about anything already living in it—this water had evolved through contact with the Tha'alani. Life was precious, if short, to the water here.

Ollarin invited me. I am not his to control here, or rather, he does not exert control. He finds comfort in the fountain. And I find him precious, although I do not entirely understand why. Some things are not to be questioned, for no answers arise. He has made a home for himself here, but it is not his home—and he wished for my presence, the only part of home that he can carry with him.

I am terrifying to the Barrani, when unleashed. They believe he will unleash me should they attempt to harm him here. But it is not himself for whom his fears are strongest. Deliver your letter, but Kaylin—I understand the whole of Ollarin, and if you can find it in yourself to do so, offer him friendship.

"He's Barrani. Barrani don't really want friends."

He is Ollarin. Yvonne is his friend. But his family, as hers, is dead by the hands of the man Ollarin finally killed. He is young, for his kin. You know I cannot command you; there is no battle of wills between us. But I ask it, friend of the Keeper. I ask it, Chosen.

Kaylin listened for one long breath. The water wouldn't drown her; she didn't need to breathe to shelter in its embrace.

But this wasn't what she had been expecting. The water loved the Tha'alani as a people, and considered them kin—or as close to kin as such wild forces were capable of having. She had never expected that it might feel the same way about a Barrani Lord of the High Court.

Did you hear that? she asked Severn.

I did.

You're not surprised?

Oh, I am. But the water wasted its time making its request. Come out. Teela's getting impatient.

How can you tell? Teela was always impatient. For an Immortal, who had nothing but an endless stretch of time, she sure cared a lot about wasting any of it. Kaylin stepped out of the water, and the water retreated; her clothing wasn't even damp.

"Are you finished?" Teela demanded, proving Severn right. The world often proved Severn right.

"The water wanted to ask me a favor," Kaylin replied, trying not to match that tone and mostly succeeding.

This changed Teela's expression, and not in a good way. "The water wanted to ask you a favor."

Hope snickered. She wondered if the water had spoken with Hope, or if Hope had spoken to the water, or if the two ancient forces had simply ignored each other.

"It wasn't a big favor."

"What was the favor?"

"She wanted me to befriend Ollarin."

Teela's eyes were blue. They got darker. She said nothing. Instead, she turned and began to walk toward the giant tree.

Kaylin had some experience with the West March version of a treehouse: it was a place in which Barrani were meant to live, not huddle and play. The tree itself provided walls and ceilings; the Barrani didn't cut down other trees to build the platforms upon which furniture and people stood. She wasn't as clear on the delivery of goods—she didn't imagine the tree could randomly produce food and clothing. Trees were not sentient buildings.

But the West March trees seemed to grow and shift—with time—at the desire of the lords who claimed them as ancestral homes.

Lirienne did not live in a tree; he lived in a large hall—smaller in scope and size than the High Halls, but similar in architecture.

She froze. The Lord of the West March was here, somewhere. He was in the High Halls. But he hadn't called for Kaylin, and Kaylin had zero desire to meet him here.

"What are you thinking?" Teela asked, the question a command.

"The Lord of the West March is probably in the High Halls somewhere. I'm thinking it would be better to avoid him today, if possible."

"Dressed like that? It is not only possible but mandatory. He has claimed you as *kyuthe*. You are his chosen kin, and your deportment and manners will reflect on him." Teela exhaled. "But you will have to see him while he is here. He understands that you have duties to the Imperial Halls of Law; duties to kin do not supersede duties to lord—in this case, the Emperor. He will, however, expect that you reach out on your own time and in an appropriate fashion.

"There are days," she added, in Elantran, "where I curse the very existence of my people." This was clearly one of them. "I know we've made clear that Barrani politics are deadly games—for Barrani. We'd like you to avoid as much of them as possible."

"She is," Severn said.

Teela glanced at him before shrugging. "Let's get this over with."

The equivalent of Helen's parlor was on the first floor of the tiered upper layers of the tree, which Kaylin considered a kindness to guests. The stairs that grew, in an upward spiral, from the tree's trunk weren't girded by something as simple as a railing. They had to walk—or Kaylin did—as close to the trunk as possible as they made their way up. She wondered if Barrani ever had a fear of heights.

Then again, Severn didn't.

But the stairs opened up onto a large platform, the trunk being its central pillar as it continued up into the boughs. Above their heads was a knotwork of twined branches, the bark a pale brown with ivory flecks. Leaves and much smaller branches had budded or blossomed, lending color for the gaze of those who might choose to look up. There was no stone; the walls, such as they were, were implied by leaves and vines. Kaylin had no doubt she could be punted through those walls.

A Barrani man was seated on a long, wide couch. Next to him, rising almost the instant she caught sight of visitors, was Yvonne.

Teela cleared her throat.

Right. Invitation. They were here for a reason. Kaylin, however, smiled at Yvonne. Yvonne, eyes green with flecks of blue, smiled back; the blue dimmed. She really reminded Kaylin of Serralyn.

"I'm sorry to bother you so soon," Kaylin began.

"An'Tellarus has been expecting your invitation since you left."

Kaylin winced. "Not patiently, I assume?"

To Kaylin's surprise, Ollarin, who had not yet introduced himself, chuckled. Out loud. "I see you did meet her."

"I'm Corporal Kaylin Neya. This is my partner, Corporal Severn Handred. And this is Corporal Teela Danelle. We serve the Hawks."

"I am Ollarin, An'Sennarin. And you have met my friend, Yvonne of Sennarin." Yvonne's eyes widened, but only a little; clearly that wasn't the name she was used to hearing. "But you are not here on official business, surely?"

"No." Kaylin took a risk. "We thought there'd be less trouble if we came as mortal Hawks."

"And not more trouble if An'Teela did?"

Teela smiled her *I'd like to see them try* smile, which wasn't exactly comforting. It seemed to bounce off An'Sennarin. "We did not mean to trouble you," Teela said to Ollarin. "But we were informed that Yvonne's residence is in the Sennarin quarters. The letter is meant for Yvonne."

Kaylin immediately crossed the distance that separated her from the Barrani young woman. "I wrote it myself." She handed Yvonne the letter. "If it's okay with you, we'd like to wait for your reply. I don't like the High Halls on the best of days, but things seem almost as tense as they were the first time I visited."

"When was that?"

Kaylin frowned. "A year ago? Maybe less?"

"Kaylin," Severn added, "has two modes of remembering dates. Anything that happened up to three weeks ago is relatively solid. Anything that happened more than three weeks ago could be months or years in the past."

Kaylin glared in Severn's direction, but she understood, from his comment, that he knew both of these people—the lord and the servant—and liked them both. Or trusted them both, inasmuch as one could trust Barrani. It surprised her. If he'd met them in the past, it wasn't as a Hawk. "I have mortal memory."

"We both have mortal memory," Severn replied. "Regardless, Kaylin's invitation is genuine and harmless. How impatient was An'Tellarus?"

"She's not with us at the moment," An'Sennarin replied.

"Barely," Yvonne added. "I think she expected you to go home yesterday and write out a precise invitation immediately. And send it by courier. Or magic."

"Not magic," Teela said. "That type of delivery must be very carefully arranged."

"Most people would just mirror—but the sentient buildings don't seem to be fond of the mirror network."

Yvonne rolled her eyes. "They like having things in writing, because it serves as evidence if things go badly."

"Mirrors can be recorded—we have Records in the Halls of Law. Mirror calls are captured and can be reviewed on command. Well, on someone's command."

"An'Tellarus isn't terribly modern," Yvonne said. "But as she points out, she doesn't aspire to modernity. She just wants to outlive every Barrani she's ever met who dared to offend her or treat her with less respect than her due."

Having met her, Kaylin thought that described most of the Barrani, because An'Tellarus was larger than life and appeared to expect large amounts of respect. And obedience.

"It is unlikely to make her life boring," Teela said, a smile enfolding the words. Her eyes were still blue, but less dark. "I would love to know how you came to be in her service."

"Oh—Ollarin recommended me. Or asked her if she could teach me how to survive in this mess of a giant stone building."

"You have not been her student for very long, have you?" But her smile lost its edge as she looked at Yvonne.

"Feels like half a century," Yvonne replied, grimacing. She didn't take Teela's barbed question to heart. "But no. Things are more complicated in the High Halls. I'm allowed less perfect behavior than Ollarin because I'm not a Lord of the High Court, and I've not been called to take the Test of Name. I won't take it," she added, folding her arms.

"No?"

"Well, I hear failure is no longer a death sentence, but if my behavior isn't good enough—and it isn't, I admit it—for a servant in the High Halls, it's definitely not good enough for a lord. If I want to exist as I've existed for almost all of my life, I'd need to be as powerful as An'Tellarus or An'Teela. I'm never going to be that powerful. Being a lord only makes my failures more obvious; it doesn't protect me from them."

Kaylin *liked* Yvonne. Yvonne's attitude about the High Court was pretty similar to Kaylin's attitude about the Hawks. She wanted to be corporal because it was a rank that didn't differ hugely from her previous rank—except for the pay, which was better. She *didn't* want to be sergeant or Hawklord. Yes, they gave the orders, and yes, she had to obey them, but . . . they were good at their jobs, and so much of those jobs seemed to be babysitting.

Or shredding hardwood desks to splinters, but she couldn't manage that either.

"I'm a Lord of the High Court by accident," Kaylin told Yvonne, matching her prior brief grimace. "I'd have to be—can you imagine the High Court encouraging the merely mortal to go take a test that will give them the status the lords there share?"

Yvonne shook her head. "In the old days, I could imagine it would be a way of disposing of inconvenient mortals, though."

Given what had existed at the heart of that test? Yes. She was right. "Inconvenient Barrani, too. Do you have to check with An'Tellarus before you give us an answer?"

Yvonne nodded.

"Kaylin will wait here for your return," Teela said. She then frowned. "If it is acceptable to you, I will escort you."

It was clearly acceptable to both Yvonne and Ollarin, and the Hawk and Yvonne headed down the stairs.

22

When Yvonne and Teela had been gone for long enough that no words from this platform would reach them, Ollarin turned to Severn. "It's good to see you," he said, his eyes a lighter blue, his lips folded in a smile that would have sat well on Yvonne's face. "You've been well?"

"I've been busy, but should have made time. I've seen Yvonne," he added in what was, for Severn, a shockingly apologetic tone.

"No one cares what an insignificant servant does; everyone watches a new lord," Ollarin said, nodding. "I assume you did not visit in the uniform you are now wearing."

"No. Yvonne left on errands for An'Tellarus, and I met her outside the High Halls. But the court itself has been more openly hostile in its various faction wars—and the Emperor has noticed." There was no warning in the tone, but the words carried it anyway. "Yvonne wasn't involved, before."

An'Sennarin's eyes became a much darker blue, the transformation instant.

"What does this invitation mean?"

Severn fell silent. Kaylin was silent because she was so surprised by the interchange.

What should I say? she asked.

You may tell him the truth; I don't believe it will harm either Yvonne or the Consort. It may be of aid. Ollarin is, and has always been, beloved of the elemental water. It was why he was pressed to come to the High Halls, and why, in the end, almost all of his kin died when he attempted to refuse. He is powerful *in his own right. But he does not wish to conquer; he will use his power only in defense of the very few remaining people for whom he cares.*

And Yvonne is one of them.

Severn nodded. *Answer as you please. I don't think, even if he considered you a genuine threat, he could kill you with the tools he has at hand.*

This wasn't a promising response. "How much do you know about Yvonne's activities outside Sennarin?" she asked, countering his question with a question of her own.

An'Sennarin was silent, as if asking himself the questions Kaylin had asked Severn. It wasn't Kaylin whose opinion he trusted here. It was Severn. She bit back curiosity; she wanted to know how Severn knew Ollarin.

"She is of my family line; I have adopted her. I am aware of some of her activities—but if An'Tellarus chooses to have Yvonne participate in activities that would not usually be considered dangerous, I am not always informed beforehand."

"So she doesn't need your permission."

"In theory she does. But you have met An'Tellarus, and if you haven't spent long in her company, I am certain Severn has told you all you need to know. I owe her my sanity, if not my life. I owe her Yvonne's life as well, indirectly; it was An'Tellarus who took Severn to the West March in search of Yvonne.

"There is some danger to Yvonne when she is not within the High Halls, but I have reason to believe while she is, she is safe. She is safe within the Sennarin quarters; she is safe—possibly safer—while she serves An'Tellarus. But she is not as we who rule must become." These last words were said softly, syllables wrapped around an endless bitterness. "And she liked you."

"You know about the test of the Lake," Kaylin said, words flat.

He didn't even blink. "It is not what you think it is," he replied, acknowledging the statement. "I, as Lord, did not instruct or demand that she submit to the test of the Lake, which is the custom in the High Halls. The Barrani have oft viewed the position of Lady as a political position—or what could be a political position should that power come into the hands of their familial lines.

"Perhaps you will not believe this, but the Lake reached out to Yvonne. I do not know how. The Lake is not the water—but it was the water that informed me. Yvonne can touch the water, but she does not hear its voice so clearly as I."

"When?" Kaylin had a sinking feeling about this.

"Within the past month."

"Does An'Tellarus know?"

Ollarin hesitated for one breath, as if breath could not be drawn. "She suspects, yes. Yvonne is not skilled at prevarication; she finds An'Tellarus intimidating. There is a reason An'Tellarus invited you to visit her quarters shortly after your meeting with the Lady." He exhaled. "The reason An'Tellarus has retained power for centuries is her lack of predictability. I do not know what she suspects or expects—but neither do her enemies. Inasmuch as I trust any living Barrani, I trust her with Yvonne's safety.

"I have enemies An'Tellarus does not have. But I am not considered a weakness of An'Tellarus's. No one of power believes that they can strike at An'Tellarus through me. People of power might otherwise believe that they can strike at Sennarin through Yvonne."

And they wouldn't be wrong.

"Her interest makes clear that there is risk involved in that approach; Yvonne has attended An'Tellarus at public gatherings, and An'Tellarus has made clear that she views the West March urchin with affection." He grimaced at the last sentence.

Kaylin frowned. "Am I known at court?"

"Of course you are known. You are both Lord of the High Court and mortal. You are Chosen, to those who care about the old ways and stories; the Marks on your skin, where revealed, cannot be denied. What can be denied is the relevance of those Marks, but the Arcanists view you with . . . caution, which implies that the Marks have power."

"And Severn?"

"He is also of interest. He is not Chosen, but he, too, emerged from the Tower. It is Severn's ownership of the unusual weapon he wields that makes him significant—and resented. But much of that enmity is centered in the West March. If the Lady did not obviously favor you, he might be more visible, but there is something about Lord Severn that evades notice."

"And not me."

"You are not a quiet presence, no. Even when you are silent, you almost seem to be quivering in place, as if you might burst into action at any moment. You are protected, to a certain extent, by An'Teela; she is, to you, what An'Tellarus was to me in my early tenure. An'Teela is even more infamous than An'Tellarus, but not, in my opinion, more dangerous." He exhaled. "Yvonne was discovered in the West March—by Lord Severn.

"You may wish to discuss this with him—but not here. Not anywhere in the High Halls. You are aligned with the Consort; she is political, because she holds that position. But you are also aligned with the Lady, who is not political. She is both of those people. She cares much for the High Lord and the Lord of the West March. It is not clear to most of the court why she cares for you, but your political relevance is minor, and your Marks might be of use to her.

"It is your visit to the heart of her quarters, so close to the Lake, that is of interest. And I assume that your interest in Yvonne arises from that. Yvonne will not, and would never, harm the Lady; even if we were born in the West March, it is here, at the seat of our people's power, that we are wakened. She has not met the Lady; her position is far, far too low for that.

"What do you intend?" Here, his eyes grew bluer; they weren't as dark as Teela's had been, but much closer.

"She intends no harm to Yvonne," Severn said when Kaylin failed to answer. Kaylin's failure was tied up in her own sense of both duty and loyalty; she was torn. She did like Yvonne. But fractured as their friendship had become, she felt a sense of responsibility for the Consort, the Lady. She'd wanted to meet Yvonne to assess the level of threat *to* the Consort, and the level of entanglement; to find out if Yvonne was a credible, useful weapon that could be wielded against one of the few Barrani Kaylin actually liked, cohort excepted.

"I do not command Yvonne, although in theory I have that right. And I believe An'Teela has returned with An'Tellarus's reply."

An'Tellarus's reply was permission. Yvonne, in theory, required it.

"An'Tellarus accepts your invitation," Yvonne said, speaking so quietly it was almost hard to hear her; there were small chimes, invisible to the eye beyond the fall of leaves, that sounded periodically—and they were louder.

The invitation hadn't been extended to An'Tellarus, but the cohort had guessed—correctly—that An'Tellarus would come as guardian, even if that was An'Sennarin's technical role.

"She doesn't think it's a good idea to have Ollarin come with us."

Teela nodded. "An'Sennarin is too new, and too untested. And An'Mellarionne resides with you. An'Tellarus has reached an age where she has proven herself in combat and politics;

she can go wherever she wants. She has ways of making clear both her alliances and her affections; it is her affection that is dangerous to cross.

"An'Sennarin does not have that luxury. If he is in the presence of An'Mellarionne and no blood is shed, assumptions about his alliances will be made. Sedarias's enemies are many—far more than Sennarin's. An'Sennarin has done much to cleanse his line, and to shed the alliances his previous lord nurtured. He has not done enough, but he has only had decades in which to do so.

"Sedarias has had months." Teela exhaled. "An'Tellarus is no fool; she knows. It would be best for all concerned if she did not insist on chaperoning Yvonne—but she does insist. And in her position, I would insist as well."

Yvonne flinched, but didn't argue.

Kaylin agreed. Sending Yvonne on her own would be like sending Serralyn to a meeting of the Lords of the High Court on her own. It was never going to happen, no matter what preferences were expressed. Terrano would follow her even if every other person had reluctantly given way.

"Did An'Tellarus demand a different date?"

Yvonne shook her head. "She said the day is up to me."

"Will you visit tomorrow, then?"

Yvonne nodded.

The Lady wishes to see you again after tomorrow's meeting with Yvonne. Yvonne should join you. Ynpharion spoke formally. He'd been listening in—of course he had—but hadn't interrupted once.

Does the Lady need to send a formal invitation? Or can we just arrive?

Arrive. The High Halls will know, and a formal invitation will be noted.

What if Yvonne doesn't want to visit?

Kaylin could feel Ynpharion's frustration, but he kept it out of his words. The Lady must have been listening. *If she is summoned, she will accept the summons. But a formal summons would draw even more attention to her than she has already received; the Lady wishes to avoid this, if at all possible.*

So it's unofficial.

It is both unofficial and of the highest priority. The Consort asks, but does not command, that you allow me to observe the visit to your home.

Kaylin shook her head. *There's too much that's likely to come up that could get messy—An'Tellarus is coming, and she's not a person who likes anyone else to be the center of attention. Sedarias will be there, and you know what Mellarionne is going through—it's just going to be too tangled. The Lady doesn't have Mellarionne's best interests at heart, if she considers Mellarionne at all.*

Ynpharion didn't respond—but he didn't berate, either.

Kaylin turned to Ollarin and offered him a formal bow at odds with her uniform.

"I trust you with something precious, Lord Kaylin." He opened his mouth, no doubt to add a warning, but closed it again before he spoke the words. He returned the bow she had offered and then offered the same gesture to both Teela and Severn. Teela returned a nod, which was proper etiquette.

"No harm will come to her while I am present," Severn said, offering assurance instead of respect.

It was the assurance An'Sennarin desired.

Kaylin turned to Yvonne. "See you tomorrow."

In spite of the color of her eyes, Yvonne managed a smile.

Helen was waiting by the open door when Kaylin, Severn, and Teela arrived.

Sedarias was in high dudgeon, but from Kaylin's perspective, this only meant she was silent. Given Mandoran's and Terrano's expressions, she wasn't silent on the inside of their heads, but

Kaylin didn't ask. Terrano, on the other hand, was willing to share.

"They're having an argument about what you should wear. If it were just Yvonne, no one would care. But it's An'Tellarus, and it's your house, so you're going to be judged by the quality of your hospitality."

Kaylin wasn't of a mind to put on a show to impress An'Tellarus. An'Tellarus was there as guardian or high-powered guard; she wasn't the actual invitee.

"No, dear, but Sedarias's concerns are not without merit. You have a few Barrani dresses, and if they are not suitable, I can create a dress you could wear. It will not persist should you be forced, for an unforeseen reason, to leave the premises."

Not, given unexpected emergencies, the smart choice. "I'll think about it."

"Teela is arguing against, if that's any help." Terrano's grin was followed by a wince.

"How's the rest of the vote going?"

"Most of us don't care what you wear. You're mortal. She's not going to expect you to be full-on Lord of the High Court. The problem is, she *can* take offense in a political fashion. You've got no traction on the High Court. You do have friends. One of them has just arrived from the West March—and he has proclaimed you *kyuthe*. Oh: you need to find the ring he gave you, no matter what else you wear."

"Teela," Mandoran added, "says you're wasting Kaylin's time, and she might need it if she can't find the damn ring immediately."

Kaylin expected dinner, if the cohort came down at all, to be more of the same. She headed up the stairs toward Annarion's chambers, and was met by Andellen, who was on the way down.

"No change?" she asked him.

He shook his head. "I have information for An'Teela, and one or two interviews to conduct."

She looked at his sword. "Will they end in bloodshed?"

"Not in the type of bloodshed that would justify the interest of the Imperial Hawks, no." Meaning he was off to talk to Barrani. "An'Mellarionne has provided me with two possible leads and several family names. An'Teela, when she is not visiting the High Halls, has been investigating some of them."

Kaylin could guess where Sedarias had pulled some of the names from. She grimaced. Why did things always get so complicated when Barrani were involved? This was petty, and she knew it. But she'd never been one for jewelry and now had to find—and wear—a very large, very expensive ring. Finding it came first.

He's not even going to be here, she said, sharing her pettiness with the only person whose namebond Helen never blocked.

It's not meant for him. It's meant for An'Tellarus to see. She will understand what it signifies. Sedarias believes it will change the way she approaches you or perhaps cause her to pause.

You don't.

No. But I have some familiarity with An'Tellarus. If anything, it's likely to make you more interesting, not less—and you're Chosen, so you're already interesting enough.

But you're not telling me not to wear it.

If we had no cause to return to the High Halls for some time, I'd tell you it's not worth it. But that's not going to happen unless and until we can resolve the Consort's difficulty with the Lake. The ring is likely to have the desired effect on Barrani who aren't An'Tellarus. The Lord of the West March is now in the High Halls.

"Severn is right, dear." Helen exhaled, which implied her expression; only her voice was in the room with Kaylin. Hope had surrendered his perch on her shoulder because she'd been crawling under the bed. Her old apartment had a floorboard that could be lifted, and a hollow space beneath it where one could hide important things.

"I'm not certain you'll find what you're looking for," Helen continued. "While these rooms were created to mimic your first apartment, they are not an exact replica—and a hole in the floor is entirely unnecessary."

"Wait—do you know where the ring is?"

"Yes."

Kaylin jumped up, which was unfortunate for either her head or the bottom of the bed.

"Why didn't you tell me?" She tried not to curse because Helen didn't like it, especially now that Mrs. Erickson was living with them. Mrs. Erickson didn't mind—but she'd spent most of her free time in the public office of the Halls of Law, and she knew how Hawks spoke.

"I wasn't certain about your decision. If Sedarias knows that you can find the ring, she will insist you wear it. Proudly. If you could not find it, she could not insist." Helen exhaled. "I understand why you chose to hide the few things you considered valuable beneath the flooring in your old apartment. There is a small cupboard at the back of your closet that serves the same function. I did not see a need to hide the dresses there.

"But the robes of the green and the robes of the intermediary are also in your closet."

"You think I should wear the robes of the harmoniste."

"I have no opinion. I understand the concern of the cohort—but An'Tellarus is coming to *my* domain. There is nothing she can do to harm you here, regardless of what you wear." Helen hesitated. "I will not make excuses for Sedarias, but only half of her concerns involve her own survival. She is very worried for you."

Kaylin's exhalation was longer. "I wish she'd worry in a less condescending way. I'm not a child. I'm not a foundling. She *knows* I can be useful."

"It is not her way. People of equal power are rivals or enemies. People of lesser power are, if she cares for them, in need of protection—and she cannot be everywhere, at every moment, to ensure their survival."

"So . . . you're saying she doesn't consider the cohort to be her equals, either?"

"She is certain Teela is."

"So, no."

"She is not a person who grew up surrounded by familial love, but she desired it in her own fashion. She is not passive; what she desired, she built. The cohort is her family, and as she always feared, her weakness. But it is also her strength. That is the nature of swords; they cut two ways; they have two edges.

"You are not part of her family, but you are part of Teela's, and she knows that if the cohort entangles you in a way that costs your life, it will break Teela's already tenuous attachment to them. In protecting you, she is protecting what she built. Honestly, Sedarias would have been a very good, very capable Dragon."

Kaylin exhaled. "I'm going to sleep on it. Unless Hope has anything to add?"

Squawk.

"Your presence is not required at the Halls of Law tomorrow, but you will need to be awake and prepared in the morning."

"Did I set visiting time for the morning?"

"Yes, dear."

Ugh.

There were no emergency mirror calls during the evening. Kaylin had been afraid, in the early days, that Helen would simply refuse to let the calls through because Helen felt Kaylin needed sleep.

Helen, however, insisted that she would never do that.

While she did believe Kaylin needed more sleep than Kaylin thought she did, she also knew the emergency calls were important to her chief tenant. Lives could, and did, hang in the balance; people weren't mirroring just to chat about their haircuts or their horrible bosses. Or their relationship troubles—although most people didn't call Kaylin for that.

Hope, usually the laziest of sleepers, was already in the air and hovering above her face. His squawk was louder and far more irritable than Helen's voice. She wondered if he'd smack her face with his wing—but he'd have to land to do that.

Kaylin rose instead. Having made something of a decision, she headed toward her closet, stumbling over her boots. "Light," she said. Helen often drew the curtains to let light in; she knew Kaylin didn't appreciate bright light first thing in the morning.

Squawk.

"Yes, yes. I'm awake now—you can stop biting my hair and settle down." She'd been so stressed out about what to wear it had taken ages to fall asleep—and Kaylin could sleep standing up if she was tired enough. She certainly had the demerit points to show for it.

The green dress—the harmoniste's dress—hadn't magically vanished the way it did the first time she'd worn it. The clothing she'd been wearing had been transformed, replaced by the clothing worn to the ceremony in the distant green. It wasn't supposed to persist; it appeared, it was worn, it vanished.

Kaylin wondered how it was that the Barrani couldn't just counterfeit the damn dress if they wanted to take over the role of harmoniste.

"It has been tried, historically," Helen's voice said. "Do you need help?"

"No—Barrani clothing only *looks* fussy. What do you mean it's been tried?"

"Exactly that. The Barrani are political by nature. They

consider respect an element of fear. They consider titles and hierarchies to be almost as important as air. The Teller's crown and the harmoniste's clothing *can* be, as you put it, counterfeited. But the roles themselves still need to be filled. Only the young or the foolish believe they can, by dressing the part, fool the green."

"Maybe they don't believe in the green."

"It is not a mistake from which they could learn."

Kaylin parsed that slowly. "Meaning they died."

"Meaning they died, yes. For their affront. But they were not the only ones. The Barrani may be foolish or egotistical, but persistent, permanent memory means they seldom make the same mistake twice. I believe you will need some help."

"Why? I'm dressed. I told you, Barrani clothing only looks fussy."

"Your hair."

Kaylin sighed. "Yes, Helen, I'd love help with my hair. And next time I set a meeting time, could you remind me to make it later in the day? Barrani don't need sleep. I do."

"I remind them of this frequently. The ring is on the dresser."

Right. The ring. "I really don't like rings," she grumbled as she lifted it and put it on her left hand. "They just feel awkward, and they bump into everything." This one was worse than she remembered. It was a thick band, and it sported an enormous emerald, although the emerald was set into the band itself.

Helen played with her hair. Teela, mindful of their first visit, had provided clothing and accessories. Kaylin didn't hate necklaces as much as rings, but Helen didn't touch any of the jewelry except the hair things.

The reason she'd hesitated to wear this dress was the Marks of the Chosen. They were exposed because the dress itself exposed more skin. Kaylin's very conservative style of dress was out of necessity. She couldn't expose her arms or the back of her neck without also exposing the Marks of the Chosen.

She didn't wear those proudly.

And maybe she should. Among the Barrani she should. She had to stop being afraid of the Marks. She had to accept them. Whether or not she was worthy of bearing them, they were hers. She wondered if confidence came in waves, rising like the tide and inevitably falling as the tide receded. Maybe it was always going to be this way, and she had to learn to live with it.

Maybe there was never going to be The Moment in which she had fully and finally become a Good person, or the Right person. Maybe there was never a time when that work was finally done and she could relax.

And maybe, if she hesitated on the inside of her room, her hand on the door, Sedarias would come storming up the stairs to inspect her, and she'd forget all the rest of the worry because immediate survival would become the priority. Thinking about it that way was almost funny: Sedarias's rage coming to the rescue, and taking Kaylin away, for a moment, from her own inadequacy.

She opened her own door. The hall was empty.

She headed toward the stairs but stopped outside Annarion's room. Annarion seldom left it, and Mandoran often kept him company through his constant vigil. Maybe the need for sleep was a gift. She hesitated at the door, and as she did, she felt her cheek—her marked cheek—begin to warm.

23

What Kaylin needed at this very moment was not to start bleeding. Not while she was dressed for intimidating company and surrounded by concerned Barrani who noticed and remembered everything. But she didn't retreat from the door. The mark had been relevant to Nightshade's survival in the end; if she hadn't started bleeding, she'd never have raced to his fief. It was heating up; she lifted a hand to her cheek both to touch it and to cover it.

She then knocked on the door. Helen could open the door but wouldn't without permission from its occupant. She accorded the cohort the same respect for privacy that she accorded Kaylin.

The door did open. It was Mandoran. He looked at her, blinked, his eyes shading into the color of surprise before returning to their regular blue. He took in the dress, probably noticed the ring, certainly noticed the hair, and stopped on her face.

"Your cheek."

"Is it bleeding?"

"Can't tell—you're covering it. You probably don't want to bleed on that dress."

"It's unlikely to be damaged or stained, unlike my regular clothing."

Mandoran shrugged. Fair enough. "Are you here because of that?"

Kaylin nodded. "Yvonne isn't due for another hour—"

"Forty-five minutes, dear."

"—and my cheek was warm, so I thought I'd check in on Nightshade before I joined the rest of our forces."

He chuckled. "Sedarias is marshaling the cohort. I'm not sure she'll like what you're wearing. The ring, yes. The dress?" He shrugged. Mandoran and Terrano had argued that Kaylin's attire was irrelevant. Helen had argued that inappropriate clothing could be wielded against Kaylin if An'Tellarus wanted to threaten her.

Kaylin privately thought An'Tellarus would come up with her own excuses if that was her intent—she didn't need to hang them on anything factual.

Teela, however, had relented. *If she needs to find offense, let's make her work for it, shall we?* That, Kaylin understood. It changed the intent behind clothing. Not wearing whatever happened to be both comfortable and lying around became a statement, an act of defiance.

"Well, Teela said—"

"I heard. But . . . I'm not sure she meant for you to wear *that* dress. Why did you choose that one?"

"It's the most significant dress I own? I mean, I own it for now."

"You're going to be in a lot of trouble if it dematerializes while it's on you." Mandoran stepped out of the doorway and allowed Kaylin to enter. "Let me go get you a towel. You really don't want to bleed on the dress."

"On the dress in specific, or on the dress before we have guests?"

"Why can't it be both?" He turned and sprinted through an arch to the right. That left Kaylin alone. She walked toward the bedroom in which Nightshade lay abed. As she approached, her cheek began to ache. Her hand covered it, because she was certain Mandoran was right: no blood should land on this dress.

She bent over at an angle to stop blood from landing on her skirts, her palm covering the Erenne mark. She could also see the faint trace of golden light from the exposed Marks on her arms.

Annarion rose from the chair he'd been sitting in. "What are you doing?"

Fair question; one didn't usually stand bent over at right angles, hand on cheek. Mandoran must have filled him in, because he approached immediately, and Mandoran wasn't far behind. Annarion took the towel from Mandoran's hand and immediately passed it to Kaylin, cupping his hands beneath her face just in case anything fell before she could cover it.

"Why is your cheek bleeding?"

"I don't know. Serralyn's research into the Erenne mark led to Androsse, who was his usual self: a lot of condescension, not a lot of information that might be useful. You caught everything he told us, right?"

Annarion nodded. "Lord Andellen has been investigating without pause. He believes—as you do—that the people who attacked my brother are the same people who've been causing difficulty for the Lady. We also now believe that one or two of the Barrani Terrano interacted with to free us from the Hallionne are among those attackers. Terrano likes to stay invisible because it means he can't be held responsible for anything he does if he can't be seen—but it's more than that.

"He doesn't want the people who were our prior allies to recognize him, because he doesn't believe we'll be on the same side now. He may have let slip his ability to move between dimensions—he'd've had to, to explain where we were and why we wanted to escape. But he insists nothing he said could be useful to anyone who wasn't us."

"You don't believe it."

"No. Sedarias was closely vetting everything he said, and he did lie—but the lies he told were her lies. They were meant to entice. Eddorian's brother was the most committed—but we know why, now. He was like my brother. Like Calarnenne. He wanted to free his abandoned brother. He didn't survive it whole—but that's why Eddorian didn't come with us. He's with Alsanis and his brother for the foreseeable future."

"If Eddorian's brother could be healed—"

"Don't think it. Eddorian knows what we know. He trusts you, as we do. But he won't trust you with his brother's safety or well-being."

"But if Iberrienne could talk, if he could tell us what the intent of his allies was, we might be able to intervene to save Nightshade." And the Consort. And possibly the Lake.

Annarion exhaled. "I know that," he said, voice low, almost a snarl. His eyes were the darker shade of blue, his expression gaunt. "But Eddorian's feelings for his brother are similar to mine. He doesn't care what Iberrienne did in pursuit of our freedom. He only cares that he tried. He will not allow us—or Alsanis—to question Iberrienne. Even if we did, without some mental cohesion on the part of his brother, we won't get the information we need." His grimace was deep, but it faded. "He's trying—for my sake. But Iberrienne is mentally a child—a young child. He's happy with Alsanis. He's happy with Eddorian—it's as if the memory of Eddorian is the only thing that allows him to function at all.

"It means that Eddorian was the strongest driving force of his actions." Annarion lowered his head. "Your life was affected by our fate. You didn't even know about us. You didn't come to the West March to rescue or preserve us. You came to the West March for reasons of your own. And the green chose you. It didn't speak through you; you weren't the Teller. But your role was to harmonize the jagged bits of story the green chose to bless us with. To make it clear. To make it resonant.

"And in the end, to free us. To bring us home. We don't

forget." He exhaled again, which was a neat trick, because his inhalation had been so quiet she'd missed it. "The second time you wore the dress, you brought Bellusdeo her sisters. You brought the Keeper back to his garden, or his garden back to the Keeper—Serralyn's not certain which. And you brought Mrs. Erickson home.

"Nothing bad has happened when you've worn that dress, but . . . it's concerning that you're wearing it now. An'Tellarus will be here in half an hour."

"Fifteen minutes," Helen said, "if she arrives fashionably early. On time is generally fifteen minutes ahead of the stated invitation time."

"It's An'Tellarus. She's far more likely to be fashionably late, which is also accepted etiquette. Too early indicates eagerness; too late indicates disdain. Too late implies the visitor believes consequences for disdain are, or will be, trivial."

Kaylin had heard all this many times. Clearly, so had Annarion—but to Annarion, it was part of the bedrock of the life he'd been born to. To Kaylin, it was unnecessary fuss. But here she was in the harmoniste's dress, a towel pressed to her cheek.

"I really think you should change," Mandoran said, his tone far more soothing than Annarion could manage right now. "You don't know what caused the Erenne mark to bleed—and you won't know if it won't start again while you're entertaining your guests."

"Start again? I don't know if it's going to stop in time."

"Have you tried to heal it?"

This was a perfectly reasonable question. Unfortunately, the answer was no. Kaylin didn't consciously heal herself; the Marks did that. Small nicks, scratches, bruises—they didn't persist in her daily life. She didn't even think about them beyond a curse word or two. But the bleeding itself, the Erenne mark, seemed immune to the power of these Marks.

"I do not advise you to make the attempt now," Helen said, her tone unusually severe. "It appears that An'Tellarus has arrived unfashionably early."

"She probably let Yvonne choose," Kaylin said, pressing the towel more firmly against her cheek.

Hope squawked.

"Sure—you go downstairs and say hello while I try to stop bleeding." To her surprise, he pushed himself off her shoulder, gliding his way to the closed door. The door opened to allow him to leave.

Her cheek still hurt. Even pressing the towel against it, she felt like her skin was being abraded. Was it because she was standing in such close proximity to Nightshade? Was it because he was trying to somehow communicate?

She placed the back of her free hand on his forehead. "He's feverish," she told Annarion—who probably knew it already.

Annarion frowned. As Kaylin lifted her hand, he replaced it with his own. "He's not. Not when I touch him."

This wasn't the confirmation either of the two expected. "Mandoran, you check."

"Sedarias is screaming in my ear," Mandoran replied. "Yvonne isn't at the door yet, but she's walking toward it." He did, however, place a hand on Nightshade's brow. "I'm with Annarion. He's not feverish to my touch." He then did what Annarion hadn't: he placed a hand on Kaylin's forehead. "You're hot."

Great.

"Barrani don't catch mortal illnesses, right?"

"Not usually, no."

"Good. I don't *feel* feverish. And if I'm hot, Nightshade should feel cooler to the touch, shouldn't he?"

"Why are you expecting things to be remotely sensible right now? To both of us, Nightshade feels normal—for a person in a coma. To you, he feels feverish. To us, you feel feverish, *and* you have important guests. And your cheek is bleeding."

Mandoran cursed—he was like Terrano; he'd adopted the Hawks' choice language. He usually avoided using it when Helen's Avatar was in the room—but Helen could hear it all anyway. He definitely avoided cursing when Mrs. Erickson could hear him, and that was probably the most important thing to Helen.

"Things are never straightforward when you get involved."

"Look—I didn't ask for this stupid mark. Or these stupid Marks. Or even this dress. I didn't ask for this heavy ring, either. I'm not involved because I'm like Terrano—I'm not just tripping over things and picking them up and saying *shiny*."

"I never said you were—but you are like Terrano. You just cause chaos wherever you go. It's not always *bad* chaos. But it's almost never predictable. If you're asking—and you aren't—the fact that you feel feverish to us and Nightshade feels feverish to you while you're wearing that dress—which you did choose, by the way—is significant. But none of us knows how.

"Serralyn thinks the fact that you can't stop the Erenne mark from bleeding is significant, and possibly in a good way—for Nightshade, not you. But you've checked in on him, he isn't waking up, and Yvonne is at the front door. Give me that towel." He held out a hand.

Kaylin dropped the towel across his palm.

He grimaced. "Your cheek isn't bleeding at the moment—it *is* red. Just—hold on a second." He ran off again, and came back with a smaller towel and a basin with water in it. His hands were gentle as he carefully sponged blood off her face. "I wish you could do something about that mark."

"Why? An'Tellarus has already seen it, and she didn't ask about it or even comment on it. Yvonne's seen it, as well."

"I really wish we'd thought of concealing it before you went to visit the Consort."

Mandoran was probably right, but it's not like he'd told her to hide it, either. Then again, no one could have predicted Yvonne and An'Tellarus.

"She doesn't know Nightshade is here, does she?"

Annarion rolled his eyes. "That possibility only just occurred to you *now*? Go downstairs. I'll be here, and Fallessian will join me after Mrs. Erickson says her hellos to the guests. Terrano will be wherever Terrano wants to be, but in theory, he's going to be in the room with you. Unseen," he added, as if that were necessary.

"Sedarias and Teela will join you. If An'Tellarus has objections, they're going to say—I'm sorry—that they're your guardians."

Kaylin almost forgot about her cheek as her jaw fell open. "I don't need a guardian!"

"Neither does Yvonne."

She snapped her jaw shut to stop any other words from escaping. "So . . . they're going to be there to balance out An'Tellarus."

"If it's necessary, yes. Ummm, I should probably warn you: Teela will be carrying her sword."

This day was not getting any better. "Just how terrifying is An'Tellarus, anyway?"

"She's unpredictable, cunning, and spiteful. But when she chooses to do so, she can protect almost anyone. Sedarias would like to be friendly with her; she could be useful to her cause. We know she supported An'Sennarin when he first took the seat. It wasn't bloodless. Had he not wrested control of Sennarin from its former lord, no one would have expected he *could* hold the seat. But she apparently did expect just that—and he's still breathing."

"He's nothing like Sedarias."

"No, probably not. Sedarias was born to power and raised to want it. The High Court is her natural element. The meeting may not go well—but you're not part of it, in theory. Speak to Yvonne. Learn what you need to learn. She won't harm you, and I'm certain you won't hurt her. But . . . try to be a little less chaotic?

"Also: try not to strangle Terrano—if you want to, you'll be standing in a long line, and it's growing longer every time he opens his mouth."

"Has the bleeding started again?"

Annarion and Mandoran exchanged a glance. It was Mandoran who answered. "For now, it seems to be okay—but the skin beneath the Erenne mark is red and inflamed. I'm not sure it won't start again." He reached into a pocket and handed her a handkerchief. "Just in case."

Teela and Sedarias were waiting at the foot of the stairs when Kaylin reached them. Hope was fluttering in place by the open door. Yvonne entered first, and Hope flew to her but didn't land on her shoulder. When she lifted her arm, he squawked but stayed in the air, moving backward as Yvonne stepped through the door.

An'Tellarus followed.

To Kaylin's surprise, her hair was not pinned and sculpted in place; it fell in a straight, perfect line from the crown of her head down her back in a glossy black cape. She wore no adornment on her head, no crown but that hair. Her eyes were blue—of course they were blue—but her expression was less dismissive.

When she bowed her head, Kaylin found herself holding her breath, because the bow she offered, she offered to Helen. Helen, in her nonintrusive, normal clothing.

Something about Helen's posture implied that the gesture wasn't out of place. To make matters more awkward, An'Tellarus held that bow until Helen bade her rise, as if Helen were the reigning noble, the reigning monarch.

"Cediela, rise. It has been a long, long time since we last met. I bid you welcome. You have met Lord Kaylin; she is my master, now, and she does not follow the customs of the High Court and your powerful kin."

Kaylin wished she was part of the cohort group mind, because she desperately wanted to tell them all that this particular surprise wasn't her fault. But Helen's eyes, when she turned toward Kaylin, weren't her normal brown. They were black, obsidian, the color of An'Tellarus's hair. Flecks of light, opalescent and shining, could be clearly seen from where Kaylin was standing.

Helen's eyes only looked like this when she had slid into defensive mode—but she hadn't exchanged clothing for armor.

Kaylin hastily stepped forward, passing Helen to take up position squarely in front of the Avatar. "Yvonne. An'Tellarus. I bid you welcome to my house."

An'Tellarus had to look at Kaylin, because Kaylin was now standing directly between her and Helen's Avatar. But her eyes shifted into an almost draconic gold: the Barrani color of surprise. They remained that way for several long breaths.

When she found words again, An'Tellarus said, "What are you wearing?" As if she didn't recognize the dress, or as if she couldn't believe that it was on Kaylin.

Kaylin, not one of nature's liars, said, "It's the dress given me by the green."

"There is no *regalia* this year, or none intended. How did you come by the dress?"

"I've worn it before, as harmoniste." She could almost feel Teela's gaze drilling into the space between her shoulder blades.

"And now?"

"It was in my closet."

Gold gave way to blue. Kaylin recovered and turned to Yvonne, but Yvonne's eyes were also gold; they were, however, unblinking. She opened her mouth and failed to speak, staring at her host. Or staring at her host's dress.

Yvonne was born in the West March; Yvonne recognized the dress. She recognized when the dress should be worn, probably even understood the role of the person who wore it.

"You were chosen to wear that dress?" she asked, finally finding her voice.

"Is it that strange?"

"Well, you're human."

Squawk.

"But you're also Chosen."

Kaylin nodded. "Please, come in. We have refreshments, and if you'd like, I can introduce you to the *kindest* member of my household." She put emphasis on that word, speaking in High Barrani.

"I would," Yvonne replied, the gold in her eyes receding far less quickly than it had in An'Tellarus's. Green joined gold, but flecks of that gold persisted. It was really a lovely color.

Helen saw An'Tellarus, Sedarias, and Teela into the parlor; she subtly cut off Yvonne from her guardian, and her guardian allowed it with a single backward glance at Kaylin. It was all smiling daggers, really—a nonverbal threat—but Kaylin had no intention of harming Yvonne, or allowing her to be harmed.

Kaylin, in her ridiculous dress with her ridiculous ring and hair that was practically starched, then led Yvonne to the kitchen, which was Mrs. Erickson's territory. The smell of baking wafted into the hall practically before Kaylin opened the door. Something savory, but something sweet. Mrs. Erickson's back, apron knots around neck and waist, could be seen as she bustled around the kitchen.

Fallessian's face could be seen more clearly; his eyes were blue. He said nothing, made no attempt to interrupt Mrs. Erickson; she hadn't heard the door.

But Yvonne seemed unaware of this. Unaware of Fallessian's stiff, expressionless face, unaware of the fact that kitchens weren't meant for lords—and certainly not people who wore the dress Kaylin wore. And the ring. Her eyes were caught—and held—by the slow, humming bustle of the kitchen's master: Mrs. Erickson.

Yvonne herself was dressed as a Barrani servant. An'Tellarus was dressed for the type of war that occurred when Lords of the High Court convened in genteel settings, although her hair fell straight down her back. So did Yvonne's. Yvonne's clothing would be considered expensive and noteworthy outside the High Halls but would blend into the background within them—as servants were meant to do.

Maybe that was a way of keeping her hidden, keeping her safe. If it was, Kaylin understood it viscerally. Safety, in the fiefs of her childhood, had relied on being unnoticed, beneath notice. It was a habit that was hard to break.

Yvonne stepped forward as Mrs. Erickson lifted a tray—it was hot enough to require oven mittens and concentration. Before Fallessian could step in, Yvonne did.

"May I help you with that?" she asked, her tone far more warm, far more musical, than Kaylin had ever heard it.

Mrs. Erickson turned to look over her shoulder at the guest, her smile instant and welcoming. "That would be lovely. There are mitts on the far counter, and you'll need them. The trays are hot. I'm Imelda."

"Yvonne," Yvonne said instantly. She retrieved the aforementioned gloves.

Fallessian's expression cracked a bit as Yvonne took his place: she helped Mrs. Erickson pull trays out of the large rounded oven.

"I don't think I've seen you before," Mrs. Erickson added. "But I'm terrible with names." This was a bald-faced lie.

"So am I," Yvonne replied, cheerful now that she had something to do with her hands. "But my name's not all that important, and I don't have to pretend to be offended when you don't know who I am."

"Some of that," Mrs. Erickson said, "is not pretense, sadly. Not in my experience. Are you one of the guests?"

"She's *the* guest," Kaylin said.

"Oh dear. And here I am putting guests to work." But she didn't panic, and she smiled as she said it—as if she knew that Yvonne helping in the kitchen was the best comfort she could offer. Yvonne certainly wouldn't find Sedarias or Teela comforting, and An'Tellarus, whom she clearly respected, was too prickly. Or maybe, Kaylin thought, An'Tellarus, like Sedarias, felt the need for comfort was a weakness that could be easily exploited.

Kaylin exhaled. "Yvonne offered, and I think she's more comfortable here than she'd be in the parlor. Hells, *I'm* more comfortable here than I'd be in the parlor, and I live with the scariest person in it."

Yvonne laughed. "I don't think An'Tellarus disliked you, but I've never seen her quite so unsettled. Helen seemed to recognize her."

"An'Tellarus is old. Helen's older than both An'Tellarus and Teela, but at one time, Helen was home to a sorcerer. Or an Arcanist. I really can't tell the difference between the two."

Hope squawked.

"Hope thinks you should be able to differentiate," Yvonne said politely.

"*Anyway*, Helen doesn't speak that much about her prior tenants."

"Tenants?"

Kaylin grimaced. "Masters, if you prefer. Especially not the older ones. She's a bit of an unusual building."

"She's like the Hallionne. I mean—they're all different, but they all take care of their guests. And they hear what their guests think."

Kaylin nodded. "Helen will hear what you think unless you're good at misdirecting."

"Which I'm not. I'm not afraid of that, though. I always wanted to spend time in the Hallionne, but Alsanis was . . . not accepting visitors for most of my life."

"He did have visitors," Fallessian said. If Kaylin's eye color could change with surprise, they'd be that color now. "Mostly, it was us. For centuries."

Yvonne's brows rose. "You—you're one of the children who were forced into the green!"

Fallessian's expression rippled, but he nodded. "We were with Alsanis for a long time. He worried about us and cared for us, but he wouldn't let us leave. And he wouldn't let anyone else visit us, either. We were younger, then—it didn't really occur to us to care about Alsanis's other friends."

"But you did leave."

Fallessian nodded, glancing at Mrs. Erickson before he spoke again. To Kaylin's surprise, Mrs. Erickson's gentle smile was accompanied by a nod—wordless encouragement. The idea that Fallessian cared about Mrs. Erickson wasn't a surprise; he'd have to, to spend so much time with her. But that he could somehow take direction from an old, mortal woman?

"We left on the day of the *regalia*. The *regalia* trapped us; the *regalia* freed us. The harmoniste on the day of our release was Lord Kaylin. She wore that dress. Her hair was far less refined, though."

"I wish I'd seen that. I imagine the Lords of the West March weren't really happy about it."

"They weren't. But the green chooses—both harmoniste and Teller. Lord Kaylin was chosen as harmoniste, and the Teller was Calarnenne."

Yvonne frowned. An'Tellarus would not have—she'd've recognized the name.

"He's outcaste," Kaylin said, voice soft.

Yvonne's eyes grew gold again, but surprise fled more quickly this time. "The green chose an outcaste lord as the Teller." It wasn't a question. She didn't think Fallessian was lying. "And a mortal as harmoniste."

"Probably because of these," Kaylin replied, lifting an arm. The Marks of the Chosen were faintly luminescent, even in the bright lights of the kitchen. Mrs. Erickson liked natural light, but not to bake by—at least not according to Helen.

"That probably caused a lot of noise as well," Yvonne replied, acknowledging the probable truth. "I think you're the only mortal the green has ever chosen for that role."

"Well, the only one in recent history—I get the sense that history about the green is scattered and not entirely reliable."

"Because it isn't necessary." Yvonne's answer was far firmer. "The green is the green. We can serve the green at the edges of its domain—but only with permission, and the service itself is akin to gardening. With extreme care. Some Barrani cannot enter the green. The gates are there, and the Warden is willing to guide them, but the green is not willing to entertain them.

"But sometimes the green will sing. And sometimes it will tell stories. The *regalia*. The stories offered by the green are transformational. They can change lives and sometimes do—but never in a completely predictable way." She turned back to the oven to rescue the last of Mrs. Erickson's trays. While she did, she continued to speak.

"The green decides, but it doesn't tell us its decisions. We have to guess. One of its decisions is, was, and will always be: no children at the *regalia*. No children exposed to the full force of the green's primal stories.

"But you were. Everyone in the West March knows An'Teela's story. Everyone. But we also know that she wasn't the only child who was sent to the green. The Lords of the High Court thought they could experiment with their own kin; they thought to learn about the green, to *use it*."

Fallessian had fallen silent.

"Yvonne," Helen said, her Avatar appearing in the kitchen. "An'Tellarus is now very alarmed."

Yvonne was confused. "But why?" She set the tray, with its pastries, on the counter, and carefully removed the mitts.

"I cannot say, but she feels this is not the conversation you were meant to have when you accepted the invitation. I should warn you she is on her way to the kitchen as I speak."

Yvonne's eyes took on a disturbing shade of blue. Something about that color reminded Kaylin of Teela at her most terrifying.

"The green is protective of the children it almost destroyed," Yvonne said, her voice louder and far more resonant than it had ever been. "I intend Fallessian of Torcannon no harm."

Nothing about the voice, the sudden shift in posture, the darkness of the eyes, reminded Kaylin of the Yvonne she had met in either the Tellarus rooms or the Sennarin rooms.

24

Fallessian moved toward Mrs. Erickson, who, hands in mitts, was frowning as she looked at their visitor. The movement was protective, as if the only person who was under credible threat was the frail baker.

Kaylin was less concerned about Mrs. Erickson because Helen had materialized her physical Avatar in the kitchen the moment An'Tellarus had started to move. The kitchen was actually large enough to accommodate all of the guests and all of the hosts, and Helen would allow no injury to come to any of them.

"If it can be prevented," Helen agreed. Her tone was cold, as unlike her normal voice as Yvonne's reply had been. Kaylin didn't have a lot of experience with Yvonne, but she knew Helen very well.

"Helen—what's wrong? What are you worried about?"

The kitchen door slammed open. An'Tellarus stood, towering in the doorway; beyond her back, Sedarias and Teela weren't far behind.

"Yvonne," An'Tellarus said. "We are leaving."

"I am not leaving," Yvonne replied. Her hair, unlike An'Tellarus's, began to move, as if a passing breeze touched no one in the kitchen but Yvonne. An'Tellarus did not step forward; Helen widened the kitchen doorframe to allow Teela and Sedarias to enter. Teela's hands were empty; she'd worn her sword, but she hadn't drawn it.

Kaylin wasn't surprised to see Severn behind Sedarias and Teela. She wasn't surprised that he entered. She *was* surprised when he moved, his steps almost inaudible, directly to Yvonne. Unlike Teela, Severn had armed himself—but he'd also unwound the weapon's chain. That was most often used as a spellbreaker, a shield of rotating blade and chain. It wasn't spinning yet.

"What did I tell you?" An'Tellarus demanded. She didn't demand it of Yvonne. It was Severn who held her attention—and most of her very chilly glare.

"Mortal memory isn't perfect," Severn replied after a pause. "I'm sorry. I don't remember."

"I am disappointed in you."

Even Kaylin flinched at the force of those words.

"I have considered you a wayward nephew."

Silence.

"But I have taken Yvonne under my protection. Had you offered a warning, I would have advised her to decline this invitation."

"Why?" Yvonne asked from behind Severn's back. "You're from the West March—even if you live in the High Halls as befits your rank there. You should know what happened there."

"I am aware. But I did not realize that *all* of the lost children now take up residence within Helen's walls. Helen can protect the rest of us from any irregularities; those children are safe here."

"And that means I'm safe here as well," Yvonne argued. This wasn't a Yvonne that Kaylin had expected or predicted; she'd seemed more like Serralyn in temperament, and far more cowed by An'Tellarus. But something about her tenacity here didn't seem to surprise An'Tellarus. She wasn't worried for the cohort.

She was worried for Yvonne. She was either angry at, or worried for, Severn, and that was also a shock.

What does she mean by nephew?

Long story, Severn replied, tension in the words. He didn't want to talk about it. Not now. Probably not ever. She felt uncomfortable and even petty, because it bothered her, and now was absolutely not the time.

Do you think of her as an aunt?

In the Barrani sense. Which was why he'd brought his weapon.

And Yvonne?

Severn shook his head. *Yvonne has reason to trust the green. She may even have reason to trust me. She has every reason to trust Ollarin. She has less reason to trust An'Tellarus—and nothing Yvonne's done here should anger An'Tellarus.*

But she said she warned you.

Severn's shrug was a fief shrug, at odds with his stance and the weapon in his hands.

Severn—what warning? What did she say?

The short version: don't anger her. Don't disappoint her. Don't let political Barrani near Yvonne.

Why Yvonne in particular?

Long story. Shorter than the nephew *bit, though.*

"You recognize the dress Kaylin is wearing," Yvonne said, as if no one else had spoken—or as if only An'Tellarus was in a kitchen that was growing more crowded as people entered.

An'Tellarus was silent.

"You must recognize the ring of kinship."

Silence again. An'Tellarus's hands were rigid, her eyes very dark.

"You know the weapon Severn is wielding." Yvonne's eyes were as blue as An'Tellarus's. "I don't know why Kaylin has that dress, because you're right: it's too early for the *regalia*. But you must sense it. You must know that we're standing on the edge of the green." She lifted a hand to touch Severn's back.

"It doesn't matter. We are leaving. Now."

Yvonne shook her head and turned to Kaylin; Severn moved slightly to allow an unimpeded line of view. "I know why you invited me to visit—and I *wanted* to visit. You might be a Lord of the High Court, but you're human. You don't have roots in Barrani politics.

"I'm not a Lord of the High Court, in case that wasn't obvious. Ollarin is. An'Tellarus definitely is. I know I've gotten myself involved in political things here—but I swear to you I didn't do it deliberately."

"Yvonne."

Yvonne shook her head. "You know it, too."

"Might I suggest we repair to the parlor?" Helen said. "It seems that only one of our guests intends to leave, and perhaps discussion might more comfortably occur in the parlor."

"Helen, I must ask—"

"You cannot, Cediela. You might speak my name as a last resort, but it will not have the desired effect. Yvonne accepted my hospitality—and my hospitality is the hospitality of my master. While Kaylin is willing to entertain guests, guests are welcome. She is not a lord who will abuse that hospitality; she will not detain you—or ask me to detain you—if you do not wish to remain." Helen turned to Kaylin. "What is your desire?"

This wasn't a question Helen ever asked.

"I need to speak with Yvonne. I'm happy to have An'Tellarus join us."

"An'Tellarus?" Helen asked.

"I will remain while Yvonne remains."

Severn rewound his weapon chain. Mrs. Erickson turned back to the kitchen counter on which trays were cooling. Kaylin exhaled. “I’m sorry,” she told Yvonne. “Things aren’t normally this tense.”

“You really don’t live in the High Halls,” Yvonne replied, a hint of a smile flickering around the corners of her lips. “I like the kitchen.”

“We can stay here if you want—but I’ve been told it’s not considered good manners to ask guests to do work while they visit.”

“Really? I wasn’t raised in the High Court—we didn’t have servants, we *were* servants. But when we gathered, when we weren’t serving our lords, we got together and we occupied the kitchen; we cooked together. It was something we could all be part of. I mean, Helen’s a sentient building, so it’s probably not really useful—”

“I like to bake,” Mrs. Erickson said. “I lived for a long time with people who couldn’t eat; they couldn’t really help, either. But what they could do, they did. They kept me company while I worked. I know you’re here as Kaylin’s guest, not mine—but I’m always happy for the help.”

Gentle voice. Thread of steel running through it. One old, mortal woman facing a handful of Barrani Lords. Kaylin spent too much of her life betting, and she knew who she’d bet on here, against all realistic odds.

Yvonne turned toward Mrs. Erickson; Kaylin couldn’t see the younger woman’s expression. But she walked toward the counters where pastries were cooling, and from there, toward cupboards she’d never opened before.

“I really was never very good at telling other people what to do,” Mrs. Erickson said, her tone entirely apologetic. “But maybe that’s why I appreciate offers of help. I can’t command other people. I’m not a fancy person. I’m not a lord. But even people who can’t give orders need help sometimes. Those plates—the long oval ones. Those are the ones we use.”

Yvonne had already begun to pull those plates down. The

kitchen was otherwise funereal—as if it were a field kitchen, and deadly hostilities might commence at any moment.

Severn exhaled and relaxed first, turning to look at Yvonne as she moved up and down the counter in harmony with Mrs. Erickson. Kaylin could believe that every word the young Barrani woman had said was true: she was at home in this kitchen, her hands doing useful work. More at home here than she would have been in the parlor, flanked by An'Tellarus, and facing An'Teela and An'Mellarionne. Then again, Kaylin, who knew almost nothing about kitchens, would have been far more at home here than in that parlor, too.

But Kaylin was afraid of getting underfoot; she always had been. She almost envied Yvonne her certainty as she moved things from trays, moved trays off the counter to the large wooden table. At some point, an apron appeared, and Yvonne grabbed it from the air in which it floated.

"Everybody needs to eat," Helen said, voice soft, eyes once again brown.

"You don't," Terrano pointed out.

"I do," was Helen's serene reply. "Fallessian, I believe things have calmed down enough that you do not need to be so vigilant."

Fallessian, to Kaylin's surprise, failed to hear Helen. Probably deliberate. Kaylin opened her mouth; Severn lifted a hand, palm out, in her direction. She fell silent.

Yvonne, however, began to speak. "You wanted to meet me because you knew about the Lake."

Kaylin drew one sharp breath. "We would never have met if An'Tellarus hadn't commanded our presence. I didn't know it was you."

Yvonne, wrapped in an apron, nodded. "But she knew you had come at the Consort's command. She doesn't know a lot about you, but she does know that you're Severn's partner. And that you're Chosen. I think she could guess."

Kaylin was almost afraid to look at An'Tellarus for confirmation.

"I think she was surprised that you were in the company of An'Teela—and at that, An'Teela when she's deadly serious—but it didn't matter. She doesn't dislike An'Teela; An'Teela and she have had very little reason for conflict in their long individual histories."

"Yvonne," An'Tellarus said, making of the name a warning.

"They were both born to the West March, and they've both made their names and power known in the High Court, not the provincial one. An'Teela has nothing An'Tellarus wants. An'Tellarus has nothing An'Teela wants. They are both capable of surviving any social irregularities they choose to indulge in. And if I'm being fair, An'Tellarus has not done much research into An'Teela and her political allies because they had, as many lords of their age—and there are few—their own interests and no desire to engage in pointless conflict."

Yvonne worked with her hands, and it seemed to soothe her, to calm her. She spoke far more easily than she had when she'd been sitting across from Kaylin in a parlor.

"I didn't take the Lake's test in the normal way—if there even *is* a normal way. The Lake almost reminds me of the green. I heard the green for so long. So, so long." Her voice softened as she spoke, and her eyes were an odd shade: green, but not the normal Barrani green. Something about Yvonne was different.

An'Tellarus pushed past Severn—glaring at him as she did—to reach Yvonne. "Child," she said, her voice soft but clear as thunder. "We should never have taken you out of the green."

Yvonne seemed almost unaware of An'Tellarus—a neat trick, given that An'Tellarus had grabbed her by the shoulder.

"Harmoniste," Yvonne said, as if An'Tellarus no longer existed. Kaylin finally recognized the green of Yvonne's eyes: they were the same color as the green of this damn dress. But Yvonne wore no crown. No one in the kitchen did.

"The harmoniste isn't the Teller," Kaylin said, her words a thin thread of defiance. *Severn, who is Yvonne? What is Yvonne?*

She was badly injured in the West March and escaped to the green. The green protected her.

For how long?

For as long as it took for someone to find her there.

Her eyes . . .

Severn was silent. He was worried, but he didn't consider Yvonne a threat. He was ambivalent about the green. Kaylin should have known that the green would make itself felt. They weren't in the West March, but they hadn't been in the West March when this dress had made its reappearance in her life.

Why, why, *why* had she chosen this dress? Because she wanted to impress An'Tellarus, an almost total stranger? Because she wanted to look *significant*? She should bloody well know better by now. She should.

"I think your choice of dress would not have made a difference," Helen said softly.

"Is there something different about Yvonne?"

Helen's eyes were obsidian, but it was Terrano who answered. "Yes. But it's subtle. You wouldn't notice it if you didn't have my eyes."

She didn't even look at his eyes; she could guess how he'd configured them, and it always made her slightly queasy.

"Yvonne," Kaylin said, drawing breath and trying to pull herself together. She'd've let An'Tellarus talk, but Yvonne was looking at only one person in the room now that the food had been plated and Mrs. Erickson appeared to be finished.

Or maybe not. Mrs. Erickson opened a cupboard and pulled down a large, brightly colored bowl. She then moved toward a different cupboard and from it pulled two covered round bins. "Helen, eggs?"

"Of course," Helen said, eyes shifting into their normal appearance.

Yvonne moved, then, as if her body was falling into familiar, comforting habits; her eyes lost the odd green, and her attention once again shifted to Mrs. Erickson's kitchen.

Kaylin had never taken comfort from kitchens. Food had been just another way of not dying. The idea of preparing it, of loving the preparation, would have required, among other things, an actual kitchen. Some hint of a memory teased her, but she wasn't Barrani: it was faint, a feeling, an echo of a sound that would never be heard again.

"I heard the Lake," Yvonne said, as if getting mixers and cooking spatulas was steadying, as if it brought her back to herself. "It was a few months ago. I could see light in the distance—soft light, not the harsh light of magic, of aggression."

Kaylin wondered what Yvonne's life had been like. Even in the High Halls, the servants were invisible to Kaylin's eyes—and they shouldn't be. But Teela wasn't a servant. The Consort wasn't. Ynpharion wasn't, not really. She wondered if Barrani servants, Immortal by birth, were a lot more like humans than she'd realized.

"I followed the sound. I thought I was dreaming. Sometimes I do. I dream of the song of the green."

Barrani didn't need sleep.

"I don't miss it," she added. "I *like* being with Ollarin. I avoid being significant in the High Halls because I'm An'Tellarus's servant, and no one messes with me if they don't want to start a war with Tellarus. But . . . I could hear a song, and the sound was off. It was wrong. It was like the green, but there was discordance in it.

"And I've heard that, too. When I slept there, when I slept in the green, I could hear its voice. No, there were no words in it—really, *song* is the best way I can describe it. But I could sometimes hear discordance there as well. It's just . . . the discordance was *me*. It was partly my hearing. It wasn't the green. I tried hard to listen to the parts that didn't sound wrong; I tried to imagine that the discordance wasn't there at all.

"I don't hear the green, now. I thought, somehow, I could hear it again. I followed the sound. For me there was safety in it. Safety isn't always comfortable," she added. "But what I found, instead, was . . . the Lake. It's what I see when I see the Marks of the Chosen."

"Did you try to touch the Lake?"

Yvonne shook her head. "But the words rose. They rose, as if in greeting—or distress. When I opened my eyes, I was there. I knew where it was. But the Lake didn't say anything else; it didn't demand anything else." She hesitated. "A path opened that took me from the Lake to the Halls, and I returned as quickly as I could to my own rooms."

The first test of the Lake.

"I know that there are others who had begun the process by which the Lake tests them. An'Tellarus said it's not uncommon. But no one expects to pass that test; they have hope, but their ambition is often political. And that's not what the Lake wants.

"But even I understand that if I've passed the Lake's first test, I become political. I'm almost certain the Consort knows."

"She's the Lady of the Lake," Kaylin said. "She knows. The Lake doesn't exactly speak, but it makes its will known."

"Be careful," Teela said.

Kaylin exhaled. There were too many people in this kitchen; caution was necessary. But caution wasn't going to help them. It wasn't going to change anything. It wasn't going to answer the questions that arose, because if she *couldn't ask any of them*, no answers would be forthcoming.

"Yes," she said, forcing herself to choose her words with care, "she does know. She knows that someone took—and passed—the first test of the Lake."

"And she knows it's me."

"And she thinks that you are the most likely candidate, yes."

"Is that why The Lady summoned you?"

"Indirectly, yes. Understand that Barrani of power consider the position of Lady to be political—possibly to be the highest political position among your people. The Lady is protected by the High Halls; lords on any side of any of the many disputes revere her; they will not touch her or attack her. Mostly." Kaylin met, and held, Yvonne's gaze as she asked the important question. "Who did you tell?"

"An'Tellarus," Yvonne replied promptly. "And Ollarin."

"No one else?"

"I don't have many friends in the High Halls and An'Tellarus doesn't have many servants."

"It is not worth the difficulty of terminating their employ should they become suspect," An'Tellarus said. Her eyes were a shade less dark, but her expression was even less friendly, which should have been impossible.

Kaylin turned to An'Tellarus. "I suppose you should know that I've passed the test of the Lake."

Silence.

"I can touch the names. I can carry them."

"Oh good. Like everything's not on fire *enough*?" Terrano snapped.

"She's worried for Yvonne. I get it. I want them both to know that I understand some of the difficulty."

"You . . . can touch the names."

"Yes. Did you think the Consort likes me because I'm human? Because I'm Chosen? She values me because I'm her emergency measure. In the worst possible case, I can continue to wake the children. No one is going to seek to bring me on board, politically; I'm useless *because* I'm human. But to the Lady, I'm essential."

I wouldn't have mentioned that, Severn said.

I know. But she is *worried about Yvonne. And now she knows both Yvonne and I are in the same boat. We're taking the same risks.*

"For how long has that been true?" An'Tellarus demanded.

"That is irrelevant," Teela replied before Kaylin could. "You did not wish Yvonne to discuss certain things for her own safety. Understand that we feel no less concern for Lord Kaylin."

"Children are always trying," An'Tellarus agreed.

Kaylin moved toward Yvonne.

"That was brave," Yvonne whispered. Every Barrani in the room could no doubt hear it, although Kaylin had to bend a bit to catch the words. "Was it true?"

"It's true."

"But the Lake hasn't called you."

"I don't live in the High Halls. I probably wouldn't survive it. I live with Helen, and I highly doubt she'd allow that kind of communication."

"I cannot prevent all such communications," Helen said. "Can you not sense it? The air is different in this kitchen. A breeze moves through it. May I suggest, in the future, that you do not wear that dress for anything but actual ceremony?"

"Sure, if I have the choice. I didn't find the dress in a closet the last time I wore it—and I lost actual clothing that cost money in the process." She exhaled. "The first time I wore this dress, it vanished after the *regalia.* I mean, not while I was wearing it—but it wasn't there after I removed it. Teela said that always happens. The second time, it . . . just appeared. My normal clothing was transformed while I was wearing it—and the transformation didn't wear off."

Mrs. Erickson said, "It's a lovely dress. But Helen, when did you bring these flowers into the kitchen? They're not from your garden."

Kaylin exhaled slowly. There *were* flowers in the kitchen—there were always flowers in the kitchen. Helen could provide them, because Mrs. Erickson loved them; they made Kaylin sneeze half the time, so she was less thrilled. But those flowers were in vases and in carefully tended pots, and they were chosen by Mrs. Erickson, because Helen had opened a garden for their growth. Fallessian helped, too; gardening was long and tiring work.

Kaylin often wondered why Fallessian had taken so strongly to Mrs. Erickson. She'd never asked because it was impossible not to like Mrs. Erickson. Conflict with the old woman would draw Helen's ire more certainly than conflict with Kaylin, her theoretical master, would. But if the cohort liked Mrs. Erickson, most of them hadn't made themselves her personal assistant.

And regardless, Fallessian hadn't helped Mrs. Erickson plant these flowers. There was no way he could. These flowers grew in only one place: the green.

Mrs. Erickson recognized them. Kaylin recognized them. Yvonne recognized them as well. She was less certain of An'Tellarus, a woman whose will and ambition implied that all forms of power were considered rivals or competitors; she wondered if An'Tellarus had ever walked the green. Now was not the time to ask.

"Serralyn says they're the same flowers we saw in the ruins of Azoria's manse," Terrano said. "She's worried."

"I don't understand." Kaylin turned to Helen. "They're the same flowers. She's right. But what are they doing *here*?"

"What is the dress you are wearing doing here? It is the dress worn when the green chooses to share its stories; those stories cannot be heard without the medium of both Teller and harmoniste. The Teller bears the weight of the green's power and intent, but there is far, far too much in the story for even a Teller of power and will to convey. It is the harmoniste who allows part of that story to be told in a way that listeners can comprehend.

"There is a story unfolding in this space."

"But this isn't the green!"

"You think?" Terrano snapped. He turned to Yvonne, and then from Yvonne to Severn, and then, finally, hands on hips, to Kaylin herself. "What did we *do* when we took Azoria down? What did we bring back with us?"

"There are no ghosts," Mrs. Erickson said, her voice soft. She hesitated. Mrs. Erickson wasn't one of nature's liars—in that, she was like Kaylin. She hadn't lied. But she was hesitant, as if she herself wasn't certain of the truth of her words.

"Terrano, ask Mandoran if—if Nightshade is awake."

"We'd *all* know if he'd woken up. What's the real question?"

"Is he wearing the Teller's crown?"

"I really wish you hadn't asked that question."

"He is?"

"He isn't."

"Then why—"

"Because the Teller's crown is now in his room. And Serralyn doesn't think that's the problem. She's worried, did I mention?"

Kaylin nodded, as if worrying Serralyn was the worst thing that was happening.

"The green shouldn't be here. It shouldn't reach here."

"But the green does touch the world outside its theoretical borders—Nightshade *had* the Teller's crown before he set out to the West March. And the dress appeared in the closet of a Hallionne when I was on the way there."

"Serralyn says that's only when the *regalia* is about to take place. It's always been true. This is different." He hesitated. "She says the green—like the elemental forces—is a power beyond us, and if it is not contained, she fears what it might do. It *has* been contained; the green is in the West March for a reason.

"But the aftereffects of the overlap between the dead and the living, and the intrusion of the green—due, probably, to Azoria's spells—are causing ripples in reality. Yvonne is part of that. You're part of that. She thought, if he were awake, that Nightshade might be drawn into it." He exhaled. "Mrs. Erickson? I'm sorry I interrupted you."

"Oh, I wasn't speaking, dear," she said almost automatically, as if to deny she'd been inconvenienced at all. That was her way. But Kaylin understood that Terrano's apology was meant to prod her to continue what she hadn't even started to say.

"You said there are no ghosts?"

Mrs. Erickson nodded, but it was a shaky nod.

"What do you see?"

Fallessian immediately interposed himself between Mrs. Erickson and the rest of the kitchen, which made it harder for Yvonne to find refuge in helping the older woman.

"Nothing terrible will happen to anyone in this kitchen," Helen said, her voice soothing, her expression the kind of soft that implied what lay beneath it was made of steel.

Mrs. Erickson then stepped out from behind Fallessian, toward Yvonne. She leaned up—she had to lean up, as she was the shortest person in the room—and whispered something to the young Barrani woman.

Kaylin could see Yvonne in profile, because Yvonne bent to catch the old woman's words. But Severn was worried. No sign of it crossed his expression, but he'd always been good at keeping his reactions to himself.

Yvonne's eyes were wide and dark. It was to Helen she looked first, and then, past Helen, to An'Tellarus, whose expression was rigid with denial. But it was to Kaylin she turned last, her eyes beseeching. "Why—why am I here?"

"Because something is happening with the Lake, with the Lady, with the future of the Barrani. And because," Kaylin added, exhaling, "I wanted to talk to you before I introduced you to the Consort. If I thought it was safe. If—as I believed—you never intended harm."

"Why is the harmoniste's dress here?"

"I don't know."

"And the flowers? The flowers are *singing*. The green is close."

"I don't know. If I had to guess, the green has slender roots in this space."

"Because of you?"

"And because of Mrs. Erickson. Because it was Mrs. Erickson who wore a wreath made of these flowers, and Mrs. Erickson who . . . touched the dead. She can see the dead, and she can speak to them as if they were children."

"What kind of a home is this?" Yvonne asked, bewildered. "I feel like I've walked into a story—and I'm not certain it isn't Barrani in nature."

Terrano snorted. "She means noble death and destruction and tragedy, in case that wasn't clear. If we're bit players, we're all dead, but we don't get *good* deaths. Well, maybe An'Tellarus might."

"What would I be?"

"Don't ask. There's a reason Barrani children don't get much in the way of stories—not the way humans do."

"That's because we don't need pointless fiction to ennoble ourselves," Sedarias—mostly silent until this moment—snapped.

"Given the High Court? We could certainly use *something*."

Yvonne coughed; it was the kind of cough that emerged when someone was surprised into laughter they definitely shouldn't share. But the coughing stopped. "Severn," Yvonne said, voice almost a whisper. "Can I trust them?"

Sedarias rolled her eyes in disgust, which was only funny when paired with An'Tellarus's equally disgusted expression.

"I do," Severn replied.

Yvonne turned to Mrs. Erickson and said, "Tell them. Tell us."

"But is it really okay?"

"If things become more dangerous," Helen told her friend,

"Yvonne can remain with us until the danger passes. Imelda—you have never caused harm. Even when speaking with Bellusdeo's ghosts, you helped both Bellusdeo and her sisters to heal. But if I understand anything now, it's important that we have as much information going forward as we can; without it, we can't even begin to ask the right questions."

"I see the dead near Yvonne."

25

Mrs. Erickson straightened her shoulders. She chose to speak to Helen, not the guests, as if Helen was the greatest source of comfort in the kitchen. Or perhaps the only woman present who felt like a peer. "I can't see ghosts with Yvonne—not the way I did with Bellusdeo. I can't hear them the same way. They don't look like *people* to me. Even the strange ghosts I brought home the last time looked like people to me, and when they spoke to me, I could hear their voices as if they were."

They weren't. Kaylin could perceive them—but she saw them as words. She couldn't hear what Mrs. Erickson heard, but, conversely, believed that Mrs. Erickson *could* hear them as if they were normal dead people. Normal.

"These look like ghosts from children's stories—phantoms meant to terrify, things that might once have been human but have no humanity left in them. They're not easy to see—but . . . they've become easier."

"Since when?"

"The flowers," Yvonne whispered. "The green."

"I think so, dear. I don't really understand what the green is. But I don't really understand what the ghosts here are, either. I think they're connected to you, but not strongly. Do you know?"

Severn said, "She doesn't remember." Maybe that was even true. But Severn's answer made clear he knew more.

"Annarion asks: can the green wake his brother?"

"We're not exactly carrying the green with us," Kaylin told Terrano.

"Yeah, but it's sort of here. I mean—the crown is here. If the green sends the crown and the dress to its chosen representatives, the green *can* reach us, somehow."

"True. Why don't you find a way to *talk to the green* and ask it yourself!"

"Might I point out that this entire complication came to our attention because of an assassination attempt? It didn't come to our attention because of the green," Sedarias cut in. "That assassination attempt involved Barrani in large enough numbers the Lords of the High Court must be involved."

"It also involved *Ravellon*, or its environs. And possible activities by former Barrani who believe Barrani shouldn't have names. Or shouldn't have fixed, unchanging names," Kaylin said, adding to her words without disagreeing with any of them.

"We are certain the green is not in collusion with either." It was Teela who replied.

That was probably true.

"And it is the green that is present here; it is the green that is throwing the house slightly off balance."

"Hazard a guess as to why?" Kaylin said to the Barrani Hawk. "Why, exactly, is everything going even further sideways? We've got enough to deal with on our hands—we really *do not need* any more!"

"Kitling," Teela said. "While we all share your frustration, some self-control is suggested."

Kaylin replied with volumes less self-control, in multiple languages.

An'Tellarus turned to Severn, her expression showing a hint of warmth. "I begin to see why you kept her from me." The tone was indulgent. "Very well. Yvonne, tell your story. Or if you cannot tell all of it, I will not punish Severn if he chooses to share what he knows."

"Why?" Kaylin demanded, suspicion in the single word. Teela's expression made clear she had resigned herself to Kaylin's lack of self-control.

"Because Yvonne ended up in the green through the actions of a Lord of the High Court. She was a target only because that lord wished to bring Ollarin to heel; it was control of Ollarin's elemental powers that was the prior lord's goal. And the previous An'Sennarin—a man I detested but could not easily bring down—was most definitely a member of the High Court.

"If what happened to Yvonne involved Shadow—even in the West March—and the Lords of the High Court are involved in some fashion with *Ravellon* and its outskirts, perhaps Yvonne is enmeshed in this far more than I originally thought. I should retreat. If you speak frankly with Yvonne and among yourselves, that is one thing—but I must retain a certain plausible deniability should things go very wrong."

Kaylin didn't believe it for a minute. But she got caught in An'Tellarus's words: *If what happened to Yvonne involved Shadow.*

Severn was silent. His silence was particular, familiar. What had happened to Yvonne definitely involved Shadow. And Lords of the High Court. And Barrani power games.

"I assumed I would be required as a hedge against the political machinations of An'Mellarionne—and her demands. That does not appear to be the case. When one is as old as I am, one learns to tread carefully where ancient, wild forces are involved. I am not, and have never been, their chosen." The last was said with both confidence and a trace of bitterness. Kaylin thought that was at the heart of An'Tellarus: strength, bitterness, and a barbed generosity.

But it was An'Tellarus who had endured.

Severn met An'Tellarus's gaze, held it until she nodded, and then exhaled. “Shadow,” he said, “was involved. Yvonne was taken into the green and held there; the Shadow with which she’d been infected didn’t taint or control the green—but it wasn’t entirely inert.”

“What does that even mean?”

“We can’t talk to the green. The green can’t explain its choices, its processes, or the meaning behind them—but I’m certain there *is* a meaning behind them.” He exhaled. “I didn’t go in search of Yvonne. We knew of her, but that’s not why I found her.”

Kaylin, accustomed to Severn, waited.

“I was allowed entry into the green, but the green has its own will. Those who understand it best are farthest from humanity. If you ask me to explain the green, I can’t. I don’t think it’s wise for me to try—there is too much I don’t understand.

“But you know that this weapon is considered—by Barrani—a weapon of the green. Like most Barrani weapons, there’s a test to prove worth.”

“You went to find the weapon?” No, Kaylin thought. It wasn’t as simple as that.

“I found the weapon. Perhaps the green assumed that I was there to be tested.” Truth, but not all of the truth; there was pain in it, as if the memory was a wound. Severn had never shared his wounds—not even with Kaylin or her mother.

Maybe she’d known him so long, she assumed he didn’t have any; that he, like Kaylin herself, would cry or rage if hurt. If there was no crying, no raging, it simply meant he wasn’t hurt. He didn’t feel pain.

She had been so, so stupid.

Pain wasn’t simply its *expression*. For Severn, it had always been private. No, more than that: he felt shared pain would cause pain. Had she ever thought of it that way?

You were a child, he told her.

So were you.

He said nothing. "I was given a choice of paths," he continued, "when I was welcomed into the green. I chose one." He exhaled, showing as much hesitation as he ever did: deliberation. Choice of words. "Yvonne was part of the test of my worthiness to wield the weapon of the green. And Shadow was involved."

"How?" Kaylin was grateful that Bellusdeo—or her many sharp-eyed sisters—weren't here.

"Yvonne had been hit by Shadow and had survived long enough for the green to find her."

"I found the green," Yvonne said, her voice at its meekest. This was the way the powerless disagreed.

Severn shook his head. "I don't know if you believe that—you might. But the green found you, and the green took you in. Something in the green itself appears to be immune to the effects of Shadow—but not in a way that prevents the damage or harm done in its entirety. You were in the green as if you'd been suspended there, waiting for someone to take, and pass, the sword's test.

"The green's test. Shadow was expressed—in the green—in a fashion I haven't encountered before or since. There wasn't a single Yvonne; there were dozens. They looked identical to the Yvonne you see here. They appeared to be suspended at the bottom of a lake, almost sleeping; they moved in concert."

Mrs. Erickson's eyes widened.

"To free Yvonne, they had to be destroyed, one at a time, until only Yvonne remained. But Yvonne *did* remain, and it was due to the power radiated by the green's weapon." He glanced, once, at An'Tellarus; she met his gaze and offered him an encouraging nod, which Kaylin hadn't expected.

"If Mrs. Erickson is seeing something that looks ghostly, it might be the remnants of those other, Shadow Yvonnes."

"Were they trying to kill her?"

Severn shook his head. "They were suspended, as she was suspended, in water." He hesitated, and then said, "Yvonne was Ollarin's closest friend. The water—even in the green—is elemental. It's possible that the water and the green in concert moved to save her. I can't speak to the water; I can't confirm."

Kaylin wasn't worried about the water. "Yvonne didn't try to harm you."

"I'm not sure she was aware of me at all; the duplicates were, but only when I attempted to remove them. I wouldn't have said they were Shadow at all, if asked."

"They were Shadow," Yvonne said quietly. "I could hear their voices when I was injured."

"Did they speak to you in a way you could understand?"

She shook her head. "But the green didn't, either."

"You could hear the green."

Yvonne nodded. "I don't think I would have heard the other voices if there weren't so many of them. Do you think that's what Mrs. Erickson sees?"

That might explain why these ghosts weren't like the rest of Mrs. Erickson's many ghosts. The multiple Shadowy Yvonnes hadn't been alive in the normal sense of the word.

"Let's never mention this to Bellusdeo. Or the Consort. Or anyone outside of this room."

"She does not bear Shadow within her," Helen said quietly. "Were you to have asked me when she entered my boundaries, I would have said she was an entirely normal Barrani—something most of the cohort is not. They, to me, would be more of a danger than Yvonne. An'Tellarus is dangerous for entirely different reasons—but those I was built to counter at need."

Kaylin walked to Mrs. Erickson's side. "I don't want you to try to hold their hands—if they even have hands in your vision—but are they trying to speak? Are they attached to Yvonne, or are they just, I don't know, haunting her?"

"They're not like Bellusdeo's sisters." Mrs. Erickson's voice was soft but certain. "I would say *haunting* might be the correct word." She trailed off. "I've never seen the dead that way.

If you asked me, I would say they aren't quite dead at all—but there's something there." She spoke almost apologetically, as if she was afraid to offer insult to whatever it was she saw.

"I can't see them," Yvonne told her, understanding immediately the older woman's gentle hesitation. "I can't hear them. I don't really remember Shadow—I remember swords, and threats. I managed to escape. My family didn't. But I was wounded in the escape, and I remember just . . . crawling. But I crawled toward the voice I could hear—the one that didn't sound like threats and death. Or screaming.

"Severn found me in the green—I knew that part. I didn't quite know the rest." Until now. "Am I danger to the Lake?" she asked, her voice so soft Kaylin barely heard the question. But it was the question that was uppermost in her mind.

This isn't why she'd invited Yvonne to visit. She'd liked her instinctively—hells, she still did. The *Lake* had involved itself, somehow. Yvonne had heard it, just as she'd heard the green when she'd been injured in the West March. She'd walked toward that sound, that voice, and found herself within the cavern that contained the Lake. Kaylin had often wondered why the Lake was situated in a cavern, surrounded on all sides by rock—but maybe that was the best way to protect it. Were the Lake open to sun and sky, it would be open to Dragon flights and magical, aerial attacks—at least, during the time when the High Halls had collapsed its focus in, toward containing the Shadow at the very heart of the Tower of Test.

If the Lake chose . . .

"Helen, could you let Ynpharion through?"

"I do not think that would be wise," Helen replied, which sounded like *no.*

"I need him to ask the Consort a question."

"If you could control your thoughts, if you could block what you see or hear, it would not be a risk. You cannot. And you are well aware that if the Lady's position is not political, that is only by Barrani standards. Should she feel something is a danger—a genuine danger, not a political threat—she will stop at nothing to remove it."

Kaylin wanted to argue further, but knew Helen was right.

"So, where are we now?" Terrano asked when everyone had fallen silent.

"We're trying to figure that out." Kaylin once again turned to Mrs. Erickson. "You didn't see the ghosts until the flowers appeared?"

Mrs. Erickson shook her head.

"I'm going to assume that the green has slender roots here at the moment. Could be because of Yvonne. Could be because of Severn's weapon. Could be because of this damn dress. I'd say it doesn't matter why, but it obviously does. I just don't think we're going to get answers to that right now."

"If ever," An'Tellarus said. "But if the dress is here and the Teller's crown is here, they are an invitation to the *regalia*. The *regalia* does not require an audience; there were early ceremonies to which very, very few were witness. What we understand is the green reveals its heart during those Tellings—but not even the Teller knows, before it begins, what tale will be formed or told.

"Somehow, the green has found purchase within the confines of Helen." An'Tellarus's smile was crooked, underlined by bitterness that no longer touched her voice. "Arcanists would envy you for eternity for what has been built here. The Arcanists of the past have tried."

"Oh, believe we know that," Kaylin muttered in Elantran. "What we need to know right now isn't why the green is here—well, maybe—but why the Lake called Yvonne, and what the Shadow contained in the green actually was. Or is. If Yvonne was injured by Shadow years ago in the West March, and it happened because the former An'Sennarin wanted to capture or injure her badly enough to make Ollarin obedient, some form of Shadow is clearly connected to Lords of the High Court—and those lords are our enemies. But they can move in ways normal Barrani, even Arcanists, can't move. They can slide past physical barriers or objects. We have some experience with that—but not the way they do."

"We've been experimenting," Terrano said, his expression far more serious. "They're not doing what we do. I wouldn't say it's remotely the same. It's more like they've created a portal tunnel through which they can travel." He cleared his throat. "Or at least, that's what we've come to believe they believe."

"Serralyn's research?"

He nodded. "Early attempts weren't successful. Notes from those experiments remain, classified as portal research, not Shadow research. She doesn't think they would ever have thought of moving the way I move—for what she hopes are obvious reasons. Not that it wasn't tried in earlier times—for war," Terrano added. "But those intrepid researchers didn't survive their early attempts.

"This, however, is different. One of the strongest elementalists of our race—a fire mage—found that he could walk through fire. With will and effort, he could use fire as a portal; the fire existed everywhere, or could. I believe Ollarin is powerful enough he could do the same: he could walk through the water to a destination of his choice. That's Serralyn, by the way."

"I guessed."

"She's thinking that Shadow might once have been very much like an element—but a different force, a later force. Life didn't depend on it—or not our lives. Not the lives of the races we know and interact with. It's possible that the Wevaran or the Ancestors touched Shadow as a primal, early force—a transformative force.

"That part, she's less certain of. Whole races were born, and whole races went extinct. The library was not yet created, and the notes about those vanished early races were . . . not like our books.

"There is evidence that some of the Ancients were aligned with all the elements, and Shadow was one—either discovered or created. Starrante thinks it was actually discovered, but he does not share a language with the archive itself, and attempting to decode the ancient recording has proved difficult. There are archives that are called *books* by the librarians—but they're not books at all. They're not writing in any way we understand writing. Starrante has been focused on Shadow as an elemental force, not as the heart of *Ravellon*.

"Shadow as it exists now seems to be a primal force with will, intent, command. Just as earth, fire, air, and water have crude will and intent."

Kaylin frowned. "I've been to the Keeper's garden. The whole purpose of that garden is to *quiet* the destructive intent of the wild elements. But that intent—and the enmity of each element for all the others—exists as part of their nature; they desire dominance and total control. Which would pretty much kill all of us, no matter which won, if there was a winner.

"We don't fear the wild elements. We don't fear their attempts to control us. But they exist. You've never seen the garden when things are unstable. I have."

"And your point?"

"Shadow isn't part of the garden. Maybe there are no boundaries and no cages that have stopped that primal force—if it *is* a primal force—from gaining dominance."

"But if that were the case, the Shadow in the green would have had some intent, some will, surely?" An'Tellarus seemed almost annoyingly amused. "Yes, Severn, I think I definitely understand why you never thought to mention the young lady."

Terrano cleared his throat. "Serralyn thinks there's some merit to what you're suggesting."

"What was I suggesting?"

"That Shadow exists in a fashion similar to elements. There's Shadow as we perceive it, which is what the Towers were created to cage, and Shadow as elemental force, as something that can, like fire or water or earth, be used as a source of power. Arbiter Starrante's research implies your guess could be true."

Kaylin frowned. "You think Yvonne's injury wasn't an attempt at invasion?"

"It was definitely an attempt to injure—but you've seen the effects of Shadow that breach the barriers surrounding *Ravellon*. It's transformative; it takes over, mutates, and changes physical forms. People don't summon fire elementals to transform things. They summon them to destroy, or threaten to destroy, things."

"So it might be likely that the Shadow used is, for want of a better word, inert?"

"Serralyn considers that not a better word, for what it's worth."

"Helen, would you sense that?"

"You carried something that definitely contained Shadow into the house, at least according to your memories. And Terrano's and Mandoran's. I cannot sense it. Hope believes it is not a danger to you."

Kaylin frowned. Eyes narrowed, she turned to Terrano. "Is it still there?"

He grimaced. "I can't see it from where I'm standing."

"Could you see it if you were standing in a different place?"

"Helen?" Terrano asked, the name suspiciously inflected with whining.

"We've been experimenting—carefully and judiciously—since Terrano's return," Helen said. "But the paths used by the assassins—for want of a better word—aren't Terrano's method of travel. I did not judge it wise to attempt to reach that space from within my own perimeters except when heavily supervised."

Kaylin opened her mouth. Closed it again. She could hear voices, now. She glanced at Mrs. Erickson; Mrs. Erickson was trying very hard not to stare at Yvonne. To Kaylin's eyes, Yvonne hadn't changed. But sound had changed in this room, and the scent of the air was heavy with growth.

"I think those of us who can should head upstairs."

"Annarion's not going to let everyone in." By *everyone*, Terrano clearly meant An'Tellarus.

She felt Severn's hesitation, but he said nothing. Yvonne, to Severn, wasn't dangerous in the way An'Tellarus could be—but she wasn't safe, either. Was it the ghosts Mrs. Erickson could see but couldn't touch or speak with? Was it Yvonne's interaction with the Lake, or before it, the green?

If he had an answer, he didn't share it. But he didn't share objections, either.

The kitchen led to the dining room, where chairs sat beneath the top of a long table. Helen had not set the table for guests, in theory—but she had set it to be seen. Yvonne hadn't been invited for a meal but had been invited for the equivalent of morning tea. Kaylin didn't love tea but understood the word as a loose description of a social event. Given Yvonne's readiness to join the kitchen, she imagined Yvonne wouldn't care about specifics of torturous etiquette—but An'Tellarus would.

Etiquette, however, was not foremost on An'Tellarus's mind. Nightshade had been mentioned, but an outcaste fieflord was not yet as important as the possible fate of a haunted Yvonne. Kaylin couldn't unsay Nightshade's name. An'Tellarus wouldn't forget it. Kaylin was certain both she and Terrano would get an earful—or eleven—when An'Tellarus finally departed.

The problem was to get her to depart.

"I think that unlikely," Helen said quietly. "While she is difficult—and she has always been difficult—she is not what the Barrani would consider malicious. Her concern for Yvonne is genuine, but her attachment to Severn is also, to my surprise, genuine. She feels Severn can take care of himself—and she is not a fool; she recognizes his attachment to you. But she feels that Yvonne stumbles into things without will or intent—and can easily get swept away by them.

"I do not believe she is wrong. But Kaylin—you, too, tend to stumble into the most extreme of situations. An'Tellarus is willing to trust you, in part because you'll be dead soon—of old age, one hopes—and in part because Yvonne already does. Yvonne's instincts are good, in Cediela's opinion. It's just that she can't act on them much of the time."

"Why do you call her that?"

"Forgive me; that was rude. It is the name by which she is called by closer acquaintances at court; it was used far more frequently in the West March than it has been in the High Halls." Helen hesitated. "I believe I can distract An'Tellarus; I can entertain her. But if I do, it will require far more concentration than it does to keep track of the cohort's doings within my walls."

"Why?"

"She is old, she is canny, and she is fully capable of masking her thoughts. She is not without personal power. And she despises boredom. She is not bored now; she is fully engaged—indeed, she was like this in the distant past."

"You liked her," Kaylin said; it was almost an accusation.

"She is not the type of person one either likes or dislikes. She is the type of person one appreciates. But buildings, as Barrani, are eternal unless destroyed. Ennui and boredom can threaten us all when we have no will or goals of our own. An'Tellarus was, to the ruin and dismay of many, never boring. I may be forced to adopt an entirely different form for my Avatar; I hope it will not be alarming."

"But if she talks to you, she won't insist on joining us in Nightshade's room?"

"I will not allow her to enter if Annarion does not agree. Annarion will never agree." Helen's smile was serene. "But Cediela understands at least this much. She may demand. She will not attempt to use force."

"Her demands are pretty forceful."

"That is true. I have let the cohort know that my physical form will be concentrated in an appearance to which they are not accustomed—and I have asked Fallessian to escort Imelda to her quarters and keep her company there over tea. Unless things become heated or physical combat ensues, he will remain with her."

If physical combat, as Helen put it, ensued, Kaylin suspected that Fallessian might remain with her as well.

"Do you expect things to be that messy?"

"People are nosing around my perimeters at the moment; they believe they are being subtle."

That shouldn't be a problem for Helen. "They're not Tellarus's people, are they?"

"No."

". . . they're not trying to enter the premises the usual way."

"Sadly, no. It makes containing An'Tellarus in a socially acceptable fashion more complicated. The cohort is also keeping watch and have expanded the domains in which they are being watchful—but only Mandoran and Terrano have any experience with some of the paths that I believe might be used. I have made Terrano aware of the possible difficulty. He has informed the others. But I believe Serralyn wishes to join the cohort, and a small argument is in progress."

"Is there *ever* a time when a small argument *isn't* in progress?"

"Yes. When things are, as you might put it, on fire."

26

Annarion accepted Yvonne's presence in the room. He also accepted Severn's. He would have barred the door and stood with drawn sword had An'Tellarus made any attempt to enter. His brother, unconscious and injured, could not defend himself against any attack she might make, nor would there be consequences if she killed an outcaste.

Kaylin didn't believe An'Tellarus would try. The older Barrani Lord had nothing to gain should she somehow succeed. But An'Tellarus was unpredictable, and her alliances almost unknown. Kaylin wouldn't have taken the chance had she been Annarion, either.

He trusted Helen to keep them safe, but it was a near thing. Had Helen been able to clearly explain *why* Nightshade wouldn't wake and couldn't be touched by Kaylin's healing power, his response might have been different. But An'Tellarus would leave the house with whatever information she gained—and she'd gained a lot of information no one had had any intention of imparting.

Everything had grown too large. Every small bit of information Kaylin had gained in bits and pieces over the past year was a thread, and the threads were tangled and messy, a giant ball of complication. Kaylin investigated murders and lesser crimes for a living and had come to understand that the most important thing she could do to solve a crime was to ask the right questions. Only then could she find the right answers.

But the disparate events and the bits of information were too entangled. She wasn't certain what information and experience were relevant to *this* problem. She would have bet against the green being involved with most of her on-hand money, but here they were.

Kaylin shook her head to clear it as she reached Nightshade's room. "You probably won't be able to avoid it if An'Tellarus is determined, but I'm asking you not to speak about anything you see in this room."

Yvonne hesitated. "If you know I can't avoid it—"

"The Teller's crown is in this room, and the person it's probably meant for is also in this room—but he's been unconscious since an assassination attempt, and we haven't been able to wake him."

". . . and you think I'm involved because of the green?"

"You didn't see the way your eyes changed color. I work with Barrani in my day job. I know the color of Barrani eyes, although I admit I almost never see green. Yours were the wrong green. And the Lake somehow called you. The green somehow sheltered you. I didn't mean for any of this to happen when I invited you."

"What did you think would happen? I mean, I didn't expect any of this either."

"I thought we'd have a talk, I'd find out why you'd taken the test of the Lake, and I'd ask you if you'd be willing to speak with the Consort. You'd like her; I'm certain she'd like you. It would disentangle some of the politics.

"But you're involved in ways I didn't even think were possible. So . . . I'm asking you to enter the room. You don't have to touch anything. You don't have to do anything. But . . . be present and keep what you see to yourself as much as possible. I won't ask for more."

"We might," Annarion said, as he opened the door. He'd heard.

Yvonne nodded. "Tell me where you'd like me to stand."

Annarion blinked. "Stand?"

"I am An'Tellarus's servant. I can serve Lord Kaylin in her stead."

Kaylin blinked as well. "You're a guest. I don't think Helen would forgive me if I made you stand invisibly in the corner."

"Helen will accept whatever makes me feel the most comfortable," Yvonne replied, a hint of a smile at play around the corners of her mouth.

Annarion shook his head as if to clear it. "Come into the room where my brother is resting."

"Your brother?"

Annarion nodded. His eyes were a martial blue, but they didn't darken when he greeted Yvonne. He turned and led the way; Kaylin, Yvonne, and Severn followed.

Teela and Sedarias did not. Teela chose to join Helen and An'Tellarus. Sedarias simply vanished into her own room.

"She is capable of doing what Terrano does; she feels it beneath her dignity as An'Mellarionne. It is likely she will join him—or anchor him. Torrisant is anchoring Terrano now, but Mandoran has joined Terrano in his planar exploration, and two anchors may well be needed. She is, of the cohort, closest to Terrano. Or perhaps it is better to say that he is closest to her.

"Go and do what must be done."

Kaylin didn't *know* what had to be done—that was the problem. All of her instincts were being overwhelmed by internal screaming, frustration, and growing anxiety. But her early training held: she didn't dissolve into a panicked mess.

Annarion was panicked enough.

The Teller's crown—as Terrano had informed them—was on the bedside table. Nightshade was lying in bed, eyes closed, skin pale. The unhealed injuries hadn't killed him yet, but it was probably only a matter of time. The greatsword he had earned in the wars lay in its sheath, its hilt against his chest, the point of the blade even with his feet, as if he were already dead and was to be buried in honor with his weapon.

That would never happen with one of the legendary Three.

But the sword was somehow protecting its bearer. Annarion was protecting his brother. And, once again, the Teller's crown was waiting for Nightshade to wake and take it. She could almost feel its presence as a weight, as if the head it adorned were her own.

Mrs. Erickson had worn a wreath of flowers.

Kaylin had worn this dress.

"Is Serralyn coming?" Kaylin asked Annarion as she bent and placed a palm against the fieflord's forehead.

"No. Not yet. She's not happy about that, and she's still arguing. Valliant is with her, and Valliant won't leave unless and until Sedarias commands otherwise. But Eddorian has been speaking with both his brother and Hallionne Alsanis as more information has come in. He thinks Serralyn might be on the right track: there could be a Shadow that can be used as elements can be used. His brother is not, as you know, entirely mentally present; something took a large hammer to his memories, and what remain exist as fragments and shards. Some of those cause panic, and Eddorian has to comfort and quiet that panic.

"But he's been doing nothing *but* that since he chose to remain with his brother." Annarion exhaled. "Eddorian is like, and unlike, me. I was close to my brother; he was close to his. But we're not the same people, and Eddorian's focus now is on the lords who made use of his brother. I believe he wants revenge."

"His brother was an Arcanist who was heavily involved with them. Anything that happened to *Lord* Iberrienne happened because of his choices and his decisions. Why would Eddorian feel he has to take revenge on Iberrienne's confederates?"

"Because he's angry," Annarion replied, shrugging. "He can be angry at you, if you'd prefer; if you hadn't interfered, his brother wouldn't have been almost destroyed. Or he can be angry because his brother is an idiot, and he can tell himself that his brother got involved because he, like my brother, intended to save us, to free us from the Hallionne, and to bring us home."

"Your brother didn't do what Iberrienne did. And your brother didn't present a threat to the Consort."

"No. No, he wouldn't. But he involved you, and he marked you—as if you could be owned. I . . . expected better."

"He tried to figure out how to reach you for centuries. Centuries of time in which you were trapped. I've changed a lot in the past few years. I've learned a lot. I've made different—better—decisions, when decisions were mine to make. There are people who *could* hate me. People who have the *right* to seek revenge. I'm not going to just stand there and let them stab me, but if they managed it? I'd deserve it. But I can't change the past. I can change the future—but I can only do that by making better choices now.

"Nightshade *isn't* dead. If I understood the reason why an outcaste was considered such a valuable, necessary target, it might help us."

Annarion agreed with this. "Barrani outcastes aren't Dragon outcastes. Their status is political. Were any of us High Lord, we wouldn't have made my brother outcaste—but he's never explained what the reasoning was."

"You think it had something to do with the cohort?"

Annarion nodded. "It's possible Iberrienne was like my brother: his goals were to rescue *his* brother. My brother was always considered a bit unusual for a Barrani Lord. He *had* power, but he didn't use it the way other powerful lords did. I looked up to him."

Kaylin lifted a hand to her cheek almost self-consciously, as if the mark itself had destroyed something precious to Annarion.

Annarion exhaled. "Yes. I know I should have let it go. You're the person who was marked, and you don't even notice it. But it's difficult. It's like my brother isn't the brother I believed he was. Yes, people change—believe we all know that, given what we've become. But what's right and what's wrong shouldn't. The Barrani aren't generally considered a highly moral people—as if morality is just a passing phase, like youth. But my brother *was*. He wasn't young when we were sent to the green. He wasn't young when he was made heir to our family line. He couldn't be bribed and he couldn't be threatened—especially not threatened.

"But he gave up our family."

Kaylin cleared her throat. "He was made outcaste."

"If he had cared—at all—he would never have allowed that to stand. Instead, he accepted it, and he eventually took the Tower in the fiefs. I don't understand why. He's never explained it. He's never complained. He's never planned to reverse his fortune. If it was something he cared about now, I'd be standing shoulder to shoulder with Sedarias in the High Halls, building alliances and making choices that would once again elevate the Solanace family.

"But even that . . . Not even that."

"Do you understand what the relationship between the current Consort and your brother was?"

Annarion frowned but shook his head. "He was never one to speak of personal things if they brought him no joy. I know that our families were close—inasmuch as any Barrani families could be close—when we were children. More than that, I don't know."

"I think it's important," Kaylin said.

"You think the attack on my brother is somehow related to the attack on the Consort?"

Kaylin nodded. The one bit of information she hadn't given up was the fact that the Consort herself was losing the ability to commune with the Lake, and to interact with the names that would wake Barrani infants. Yvonne's presence—Yvonne's open admission that she'd managed to just wander her way to the Lake without intent—would make clear the threat to the Consort's position. Probably.

But she couldn't explain why she was certain the two events were connected without divulging that one thing.

"If my brother could openly support the Consort, that would make sense—but he can't. The Consort can't accept his service. He's outcaste. She's the Lady."

"He's outcaste, yes. But that hasn't stopped him from becoming the Teller for the last *regalia*, and it hasn't stopped him from entering the High Halls—with his sword—to great effect. No one attempted to murder him for that. I don't think the Consort asked for his aid, but she was clearly happy to see him when we went to the West March, and she treated him as a Lord of the High Court, as if outcaste was irrelevant.

"If it weren't for the fact that the High Lord clearly adores her, I might have guessed that the High Lord had an interest in removing Nightshade. But what if it's the opposite? What if the High Lord is considering reinstating Nightshade? I'm certain the Consort would support that."

Annarion was silent.

"What does Sedarias think?"

"She thinks it's a possibility. But that would imply that having the Consort out of the picture is necessary. If they believe my brother would interfere with that—and could—removing him would be essential.

"Teela thinks your hypothesis is worth considering." Teela

was the only other person who was aware of the problems the Consort had with the Lake. "Lord Andellen is pursuing a line of investigation. Lord Nightshade—as lord of a fief, even if outcaste—had connections with the Lords of the High Court, or rather, with their satellite families. Usually those low enough in the hierarchy that they could be relied on to do labor unfit for noble hands.

"But those families serve different lords. We are attempting to discover the person who commanded the war bands into a service one would consider beneath them." Annarion's expression grew remote as he listened to Teela. Kaylin was familiar enough with the expression: it was Teela's Barrani Hawk expression. "I am uncertain that we will be given information that will lead immediately to the culprit, as those involved in the attack are dead."

"What about the third war band?"

"Almost certainly dead as well. They scattered. Either they fled to *Ravellon*—a crime in the Barrani High Court—or they returned to those they served to explain, or pay for, their failure."

Annarion sounded more and more like Teela, who was theoretically in discussion with An'Tellarus in a different room. Teela could withdraw herself from the group mind, and Kaylin assumed she often did. But she could *also* bring herself right into its heart, with permission of the individual cohort member. Kaylin suspected that she was doing that know. "This plan started before you were born, kitling.

"You have been the most magnificent kink in their plans. They could not predict a mortal Chosen. They could not lay hands on you without drawing both the attention and ire of the Eternal Emperor. And An'Teela." Annarion's smile was Teela at her coldest.

"The Consort is a known quantity, but she, too, is new. Her mother was Lady before her—it is historically rare, but does happen. If these plans were in the making, they were probably intended for the previous Consort. She was an austere woman—one, on the surface, as unlike her daughter as two Barrani women could be.

"Throughout history, in ones and twos, young women are subject to the test of the Lake. All fail; that is the expectation. They could not have anticipated the presence of Yvonne. Yvonne and An'Tellarus. The former Consort had no love of Nightshade, and little interest in him, except perhaps as the bearer of one of The Three.

"Clearly someone believes the current Consort does. Or perhaps they believe Lord Nightshade had no love for the previous High Lord and his Consort, but cares for the current set."

"I just don't understand why he'd be considered a threat, given his status."

A ripple of pure annoyance crossed Annarion's face. Teela's annoyance. "Given *what we've just said*, you should by now. If you don't, that is not our problem." Annarion's lack of interference made clear that if he didn't entirely agree with Teela, he felt she had a point.

Fine. "So Nightshade was collateral damage. He was kept informed about the Lords of the High Court, although information probably wasn't perfect, given his status. Outside of the Consort, no Barrani of note would be seen so much as waving at him. If the original target wasn't *this* Consort, it was the Lake."

If the new High Lord had not ascended the High Court's throne, the previous Consort would have been the one who lost the ability to commune with the Lake, and the names it contained; she would have been the one who could no longer guarantee, or usher in, the future.

Yvonne was a wild card. Kaylin was a wild card. The current High Lord and the Consort, as well. They were elements that had to be taken into account. The cohort was a wild card—it was likely, until Terrano made contact with them, that the conspirators had all but forgotten the discarded children.

Terrano would have made contact *before* the current Consort, the current High Lord. He'd been struggling to find freedom for a long, long time.

With Terrano's help, they'd made inroads into the Hallionne. The Hallionne had been built as sanctuaries and used as such during the long, long period of the Draco-Barrani wars—but they hadn't been built, hadn't been designed, to withstand Shadow. The Towers had.

Nightshade was a Tower lord, a fieflord. Nightshade could be expected to support the Consort from the figurative shadows. But that could be said of *any* of the Lords of the High Court; the Consort was not without significant support.

"What are you thinking?" Annarion asked.

Kaylin lifted a hand to shut him up. Thoughts were often scattered, and sometimes like very slender threads; if she was distracted, they'd escape.

Nightshade was a fieflord. Nightshade held one of the Towers. Nightshade had protection from, and knowledge of, Shadow across a much broader spectrum than any of the other lords who would offer the Consort support and power. He would not have offered the previous Consort that same support.

She thought of Barren, the fief to which she had fled when she'd run from Nightshade. Barren, aptly named, had been ruled by a mortal; the Tower's captain had grown bored, and had pursued a single goal: freedom from the tyranny of a True Name. The borders between Barren and *Ravellon* had grown porous enough that Shadow could break through the containment—both in obvious, military ways, and in subtle ways.

But Tiamaris had taken that Tower in the end; Tiamaris had become its captain. The Tower had become both his servant and his lord. The conspirators—whoever they were—had clearly used Shadow, possibly believing the power granted was elemental in nature: where will was strong enough, the summoner ruled rather than served.

"Maybe it's not just the Consort," she finally said. "I mean, Nightshade would support the current Consort. I'd bet everything I own on that. But he's also a fieflord; he captains a Tower. We know the Towers were built around living people of different races; Nightshade's Tower is terrifying.

"But it's captained. If Nightshade dies, I don't think his Tower will accept just anyone. There's bound to be a test, and a large pile of corpses who fail that test. If the Tower is empty, it can endure for some time; it can continue to guard the borders that enclose *Ravellon*. But the protection weakens with time.

"Dead, Nightshade can't captain a Tower, and he can't bring any knowledge he gained in his tenure to bear in defense of the Consort." He might have some understanding of what was happening with the Lake. She exhaled. "If Logia is right—if Bellusdeo's sisters are right—there is a different stream of names, one that doesn't seem entirely dependent on physical location.

"The High Halls were created in part to protect the Barrani Lake of Life. It's where all Barrani babies are taken. But if the babies don't wake . . ."

"Kitling." Teela's voice, through Annarion's mouth, was severe with warning.

"Then another Lady might rise who can offer wakefulness, right? She can guide parents with sleeping infants to different names. Let's say those names do wake the infants." Kaylin frowned. "Let's say those names *have* woken *some* of the infants. I mean—before they put this into practice, they'd have to test it, wouldn't they?"

Teela fell silent.

Annarion, in control of his own vocal cords, said, "Yes. If they want to offer this new source as an alternative, they'd have to test it. They'd have to have enough witnesses who could confirm the truth of the claims. Barrani are not notoriously flexible as a people. The Lake exists to wake our children; the Lake is protected from contaminants or harm. If, for some reason, we lose the Lake, and an alternative is offered, most will stand back and wait to assess.

"No one of power will take the risk that their children will be endangered; we do not bear young as frequently as mortal races. But they might send their servants to confirm that their children could, indeed, be awakened. If they did this, they would observe. Should the children be flawed in an obvious way, it would be noted immediately—just as it was noted that we had been transformed by the *regalia*. But if there was no such obvious flaw, they would want to observe the results for some time.

"Do you think this is what's happened?"

"Births are recorded, right?"

Annarion nodded.

"In the High Halls?"

"All children must be brought to the Lake. Yes, all such infants are recorded. Even if they live in the West March, they must make the pilgrimage to the High Halls when their young are born. There aren't as many Barrani births—we might be able to find people who are alive but not listed." Annarion turned toward Nightshade in his almost deathly repose.

"Is Serralyn there?"

"She's there. Not here, but I think Sedarias may lift the prohibition."

Kaylin shook her head. "I don't want her here because it might not be safe to get here. We might need any hints Starrante can give." Shadow. Shadow as power, as an elemental force. Shadow as underpinning of a portal path that was more flexible than the paths that existed even in the Academia. Would Nightshade know? Would he understand? "I'm not a summoner, and even if I were, I'm not sure I'd try summoning Shadow."

Silence. It had the quality of a cohort argument; she'd become accustomed to that kind of silence—one that was filled with words and emotions that didn't include her. Sometimes she was grateful for it.

"Arbiter Starrante believes if anyone could summon Shadow, it would be you."

The silence this time had a different weight.

27

"Can he explain that?"

"He says instinct, but Serralyn doesn't believe him. Arbiter Starrante is thorough, she says. He doesn't *like* guesswork. When he makes guesses, they become the foundation of research, and research will either confirm that suspicion or kill it.

"But in the absence of time and research, he is willing to say that he doesn't make this suggestion because you're Chosen, but because you're mortal and nameless. Mortals were designed with different intentions, in his opinion.

"Shadow is not quantified as an element; it's possible that, when the original garden was created, Shadow was not a force recognized by the Ancients. It is possible that it was not a force that existed; that it emerged later, or perhaps concurrent with, the birth of the Ancients. For obvious reasons, almost nothing is known about that.

"But if fire burns, if water drowns, both provide succor in other ways, and both are necessary to life as we know it. It is possible that Shadow is, if you will, the chaotic factor, the change factor, that arises *from* life itself. If that is the case, it implies that it is necessary for life, just as fire, air, or water are, because all living things change.

"There is very little research done—as you are well aware—

about that possibility. But there is some, and there are hints of its existence in magical theory and research papers that were written during the rise, and height, of *Ravellon* before its fall. None of those papers reference Shadow in any fashion, but they reference new forms of magic, new forms of power. And, of course, multiple worlds.

"He has been focused now on the magic of transformation, where he feels hints of Shadow might be found. Certainly the fall of *Ravellon* caused the fall of many worlds—but its fall was accelerated, and by the time the danger was understood and credible, there was very little time to research and take notes. There was time to flee, time to build fortifications—such as the Towers, although those rose only after all hope was lost.

"It is Arbiter Starrante's belief, and Arbiter Androsse concurs, that research of that nature, or papers, or even desperately written warnings, were trapped within *Ravellon*. They did not emerge to join the library's extensive archive. Whether they could not leave or could not be added due to the precautions taken by the Ancients, we cannot say; we are aware that there are some few Arcanists and sorcerers who could prevent their work from becoming part of the archive.

"Before you ask—because he's certain you will—investigation into the cause of *Ravellon*'s fall has been done in the library, but the library was inaccessible for a long period because the Academia was submerged to make way for the Towers. The records pored over in those investigations—anything researched while the city stood and shone as a beacon—are records all three of the Arbiters know relatively well.

"Starrante is familiar with research into transformation. That research was not considered part of *Ravellon*'s fall; it is a separate field of interest. Early transformation research did not involve sentient beings; much of it involved materials for building or crafting. The highest of spires in the city itself were not created with quarried stone and grown wood but magically transformed goods. Short-term transformation was apparently trivial—for a value of trivial that confounds most of the Arcanists of the present day who have recently begun to visit the library. But permanent transformation was, where it could be achieved, reliable and persistent.

"Where sentient beings were concerned, however, it was far less reliable—and far more researched. We do not have records of the completion of that research but have retained some of the initial research itself. In this merging and blending of disparate spells and powers, some research was done in the green; most was conducted within the city itself.

"Arbiter Starrante believes that it is the living transformation research that might have the strongest bearing on the question of Shadow as an elemental, separate force."

"Was there a lot about moving between planes?"

"He says there was, although this was considered an entirely separate school of research; in some cases, it was weaponized research. It arose from the study of portals—but the portals being studied were constructed by the Ancients for their own convenience."

"So transformation and multiple planes didn't cross over."

Annarion grimaced. "Starrante is apparently whirring like a machine because you asked that question. Serralyn had to remind him she was there because he spit a web and almost vanished into the archives."

"Why? Was it a smart question? I don't usually ask those, if you believe my former teachers."

"I think it's a combination of both the question and the context. I'd say the answer is a definite maybe. But . . . we sort of know that because of Terrano. The most obvious example is his eyes—he can alter those here. None of us enjoy it, and while most of us can do it, it gives us wicked headaches. But he's just a lot more flexible with form and shape when he needs to be. There are places he can walk that require changes—

but he walks those planes the way he walks this one when he doesn't want to be seen: not quite there, not quite here."

Kaylin exhaled. "One more question for Serralyn to pass on. Did the transformation research involve reaching into the Outlands? The potentia?"

"Yes, in some cases. The potentia is powerful, but the power is localized. You've seen that with Helen, Killianas, and the Hallionne. Helen can create anything her occupants desire—but it will not persist beyond Helen's boundaries. Some sought to make those creations permanent; others simply considered a building such as Helen a perfect place to house or create art, or to store it safely so that visitors might see it. There were artists who created their masterpieces in buildings such as Helen, limited only by what they could envision.

"And he apologizes for the digression. The green is not well-studied, but he believes it is, in some fashion, the earliest possible iteration of a sentient space."

Yvonne snorted. Loudly.

"That's not what is believed in the West March, I take it?" Kaylin asked.

"The green doesn't care what we believe," she replied. "But if what Severn said was true, the green can't be affected by Shadow, except at its own will. And no, before you ask, I wasn't a servant of the green. Maybe, in time, I might have aspired to that, but I speak with the authority of one who lives in its lee, not one who has studied or communed with it."

"But the green might have communed with you," Kaylin replied.

There was just too much information to take in, too much to untangle; some of it would have to be disentangled—if possible—at its source. In this case, that was the High Halls. But the green wasn't reaching out to the High Halls; it was reaching out to Helen, or to her numerous tenants. To Kaylin, in her poorly chosen dress. To Nightshade, who couldn't respond to the call of the Teller's crown.

And to Yvonne, who had been saved by the combined effort of the green and Severn.

Not all change is dangerous. Kaylin blinked at the voice and then turned to look at Hope. Hope was standing on her shoulder, his neck elongated, his eyes on Nightshade. *Not all change is positive. Positive, negative—often they are decided after the fact, but from very different viewpoints.*

"Can you wake Nightshade?" she asked.

There is very little I cannot do if you are willing to pay the price.

"And the price?" She almost never asked this question but felt a growing sense of urgency.

You would not pay it, Chosen. This is not a situation that requires my intervention, if you are careful.

"Serralyn actually agrees with Yvonne, for what it's worth." Annarion's eyes widened. "Whatever you think you're going to do, Terrano suggests you do it now."

"Helen?"

"I am currently in communication with Terrano," Helen replied. "Something is attempting to create a door within my boundaries."

"Would you have noticed it without Terrano?"

"Not immediately, and perhaps not in time."

"Is it the same path Terrano got caught on the last time?"

"He believes it is. But . . ."

"But?"

"The planes of existence, the planes he crosses and moves between, do not exert gravity, for want of a better analogy."

"And this path does."

"It appears to; it is subtle. Without caution, the path will draw people to it."

"It took Mandoran some time to reach Terrano in the fiefs."

"Mandoran is naturally more cautious than his brother. And as I said, it's subtle."

Annarion shook his head. "Mandoran doesn't think it's subtle this time—his guess is they're walking that small, created planar tunnel, but they're also using magic within their defined space; he says the pull is noticeable."

"Are people trying to enter?"

"I cannot sense people," Helen replied. "Just the entry point. But if the point is anchored here, people are certain to follow."

"You want to trap them here."

"I believe it would be to our advantage to have them here, yes," Helen replied. "But the idea was not mine. It was Teela's."

"Nightshade is here—it's too risky. It wouldn't be difficult for his enemies to find out where he is. They're probably here to finish the job."

"An'Tellarus is here. She is not pleased. Fallessian has left Mrs. Erickson in her rooms and has joined Sedarias. Allaron is with her now, as well."

"Serralyn better not be on the way."

"She is not. Valliant remains with her; they are both in the library. She is possibly the safest person in the cohort at the moment. Arbiter Androsse, apprised of the presence of the green here, has joined Arbiter Starrante in his research."

Annarion cleared his throat. "Androsse suggests that you attempt to use the Erenne mark to reach my brother."

Kaylin had no idea how to use the mark. A slave mark—or so it had been called—didn't generally go two ways. But the mark bled periodically, and had since Nightshade had been attacked. She assumed he was—somehow—trying to reach out to her.

"Ask Androsse if the more powerful person in this arrangement can unconsciously reach out to the person bearing the mark."

"Yes. There should be some hint of subconscious, some hint of actual intelligence, in the attempt; the binding can become attenuated, but the connection persists until the mark is released. He adds that this was true of Immortals of disparate power; he is uncertain that the rules that govern the mark's use even work in a situation in which a mortal is involved.

"Given that caveat, Androsse believes you should never have lost contact. The binding isn't a binding based on True Name. It's a binding of a more personal nature, if the spell was properly executed. The nature of the mark applied would change depending on the person who applied it, but the essential nature of an Erenne should be preserved."

Silence. Annarion bowed his head; Kaylin couldn't see his expression. Yet another argument was in progress.

"Yes," Helen said. "Arbiter Androsse informed Serralyn that the problem may be you. As the historical significance of the Erenne mark was lost, the application of that mark lost power; it became a symbol of ownership, but not a symbol of communion. It is clear to Androsse that Lord Nightshade held you in some esteem, or the mark could not be activated at all.

"You did not accept the weight and the truth of it, or of what it once was. He believes the reason the mark causes your cheek to bleed is your resistance. Annarion does not wish to pass this on; the mark is the cause of much conflict—and it was not applied as it once was by its creator. It *is* a simple brand, as Lord Nightshade used it. I believe it was meant to warn Barrani of your value—and the consequences of harming you.

"But Arbiter Androsse is disgusted by that notion. Or perhaps angry. He is surprised that it functions at all. Serralyn adds that surprise is perhaps not his primary emotion. But he believes that you can reach Nightshade because of the Erenne mark and binding. At the moment you are on the outside of the barrier that prevents communication through the namebond.

"If you make proper use of the Erenne mark, you will be on the inside of that barrier rather than the outside of it. Or at least, that's Androsse's theory."

Annarion paled. Clearly, Androsse had had more to say. He repeated none of it.

Helen took Mandoran's role. "Arbiter Androsse is uncertain what effect Nightshade's death would have on you, given the Erenne mark. As you haven't fully accepted it, he thinks you might be safe."

Might. What an awful word. "Did he explain any of that?"

"Not in so many words. In the best case for you—not for Nightshade—you will not be able to utilize that connection, and his death will merely cause the mark to disappear."

"When is my life ever best-case? What's the worst case?"

"You will die with him. He doesn't think you are in that position now. You are left with two choices: accept the mark properly or reject it utterly. But in the latter case, Nightshade is almost certain to die."

Kaylin fell silent. She understood the theory. If she could make contact with him at all, she could heal him. She couldn't reach him through the namebond, but the connection from the Erenne mark persisted. If he were awake, if he were healed, he might be like the Consort; there would be no obvious, visible sign of the interference at all.

But the Consort's decline had been subtle. Nightshade's had been instant.

Annarion wouldn't even meet her gaze; his shoulders were almost bunched up around his ears. He couldn't ask her to do what Androsse said was necessary. She wasn't even certain she could. She felt she'd accepted the mark's existence; she didn't even think about it anymore. Barrani with whom she interacted were familiar enough with it that they also ignored it.

An'Tellarus had barely lifted a brow, and Yvonne hadn't seemed to assign significance to it either.

Kaylin lifted a hand to her cheek. It wasn't bleeding at the moment, but it was warm where the Erenne mark lay.

How much more could she do to accept it?

If Androsse's research was correct—and she was absolutely certain it was—the spell had been created by an Ancestor who wished to form a lasting bond with a person he loved. His power was such that the namebond was overwhelming, and the person he loved likely to be absorbed by it, changed by it, devoured by it.

Why he couldn't just love the person, she didn't know. Why did there have to be a mark at all? Why did there have to be visible proof of that bond? If love was what was felt between two people, why did it involve others at all?

But the Ancestors were basically Barrani to start—with longer, more complicated names. Ownership, claim, elements of power were things it might not occur to them weren't necessary.

"Some cultures have wedding bands," Helen said, possibly attempting to be helpful.

Kaylin didn't really understand those, either. Why was it necessary? Why did someone else's claim matter so much? Was it *always* about power and ownership? Ugh. Her cheek was warm. Possibly the rest of her face had warmed up as well because she was flailing. Asking all the questions, but not in a way that would actually get useful answers.

What was acceptance?

Did it mean that she had to somehow love the fieflord? She cared very much for Annarion, his brother, but she'd hated life in Nightshade, especially after she'd seen what Tiamaris had begun to build. Her life in the streets, her hiding from Ferals, her scrounging for scraps of food—that was a function of a lord of territory who considered the people living in it like any other form of wildlife. They survived or they didn't.

She even understood it on some level.

But the Emperor's Elantra and Nightshade's fief were so different. It wasn't that people on the right side of the Ablayne were somehow richer—Kaylin had struggled to make ends meet before Helen—it was that they were safer. There were orphanages. There were doctors in their large medical buildings. There were Hawks and other officers of the Halls of Law. There were *laws*, and people like Kaylin were meant to enforce or uphold them. They were *paid* for their allegiance to those laws.

Nightshade hadn't cared. He barely saw the fieflings as people at all. Before Kaylin met the cohort—and Annarion in particular—she would have said Nightshade was incapable of what she herself called love. He saw power—all Barrani did. He *had* power. But love existed outside of power, didn't it?

The foundling hall was run by a Leontine who treated the orphans as if they were her children. What did she gain from that? Kaylin at least got paid.

It was impossible to accept the Erenne mark as a symbol of love, because there *was no love* involved with its placement. Not on his part. Not on hers. But there was attachment or maybe hope. She was Chosen. Annarion had been trapped in the West March. She'd suspected, since meeting Annarion, that the purpose of marking her, of staking that claim, was to bring the Chosen under his control, or at least into his orbit.

She'd never asked.

"Serralyn," she said to thin air, "I understand what Androsse thinks he's asking me to do—but I don't think it's relevant. If he's saying the mark itself was placed one-sidedly, and the bleeding I've been experiencing means that it was placed there as an act of love or communion, he is totally, utterly wrong. If there was love, it wasn't something I recognize *as* love. And maybe that's how the Barrani operate—but the cohort is what I would consider loving, which is proof that it's possible that not *all* Barrani do."

Think. If it weren't for Annarion, would she care what happened to Nightshade at all? He would be like most of the High Court to her: irrelevant to her life, her work, and her job.

Except she was here, trying to figure out how to use a mark she'd never asked for and didn't understand. Maybe because of Annarion. Maybe because Nightshade had saved her life, possibly more than once. Maybe because he'd given her his True Name, but he'd never tried to use it to control her.

Did it matter why?

She wanted to save him. She'd wanted that on the day he'd been attacked. She'd brought him to Helen, where he'd be safe, because she wasn't certain she could get him to his Tower in one piece. He was here, in her home, his brother hovering over him.

"I need to know how to accept it," she finally said. "I can't love him the way the Ancestors loved. I don't think I could love *anyone* the way the Ancestors loved. And I can't love him the way *I* might, in theory, love someone in the future. But he didn't love me when he marked me, either. If Androsse is right, there's no way the Erenne mark should work in either direction."

"Serralyn says Androsse finds the question upsetting. He is not impressed by either your ignorance or Nightshade's. He is, however, willing to allow that Ancestral love and possessiveness were almost inseparable. In the absence of love, one might call the result slavery; in the presence of love, one might call it exaltation."

"There was no exaltation, believe me."

"But no slavery either?"

"If Androsse is making the argument that Nightshade actually cared about me as a person, he's clearly been stuck in the fiction section of the library for too long." She hesitated. "I've seen the fate of those who love him. They're living statues. Sometimes he lets them out to breathe—but otherwise they're stone. Whatever I felt, whatever I accepted, would lead to that fate."

"Are they mortal?" Helen asked.

Kaylin nodded.

"And they chose to be so transformed?"

She nodded again. "I think, maybe, time doesn't pass for them unless they're with Nightshade. In his way, he cares for them. But it's not a way I could ever accept. My whole life isn't Nightshade—and it would never be Nightshade, even if I could convince myself I loved him."

"I doubt you could join that statuary, regardless. You bear the Marks of the Chosen. You have Hope. What do you, Chosen, sorcerer, Hawk, want to do?"

"I want to kick his ass out of bed. I want him to wake up, to be healed, and to figure out what the hells is going on in the Barrani High Court."

Annarion coughed. To Kaylin's surprise, he was almost laughing. How long had it been since he'd done that?

"Honestly," she said to him, "I want the two of you to stop fighting. I want you to forgive him because you're the only other person I could say, with no hesitation, he loves. And the fighting seems like a waste of love, because it's clear you love him, still. You're not ready to cut him out of your life, and he's willing to endure your anger and disappointment until you can see beyond it. I understand the disappointment. I get it. But there's more than just disappointment there."

"Do you think he'll know what's happened?"

"He'll know what's happened to him. If nothing else, it gives us more information. This is bigger than your brother—but he's central to some of it. The first time I encountered Barrani who'd ditched their names was in Nightshade. And if our enemies consider Nightshade enough of a threat they'd send war bands into the fiefs, he's someone we need."

That much she could accept.

She bore the Erenne mark, but she'd always been a fraud. She'd never been his. Would never belong to anyone, even if she grew to love them. History informed his place in her thoughts—near-starvation, cold, cold winters, hunting Ferals, the thugs that intermittently roamed the streets collecting the equivalent of protection money from people who had so little of it.

She learned to live with fear; fear guided her. She could pretend it was caution—but at this remove, there was almost no difference between the two. Nightshade was his fief; his fief was Nightshade. She couldn't separate them and had never tried. She had accepted the Erenne mark because she'd grown up with no real choices when confronted with people in power.

But she'd refused the High Lord's offer to remove it.

She wasn't certain why. She'd felt hesitant; it had been instrumental in saving her life and might in the future. She wasn't a fiefling anymore. She didn't have to fear the fieflord and his band of thugs. She genuinely liked Andellen—enough that she was willing to ask the High Lord to allow him to enter the High Halls, even if his oaths were sworn to an outcaste.

Was that all? Was that hesitance just a blend of fear and familiarity and pragmatism? The mark had changed the way the Barrani who served Nightshade treated her. Even if she were still a denizen of the fiefs, that would remain true; it was a form of protection, there. It was probably a red flag in the High Court itself, which would make it far less useful—but she'd managed to avoid the High Halls in her normal life.

The situation with the Lake wasn't normal. The situation with Nightshade and the Consort wasn't normal. The inability to interact with the namebond was definitely not normal.

And having Nightshade as an emergency tenant? Not normal, either.

Would she have brought him here at all if it weren't for Annarion? Would she have gone flying to his rescue—his possible rescue—if Annarion weren't living with her?

She exhaled.

Yes, she would have run to his rescue. But she would have

run to Andellen's rescue; she would have run to the cohort's rescue—and had. She would run as if the hells had been unleashed if Severn were in danger.

What was love, after all? Was it sexual attraction? Was it desire? Possessiveness? Impulse? What did Androsse mean when he said she had to accept the Erenne mark?

She looked at Nightshade. He was breathing, but his breath was shallow. Once he had been the fieflord, a person whose displeasure was almost a guarantee of death. Now he was Anarion's brother. The Consort's support from the shadows. But he wasn't Kaylin's in any way. She didn't want him to *be* hers.

The Ancients had chosen Kaylin. Nightshade had chosen Kaylin. Both had applied marks she didn't understand to her skin. But she didn't love the Ancients. She couldn't know them. Couldn't communicate with them. They'd chosen and they'd left. Nightshade was an echo of the same thing.

"Serralyn, ask Androsse why the mark could be placed on my cheek at all. I didn't accept it as an act of communion. I didn't accept it as anything other than the fieflord's will. And I spent a lot of my life cursing the fieflord's will. Is it only the power differential that defines the mark's placement?"

"Androsse says that's not the way it's supposed to be."

"I don't think the Barrani truly know any other way. Present company excepted," she added.

"Starrante thinks the power differential was possibly the deciding factor. He's speaking slowly and carefully—Androsse has some history with the Erenne mark, and he's even touchier than usual."

Kaylin had no trouble acknowledging that Nightshade was the greater power. Yvonne would be, absent the Marks of the Chosen, the greater power. Barrani were Immortals. They had forever in which to amass knowledge. They were physically more naturally fit, immune to the need for sleep; they didn't even need to eat as often as Kaylin did.

Did she envy them? Yes. On bad days, she envied them a lot. But she wasn't Barrani. She wasn't Immortal. She wasn't born Chosen.

But she was Chosen, now. And she bore the Erenne mark; if it had required communion or permission, it couldn't have been placed on her cheek without her consent.

Androsse's advice was impossible to follow. She couldn't bring to the Erenne mark the emotional resonance the mark had once required. It wasn't in her. Had she been younger, it might have been. Nightshade's power, a sign of Nightshade's favor, was armor. He knew far more than her; he could make decisions that could keep her safe. She would have been far less likely to starve, and far less likely to be Feral food.

But she was no longer a fiefling. She wasn't that starving, homeless child. She would never be as powerful as Nightshade, but she had chosen to use her power in defense of people who had even less power than she had. The Hawk. She'd chosen the Hawk. She'd chosen to believe—however imperfect they were—that the Imperial Laws were better protection, better foundations, for daily life; that they made it harder for the powerful to prey on the powerless.

That maybe, if the laws were followed and enforced, the powerless would—as Kaylin had—find their power, grow into it, become stronger as themselves.

The Erenne mark was a sign of the imbalance of power, a way for the powerful to coexist with the far less powerful without overwhelming them. Love might have been the motivation for the creation of that binding spell—but it wasn't a necessary condition. It couldn't be. How could anyone love what they feared so much?

Kaylin inhaled slowly, as if counting. She exhaled the same

way. She couldn't touch Nightshade with the power of the Marks of the Chosen; she'd tried. Helen didn't need to protect her from the namebond—or hide the details of her daily life—because it no longer reached him.

She couldn't be what the first Erenne had been. She wasn't an Ancestor. She wasn't Barrani. She wasn't Immortal. He hadn't marked the mortals in his statuary. They'd come to him—they were *happy* to spend their lives waiting, untouched by time—and they'd given everything.

She couldn't.

But if she could have, he'd never have placed that mark on her cheek.

In return, he'd offered her his True Name. She'd never tried to command Nightshade with the power of that name, and she never would. Partly because she was certain to lose any contest of will.

But . . . the name had been a vulnerability. Maybe that had been his way of balancing the implications of the Erenne mark; the mark was his, but in return, she knew his True Name. Right now, she couldn't call it. Any vulnerability was theoretical.

Maybe Barrani who were otherwise reasonable would actually appreciate the magic affecting Nightshade because it would protect their names from being used against them. But it didn't prevent the affected Barrani from accessing the source of both their life and their power: their True Name.

And it couldn't prevent Kaylin from accessing the source of her power: the Marks of the Chosen. It prevented her from using that power on Nightshade. But if Androsse had given the wrong advice, not all of it was useless.

It wasn't Nightshade Kaylin had to change. The Erenne mark was on her skin; it was part of her space, part of a place her power could touch. It was the mark itself that had to be altered.

28

Kaylin had ignored the Erenne mark. It had become part of her skin, a tattoo. That's how anyone who wasn't Barrani saw it in the Halls of Law; it's how people at the market stalls saw it. It's how residents—and customers—of Elani street saw it as well. One or two had even asked her where she'd gotten it done.

She didn't ignore the mark now. She didn't accept that it was a passive statement of her power—or more specifically its lack. She knew a connection existed; she wasn't making *herself* bleed. Power flowed toward that mark. Her guess was her inability to *process* that power, that connection, caused the magic to disperse across that small patch of skin—which was what likely caused the heat and bleeding.

She should have thought about this before now. Maybe if she had, she could have untangled at least Nightshade's fate. She didn't understand how any of the rest of the interference worked; she accepted that it did. What she could do for Nightshade, she couldn't do for the Consort—or anyone else affected by whatever magics had been cast.

But this Erenne mark had existed before the magic cast on Nightshade; it was already established. As was evidence of the continuing connection.

She lifted a hand to her cheek. Her skin felt cool; the bleeding and the heat had stopped. She closed her eyes. The power of the Marks of the Chosen couldn't reach Nightshade—but she wasn't Nightshade. She'd never really examined herself with that power; healing had been almost automatic, and she hadn't caught so much as a minor cold since the Marks of the Chosen appeared on her skin.

She lived her life by instinct. What she was doing now wasn't instinctive, and she was certain someone who'd been more deliberate in their life choices would have had a stronger sense of how to progress. But she was sensitive to the power of the Marks of the Chosen, and of the bindings of True Names. She listened for a long breath, but the Marks were silent against her skin.

They weren't necessary right now. What was essential was the mark on her cheek. That had never spoken to her the way the True Words could; she had never heard it as if it were a word, as if it expressed thoughts through language.

The Erenne mark had been used before—by Nightshade. She had a sense that words had been conveyed at a time when she wasn't quite in the same place and cursed mortal memory. Or maybe it was just Kaylin's memory, honed in childhood in the fiefs. If it wasn't a threat, if it wasn't a danger, she didn't think about it at all. Her focus had always been on survival, and the Erenne mark wouldn't end her life.

She felt like she was always fumbling in the dark; there were glimpses of light here and there, and she tried to follow them—but she couldn't see the actual destination. She could make choices. She could act on them.

This, then, was a choice. She could feel her cheek, could feel, just beneath the surface of the skin, the tiny roots of the spell, the magic that grounded the Erenne mark. She couldn't feel Nightshade.

Why had he done this? Was it, had it ever been, about her at all?

Kaylin. Hope's voice. She resonated with the sound of her name; it was a tremor that steadied her. Reminded her that even if she was connected to people, through their names or hers, she was still herself. Whoever that was. The person she'd been in the fiefs was not the person she was now. But that distant person, broken, angry, and afraid, had had dreams—and nightmares—that had led her to become Kaylin, Imperial Hawk.

The Marks of the Chosen, like the Erenne mark, had been outside both her intent and control. But the Marks of the Chosen had become part of the way she interacted with the world. They'd become a tool she could use.

But if she'd accepted the Marks because she had no choice, she learned to use them. The Marks of the Chosen didn't make her feel like a victim; they didn't make her feel like less of a person. In theory, they made her more powerful; among the Immortal, they made her worthy of a grudging, condescending version of respect.

They hadn't changed who she was. They'd given her the opportunity to do more. To help more. To heal. Not all things that happened without her permission became terrible, unwanted things. Birth, for one. No one had asked if she wanted to be born. No one had asked her *where*. She would never, ever have chosen the fiefs if the choice had been hers to make.

Life was made up of things that weren't her choice. But her choice still mattered. She wasn't a god. She wasn't an Ancient. She couldn't have perfect control over her life and what happened in it.

But she had enough choice that she could clear the rest of her thoughts. She could focus on the subtle, tiny roots of power that seemed to rest just below the surface of her skin—the skin that bore the Nightshade. She could feel warmth in them, not heat—but even as she thought that, they grew warmer beneath the palm of her hand.

She couldn't heal Nightshade—not yet. She could heal herself or at least reach her own body with her power. She did, examining the one element that wasn't hers, although the Marks of the Chosen weren't really hers either.

She could feel warmth, could feel it as a trace of magic, of enchantment. It had no sigil, no signature, no name—but it wasn't that kind of magic. She was surprised it had power at all, but it did. Power was apparently required to maintain the mark. She wondered if Nightshade was aware of it. Beneath the visible tattoo lay small roots that were almost skin-deep. They were warm to the touch; her cheek was warm.

If it grew heated, she bled. But the bleeding was a result of the power that seemed to pulse into those roots, those traces of magic.

She'd assumed, from Androsse's research, that the point of the Erenne mark was the connection itself. It was laid where it was both desired and accepted; it required that level of emotional communion.

Kaylin didn't *have* that level of connection. The reasons didn't matter. If Androsse was right about the origins of the spell, he was wrong about its nature; the mark existed. It didn't elevate her interaction with Nightshade. It didn't change it. It certainly had a negative effect on Annarion—but Annarion's understanding wasn't the historical, Ancestral understanding: it was modern, for want of a better word.

Still, this was the only hope they had. These tiny filaments. Her eyes were closed; the Marks of the Chosen were glowing, which made it hard to see any other light. But she breathed slowly, inhaling and exhaling, balancing breath as if she were about to enter the training ring against a Barrani opponent.

She could feel warmth spread across that patch of skin. It wasn't her own skin she needed to find. It was the source of the power that caused the bleeding. She'd used her natural ability to see magic—and the sigils left in the wake of powerful spells—to examine spells, but none of those spells had been cast on the living. Nightshade had never cast a magic powerful enough that she could see his signature and recognize it. Or at least not where Kaylin could examine it.

This wasn't a powerful magic. Had it been, she would have sensed it instantly. But it was a personal one.

This Erenne mark drew no power from Kaylin. All of the power that sustained it must come from Nightshade himself.

She could, with effort, follow the trace of magic that led from her mark to the man who had placed it there—but it was hard work, and it required intense focus. Noise broke that focus. Light broke it. Even the Marks of the Chosen were a disruption. Thinking that, she noted the golden glow of the Marks diminished as if responding to her irritable thought. It left the darkness behind closed lids.

It left a single, very dim light, so faint it might be an illusion brought about by her need to see it. The color was odd. The Marks of the Chosen were often gold—a warm gold—or blue; they were sometimes a haze of white light in which individual words blurred. This was a green-tinged ivory; it reminded Kaylin of the green.

Even thinking of it, she felt the movement of words, the impulse of story—something yet to be given voice but building as if it were a gathering storm.

Nightshade couldn't tell the story, but the story needed to be told. That was the power of, the demand of, the green—something that existed without the need for True Words, although True Words were spoken during the *regalia*. The words, Kaylin thought, were offered by the Teller and the harmoniste—the green had no easy way of communicating with anyone else.

She could see Yvonne, ghostly and pale, images of her face overlapping. She couldn't see anyone else because her eyes were closed. Even her Marks were visually silent.

But the green thread that led from the Erenne mark, so slender it evoked spiders and other things Kaylin often found pointlessly disturbing, continued past Yvonne. Through her. Had she moved? She'd been standing in the corner.

She hasn't moved, Severn said.

Kaylin felt her shoulders relax at the sound of that voice. *But the thread doesn't seem to be going to where Nightshade is.*

Follow it. Follow it for as long as you can.

Kaylin nodded. She expected to lose that thread as it passed through Yvonne; she hadn't expected that these blurred, overlapping images would suddenly separate as she approached. She moved toward them, wondering if her body was moving, too.

No.

Can you hear voices?

No.

They're not quite voices. I can't hear words. It's more like the murmurs of a crowd. As she moved, she added, *There's too much low-level noise to hear individual words.* She exhaled. *I can't tell the mood of the crowd.*

She'd seen mobs form, crowds transforming, through fear and anger, into something dangerous and unpredictable.

Severn wanted to join her. *Is the noise directional?*

She shook her head. Frowned. *It's louder in the distance—behind me.* She could hear, absurdly, the sound of a sword being drawn. It wasn't Severn's.

No. It's Teela. Helen was right: there are intruders. Fallessian has let Terrano go, if you hear a second sword. The third is Sedarias. He hesitated, which was unusual when things were starting to heat up. *The fourth is An'Tellarus.*

Kaylin didn't understand why swords had to be drawn. They were all standing within Helen's perimeter. Nothing should be able to make it into the manse itself. But Helen had mentioned a possible avenue of attack.

Kaylin was already in a state of heightened tension; she knew time was rapidly evaporating. And she knew that the slender thread she could barely see was the answer, if she could follow it through to its end. An end that should be Nightshade, except it was going in the wrong direction.

Or maybe the power of the Erenne mark wasn't derived entirely in the space in which people mostly lived. Maybe the thread that ran from Kaylin to Nightshade passed through something else. Given Yvonne's presence, and the Teller's Crown, and the dress—which she'd stupidly worn to impress An'Tellarus—Kaylin could guess what that something was.

She did what she always did when nothing made sense: she kept moving forward. Moving was better than fear. Anything was better than fear.

Even the ghostly Yvonnes in their multiple forms were better, although she sucked in air when they began to separate, each copy a perfect representation of the Yvonne that Kaylin had met in the real world. Their eyes were flat, though; they lacked pupils. Their color was a muted shade of green—like forest green, if forests were dark with lack of sunlight.

Those eyes were turned toward her, and they moved as she moved, although they reflected nothing. But the Yvonnes stood to either side of the slender thread, as if they were human walls meant to protect it and to emphasize its existence. Their mouths moved as if they were speaking, and sound emerged—but it was wordless, almost keening, although their expressions were placid, even neutral.

Severn said there had been multiple Yvonnes when he'd found her—Shadow Yvonnes. If these were somehow the Yvonnes he had destroyed to reach the real Barrani woman, Kaylin shouldn't trust them. But they had been in the green. They had been, according to Severn, the test of the weapon he now bore.

Had the green made guardians of them?

Had they somehow remained, nebulous and unseen by all save Mrs. Erickson, as guardians of Yvonne? Why were they here at all?

They didn't move as she approached them; they didn't move as she passed by, following the barely visible thread of power that flowed from the Erenne mark to an unseen destination. She could hear steel clash as it struck steel. Her arms began the slow burn that announced the unwanted presence of magic.

The magic of the green had never affected her that way. Nightshade's mark hadn't, either. She froze for one moment, and everything wavered: the many Yvonnes, the absence of light in the Marks of the Chosen, and the slender thread that was still, somehow, attached to her.

The power of this mark wasn't hers, but she needed that connection now, in a way she'd never needed it consciously before. She had to focus, had to ignore the sudden pain that flashed, like brief, intense fire, across her skin. If the cohort was fighting, this was their battlefield, and Helen was on their side.

Even Annarion had drawn his sword.

Silence, then. Even Annarion had drawn his sword. How did she know that? She hadn't asked Severn, and she was certain she hadn't reached for him, either. But she did know. She could feel the slow trickle of blood down her face. She could feel heat, and the light of the thread that had almost evaporated grew stronger, more certain.

But it wasn't certain enough. She understood, as she stood, ghostly Yvonnes to either side, that the connection wasn't strong enough. Androsse had said that she had to accept it. She'd spent too long worrying about love, about what love meant. Maybe there was a True Word called *love*, but Kaylin had never seen it. What she'd seen and heard were mortal variations, different languages, different attempts to approach love, own it, deny it.

Androsse's version of *love* was not Kaylin's. Kaylin's version of love would not, could not, be what an ancient, Immortal, unknowably powerful being felt. But clearly it wasn't necessary; Androsse was wrong. Except in one way.

These small filaments rooted in her skin had weak purchase there. They'd never grown stronger or deeper—whether by her will or Nightshade's. Why had he placed the mark on her cheek at all? She remembered, as she concentrated on moving forward, that she had met a young Nightshade, and he had seen the mark on her cheek; he had been surprised.

But that man, and the man who placed that mark on her skin, were not the same; they had not—yet—lived the same lives. Had he placed his mark on her cheek because he had seen it, in his distant youth? Did it matter?

She stopped walking. She didn't open her eyes—if she opened them, everything else would be overwhelming. Who stood still, unarmed, and silent when combat was unfolding all around them?

You, Severn said. *And Yvonne. Watch the path you take, now. Helen says it will be unstable.*

Yvonne's many ghosts had formed two walls; she passed between them. Stopped there. She understood some part of what had to be done. Inhaling slowly, she allowed the tiny filaments to extend, not outward, but in. To take root properly. To become part of more than just a flower, more than just layers of skin.

She felt Severn's drawn breath, his worry. She understood it. But they were standing on a cliff's edge, and all other options led to a fall. She could hear the crowd; she thought of it as Yvonne—as Yvonnes—because all of their mouths were moving, but none seemed to move in the exact same way.

It was much, much harder than she'd thought to let the small roots that emanated from the Erenne mark spread. She could feel them grow as if they were physical; she was certain her cheek was bleeding more heavily; it felt like pain. It felt like invasion. Her instinct was to pull it out—or push it out—and be done with it.

She let the Erenne mark sink in. She let its roots spread beneath the surface of the skin, into flesh, growing—almost burrowing—as they did. And then, with a healthy Leontine curse, she added power to it, almost as if it were a living thing, an injured creature. It was the power of the Marks of the Chosen.

As the tiny filaments spread, she felt them thrum; they were warm, not hot. They didn't add to the bleeding of her cheek; they didn't change the nature of her body. They wrapped themselves around Kaylin, but they never touched the Marks of the Chosen.

The thrum was almost rhythmic, a beat, too soft to be drumming.

Oh.

A heartbeat. She could hear her own heart beating a little bit too quickly; this one was different. It was foreign. It was familiar. The sound grew louder and more steady as she listened.

When she looked, once again, at the thread of light between the Yvonnes, she squinted—which was awkward, given her eyes were closed. It had grown so bright, she couldn't miss it. Bright, heart of white, edges of green—and that green was the color of the Yvonnes' eyes. She moved quickly, aware that she was no longer following something attenuated; she was bringing the source of that light with her as she moved.

Step by step, the light cast by this single, wordless connection grew brighter.

This time, when the Marks of the Chosen began to glow, she ignored them; she didn't attempt to squelch their radiance because they no longer overwhelmed the thread she followed. She could hear the distant sound of swords; she could feel the thrum of magic—other people's—across the Marks. Instinct screamed: *stop what you're doing and get ready to fight.*

But she *was* fighting, now. She had to hold on to that.

The cohort were here, just beyond her closed eyes. They could wield swords. She could wield daggers and long knives. Against good swordsmen, unless she could lead them down very tight alleys where their weapons were constrained, she was just another target.

None of the cohort could do what she was doing now. None of them bore Nightshade's Erenne mark. None of them wore the Marks of the Chosen. None of them were healers. None of them had any chance of doing what she *might* be able to do if she could follow the slender green thread to its end.

The clangor of swords was so very loud; she bent into her knees without thought, as if she would be forced to leap to survive. Her hands found knife hilt and clenched. The thread flickered; the Yvonnes became more ghostly.

No. No. She forced her hand to release her knife. Against any Barrani wielding a sword, she was a profound embarrassment, and that kind of embarrassment led to injury or death.

They do.

A familiar voice. A voice she felt like she hadn't heard in months. She couldn't see Nightshade—but she would recognize that interior voice anywhere.

29

Kaylin.

She exhaled. *Nightshade.* Then: *Calarnenne.*

What are you doing? The question was asked in a tone of almost idle curiosity. At another time, she would have found it enraging; now, she was just annoyed.

The annoyance amused him.

I'm trying to reach you.

Ah. Perhaps I was not clear. What you see, I now see, and you appear to be surrounded by the ghosts of a young Barrani woman.

Yes, but it'll take time to explain, and given the sounds I'm hearing, we're really short on time. She exhaled. *Teela is here, and she's drawn* Kariannos*; we apparently have invaders.*

Are you not within Helen's perimeter? The question was much sharper.

We are. She followed the thread, leaving the last of the Yvonnes in her wake. But when she turned to look back, she saw that the formation that had protected the trace Kaylin had tried to follow to its source had closed; they stood behind her, their eyes the one feature that didn't look Barrani. *You've been unconscious since you were attacked by Barrani assassins. We reached you in time, but you were injured. I think by a magical poison—but that's not my specialty, so that's just a guess.*

Are you saying I am also within Helen's perimeter?

Andellen didn't think we could get you back to Castle Nightshade safely. You were unconscious. Apparently, your sword was protecting you. I know Barrani hate to be healed—but you were in really bad shape. I tried to heal you.

Again, she felt a flicker of amusement. *I understand the reluctance on the part of my people, but you already know my name. There is nothing in the healing that could be a greater weakness than that. But I see you've been busy.*

Very. She found his amusement annoying. She was almost certain there would be no attack mounted against Helen if Nightshade weren't in residence.

Very well, Chosen. If you can reach me, if you can heal me, I will not fight you.

Did I mention you've practically been in a coma?

Ah. Yes. You believe that means I could not defend myself should your healing be unwanted?

If Annarion could hear his brother now, he'd be less frantic with worry.

Kaylin opened her eyes.

To her surprise, the room was empty of everyone except the convalescent, Yvonne, and Kaylin herself. Severn was no longer in the room; neither was Mandoran. She knew they'd shifted to meet the enemy; she'd heard—could still hear—the distant echo of swords. An'Tellarus had, according to Severn, joined the fight, and An'Tellarus didn't have the ability to shift across planes the way the rest of the cohort did. Neither did Severn.

Her hand still rested on her cheek; she lowered it. Blood had dried, darkening the lines of her palm. Yvonne met Kaylin's gaze as Kaylin glanced toward her; the young Barrani woman's eyes were normal, given the circumstances; they were blue. Flecks of green appeared as Kaylin moved toward the Teller's crown.

"I don't think you can touch that," Yvonne said, voice soft. "I think he has to wear it."

Yvonne hesitated.

"What do you know?"

"Not yet," Yvonne whispered. Kaylin couldn't tell if she meant that the *regalia* wasn't ready, or if Yvonne wasn't willing to talk about what she knew. But Kaylin thought she could lift the crown, could place it across Nightshade's brow. He'd worn the crown on the way to the West March. Even as outcaste, he'd been spared the contempt and murderous intent of the Barrani who traveled with the Consort to the green itself.

Kaylin didn't understand the purpose of the *regalia*. She didn't understand how a ritual that occurred in the distant West March could hold so much meaning for the Lords of the High Court. She knew that children weren't meant to witness the *regalia*. The cohort had arisen from the breaking of that ancient law. She wondered if Yvonne would be considered a child.

But Yvonne had spent time in the green, according to Severn. How much, she didn't know. Enough to understand the will of the green?

Kaylin sat on the chair beside Nightshade; she lifted a hand to his brow but hesitated. If she still couldn't reach him with the power of the Chosen . . .

You can, Nightshade said. *You already are.*

She nodded. The crown, she left where it had appeared. Yvonne might be right, and if she could heal Nightshade fully, he could put the damn thing on his own head.

Once again, she felt a familiar amusement.

Grinding her teeth, she placed her left palm across Nightshade's brow. She realized she was holding her breath only when she released it. "Helen—can you tell Annarion that I can finally reach his brother?"

Helen didn't reply.

Where is my brother? Amusement left the fieflord instantly.

He's fighting intruders. Barrani intruders who managed to find a back door in.

Do what you must do. Do it quickly. There was no force behind the command.

Kaylin, far more aware of Nightshade than she would have been otherwise, let the power of the Marks go, pushing it out to meet the fieflord, and to examine the injuries he'd taken. She couldn't heal blood loss, and he had lost blood, but he'd been unconscious and recovering as much as he could; it wasn't the major problem.

She'd assumed poison, or magical poison—if that even existed. The Barrani were endlessly inventive when it came to causing death and destruction, as if the tools they created could be contained and aimed only at their chosen enemies. Kaylin had worked in the Halls of Law for long enough that she would never believe that.

Poison was present, eating away at organs; the damage done was not enough to kill the fieflord—but it was very close. She could sense traces of it, carried in Nightshade's blood, but she could also touch the traces of a strong, protective magic, fighting the damaging invader. *Meliannos.*

She heard the sharp reverberation of thunder even as she thought the sword's name. She knew better than to touch it. In some indefinable way, it was part of Nightshade.

For now, the fieflord said. *Hurry. I* must *wake.*

She heard Annarion's name beneath the syllables he shared with her; felt the force of intent and—rare for Nightshade—fear. This wasn't caution, which was fear's smarter, wiser, older sibling. This was just fear.

As if Annarion were the key to Nightshade's injury, Nightshade's intent, images of Annarion flooded in through the healing connection: Annarion as a baby. Calarnenne had been calm upon waking; Annarion's furious, infant cries showed outrage at the very idea. He had been fast to walk, fast to grow;

he had been better with a sword than Nightshade, but had taken poorly to magic, to start.

He could speak almost before he could walk.

He could bespeak the animals kept for use by the Solanace clan. He couldn't sing, although he loved singing, and often joined in with a voice far stronger—if off-key—than the other infants. But to Nightshade, Annarion was gentle—far too gentle for the Solanace fray. It was not a trait that was prized by their kin.

It was a trait that had always seemed precious to Nightshade, perhaps because it was so rare. He had become protective of his brother and had learned to do so with subtlety. His father—and mother—believed that a child who could not survive their youthful naivete was pointless; it would not strengthen the family. It would not add to their prestige.

Being the parents of a weakling was, in fact, an embarrassment. Annarion was the perfect test subject in the eyes of his relatives: he was weak, he was naive, and he did not grow out of it. He was good with a sword. He could wield basic magic. He had the *potential* to become a good son, a worthy child.

Calarnenne attempted to train his brother. To teach him the rules of power. He made clear what the cost of his brother's warped sense of right and wrong would be—to both of them—if Annarion could not hide his views and beliefs. But he could not do as his parents had done: he could not break the child, could not disparage him, could not humiliate him. Nightshade himself had undergone similar things in his distant, dim past.

He had proven the right of his parents' approach. He had grown strong—much stronger than the cousins who nipped at his heels in an attempt to remove the most promising candidate for heir of the line. He had learned magic, and found it fascinating, but even that fascination, he hid; it was not seemly to be too interested in anything.

But he could not surrender his brother.

To Calarnenne, that child was a spark of hope, of a kindness, a joyful loyalty, that was absent in his life. His parents could not see it, or did not desire it. Perhaps Calarnenne himself was broken in dangerous ways. He attempted to feign disinterest in his brother, but that was all he could manage—and his family's many servants were the eyes and ears for his parents, his uncles, his cousins.

The first person he had killed, when he stood on the edge of childhood, was a cousin. The second, a cousin as well. He'd been injured in the second death, and that had taught him to focus, to practice, to become strong enough that he wouldn't face injury again. He accepted that death was the natural outcome of laziness or weakness.

He accepted, as well, that Annarion, if weak, would face that death. His attempts to deny affection for his younger brother had ended with an ultimatum: kill Annarion or be killed. A test. Life was full of bitter tests.

Kaylin almost pulled back at the searing rage, the pain, the fury, that blossomed in the wake of that memory, understanding again why healing was so inimical to the Barrani. Their lives depended on their ability to keep secrets, and the older the Barrani, the more secrets they had.

She didn't pull back; it took effort. For just a moment, she was swamped with a murderous rage and an endless hollow of despair.

What stilled them, what interrupted them, was a young woman. Kaylin recognized her because the color of her hair was so different from the Barrani norm: the woman who would become the Lady. The current Consort of the High Lord. He had been drawn to her because, in her, he found some of the warmth and affection he found in Annarion. But she was drawn to him for the same reason.

If you attempt to unseat your parents now, you will die. If you die, your brother will die. There is no one within Solanace who will protect him. Her tone was bitter, which was unusual—maybe because she was young. *There's no one in my family that would, either. Not yet.*

That will change. It will *change. My brothers remind me of you and your brother. But they have the same power we have.*

Almost none.

Almost none, in the time when Nightshade wasn't outcaste, his brother wasn't a member of the cohort, and the Consort wasn't the Consort.

Kaylin tried to focus on the healing. Most of the thoughts that flowed into her as she healed were almost incidental; they came through the channel of her power. These weren't that; they were far too strong, far too immediate. She felt as if she could join the two who spoke, huddled in the garden, their voices low, their gazes watchful.

She felt that even in this private moment, worry and fear and anger causing a collapse of shoulders, she could have touched them. She could have reached out with both arms, drawn them in toward each other and toward her, and neither would have pushed her away.

You still have us, the young woman said. *You still have me.*

No. Your parents are the High Lord and his Lady.

But I'm not them. We're not them. I'm Ellorinel. You're Calarnenne. You don't have to change. You don't have to be a different person. I won't, either.

Kaylin had a terrible feeling, a premonition of doom.

When healing, she accepted the blending of memories as part of the process. She had never consciously attempted to separate or distance herself from the person she was healing. She touched their memories; she was certain they touched hers. This was not a memory she wanted to touch, to know.

Calarnenne, look at me. Look. I trust you. I trust you as much as I trust my brothers.

You shouldn't. But even as he spoke the words, she felt an odd glow, a terrible relief; it wasn't without fear, without dread—but it was almost as strong.

She forgot the damage done to him by the poison—the organs that were near to failure, the odd way blood flowed throughout his body. She'd been correcting them, rebuilding damaged connections. Had he been human, had he been mortal, she'd have been examining him in the morgue.

You should not do this, he said.

Kaylin screamed the same phrase silently, trying to separate herself from his memory. Trying to preserve her ignorance—to leave it in the realm of suspicion. This younger Nightshade wasn't a person she knew. He had a home, a family he disliked, and at least one friend.

One friend, eyes green; Kaylin could see her pale hair, could see the strength of determination in her expression. It contained eternity. And she saw the woman's eyes shift from green to the lambent gold that was Barrani surprise. The surprise faded as green overcame it. The woman laughed, delight in the sound.

He had offered her the truth of his name—a truth it was never safe to offer, as if to forestall her, as if to make his escape before she could offer him the same truth, the same vulnerability.

Annarion would have made this choice.

I would not take this risk, the young Barrani woman said, *if you were not who you are. Time changes all things. I know it does. I cannot see the future. I cannot see where our lives will diverge. But the person you are now is worth preserving. Do not become what your parents tell you you must become. Do not surrender your kin without a fight.*

By kin, she meant Annarion.

By risk, she meant her name. Her True Name.

Ynpharion would kill Kaylin if he knew that she knew it;

the Lady had never taken that risk with Kaylin and never would. But absent choice, the consequences were profound. Kaylin didn't want to know.

She healed by instinct; she'd never had to work at healing the way she'd had to work at lighting a candle. She just did what she did; it came naturally. When she reached out to heal, she held the whole person in her hands. The barriers that separated two individuals vanished.

She'd healed Bellusdeo before; had seen parts of Bellusdeo's history. She hadn't chosen which parts. She hadn't searched for memories. Some came to her, as if life was a stream; as a healer, she had to stand in that stream. She couldn't avoid seeing something, but there was no reason, no choice, in what she saw.

That had to change.

That had to change now, because her entire body reverberated not with Nightshade's True Name—which she already knew—but the Consort's. She heard the Consort's True Name. She felt it as a blow, as a warmth, as a sudden door that opened into endless possibility, endless *trust.*

She knew the names of other Barrani. She knew Nightshade's name. But she had never felt, in the gaining of that knowledge, what Nightshade felt in that long-ago past.

She wondered if this was what the cohort had felt when they, as a group, had chosen to take the same risk. As if the world had, for a moment, opened up into endless warmth, endless trust. She had never felt that way about the names she'd been given—maybe because those who'd allowed her that glimpse were so certain of their own power, they did so without fear, without a true sense of risk.

Ynpharion was the lone exception; he hadn't offered. He'd hated her with an intensity she hadn't experienced before, even in occasionally heated office politics. That hatred had been whittled down to grudging resentment, until the moment he had offered the Consort his name. He understood that he was the link between Kaylin and the Lady he would have died in a heartbeat to save.

She wondered if Severn had felt the way Nightshade did when she had casually offered him the name she had taken from the Lake for herself.

And she wondered all of this while she worked to fix the things that were broken in Nightshade. The invasive, inimical magic was so faint that, were it not for the damage it had caused, she wouldn't have noticed it as foreign. She removed it, eradicating it as she repaired the injuries it had caused.

Wondering, as she did, what it might have been like to be the Consort, to be the source of so much joy, however brief the moment in their lives.

The Consort had never stopped trusting Nightshade. She had never stopped believing in what she had seen, what she had known, that day. He hadn't seen her since the moment he was ejected from the High Court—not until the *regalia*. And she had been the same woman, when they had at last crossed paths, that she had been on the day she had offered him the knowledge of her name.

Nightshade could hide his own thoughts. There was almost nothing she could read that he would not allow. But this knowledge was poison to the Lady. If it were known, it would damage her in far too many ways. He did not speak to her through the namebond. He isolated the bond, and the truth of the bond, moving further away from the naivete and idealism of distant youth.

What she had given him he could not keep. But he could never keep it, in the end: she was the heir to the Lake. If not Consort, she was the Lady, as her mother had been. Her mother, who had not prevented the children from being sacrificed to the green.

His naivete, his idealism, had been all but destroyed when Annarion had been sent to the green—and he had been sent while Nightshade was on the frontlines of the war. Everything he had done in the long years between that loss and the *regalia* that had finally brought his brother's freedom, he had done for the sake of the only family he graced by that word: Annarion.

Annarion, whose sense of rage and pain and betrayal reminded him of the man he had once been. Nightshade had destroyed the home of his childhood without care; home was, and had been, Annarion.

Kaylin, stop. It wasn't a command; it was a request.

She wanted to stop. She wanted to withdraw, to give him privacy, to forget everything she'd seen and heard. *I'm not done yet. If the source of this affliction was magical in nature, the magic's still there.*

I am capable of diffusing it on my own now.

I'll be the judge of that.

Then judge, but judge quickly.

When this is over, I'm going to suggest a new course be taught in the Halls of Law. She focused on that. On the existence of magical poison. On its possible use. Something had penetrated skin, which was how poison generally worked if it wasn't offered in food. This hadn't been. Maybe Nightshade was immune to regular poison.

Maybe the poison was a backup in case the war bands failed. And they had.

She understood assassination; she usually understood its motivation. She didn't understand why an outcaste fieflord was so important. This was almost foreign.

But the magic that was also foreign lessened as she uprooted it, gathering it around her hand as if it were thread. No healing had ever been like this. The damage to the organs, she repaired; it was the magic itself that was much, much harder to remove. But she felt, as she worked, that it was the most important task. She could not leave it spread inside Nightshade's body, a fine web waiting for its hungry spider.

Kaylin. Severn's voice. He added no words, but they weren't necessary.

She found the last thread—what she assumed was the last thread. *If I don't finish this, they'll just grow again*, she told Nightshade. *They'll spread again. They'll wrap themselves around your heart, your lungs, your kidneys—and they'll squeeze.*

He should already be dead.

If you're actually awake, and you believe the magic that almost killed you *is so trivial, you can help me eradicate it.*

He couldn't. She knew he couldn't. But he fell silent, examining her thoughts, her focus, her certainty. She felt a wild impatience, and it came from two places: Severn and Nightshade. But all their efforts would be wasted if she couldn't finish this one thing. It wasn't the damage that had been done that would kill him; it was the future damage.

I do not sense what you sense, he finally said. *You are healing the damage; that much is clear. But the source of the damage remains opaque to me. We do not have time. If you must, finish this after we are certain to survive this moment.*

There was urgency to the words. There was no command.

Kaylin had healed Terrano when he'd been standing on a different, constructed plane. What she had seen there was not what she could feel here: Shadow had bled out of the wound Terrano had taken. That Shadow had coalesced because Hope had chosen to breathe on it; it had become a darkly glowing orb, a ball of not-quite light.

She could now feel its contours in her palm. She hadn't seen it since Mandoran had retrieved her from the place in which Terrano had waited, injured, for healing.

This magic was like the dark wisps of smoke that rose from Terrano. She really, really wanted Terrano's name; if she had it, she could ask. Severn could hear her. Nightshade could hear her. But given the distant sounds of battle, neither would shout the question so Terrano could hear it.

He'd been aware of the Shadow that poured out of his open wound. Had he somehow, changed physically by exposure to the green, been able to do what Nightshade couldn't? Had he sensed the Shadow and remained trapped where he was so that he didn't bring it back to the cohort—or Helen, or Kaylin?

She hadn't drawn that smoky Shadow from his body; hadn't had to struggle to remove its tendrils. It had emerged on its own. Hope's breath had changed it, solidifying it, maybe rendering it inert. But she couldn't ask Hope to breathe on Nightshade. She knew he wouldn't do it unless she was willing to sacrifice something important to her.

She wasn't. What she would be willing to offer wasn't of interest because it wasn't fundamentally valuable to Kaylin.

But here, as she drew out the burrowed threads, she realized that it wasn't her palm she was wrapping them around; it was the orb itself. Somehow, to heal Nightshade at all, she'd approached not Nightshade himself, but the source of his injury. They weren't on the same plane. The one reached out to the other, anchored by the physical body—but it didn't belong where it had taken root.

She continued to wind the thread of that magic around her hand—or the orb that rested in it. It resisted, as stubborn roots will. If she'd had the ability to just destroy the roots without destroying their host, she might have tried that, instead—but it was hard to use healing power to destroy.

Oh.

That was what was wrong. She'd used the word *thread*, the word *roots*, to describe this magic, but it was the latter that was the most accurate. The magic itself felt *alive*. Alive, and part of Nightshade. She'd seen the damage Shadow could do to the living: it transformed them, sometimes almost instantly. Mortals could be overtaken and transformed with ease; Immortals, less easily. Was it the True Names? Was that why Immortals were more protected?

But they could be transformed as well—it just took longer. It gave Kaylin time to heal their damaged body, to force it back into its natural shape. Nightshade's body didn't have that kind of injury. This Shadow was meant to kill. It hadn't changed anything that she could see.

I'm almost done. She spoke to Severn. She spoke to Nightshade. She felt the last of the tendrils finally let go, as if she had spoken to them as well. She wound it around the orb she could feel but couldn't see.

Yes. Nightshade was the only person to answer. *You are finished. I, on the other hand, am just beginning.*

His voice was the endless depth of a winter that could kill children like Kaylin in the streets of the fief just by existing. She felt it in her bones as her hand fell away from Nightshade. She opened her eyes.

Yvonne was leaning against the wall, her chin tucked toward her chest. Nightshade was standing, his greatsword in hand. Severn was gone; Annarion, Mandoran, and Terrano were elsewhere. She could hear the clash of swords and feel—much more strongly—the evidence of magic and spell; her arms ached, and the back of her neck felt as if it had been rubbed raw.

There was only one Yvonne in the room. This was Helen's space.

"Did they tell you where they were going?" Kaylin asked, squinting at the ambient light as her eyes adjusted.

Yvonne shook her head. "I would have gone to check, but An'Tellarus made *very* clear that if I were that stupid, she'd just remove my head from my neck to spare me future pain."

"You saw her?"

"I heard her. I'm surprised everyone didn't."

Everyone else heard her, Severn said, his internal voice almost as grim as Nightshade's.

Well, she's not going to cut my head off.

"No," Nightshade said, glancing around the room as if he

expected invisible assassins to materialize from its walls. "She believes Yvonne is her responsibility. But Kaylin, you are not. You are mine."

"It's my house—"

"Yes. And it would not be under attack if you had managed to remove me to Castle Nightshade. You will remain here with Yvonne."

Severn wasn't as certain. *We may need you*, he said. She trusted his take on things but waited until Nightshade sprinted to—and through—the door. She approached the door once Nightshade left but felt Yvonne's hand on her shoulder. She turned back.

"It isn't safe," Yvonne said, her voice soft and tremulous.

"I know—and I'm sorry for that. It makes me a terrible host."

"You should remain here. Mrs. Erickson is in her room, as well. Helen told me."

"What did Helen tell you?"

"There's no shame in not being able to fight or to kill. Mrs. Erickson can't, either. Helen said her first tenant could cook and clean and tidy. And grow flowers in the garden. But she couldn't use magic. She couldn't lift a weapon—not to use *as* a weapon. Helen loved her. The fact that she couldn't fight and kill like most of the Barrani didn't make her useless or worthless."

"I can't cook, I can barely clean, and my room is a mess," Kaylin said, gently removing Yvonne's hand from her shoulder. "But I can fight, and I can kill if it's necessary. An'Tellarus and Helen are right—you should stay here. If the green has roots in Helen right now, it's because of you."

But Yvonne shook her head. "It's because of Mrs. Erickson. I'm sensitive to the green; I feel its reach when I'm close. It's strongest in her—and *she's* in her room." Some hint of the girl Yvonne had once been showed in her eyes and her expression.

Kaylin wanted to ask questions, but that would have to wait. The hem of her dress was moving around her legs as if caught in a strong gale.

"Helen," Kaylin said, raising and strengthening her voice. "Have the attackers actually entered the house?"

"Yes—but not all of them; the cohort is fighting on the path they created to enter."

"How many of them are there?"

"In Teela's opinion, there are at least two war bands."

"Is Teela fighting on that path?"

"Yes—but An'Tellarus is fighting within my walls."

Helen should have been able to crush those intruders. That she couldn't or hadn't was not a good sign.

"Lord Nightshade has joined that fight. He is here, as An'Tellarus is here. Fallessian has remained here as well." Helen's voice stopped.

"They're not—" Kaylin stopped too. "Helen, have they approached your core?"

"Not yet."

"Are they trying?"

Yes, Severn said, answering Kaylin's question. *That's Teela's guess.*

Why can't Helen just kill them or send them to prison? That's what she usually does with intruders.

I believe she tried. If they've left the path they created to get here, they're still attached to it—and Helen is having difficulty because of that. The cohort aren't.

Are you fighting beside the cohort?

Yes. Mandoran decided I would be helpful there.

Come back—it's not safe for you to be there. You don't have the Marks, and Mandoran usually keeps people like us anchored by being in physical contact with them.

Severn didn't reply immediately; it was the hesitance of thought. *I believe the edges of their portal or their path anchor them in a way Helen finds it difficult to break—she says it's not what the cohort does. Invaders who walk existing planes are easily seen and accommodated.*

"Helen—I'm sorry, I know you're busy. I just need you to ask Terrano or Mandoran if we can cause that path to collapse." She opened the door and headed into the hall.

30

There were intruders in the foyer; they were armed and armored, and Barrani to a man. Or woman. Nightshade was in the foyer; An'Tellarus was beside him. She wielded a sword that seemed more slender than the usual Barrani long sword, and she moved like a localized storm. There was blood on her dress. Kaylin guessed it wasn't hers.

What she couldn't see was Helen's Avatar. Helen had surrendered the fray to the two who fought it here. To Nightshade, armed with one of The Three, and An'Tellarus. Kaylin knew nothing about An'Tellarus, but the way she carried herself implied a history of violence and war.

Hope lifted a wing and smacked it across her face. *Squawk.*

He was right. Now was not the time. But she wasn't armed with anything but daggers, and she knew she couldn't stand for long against this many Barrani assailants. Nightshade was attacking so quickly she could barely track his movements; the reach of his sword was greater than An'Tellarus's. She wasn't letting that slow her down.

They fought at the foot of the foyer stairs; the chandelier above them created diamonds and sharp flashes of light as it bounced off armor and blade flat.

This wasn't where she needed to be. She moved down the

stairs, taking them two at a time; she used the banister and momentum to leap in a circle that sent her down the hall leading to the kitchen. She felt Severn's worry, but ignored it as she sprinted, skirts flying, toward the door that led into the basement, for want of a better word.

Hurry, Nightshade said, in contrast.

The rooms Helen brought into being beyond this door were rooms meant to contain the cohort when they practiced. What they practiced looked, to someone who didn't understand what they had become, a lot like disintegration. Kaylin had once walked into a room in which it looked like an insane interior decorator had thrown different colors of paint against the walls in a rage. That paint was the cohort in conflict.

She didn't expect that now. Helen's training room was her most secure room—it had to be. Not because she needed to protect the occupants from intruders, but because she needed to protect them from themselves. She was aware of them, no matter where or how they moved through the house, and she was fond of them.

Even the prickly Sedarias. Sedarias wasn't in the foyer; she wasn't immediately visible. But Kaylin could hear swords and shouts. Those shouts were likely meant for Severn, the only person fighting alongside who wasn't part of the cohort; he wouldn't hear what they said to each other.

What she didn't understand immediately was *why* she could hear them.

"They are attempting to stand to one side of the path that's been constructed. It is dangerous, for the cohort, to stand and fight on it."

"Because Terrano was injured there?"

"No. He could have been injured on *this* plane in a similar fashion to Nightshade. But he was anchored by the injury—he didn't choose to return. He knew that something was wrong—beyond the bleeding."

Kaylin looked at her hand. To her surprise, she could see the orb that had vanished when Mandoran had taken her to where Terrano stood, bleeding, and then brought her back. "Helen—can you still hear me?"

"Yes."

"Can you see me?"

"Yes."

"Have I wandered into another encroachment?"

This time, Helen didn't respond immediately. Kaylin didn't press for an answer, because she could see the Yvonnes. Kaylin's eyes were open; she stood on the winding stairs that descended into a darkness unlit by torch or vision. The eyes of the Yvonnes were once again that odd shade of green, and they were focused on her as she made her way down the stairs, one hand on the wall. They formed a human railing, because these stairs had no rails or guideposts.

If they'd spoken at all, they'd be far less disturbing. They simply watched, their expressions neutral.

"Yes," Helen said. Kaylin had to work to remember what her question was; the presence of the Yvonnes had driven it out of her mind. "Yes, you stand at the edge of an encroachment—but it's not one our attackers are using. It is far more like the planes Terrano wanders; it feels natural, not constructed."

"It's the green," Kaylin said, her voice a whisper. "The green is encroaching." Maybe she shouldn't have invited Yvonne to visit. But there was no doubt that An'Tellarus was helping the cohort. And Helen.

"Cediela is, and has always been, powerful in her own right. She is often bitter, and her resentment is undeniable. But she has, as she said, been forced to stand on her own feet and make her own way. In other circumstances, she would resent you—you are Chosen, after all. But I believe she has chosen to pity you instead."

Kaylin would have found that infuriating in different circumstances.

"She has come to understand that being chosen is not the same as choosing, even if it has taken her centuries to fully accept that truth. She will not harm you here."

Kaylin had taken that for granted until this moment. Nothing could harm her when she stood within the safety of her own home. But this wasn't the first time Helen had been attacked. It wasn't the first time the visiting cohort had had to defend themselves—and Helen—from forces that were ancient before Kaylin had ever been born.

This time, it was Barrani. That should have made things easier, in theory. Theory was often garbage. She continued down the stairs. She knew where she needed to be—but she wasn't certain she could find it without Helen's intervention. Helen didn't have a room in the hall where tenants lived. She had a table beneath an evening sky where she might meet and interview possible tenants, but as she was meeting relative strangers, it wasn't where she *lived*, if she could be said to truly live at all.

The heart of Helen was the words at her core, True Words, all.

What would happen to a sentient building if they couldn't reach their own words? Would they die? Would the words sustain them? Would they be like the Consort, whose True Name sustained her life, but in isolation?

"No, as you suspect." Helen's voice was soft. "It has not happened to my knowledge—but all living things can die; it is the ability to die that defines life."

"That's pretty grim."

"Is it? My tenants, as they aged, feared death less and less. Perhaps when it arrived, they greeted death with resignation, grace, and peace. Their only worry was that they would leave me behind—because to them, I was always the one being abandoned."

Kaylin could follow the sound of the voice. It brought her, finally, to the end of the stairs, rather than a door that opened up in the wall. The Yvonnes came with her, abandoning their positions as guideposts and railings.

Kaylin stopped. She realized that the Yvonnes intended to follow her, and she wasn't certain this would be a good thing for Helen. "Can you guys stay and wait for me here?" she asked without much hope. She wasn't surprised when they failed to acknowledge her words at all.

Would the real Yvonne have been able to reach them? Or would they have looked past her, the way they sometimes looked past Kaylin? She didn't know what they were looking at. But she felt a very real fear because she suspected they were seeing Helen. Helen's core.

The Barrani understood that this was the way to attack a sentient building. But reaching the words at the heart of that building was almost impossible. Had she led the Yvonnes here?

"Yes," Helen said. "But it is not the ghosts that I fear. Come, Kaylin. Quickly. Whether they follow or not, they are not the gravest threat."

Kaylin could see stone walls, stone floor; she could see the golden glow of her exposed Marks. She couldn't see the connection that bound her to Nightshade but suspected it was no longer necessary. Her eyes were open. She wondered if she would see the Yvonnes at all if it weren't for Hope's wing; he'd spread it across both eyes as if he knew it would be necessary.

Kaylin Neya was the tenant Helen had chosen; in the parlance of sentient buildings, it meant Kaylin was master here, Helen servant. But that wasn't what Helen wanted from a tenant, and it wasn't what Kaylin wanted from a home. She wanted Helen to be Helen, to be as much of herself as possible, even if Kaylin didn't understand all of it. Or even most of it.

But she was certain that the goal wasn't to kill Helen; it was just a means to an end. Killing or injuring Helen would allow the Barrani to kill Nightshade. She shouldn't have brought him here. If Nightshade could be mortally injured by Barrani, there was an unknown power in play, and it was a power that even Nightshade didn't understand. She shouldn't have assumed Helen would be safe, that Helen wouldn't suffer consequences.

Her choices exposed Helen to mortal danger.

"You did not command me," Helen said, her voice much softer. "Had I refused, you would have found someplace to take him. Perhaps you would have risked the Barrani in the fiefs. If your decision led to this, it was my decision as well. I was, perhaps, arrogant; I assumed what you assumed. Come in.

"Come, Chosen."

The Marks on her arms were glowing brightly; as Kaylin watched, they pulled themselves up, off her skin. This wasn't the first time it had happened, and it wouldn't be the last—if she survived. If she didn't, the Marks of the Chosen would depart; they would, in time, be offered to some other person. Maybe someone who would understand what they meant. Maybe someone who could *use them properly.*

Kaylin took one step forward and found herself in the heart of Helen's power, the words now risen from stone as if they were like the Marks of the Chosen. She saw no one here, no Avatar of Helen, no invaders. None of the cohort were here, either.

But Severn's voice reached her; Helen hadn't done anything to prevent it. *We're closer than you think*, he said, the tone one that reminded her of speech that came from clenched jaws.

"Helen, I need you to ask Terrano—privately—if the created space our enemies are using can be safely collapsed. Is he standing in it, now? Are any of the cohort?"

"Only Fallessian, Teela, and Severn," Helen replied. "Everyone else is outside its perimeter. There is a danger to standing in that space for any length of time; we've tried to get Fallessian to withdraw."

Tried implied both attempt and failure.

"Why is it safer for Teela and Severn?"

"They're older."

Severn was certainly not older than Fallessian.

"They are more fixed in themselves. They have made choices, and those choices have helped them define who they are and who they must be. They are not immune to change—but they are less easily altered."

The same could be said of Nightshade, and that hadn't saved him.

"He was not fighting on that path."

"If Severn can get Teela and Fallessian to leave, can we collapse the space?"

"Terrano believes it can be done."

"But he thinks it's a bad idea."

"None of us understand how that space came into being," Helen replied. "We exist as one plane, one facet, of the creations of the Ancients when they walked both this plane and all the others. Those planes overlapped, and some of their creations lived in a way that bridged them. In the deep planes of the world, sentiences that you will never encounter made their homes and built their civilizations. Terrano is, of the cohort, the most unanchored. He knows what he can navigate and what he can't; he can alter his physical form to obey the laws of the planes into which he steps.

"This, he says, is entirely unlike that. It's like an artificial tree, not a natural one. Those unfamiliar with trees might consider them identical. The path can accommodate Barrani who can't do what Terrano or the cohort can do. They haven't shifted in place at all; they are physically as present as Nightshade or An'Tellarus. He believes they will perish; he is, he says, fine with that.

"But he feels there's a danger. It's the danger that flows in the wake of destroying a very large glass window. It's very difficult to crack a window and remove pieces of that glass safely. He can't think of a way to subtly collapse the space, and that means detritus. He can't say for certain that detritus won't be harmful."

"If we can collapse the space and kill them all," Kaylin said, "they'll think twice about ever trying this particular method of invasion again."

"They are likely to be dead."

"The people in charge almost never risk their own lives." She thought of the attack on the Academia. "Can Terrano collapse it, though?"

"He says no."

Meaning he'd tried. She doubted he was fighting alongside the cohort members who could really handle a weapon.

"He thinks you might be able to do it."

"Did he happen to give you any clues as to how?" Kaylin didn't try to keep irritation out of her voice; it was better than panic.

"No, dear. He said *you figure it out*." That sounded more like Terrano.

But she had managed to reach Nightshade. The magic in his body, the magic that had attempted to destroy his insides, was part of this other space, this other plane. It was part of the Shadow that had attempted to do the same thing—she was certain of that now—to Terrano.

But Terrano hadn't been where Nightshade was; he'd been on that narrow constructed path—and he hadn't moved off it until Kaylin had reached him. That meant *within* the path, the Shadow that divided Nightshade and Kaylin—or the Consort and the Lake—didn't have that effect. No, she was sure it was more complicated. Terrano could talk to the cohort on that path; he could talk to Serralyn from it.

She stopped. That wasn't important right now.

Something she had done had allowed Nightshade to return to what passed for normal for a centuries-old fieflord who also wielded one of The Three. Something.

The Yvonnes had followed Kaylin into the very large, cavernous room, with its rough stone walls and its uneven floor. She couldn't see their feet at all—if ghosts of this nature even *had* feet. But she was afraid that they did; she could see ankles. The feet rested below the surface of the stone. This was where Helen was both her strongest and her most vulnerable. This was the seat of her power.

If the Yvonnes noticed, it didn't show. But they stopped at the edge of the circular formation that contained True Words, and as Kaylin watched, they spread out around that circle and then lifted their arms. They locked hands.

Kaylin was on the inside. The Yvonnes were positioned to look inward, not out.

"I don't think I can do this from here," Kaylin said. "I'm not in contact with anything."

"You are carrying something in your hand. Hope can sense it; I cannot. But I am aware of what you can see. What do you carry, Kaylin?" Helen's question was gentle and measured, as if it had been asked in a classroom and not an emergency.

"I don't know." But she held the orb up. The threads that had been pulled from Nightshade—the threads that had spread throughout his comatose body—had been absorbed by the orb; it looked the same as it had looked when she had first taken it from wherever it was Terrano had been.

But she'd never seen it in this house. She'd never seen it, as she did her Marks, with her eyes closed. She hadn't seen it—before—through Hope's wing. Something had changed, or was changing, and it was happening here, where Helen was the most vulnerable.

She held the orb up, and saw, as she did, that the eyes of

the Yvonnes followed it. They could see what she held. But in their eyes, the reflection of that orb was much, much brighter; it changed the color of their eyes. It changed the pallor of their skin. Ghostly skin seemed to gain the warmth of flesh tones that had been absent, as if their Barrani roots were reasserting themselves.

Mrs. Erickson had seen them as ghosts—as ghostly ghosts, which the dead didn't look like most of the time. Maybe that was because they weren't actually dead. Maybe it was because they'd never been alive. Yvonne herself was alive. The many Yvonnes had, according to Severn, been surrounding the real Yvonne without harming her.

They would have hurt Severn if he'd allowed it. If they had appeared to be Yvonne, they weren't. They'd taken her form, her shape, for reasons that weren't clear to Severn. If he didn't understand it, Kaylin wasn't going to—not right now. But he had found Yvonne, found the many Yvonnes, in the heart of the green, in a place even the most respected of the Wardens had never seen. They were Shadows to Severn. No one who grew up in the fiefs thought of Shadow as anything but death.

Not all Shadows were death. Kaylin knew that. If these Shadows, these ghosts, these Yvonnes had existed to guard and protect the Yvonne who was in Nightshade's guest room, they couldn't be enemies.

She felt Nightshade's brief flash of anger. She hadn't really missed that. But he could lecture her later.

If you survive. If Helen does.

Definitely angry. Or disgusted. Sometimes it was hard to separate the two.

She exhaled. As the orb remained in her uplifted palm, the Yvonnes continued to stare at it. None of them blinked. Even if their eyes had been normal Barrani eyes in appearance, the lack of any blinking would have been disturbing.

But not so disturbing as what happened next: all of the

Yvonnes opened their mouths, as if they were part of a harmonious choir. No words emerged, no song, no harmony; it was a storm of sound, syllables, notes, oral textures, overlapping and crashing into each other. Kaylin would have lifted her hands to cover her ears if one of them hadn't been occupied.

The orb in her hand began to vibrate as the sound of the Yvonnes touched it, coming from all directions. It began to wobble as if it were an egg. Kaylin almost dropped it in her shock.

Squawk!

"I don't want something to hatch!"

Squawk. Squawk.

She would have argued. Opened her mouth and drew breath to do exactly that. But the sound of cracking stone filled any small space left between the sounds of the Yvonnes.

Helen cried out a warning in a language that felt like a physical blow. The Yvonnes replied in actual concert, the cacophony of different sounds blending and cohering into one extended cry. Kaylin's Marks, suspended above her skin, began to lose their gold, as if the power at their core had cracked the surface of their shapes to reveal what lay within them.

She'd never seen the Marks like this before. Couldn't tell if it was in response to the Yvonnes or Helen's warning.

None of the cohort entered this room. None of the guests did, either. But something had broken the floor just ahead of where Kaylin stood; she could see the crack clearly; beneath it was darkness. She knew the stones with engraved True Words were just an appearance. But as the crack began to expand, she wondered what would happen if the stones themselves broke; the crack had appeared between words.

She'll die, Severn said, the words sharp with worry. *We can't come to you.* He wanted her to leave; she felt that clearly—as if he'd spoken the actual words. But he knew she couldn't. She understood that no one else would come to her rescue—or Helen's, more importantly—here; they couldn't reach the space that Kaylin now occupied. The only person in residence who could was Kaylin.

Kaylin, and whatever it was that caused these cracks to form.

She looked to the Yvonnes as the Marks of the Chosen grew larger. Although they weren't attached to her skin at the moment, she felt their weight, their feverish heat; she would have closed her eyes if she thought it would help; she squinted instead. The light was so bright, the dim Yvonnes could only barely be seen.

But the orb in her hand remained visible, blocking light, quivering with sound.

"Hope—tell me that this isn't some kind of weird egg."

Hope said nothing.

"If we were standing anywhere else, it would be fine—but not *here*. Not at the heart of Helen!" She'd come here because this was where Helen was concentrated. If this space vanished or broke, none of the protection she offered her residents and guests would hold. Helen had always stood alone, above the passage of time and the changes time inevitably brought.

"I am not alone now," Helen said. Her Avatar didn't appear. "You are here with me. I understand the fear of risk, but I trust you. Trust yourself. Do what must be done. There is more than one force that seeks to root itself within my domain. I cannot see the guests you brought with you; I am uncertain that they can see me at all.

"What is it they seek to do?"

As if they could hear Helen, the ones Kaylin could see beyond the light of the Marks of the Chosen opened their mouths. This time, there was no sound. But it was worse than that. This time, Shadow tendrils emerged from their mouths.

Before Kaylin could react, those tendrils shot out as if they were quarrels; they hit not Kaylin but the orb in her hand. The orb around which the poison that had almost killed Nightshade was twined. The orb that had been Shadow until Hope had chosen to breathe on it. They struck the orb with force; had they not come from all the Yvonnes, the orb would have gone flying from her hand. But all the Yvonnes had done this, and they had been spread in a perfect circle around the area that Kaylin needed to protect.

The orb began to glow—if *glow* was the right word; it darkened, but a nimbus of light surrounded that darkness. Kaylin recognized the color: it was the same as the Marks of the Chosen. Around the orb, those Marks began to rotate, as if the orb, not Kaylin, were their anchor.

What was more disturbing was the Yvonnes. They began to lose form, cohesion, shape, as if the tendrils were their insides, and those insides were being emptied. The orb absorbed it all. Kaylin shouted at the Yvonnes. She told them to stop—not for her sake, but for theirs. As if they were actually people. As if they were sacrificing themselves needlessly.

They couldn't hear, or maybe it was more than that: her words, her concern, made no sense to them. Mrs. Erickson hadn't seen them as people the way she did the other dead—even the ghosts Kaylin saw as words. She probably couldn't converse with them. She certainly couldn't command them if they couldn't understand or interact with her.

But this was the first thing they had done that felt like a deliberate sacrifice of literally all that they were: there was no coming back from this.

Severn understood. He didn't argue with her—but he was too pressed by Barrani invaders. He'd adjusted well to the space—probably better than Kaylin had. She wondered if it had something to do with his weapon, because he wielded it fully; the chains were unwound, one blade in hand and one spinning, a wall of metal with gaps for air and blood.

Helen said there were two forces attempting to take root in

her domain. One of them must be the green. The other, the Barrani Shadow. Kaylin wore the harmoniste's dress. Yvonne had come from the green. The green had sent Yvonne to the shores of the Lake of Life.

Kaylin felt cold as the orb in her palm suddenly froze in place; white spread from its surface as if emerging from the roiling mass of Shadows it had drawn in. The shape of the orb remained round, but the surface, glowing brightly, looked like an opal—a white opal. Even as she watched, she understood that it was becoming an egg. An egg that shouldn't hatch.

But it would; as the last of the Shadows that had erupted from the circle of Yvonnes disappeared, the orb began to tremble. It might have been because Kaylin's hand was no longer steady; the ground was trembling, and cracks were spreading. She frowned even as she squinted; the Marks of the Chosen had not returned to her arm. But those that remained on her skin were the same overly harsh white.

She knelt.

She placed her free palm against the trembling, cracking stone. What she could not initially do for Nightshade, she could do for Helen. Helen was injured. Kaylin was a healer. She didn't know if the healing originated in the Marks of the Chosen, as she'd assumed; the Arbiters' research implied that healing existed—if rarely—without the Marks.

But she could use the power of the Marks to heal Barrani, Dragons, and mortals. Children. Adults. People with injuries that would otherwise be fatal. Helen was a sentient building—but she was a *person*. She was a person Kaylin had grown to love; she'd always trusted her.

Helen was home. But home wasn't something that existed in isolation. Home was built of more than a single person. If Helen was Kaylin's home, Kaylin was Helen's—for now, for as long as she survived. It was because of Helen that Kaylin could offer the cohort safe homes, could house Bellusdeo when the

Barrani High Court wanted her dead. It was because of Helen that Mrs. Erickson had a home, when her dead children had been so afraid of leaving her alone.

Helen could not die here. Yes, Helen had attacked her own core in the distant past. She'd injured herself, broken the threads that kept her memories intact. Kaylin began to push the healing power of the Marks into Helen's stone floor. She didn't ask Helen's permission; Helen made no attempt to deny her. They were a home built of two people, and Kaylin's attempt to protect her home was wanted, needed.

But the power that flowed into the heart of Helen flowed, at the same time, into the orb.

The bright, harsh glow of the floating Marks faded—as did the Marks themselves; she couldn't tell whether or not they'd returned to her skin, and didn't have time to check. She could feel something push back against the healing itself; it almost reminded her of Nightshade's body and the roots spread throughout it.

"Terrano asks that you continue what you're doing. Whatever it is."

What was she doing? She was healing Helen, but power flowed from both of her hands. She couldn't sense Helen the way she had Nightshade. She couldn't sense the orb. The egg. It was the beginning of possibility—and hatching might be the end. But it felt as if both of her hands were somehow touching the same thing.

The orb had absorbed the entirety of the Yvonnes. Not even the faint hint of their outlines remained. But if the egg was absorbing Kaylin's healing power, it was also absorbing something else. Something outside of her.

For one panicked moment, she thought it was Helen.

Kaylin!

Kaylin.

Two voices.

"I am not connected to the egg you hold," Helen said, as if to calm three people's sharpening fear. "Terrano is right. If what you carry was born in, and of, Shadow and Hope's breath, it is not yet strong enough. You are stabilizing something. And the egg is drawing in what remains of the Shadows that sustain the path upon which our enemies stand."

The orb was absorbing the infestation of the Shadow under the Barrani command? Good. But it also appeared to be absorbing the healing that Kaylin meant for Helen.

Everyone who was still alive was safe because Helen remained the master of her domain. But Kaylin could feel the power of the Marks of the Chosen pass through her, as if the Helen she hoped to preserve had become a sieve. Helen was far more complicated than any Barrani Lord, even one as old as Nightshade.

She felt, as she desperately sought to heal the injuries to a being so vast and Immortal, that it was Kaylin who was being examined, Kaylin who was in some fashion being overwhelmed. That it wasn't the Marks of the Chosen alone whose power was being used.

There was another power. As if to acknowledge that, the Marks of the Chosen began to glow a familiar green color, the edges of the runes ivory. She might have expected it; she wore the dress the green granted those who were its intermediaries.

She was touching the green. The green was here. Helen was here. Kaylin was here. And the green held a power so ancient even the Arbiters didn't understand it. It offered that power now, wordless; she reached for it instinctively. Reached for it, joining it to the healing power she had always used.

The cracks in the floor began to close, the words engraved in them to brighten. Had that been all, she would have been grateful, if exhausted.

But the orb in her hand began to crack as well, small fissures spreading from a point at its height and traveling down the whole of the sphere as if the cracks were liquid.

31

The most disturbing thing about the cracks that spread across the opalescent surface of the orb was their color. They were red and glistening in the light as if they were blood.

She tried to put the orb down but wasn't surprised when it wouldn't leave her hand. She'd been carrying it ever since she'd healed Terrano. It wasn't the only Shadow she'd carried; it wasn't the only Shadow bound—as Marks were—to her skin. It wasn't even Shadow as she understood it, now.

She'd never healed two different things at the same time. She didn't even feel like she was healing the orb, because to heal something, it had to be alive. By feel alone, *both* of her hands were touching Helen, and only Helen, even if reality disagreed.

Hope squawked. She didn't recognize the tone: it wasn't angry. It wasn't irritated. It wasn't the near croon the familiar sometimes offered when Kaylin was at her lowest. Hope lifted his wing from her eyes. Nothing changed. Kaylin could see the orb; it was now the color of blood as the red that peered out between cracks expanded. She could see the stone floors etched with True Words she couldn't read. She could see her Marks, far dimmer now, as if the enormity of the healing was draining them of their very essence.

"Helen?"

"I am here, Kaylin. I will be here until the end." Helen's voice was stronger, more resonant. "Yes. You are healing me."

"And the orb?"

Squawk.

"The orb is trying to heal itself; it is reaching for whatever power it can consume. Some of that will be yours. But some will be the Shadow the Barrani invaders rely on. The path upon which they stand is becoming thinner and more attenuated," Helen said. "I . . . am better able to defend myself, now. In the healing, I have seen how the invasion was accomplished, perhaps because of the orb you carry. I can see its tenuous connection to . . . everything. I can cut off the almost unseen anchors that are binding their pathway to me.

"Let go of me, Kaylin. There is danger to you should you continue."

What she will not say, Hope squawked—and she could hear the squawks as a kind of punctuation—*is that there is danger to her. Mortal bodies are not beings such as Helen. When she chose to damage her own core for the chance of freedom of choice, she broke things. If you continue, you will remake what was broken at such risk.*

Hope had risen from her shoulder and fluttered in front of her face as he spoke.

"Helen—is Hope right?"

"The Marks of the Chosen are the will of the Ancients," Helen replied. "I cannot say for certain that he is—but I can say it is a fear. There was a chance—there was always a chance—that even with my knowledge of myself, I would die. The harmonies between the many words at my core are interlinked in ways I could not discern precisely. I chose, but a wrong choice, a wrong word, might have shattered the core.

"If you heal me, if you bring my body back to its initial state, I will have far more power—but less freedom, in the end, than I have had. I trust you," she added. "As tenant. As lord.

But you are mortal, and I cannot be certain to trust those who come after. Cannot be certain to trust visitors from long ago who knew the words of command."

Kaylin stilled. Helen was speaking of An'Tellarus.

"Yes." Helen's confirmation was chilly as she glanced at the Barrani Lord.

Kaylin changed the subject. "But the attackers aren't gone."

"No. But I am not alone. My tenants are fighting alongside me, and you are here, protecting my heart. Let go, Kaylin."

She could still see tiny cracks in the stone.

"They will always be there," Helen told her.

Kaylin took a deep breath and lifted her palm from stone that didn't feel at all like stone when she touched it. She stumbled immediately; she'd been on bent knees for the duration of the healing.

It was more than that. Helen had provided an anchor against the growing weight of the orb.

Hope continued to flutter around it, tilting his small head from side to side. When he opened his transparent jaws, the only part of him that had color was revealed: the interior of his small, but effective, mouth. His teeth glittered with light that had no obvious source as he bared his fangs.

She wasn't expecting the genuinely draconic roar that emerged from his throat.

She wasn't expecting the orb in her hand, reddened as if with blood, to vibrate at the sound. She'd half expected Hope to *eat* the orb. He'd eaten words before.

But no. He continued his roaring, which would have made her laugh out loud at any other time. It was as if a tiny lizard was trying its earnest best to prove it was a dragon.

"Hope—I don't think it's got *ears*. I don't think it's listening. And the rest of us would like to be able to hear in the near future."

As if in response to her comment, his roar grew loud enough

she could feel it in her jaw and shoulders. The arm that held the orb trembled, not with sound but with weight; the orb had grown heavier.

She wasn't surprised when he breathed on it; she would have leaped to the side because his breath was the fine spray of glittering silver mess that panicked Barrani who knew anything about ancient familiars.

Helen spoke. It was hard to recognize her voice because she spoke as Hope had been speaking—in a roar so loud it made of sound a sensation.

Hope replied in kind. Kaylin couldn't tell whether it was meant for Helen or the orb he'd been screaming at.

"He says what he does is necessary," Helen told her.

"And you believe it?"

"I believe he believes it, and Kaylin, something has happened to the intrusion." She hesitated. When speaking with Kaylin, Helen seldom hesitated, and when she did, it was because she was trying to find the right words to express her thoughts. "I think the orb has absorbed much of the power required to assert the path they've taken. Annarion believes that the attacks have lessened because the path has become unstable. Someone will have to stabilize it."

"And they're trying?"

"Yes—but not from the inside. Nightshade has mortally wounded a dozen people and killed two. An'Tellarus has killed four."

"And the invaders are using magic."

"Both sides are using magic, yes. Hope must finish as quickly as he can. I have slowed time in this space, but I cannot stop it—it requires too much power, and I am attempting to keep track of everyone within my domain."

"Did they come in through the outlands?" That was how Hallionne Alsanis had been breached. She grimaced. "And can you do anything to help me with the orb's weight? I don't want it to touch the floor."

"To help you, I will have to touch it. Everything created, everything affected, within my boundaries is me. If I help to lessen the orb's weight, it would be my power exposed to it."

Hope squawked in fury.

"Damn it! I already *know* that's a bad idea or I *wouldn't care* if the orb touched the floor. Whatever you're doing, hurry." Her arm had fallen; the trembling was worse. She could lift and carry almost anything for short distances or small periods of time. The orb's weight, when it had first come to her hand, was as substantial as smoke. Now it was heavy—heavier than its size implied and becoming heavier as the seconds passed.

Hope roared again. This sound was loud but short, a bark with an earthquake behind it.

The orb—she'd avoided calling it an egg with effort—began to open, the tiny cracks widening to reveal blood and darkness. And eyes. If she could have dropped the egg, if it weren't attached to her palm, she'd have thrown it as far as she could. The eyes were open, and they were looking at her. They were red-irised, but the pupil was a pale gold—so pale it might have been white.

The eyes belonged to a face; the face rose out of the broken shell, although pieces clung to its cheeks and ears. It had a lizard's head; it reminded Kaylin of Hope. It was the wrong color—it had some—but the right shape; the problem was its weight.

As she watched, red eyes fastened onto her gaze as if to hold it forever. The rest of the shell cracked and fell, becoming white ash before it touched the ground. Wings of silver, red, and ebony shot out. What emerged from the egg looked very much like an oddly colored version of Hope. She only wished it weighed as much.

It didn't squawk. It didn't have Hope's voice. But even its

newborn wings were the length and shape of Hope's. It didn't look friendly; it bared its teeth at Kaylin.

Hope squawked.

The newly hatched creature didn't seem to hear him. Kaylin didn't need to understand Hope's words to know that Hope was about to lose his temper. What she didn't expect—what was almost horrifying—was Hope's jaws. They opened—they had to when he was complaining—and then just kept *growing*.

The hatchling turned, opening its jaws; Hope got a face full of fire. The wings, still wet and red, shot out as it rose to face its attacker. This was not what Kaylin had assumed would happen. Some small part of her had assumed she'd have two familiars, or at least two tiny winged lizards.

Hope clearly had always had other ideas.

The newborn hatchling breathed fire. The flames were purple. Hope breathed silver mist. Where the two collided, they seemed to seep into each other. At least the roaring diminished.

The hatchling hopped onto Kaylin's left shoulder—and wound its tail around her neck as if to balance itself. Hope roared at it.

The hatchling's croaking roar was its reply. Its tail tightened. Hope swooped down, far more agile than the newborn, and fastened its jaws to the tail as if to remove it. Predictably, the tail tightened. She didn't understand what Hope wanted, expected, or needed from this—but the hatchling, dark and red and utterly unlike Hope in anything but shape and size, turned its head toward her, closing its jaws as she attempted to pull Hope off its tail.

"Helen—what are they doing? What are they trying to do?"

Helen was silent for so long, Kaylin felt a knot of anxiety begin to form. When she spoke, it was in a language Kaylin didn't recognize and couldn't understand. But Hope did, and the hatchling, newly born, seemed to as well; they both stopped their fight. Hope let go of the hatchling's tail but breathed on it before he withdrew to Kaylin's right shoulder. He lifted a wing to cover her face but didn't smack her with it.

To her surprise, the hatchling mirrored his movement, lifting his wing to slap it across Hope's. She shouldn't have been able to see through the substantial new wing. She could. She could see the darkness and Shadow that existed beneath her feet, could see it at arm's length. And she could see, as the Marks on her arms began to glow a strange purple-blue, the tendrils of that Shadow, as if Helen no longer existed.

She could see her hands.

She could see the intricate lace of black on one of them.

She understood.

Kaylin! Overlapping voices. Distant voices. Voices she knew. She heard Helen's voice. She heard Nightshade's. She heard Severn's. Over them, around them, she heard familiar cursing, familiar beloved invective. Terrano.

She had no words to offer in return; she had a silence built of fear and determination. She stood on the edge of hope, the edge of despair—really, was there that much difference? If she failed, she would fall. If she succeeded, she would fall. Where she landed defined what she needed to do.

She reached for the tendrils of Shadow she could now see so clearly. Reality faded. She could see Helen's floor as gray, lifeless stone. It reminded her of the buildings in the border zones of the fiefs.

Yes. Hope's voice.

Yes. The hatchling's.

It was the hatchling's wing that revealed Shadow—but the Shadow itself was like flickers of fire, small streams of water, damp soil; it existed, but it didn't seem sentient. The Yvonnes were gone. What was left of them was this new lizard, far more physical, far more present, than Hope.

She no longer held the orb—the egg—in the palm of her hand, but the egg's weight rested on her left shoulder, almost unbalancing her as she shifted her stance to accommodate it. She then reached out for the closest tendril of Shadow.

It was a thread. It reminded her of Wevaran webbing, it was so slender. If she blinked, it vanished, and she had to work to reassert her vision. But she'd had to do that with the magic of the Erenne mark as well. Throughout, the Yvonnes had helped her, forming a tunnel, a passage that she could traverse to reach Nightshade. Or to reach enough of him that she could heal him and send him into the battle.

What will had created the Yvonnes? What will had driven them to Kaylin's aid? Not Yvonne. Kaylin would have bet her own money that Yvonne had been unaware of their existence until Mrs. Erickson had seen them.

Light rose from her legs, her chest—a green-gold light. The green.

But there was no story being told—not in the words of the Ancient, wild green. She could hear it in the clang of steel against steel, the sharp explosion of spell against spell, the whistle of a weapon chain that broke spells before they landed. She could hear it in the shouts and commands of unfamiliar voices. It was an unfolding story of its own. She wanted it to end—but *end* had many meanings, and she was terrified of the wrong one.

She knew the silence of death. The absence. The loss of warmth.

She'd found a home. She'd built a family. The Barrani were attempting to destroy that—and they couldn't do it the usual way. Nightshade's near death was the Barrani norm. Anything their enemies did here could be prosecuted under the full force of Imperial law. But prosecution didn't bring back the dead. She knew it. She'd known it for years: her job was to bring criminals to justice—but that didn't repair the damage they'd done.

She caught Shadow strands and began to pull them, to wind

them around her gloved hand. The hatchling growled and bit her ear—much harder than Hope usually did, but probably not hard enough to remove part of her lobe. She didn't like that the immediate result was a shift in color; the threads themselves were multihued: purple, dark turquoise, blood red. She understood that these were what she needed to pull, to gather.

The Shadow-created tunnel was a tapestry; it was the colored flecks and threads that seemed to hold it together. She pulled and they came, with resistance, to her hand. But she saw, as they did, that they weren't threads. They weren't like whatever became laced gloving. They felt like . . . vines. Like stems.

She was unprepared when they grew buds, and utterly silent when the buds immediately blossomed. The shape of the bloom was familiar; the color wasn't. These were the flowers, in green and white, that Mrs. Erickson had worn as a wreath; they were the flowers that had bloomed in the ruins of a displaced mansion.

But these were blooms of livid, brilliant colors, and the colors seemed almost liquid in the way they moved across the shape of petals. She continued to gather them, continued to uproot them. She was almost afraid to put them down, but they eventually grew too numerous to easily carry.

Hope squawked loudly in her right ear.

The hatchling hissed, digging dark claws into Kaylin's collarbone as if to stand its ground. Hope's neck craned forward, and he began to *eat* the flowers. The hatchling hissed in obvious rage, and his neck, less graceful, snapped forward as he lunged to do the same. If they could have done it without unbalancing Kaylin, it would have been better, but at least the flowers weren't touching Helen.

"Anymore," Helen said, her voice stronger. She sounded worried. To be fair, she often did—it was familiar and comforting, even in this odd space. Perhaps especially in it. "I believe you must continue what you're doing as quickly as you can. But I caution you strongly against feeding the hatchling any more of your blood."

The hatchling, having bitten her ear—and the ear did sting—was busy making short work of the flowers; droplets of different colors trickled down its jaws. Hope was a far tidier eater. What Kaylin uprooted, the two ate—snapping and hissing at each other as if they were siblings afraid that the other child would get more.

Hope seldom ate. Here, he was voracious. So was the much weightier hatchling. Kaylin continued to uproot these odd flowers, and the two continued to devour them as they blossomed. The hatchling snapped at her hand once in an effort to get to a flower first; it bit her finger twice for the same reason. It didn't happen a third time because Hope bit the hatchling, hard. The wings were the only reason they couldn't fully engage; one of each was still plastered, like a mask, to her eyes.

Kaylin put a hand between their snouts before they could resume fighting. She could feel the air grow cleaner as she worked, could almost feel the touch of sunlight, of warmth, even if she couldn't see it. Her Marks were faintly luminescent, and Hope shone with the same light; the hatchling didn't. He radiated a red darkness—the kind of darkness she could see in broad daylight if she closed her eyes.

Its eyes, however, became an almost milky white as it ate. The stems that Kaylin pulled from the stone ground continued to bud and blossom in her hands, and the two—Hope and the hatchling—continued to eat as if they were ravenous, starved pets owned by a neglectful master.

One of them seemed to gain substance and weight as it ate. Kaylin noticed, as the flowers were consumed, that the silence was also consumed; the hush, the wall that had kept all sound out, was being weakened as she worked.

The hatchling finished eating first. Hope continued, squawking at the hatchling in disgust, annoyance, or concern—

she couldn't tell which. But she'd made her way around the rough circle the Yvonnes had traced by their chosen positions. She had handled the stems with care, pulling them up by the roots before they budded and blossomed. It made no sense, but she'd given up on sense.

Only one stem resisted. It felt no different to the touch than any of the others, but she couldn't pull it up as easily; it felt almost as if something was pulling it from the other side.

"Not that one," Helen said, her voice much stronger.

It felt no different to the touch.

"No. That one must remain if you do not wish to lose your friends."

"Why?" It didn't belong here. Kaylin's sense of that was visceral and immediate.

Helen's reply was in a resonant language Kaylin did not understand. Hope hummed, and the hatchling joined in; she felt the sound travel through her body as if she were a bell that had just been struck by an unseen force.

Hope squawked. The hatchling growled. As if they were two halves of one body, they rose from her shoulders, lifting both of their wings simultaneously.

Kaylin looked at her hands; they were empty. But she could feel the stem of something that hadn't budded or blossomed, waiting.

She squinted as light and reality returned to her. She stood in the heart of her home, and Helen's Avatar stood beside her. Helen wore her usual clothing, but her eyes were the color-flecked obsidian they became when she made no conscious effort to change their appearance.

"I will send you upstairs," she said. A door appeared directly in front of Kaylin. "It should not cause discomfort."

"The intruders?"

"I have two in isolation," Helen replied. Her smile was granite and ice. "Two escaped. The rest are dead. Lord Nightshade is speaking—somewhat casually—with An'Tellarus. Teela has joined them. Sedarias is with Terrano and Mandoran; Terrano believes he can follow those who escaped."

And Sedarias thought this was a good idea?

"No; she thinks it's a terrible idea."

Kaylin reached for the knob. "What did we do here?" she asked, voice soft.

"The Teller's crown remains in Lord Nightshade's room." It wasn't really an answer. She turned to Hope, who settled slowly back on Kaylin's shoulder. "You are responsible for Kaylin's safety."

Kaylin exhaled. The hatchling came to rest on her left shoulder, folding its wings and glaring at Hope. "Do you think the hatchling is going to be visible to everyone? He looks . . . less solid, now." To Kaylin's eye, it looked like smoke and shadow, although its eyes were clear. Rings of swirling color served as irises, but the pupils they surrounded remained white.

"Yes."

"What *is* it?"

"You will have to ask Hope, and Hope will have to answer. My attempt to answer is fundamentally broken; I cannot translate it into the words I am speaking now. Please join your friends before Teela destroys half the manse in an attempt to find you."

The door didn't lead to Teela.

It led to the room in which Yvonne now sat, shoulders curved inward, eyes a wary blue. She lifted her head the moment Kaylin stepped through the doorframe, her eyes shedding blue until very little of it remained. Green-eyed, she rose. Her eyes, while an unusual public color for Barrani, were the normal shade of happy green. Her hair was Barrani black, her skin flawless. But her expression was far more open.

"Is the green still here?" Kaylin asked.

"You're still wearing the dress."

"And I should have known better. I really should." She listened. She could no longer hear the sounds of combat. "I think it's safe to go downstairs, if you're willing to face An'Tellarus. She . . . didn't exactly cower from fighting."

Yvonne grimaced. "She never cowers from a fight. She believes anyone who attacks her is committed to death. Usually their own. But she's not going to be happy about it. This isn't something set up by An'Teela and her friends, is it?"

"Gods, no. If it pushes An'Tellarus into reluctant support of An'Mellarionne, that'll be the silver lining of a really bloody awful storm cloud." She hesitated. "Nightshade is outcaste."

"So Helen's mentioned. But she isn't likely to care. If he doesn't attack her, she'll consider him largely irrelevant."

Kaylin doubted that.

She heard raised voices and winced. "Helen, could you tell Annarion to calm down in front of our guests?"

"I believe the attempt has already been made. But as you are host, you should join An'Tellarus before she feels insulted. Cediela can find fault with almost anything, but in this case, she would not have to search very hard."

Annarion was not in the foyer when Kaylin reached it. She wasn't certain where he was, but didn't ask. Nightshade, An'Tellarus, and Teela were in the foyer, and Helen hadn't moved any of the bodies. She hadn't cleaned up the blood, either.

Teela's head turned toward Kaylin in her very green dress as she made her way down the stairs, both shoulders occupied. She noted Yvonne's presence behind Kaylin and nodded in the young woman's direction.

"What have you done this time?" she demanded, her eyes the color of midnight, but lightening into wary blue as she saw Kaylin was uninjured.

"I don't think this one is entirely on me."

"And that new shoulder ornament?"

"Definitely not entirely on me. In fact, if I was going to waste time pointing fingers, I'd say Barrani, Terrano, and—I'm sorry—Yvonne, in that order. With a large component of the green thrown in." She glanced at her dress very pointedly. "The Teller's crown," she added, looking past Teela to Nightshade, "is sitting in your room on the bedside table."

"It is not yet time for the *regalia*," he replied, his tone very subdued. Her eyes narrowed. If he had been fighting—and he had—he had no obvious injuries, but he was the wrong kind of pale.

Oh. That was probably why Annarion had raised his voice. "I'd say it's time for rest and recuperation."

"Yes, dear," Helen agreed. "Lord Nightshade felt it premature. He wishes to speak with the two who are currently detained before he returns to his rooms."

Kaylin glanced past the fieflord to the most intimidating of her guests. An'Tellarus's dress was wet with blood. The cloth had actually been cut at the sleeve, and the left side, near her ribs. She had chosen to sheathe her weapon. Her eyes were blue, but they weren't as dark a blue as Nightshade's.

"Yvonne," she said.

"I wasn't attacked. Nothing entered the room I was in."

"Good. I would have been highly displeased were that not the case. I must say your hospitality is refreshing and slightly nostalgic. Helen, if you would be so kind as to provide repairs to my clothing while I am visiting, I would greatly appreciate it. While I have attended events wearing bloodstained clothing, I chose to do so to make a point, and I believe that point is unnecessary in this gathering.

"I believe," she added, turning to Teela, "we have much to discuss. While I am certain that I was not the intended target, I believe I am slightly offended that I could be so easily overlooked." She grinned. It seemed disturbingly genuine.

Helen's Avatar appeared in the foyer. "An'Teela, may I now remove the bodies?"

"I don't think they bother An'Tellarus," Teela replied, "and I'd like a chance to examine them more carefully." Which meant no.

Helen turned to Kaylin.

"It's Hawk work," she said. "And there may be some clues on the bodies. We'll have to interrogate the prisoners, but the corpses might serve as confirmation of either truth or lie. Teela?"

Teela nodded.

"You might as well start now," An'Tellarus said. "Lord Kaylin, please lead Yvonne to the parlor. Severn may join you. I wish to speak with An'Teela and Lord Nightshade." Without, her tone implied, the interference of children.

Kaylin was old enough now that she didn't bridle. She didn't even attempt to take the reins of control from her guest. She owed this ancient Barrani woman at least that much. She turned to Yvonne. "Will you join me? I could use a stiff drink."

Yvonne nodded, looping an arm through Kaylin's. "I'd love to. I know the old warriors are so accustomed to corpses they don't look at them as if they used to be living people—but I'm not, and I'm feeling a bit queasy. They don't bother you?"

"Corpses are part of my work. And . . . yes, they bother me."

"Don't force yourself to smile," Yvonne said—in Elantran. "It's your home. I'm your guest, and I say it doesn't matter. Who could smile when things are like this?" As she spoke, she glanced at the shadows on Kaylin's left shoulder.

Teela had already begun her examination of the bodies. This was Kaylin's home. The crime had occurred in it. Laws of exemption couldn't be invoked.

That did make Kaylin smile.

EPILOGUE

"I want you to meet the Consort."

Yvonne flinched.

"You could approach the Lake of Life. So can she. She isn't political, even if she occupies a very political position. She loves both of her brothers. I'm not sure she was as fond of her father. Word's going to spread."

"I've never mentioned it. An'Tellarus said it wasn't worth my life."

"I'm not sure anyone would kill you—but I think if people know, the Consort is vastly less safe. And she won't care about that. She'll only care about the Lake, and the future of the Barrani people. If she knows you can do what she does, she'll feel relieved."

Helen had opened the parlor for Kaylin and Yvonne. But the doors that normally opened into a fancy room with equally fancy furnishings opened, instead, to a late afternoon sky. A path led from the doors, of interlocking stone in pale colors, hemmed in by grass and rows of flowers. None were flowers that grew in the green.

"You could help her," Kaylin added. What she'd managed to do for Nightshade, she'd achieved *because* of the Erenne mark that had driven such a wedge between the two brothers. She didn't have a similar mark placed on her by the Consort. Given it was a sign of vast disrespect, she'd never have one, either.

Yvonne swallowed. "You like her."

"We've had our arguments," Kaylin replied. "But . . . yes. I think the hardest thing about those arguments was her sudden coldness."

"I'll have to speak with Ollarin."

Kaylin nodded. And hesitated. She knew she'd be grilled by the cohort when they finished their interrogation—and after they actually managed to get Nightshade to rest. Kaylin had her own reasons for wanting to avoid the Consort, but she knew Yvonne wouldn't visit her unless she were also present.

Not that Kaylin's presence was a guarantee of safety; these days, it seemed the exact opposite.

Yvonne reached out, almost hesitant, toward the new lizard. It turned its head in her direction, but she withdrew her hand before she could touch it.

"Does it feel familiar?" Kaylin asked.

"It does."

"Dangerous?"

Yvonne shook her head. "It—I know this is going to sound strange—but it feels like sleep."

"Does it remind you of the green?"

Yvonne glanced at Kaylin's dress and considered the question. "It wouldn't if you hadn't asked, but yes. Your dress really does. And the Teller's crown. But Lord Nightshade is right: it's too early for the *regalia*. And I don't think the green means for us to go to the West March. I think . . . the green intends, somehow, to come to us."

That wasn't what Kaylin wanted to hear, but it didn't surprise her. The Lord of the West March had already arrived. She wondered if Yvonne had been sent from the green *by* the green. But Yvonne had been here for years. The green and its flowers hadn't figured much in Elantra until Mrs. Erickson.

No, be fair. Until Azoria and her flowers and her terrible paintings, and her attempt to become something other. "Was it the green that led you to the Lake?"

". . . I think so. It felt like a dream, a waking dream. But I slept for a long time in the green, and I dreamed there."

"What did you dream of?"

"Flowers and shadow and death," Yvonne replied, and turned her face to the side. "Death was the last thing I saw. I wasn't afraid of death in the green. I wasn't awake enough to be afraid of anything. I knew—I knew that if the green took me in, I would be safe."

"But you didn't want to stay there?"

"I didn't have the choice. I was found, I was alive, and the very few people I cared about were happy. I offered to stay in the green where I'd be safe, but the green wouldn't let me back in. So I came to Ollarin. An'Tellarus made certain I arrived safely. And I've been there ever since. How do you know Severn?"

"We were children together in the fiefs. In Nightshade," she added bitterly. "You?"

"I was part of his test. Because he passed, he could wield the weapon of the green, and I could wake up and emerge." She hesitated again. "You're friends, right?"

Kaylin nodded. "We've had our disagreements as well."

"It's just . . . I think I heard your name while I was sleeping."

Kaylin fell silent.

"I don't think Severn's test is over yet."

The silence changed. "What do you mean?"

"The weapon he wields—it's the weapon of the green. The green tests those who want to wield it. He passed the test. But I don't think it was the last test."

They were silent again. The silence was broken by Hope

and the hatchling, their voices a much quieter clash of sound than their roaring had been.

Squawk.

"What now?"

Yvonne looked at Hope as if he'd expended enough power to make himself understood. The young Barrani woman swallowed and nodded; she didn't answer in words Kaylin could understand.

But the shadow on Kaylin's left shoulder opened its mouth, and a spout of purple fire left its jaws.

"Tell Lord Nightshade to wear the Teller's crown if he leaves this place," Yvonne said. "I will do my best to convince An'Tellarus and Ollarin that meeting the Consort is safe."

When Yvonne left, Kaylin walked her from the garden to the front door. An'Tellarus was waiting. The moment she left Helen's boundaries, her clothing would revert to the bloodstained remnants of her very fine dress. She knew it and seemed unconcerned.

"Sedarias offered her more suitable clothing. An'Tellarus declined," Helen said. "I believe she wishes to make a statement—and she will, when she arrives at the High Halls. She is feared for a reason."

"Probably because she's not sane," Terrano muttered. He was invisible.

"She doesn't have to worry about social grace, no," Helen replied, a hint of disapproval in her tone. "But she is not bored, and boredom, where An'Tellarus is concerned, has always been dangerous for anyone who isn't An'Tellarus.

"You should eat," Helen added, turning to Kaylin. "And sleep. I'm afraid your color is terrible."

Kaylin was exhausted. Her shoulder hurt. She'd never truly appreciated Hope's lack of weight before. "Helen, can you see the hatchling?"

"Yes."

"Terrano?"

"You mean that smoky shadow sitting on your left shoulder, glaring at the world?"

"That one."

"Where did you find it?"

"Later," Kaylin replied. "I'll tell you all later."

"Sedarias wants to hear it now. Teela agrees with Helen. She wants you to eat in your room, hopefully before you fall over."

"Is there a reason you're hiding?"

Terrano materialized. "I was avoiding An'Tellarus. I think Yvonne is a bit like Serralyn, just interested in different things. I think An'Tellarus is terrifying." He winced. "Annarion also agrees with Teela, and he's coming downstairs to make sure you actually make it to your room without tripping on the stairs on the way up."

Annarion was standing on the last step, arms folded. He reminded her of Teela in that moment. His eyes were an odd color, not the dark blue the combat had all but demanded, but not the green-flecked blue that meant danger had passed.

She frowned. "You're injured."

"It's nothing."

"I'll be the judge of that."

"She will," Helen added.

"My brother took worse, and he's *fine*." The wealth of sarcasm turned the sentence on its head.

"Did you get him back to bed?"

"He's resting." Which meant no. "He doesn't need sleep. He says he's slept enough for a decade."

"That wasn't sleep. He was unconscious."

"What's the difference?" Before Kaylin could answer, Annarion frowned. "Mandoran thinks you're trying to distract me. He says it doesn't matter whether or not my brother needs sleep—you need it. You look awful."

She felt awful, truth be told. As if the days of terrible tension and anxiety she'd been bracing herself against had suddenly folded, and she was left pushing back against nothing.

Annarion slid an arm around her shoulder. She tensed—she always did—but accepted it and let him take on some of her weight. They made it halfway up the stairs before he took on all her weight; he lifted her off her feet. His gaze skirted the Erenne mark and shied away.

"Can you forgive him now?" Kaylin asked, her voice soft because she was so exhausted.

Annarion opened his mouth, closed it, and continued up the stairs. Hope had adjusted his position. The hatchling had not, and almost fell, because Hope had pushed him off the shoulder he'd occupied. "What is that?" Annarion asked with obvious relief. "Another familiar?"

Hope squawked. It was the unhappy, disgusted squawk, but at least it wasn't aimed at her.

"I don't know. Right now, it's not my problem. It's not biting me, it's not trying to burn me to ash, and it's not hostile. I'll figure it out tomorrow."

"Serralyn asks if you'd like her to speak with the librarians."

"As long as I don't hear what they have to say until tomorrow, sure. She can use me as an excuse to get into the library."

Annarion chuckled. The sound faded. Kaylin had closed her eyes. "I never hated him," he said. "I was so angry, and so disappointed."

"You know he probably did this—the mark, I mean—because of you, right?"

Annarion's arms tensed. That had definitely been the wrong thing to say, but she really didn't have enough energy to make sure only the right things left her mouth.

Kaylin made sure she met, and held, Annarion's gaze. "He wanted to rescue you."

"Did he ever say that?"

"No—but why would he? He was the fieflord. I was a fiefling who'd managed to escape. I knew nothing about him besides that. Why would I care about his brother? I hadn't met you yet." She hesitated. "I met him once when he was younger. There was a big upheaval—a time storm, I think someone called it? The fiefs are unstable when the Towers aren't properly captained.

"He was different, then. I couldn't imagine that he would become the Nightshade I knew."

"Neither could I."

"But he recognized the Erenne mark. And he knew he hadn't put it there—not yet. It was one of the first things he did when I met him for the first time." She swallowed. "I was Chosen. I had the Marks of the Chosen. No one knows for certain what power comes with those Marks. Maybe he thought if he kept me close by, I could help you, somehow.

"And he wasn't wrong. He never forced me to do anything. He never hurt me, beat me, or commanded me. And his thugs treat me with respect."

"The High Court doesn't."

"They wouldn't even if I didn't have the Erenne mark."

"They might. You have Hope. You have the Marks of the Chosen."

"The Erenne mark makes me seem lesser to them. Your brother is the threat, not me. On the other hand, it probably makes him seem like *more* of a threat. He has the Chosen in his pocket. If he removed the Erenne mark—or if someone else did—it would make me more of a threat, not less of one." She grimaced. "But because it's still on my face, people know he's alive.

"Annarion, I made my peace with it. I don't even notice it's there on most days."

"Except when it's bleeding?"

"Except then, yes. But if it weren't for this mark, I'm almost certain your brother would have died. We wouldn't have been able to reach him or heal him. Please—find another reason to fight with him. Hate him because he treated the citizens of his fief like less than garbage, for instance."

Annarion fell silent but carried Kaylin to her room. He didn't stay to make certain she got ready for bed—but Helen was determined. It wasn't a fight Kaylin wanted to have. She did need sleep.

"You should be resting," Annarion said as he entered his brother's room. The door wasn't locked, but even if it had been, Helen would have opened it for Annarion. He would not have asked. He understood sentient buildings and their hospitality; Hallionne Alsanis had been both prison and home for the majority of his life.

Calarnenne was not resting. He appeared to be talking with Helen's Avatar. She was, to Annarion's surprise, aiding his brother in bandaging a wound on his right side.

"Your brother's ribs protected his internal organs," Helen told Annarion. "And your brother is far too proud to acknowledge trivial wounds. But these blades weren't poisoned in the same fashion as the weapons of his first assailants."

"They weren't?"

"Not when they were drawn in the foyer." Helen exhaled.

"Did the attackers in confinement survive?" Annarion asked. The question was meant for either Helen or Nightshade, but it was Helen's answer he expected.

"Yes. But their survival requires suspension of time in a very, very localized way. It is possible Kaylin might heal them;

your brother is against even the attempt, although he knows that the attempt comes with memories that might prove of critical import.

"Sedarias argued for the healing. Teela remained neutral. What are your thoughts?"

"You know what they are." Annarion's eyes were very blue.

Helen's smile was harsh but genuine. "Yes. I have not asked Kaylin for her opinion yet. If we ask, she will make the attempt." Helen finished bandaging the wound that Calarnenne had refused to acknowledge when his own brother asked.

Annarion waited. His brother's clothing was real; it wasn't a courtesy or an artifact of the house; he had no attendant to help him dress. Calarnenne had always been graceful, elegant, and effortlessly powerful. Solanace had enemies—any family of note did. This much weakness he had never shown to anyone. Not even to Annarion.

Perhaps especially not to Annarion.

There was so much he wanted to say to his brother. He swallowed most of the words but found no way to soothe the anger, the bitter disappointment. Annarion was the one who had vanished, but Annarion felt abandoned in place. That was the truth.

He felt abandoned by the brother he had respected and trusted.

But . . . had he? It was not Calarnenne with whom he shared his True Name; not Calarnenne with whom he was tied by the namebond that Barrani were taught, from the moment they first opened their eyes, to fear and hate. He would never have taken that risk before he was sent, by his elders, to the green. He understood—everyone did, except Sedarias—that they were disposable tools. If they were fortunate, they would be powerful disposable tools. If, as people expected, they failed, their loss would cause the least harm to the family.

The war had been waged across the continent. The Dragons

had come far, far too close to the heart of Barrani life; the Barrani had responded in kind.

Calarnenne had not known of the plan. Calarnenne could not act—in time—to save Annarion. He had what Barrani had had for the entirety of their existence: vengeance. Destruction of those who had wronged them. Calarnenne had that. He was a renowned war hero. He was the master of one of The Three. He was the undisputed heir to Solanace.

He destroyed them all; only the sword he did not forsake. He never forgave their parents. He never forgave the extended family. And he never surrendered the hope that Annarion could be saved. The family, he buried. His revenge was akin to Teela's—maybe it was no coincidence that they had both been chosen by the greatswords. They had not built their reputation on the swords; the swords had chosen because they had already achieved power.

Annarion discovered the extent of the destruction—the extent of all the loss—only when he was free to leave Hallionne Alsanis. He was not his brother. Had never been his brother. If he felt anger at being thrown away, it had never fully taken root. Not to assuage that anger would he have killed whole family lines, branch and root, but his brother had done that—starting with their own.

"I was alone for centuries," his brother said, as if he could hear what Annarion did not say aloud. "I was not as you were. We have never been the same. I believe you would have earned great renown in wars, if wars still existed. I believe you would have brought glory to the Solanace name. But the family that occupied it did not deserve even the ashes of that glory."

"I wouldn't have killed them all," Annarion said, voice low.

"No. But they had not finished. They desired power—glory for Solanace, and for themselves by extension. Were I to bring you home after the *regalia*, you would never have been free. They would not countenance my attempt. Had they left me to research on my own, they would not have died. But we are not mortals, whose familial bonds need only survive paltry decades. What affection I might once have felt could not be sustained.

"This was not the first assassination attempt. I wished to make certain there were few others. The fiefs were less approachable for those who might seek my death. I might have chosen to take the Tower even had I not been made outcaste. Yet you have returned. You have passed the Test of Name. You are a Lord of the High Court.

"You style yourself of Solanace. An'Solanace. It is an empty title. You must know it is an echo of your abandonment."

"To you. To you that's all that it was. But I am not dead." Annarion turned away from his brother. "The brother I knew would not have destroyed Solanace."

"Then perhaps we did not know each other well enough," Calarnenne replied. "The only kin I valued was you. Perhaps I was overprotective. Perhaps what I sought was to preserve who you are. Your life within the Hallionne had very little of politics in it. You built a family that was far more steady, far more true to you, than the family to which you were born.

"But you have not lived in the High Halls; you did not fight in the wars. You did not lose what few friends remained to you to Dragons and treachery. You did not see them fall to despair; did not see them surrender to what they believed survival required. You did not see them bow, bend, and even break. And perhaps you will not. What I have seen and what you have seen are different.

"What I wanted was to have you back. You were my only weakness, and you could not be threatened, could not be used. Not against me. But you are home, now, in a very changed land. You are the child I remember. I am not the brother of your memories. But that is the outcome of experience. You did not see my struggles; you did not evaluate my choices—my many choices. You could not weigh the losses you could not see—but you could judge. And you have.

"And perhaps I even expected that." The words were not bitter. "What I did, I did for my sake. But I find that having achieved that goal, I am adrift. I am fieflord; I am not An'Solanace. I will never become that while I breathe. I have prevented anyone from taking that title, and there were those in the early centuries who tried.

"Perhaps all my efforts were wasted in the end. It was the Chosen who freed you."

Annarion was silent.

"But you are still the only person alive I would claim, willingly, as kin. What I wanted, I have achieved. Tell me, brother, what you want. Do you wish to take up the mantle of Solanace? There are none, now, who would deny you. You will not have the power of alliances that Solanace once boasted—but I see a future in which your friends will become those allies."

What had Annarion wanted? What had he wanted to hear?

What had he hoped for? That his brother, separated from him for centuries, would somehow be exactly the same person he had been when Annarion had been sent to the green? Why had he expected that? By the time he'd arrived in Elantra, he knew the fate of Solanace. He knew his parents were dead, and his aunt, and his cousins.

He knew no one had stepped up to become the head of the family. No one had rebuilt it. And he knew that his brother had been blamed for the destruction. Had he not believed it? Had he somehow hoped that his brother had been framed? His brother, who had never joined games of murder and assassination just for personal power, personal gain?

No. It was Sedarias, not his brother, who answered because he hadn't spoken the words aloud. *You believed it. But you believed in your brother; you believed that if he'd made that choice, it was the right choice. And Annarion, we all agree. It was the right choice.*

Had our own families made similar choices in our defense . . . I always envied you your brother.

And now?

I still do. Maybe I understand his choices better than you do—maybe I'm more like him than you are. But he's never going to fight against you with anything but words, and his words aren't meant to wound. What do *you want? What was Solanace to you?*

There was only one answer to that question. One, and he had not answered anyone who'd asked. He had learned from observing Teela how to compartmentalize his thoughts. He had never needed to until his return to this city in which the High Halls stood. From which the High Court ruled.

But it was a question he had to answer. His brother waited. Calarnenne had survived. He'd survived because he had placed that mark on Kaylin's cheek.

"I will do anything in my power to support you, should you decide to revive the ancient Solanace fortunes. Anything," he added, eyes an odd shade of blue, "except harm the current High Lord and his family."

"They're the children of the people who sent us all to the green."

"Yes. My enmity for the previous High Lord was bitter for that reason. But had his son assumed the mantle far earlier, you would never have been sent to the green. I will not attempt to unseat them; I will not attempt to harm them. Anything else I will do."

Annarion had no desire to destroy the High Lord or his family. But that had not always been the case. He felt no anger when he asked a single question. "Why?"

Perhaps because his brother heard no anger, he replied. "The Consort was the only lord of note to argue against the expedition to the green. She was the only person of power who refused to even acknowledge my status as outcaste. Because she could speak to the Lake, and because the Lake accepted her, she was immune to the consequences of such an act of defiance.

"I will not repay that friendship by deposing her. I will not see her harmed."

"And if that's what we need?" Again, there was no anger. There was curiosity, and it was genuine, as if he was only now looking at his brother as a person he did not fully know or understand.

This time, his brother smiled. "It is not what you need. Kaylin would never countenance it. You collectively need Helen. And if you spent any time with the Lady at all, you would not countenance it, either. Strategy is theoretical, but the Lady is not. Meet her, spend time with her, and you, too, will understand.

"What would you have me do? I failed to protect you. What you experienced—"

Annarion lifted a hand. "Enough. Solanace, to me, was you."

Calarnenne fell silent.

"It was you. It was us. I believed that you would become An'Solanace and you would remake Solanace in your image, not our parents'. I don't know if we can become what we were. We've both changed. But if I could . . . I would rebuild Solanace."

"I cannot leave the Tower. I do not believe I could become the family head if I remained fieflord; it has never been done to my knowledge."

"Then I will become An'Solanace. And I will have you reinstated."

"That was not of concern to me."

Annarion nodded. He knew. "But that was before I returned." His exhalation was long, and as he found his words, he finally lost the sense of betrayal that had driven his interactions with his brother since he had first set foot in the city. He reached out as if to touch his brother's shoulder, but let his hand fall away.

"Solanace was you, to me. It was my home because you were its future. Join me. Build that home."

"We have very few allies." It was not a rejection.

"We have almost a dozen. And Lord Kaylin."

"She is mortal. We will only barely begin to rebuild before her life reaches its natural end."

Annarion's smile was soft but genuine. "I think her influence will be felt for far longer than that. Will you help?" The words hung between them, the injured wielder of *Meliannos*, hero of wars long ended, and his only surviving kin.

Nightshade was silent, his expression inscrutable.

"Will you come home?"

The fieflord closed his eyes. Eyes closed, he reached out; his arm trembled as his hand found his brother's shoulder and remained there until it steadied.

★ ★ ★ ★ ★

ACKNOWLEDGMENTS

This has been, without question, a tumultuous year. Most of the book you've read was written in 2024 and the first two months of 2025. Change is a constant in life; we struggle to reach a stable place in which to stand and live, but stability, once achieved, isn't static.

Struggle and success are a cycle. There will always be ups and downs. I tell myself this because when struggling, it can feel like things will never be better again. The noise of struggle, the sudden swell of uncertainty in almost every aspect of life, overwhelmed the voice of the book for me, and for weeks I couldn't write a word. I couldn't read a word, either.

If I were living alone, that would be difficult, but it wouldn't affect other people. But I'm not.

My husband, Thomas, kept my household sane and stable—or as stable as a house full of geeks can be. He's the core of the home team. My sons, Ross and Daniel, my godsons, Jamie and Liam, their parents, Kristen and John, and my brother Gary and his wife Ayami. My mother, whose presence, replete with affectionate nagging, held the fort while I hid under a rock, recharging. Or surviving. One of those two.

My book came in too long, a few days too late, and Mary-Theresa Hussey had more than her usual editing duties because of it. I'm grateful. Eden Railsback had to deal with the chaos of my move from my home of many years to a new line and a new editor and the delays and confusion that arose—which also took time.

At this writing, the book hasn't gone through all of the publication stages, but the Harlequin Trade Publishing's in-house proofreading has always been one of the things I appreciate most. So: thank you, as always.

But during the writing of the book, I also took time off from the bookstore at which I work, because the manager there—a redheaded troll—is *also* incredibly supportive of my writing, and makes space for it when I ask. I try not to ask too often.

All books take a small village. If the writing is done by the author sitting at their computer, there are a lot of hands through which that initial draft must pass before becoming the book you hold in your hands.

And if it weren't for my readers, there would never be light at the end of that tunnel, which sometimes seems short and neat, and sometimes seems long and endless. Thank you for joining me. I'm beyond grateful to have you all.

Read on for an excerpt of Michelle Sagara's *Heir of Light*, available now!

The Academia required students. Apparently, it also required vast quantities of paperwork, much of which appeared to be stacked in teetering piles on the chancellor's desk. The chancellor in question eyed those piles with narrowed eyes. Lannagaros had a large desk, although it was almost buried at the moment beneath bureaucratic detritus.

"I do not suggest burning them," the voice of the Academia said, tone dry as good tinder. "Some of those papers are student applications."

"I am aware of that." It was not the student applications that the chancellor wanted to reduce to ash. Students were the life's blood of the Academia; their presence gave Killianas, the sentience behind the Academia's many buildings, strength.

An influx of students, however, required teachers. Professors. Experts in their fields of knowledge.

Lannagaros's choice—at the start of his tenure as chancellor—had been limited. Barrani scholars came, of course; the Barrani had famously long lives and memories, and if most had not attended the Academia in its golden years, they had heard of it many, many times.

Lannagaros was currently inquiring into two possible Dragon scholars—both of whom had chosen the long sleep some centuries past. It was Imperial custom—and law—that those who slept remain undisturbed in their chosen slumber; Dragons did not always wake gracefully, and if they were startled into their new surroundings, could be quite proactively defensive. He had requested permission to disturb, or attempt to disturb, that slumber. The Emperor had yet to make his decision.

Lannagaros had accepted a handful of mortal scholars with far less pickiness than he had similar Barrani professors; he felt that their presence would prove a comfort to those mortals among the student body, given the number of mortals who comprised it.

This had not, in at least one case, proven true.

But now, on his desk, he had over three dozen applications and requests for professorial positions, all from humans. Some of the names he recognized; some, he did not. Of the nearly forty requests, only two had family names that were not immediately familiar to a lord of the Dragon Court, and he set those aside for further investigation.

His sigh had smoke in it.

The interest of so many people of note in the human caste court was not a coincidence. None of these scholars had shown any previous interest in the Academia. Some of these scholars were Imperial mages. He had a natural suspicion of the Arcanum, but many of the current Barrani professors had been trained and schooled in higher magical arts in that very place.

Some of their Arcanum confederates had carelessly experimented in a fashion that could have become literally world-threatening.

"Their studies within the Academia could be more easily curbed. The Arcanum was never hosted within a sentient building," Killianas said.

"The Barrani tend to avoid sentient buildings, where at all feasible." The chancellor's very toothy grin was possibly petty;

the High Halls from which the caste court ruled the Barrani was now subject to a similar sentience, which had been trapped for almost a millennium in its effort to contain a dangerous Shadow imprisoned at its heart. The Barrani who wished to be Lords of the High Court had no choice but to subject themselves to the inspection and knowledge of the new High Halls.

Killianas agreed. “Mortals would not avoid them in the same fashion.”

“They would, if they were wise.”